OUT
OF
ASHES

A NOVEL

by

Sutton L. Avery

Dog Ear Publishing
4010 West 86th Street, Suite H
Indianapolis, IN 46268

First Edition: January 2014

Out of Ashes 1638119

Some people, places and events are actually historical event that are public knowledge.

Historical Fiction

Editors
Geneva J. Chapman, Bachelors of Arts English, Cameron University
Masters of Education, Wichita State
Education Specialist, University of Toledo
Dan C. Sullins, Bachelor of Arts Journalism Texas A&M,
Masters of Arts in English University of Texas at Arlington

ISBN 978-0-615-87913-0

Additional information & Books; www.outofashesthenovel.com

10 9 8 7 6 5 4 3 2 1 0

Printed in the United States of America

Prologue

BIRMINGHAM, ALABAMA
1960

A frightened Negro child is dragged across the floor. She sees only a dark image hovering over her, as her hands and wrists are roughly bound together. A utility light, swinging above, briefly illuminates her attacker. Recognizing him from town, she repeats the man's name, over and over, again. But he does not answer. Now, she knows. Uncontrollable tears run down her cheeks. He never says a word and the look on his face shows no remorse. His large hands cover her nose and mouth tightly. It is silent. Her body goes limp and in an instant, she is gone. Like so many before her, she will never be heard from, again. Her family and friends will never know her fate.

In loving memory

Barbara Lee Stubbs

"I refuse to harbor hate in my heart,
because I know the true meaning of love.
Love, true love, is my salvation and my peace."
Sutton L Avery

PRESENT DAY 2017

I am awakened in bed by the smell of bacon and coffee, wrapped in my nice, warm down comforter. I climb out of bed after being up all night working on a big case in New York. My toes touch the cool marble floor that I imported from Italy for my Manhattan penthouse. I walk just feet away to open the curtains and patio sliding doors to feel a cool breeze that eventually fills my room.

"Fall is here," I think, as I make my way to the ledge where a visitor would be overwhelmed by an array of colors that blankets the trees down below over Central Park.

"I did it! I made it! A Southern girl from Birmingham, Alabama!" I whisper in my hoarse early-morning voice, while looking down below at New Yorkers rushing to and fro in the busiest city in the world. All the hard work I had to endure to get where I am today fills my mind.

I reminisce about the long nights studying on campus at Yale University while most of my friends went to sports activities and countless parties. Who would have believed that I, Emily Rose, would be the head partner of Stevens and Silverman, one of the most powerful and prestigious law firms in America?

Anyone who knows me personally does not find it odd that I never married nor had children. I guess it comes with power that a man would feel threatened by a successful woman. I deeply inhale the morning air, starting my daily purification ritual, and then, just as I start to slowly exhale, I'm disturbed by a knock and a "Good morning, ma'am!" from Maria, who barges in with breakfast, coffee, and freshly squeezed orange juice, placed on a silver platter.

"Can I get you anything else, ma'am?" Maria asks softly, as she sets my breakfast and *USA Today* on the patio table next to me before ducking into my bathroom to start my shower.

"Yes," I reply, as she returns to pour my coffee. I'm smiling at the front-page headline on the paper: "President Harris' administration will soon nominate pick for Supreme Court."

"Please have my driver come earlier, at eight, Maria."

Everyone knows that I am particular about time. I decide to leave from home earlier than normal to avoid some of this morning's commuter congestion. It will only take ten minutes to get to my office if I am lucky.

"Yes, ma'am," Maria says, leaving immediately to take care of my request.

After showering and getting dressed, I gather the files I worked on last night, now scattered across my bed and tuck them inside my briefcase. I spoke with my father last night, and was told that my mother is happy about the news he said would be in today's paper, and she can't wait until she can finally rest, now that she is home in Birmingham. I told my father I will come home later this month and maybe we can go fishing. He sounded pleased when I suggested our favorite outing.

Downstairs, the doorman in the lobby greets my limo driver, who is ready to take me to my office.

"How are you today, Ms. Stevens?" the driver says politely.

"Good morning, Bob," I reply cordially, while looking out the limo window, smiling at pedestrians. We drive down to Lower Manhattan, where we come to a stop. I notice a small coffeehouse and see the people inside sipping from coffee mugs, while they sit in front of computers perched on small tables in front of them.

"Bob, pull over please."

"Yes, ma'am," he says.

Inside, I am greeted by wonderful aromas that fill my nostrils with the pungent odors of dark roasted coffees. I also notice freshly baked crumb cakes and pies in a glass covered patisserie just a few yards from the coffee bar.

"You should get the pastry with the cream cheese."

The young gentleman next to me smiles, holding a beautiful young woman's hand. The couple is in their mid-twenties. His skin is a wonderful cocoa brown complexion that you would expect to see in Jamaica and she is blonde with beautiful bluish-grey eyes. I can tell they are a couple in love, because when their eyes meet they both smile and pull each other closer and kiss. I smile at them, envious of their love, yet happy to be reminded that New York is definitely a melting pot. It is good to see people who are just in love, not caring about things like race, ethnicity, or nationality.

"Yes, ma'am, can I help you?" the lady behind the counter asks.

"Thanks. I think I will have the cheese pastry, please," I say, giving the couple a wink as they head for the coffee bar. "Make it a dozen."

I hand one to Bob as I return to the limo before he pulls back into traffic.

"Bob, you made this drive in record time," I say as we arrive at our destination.

"Thank you, ma'am," he replies. "I know this is an important day for you."

The doorman at Stevens Towers politely nods while opening the limo door.

"Good morning, Matthew," I say, as I head to a lobby full of designer furniture and cathedral ceilings that looks like it has been staged for a magazine. I am greeted by Stephanie, my assistant. She walks with me, taking notes as she's done each morning for the past ten years. I'm thankful for her patience and the way she handles my daily appointments. It seems she is always one step ahead, making my transitions run smoothly. She takes my briefcase and hands me the day's schedule.

"You have a partner meeting at 9 a.m. and an interview with Oprah on *OWN* at 10:30. Oh, and yes," she says as she looks at her task and appointment book, "your dress will arrive at your residence at 5 p.m. for your *Time Magazine* award ceremony at the Waldorf at seven o'clock."

"Here are the documents you requested," she says, handing me a pen while walking beside me, trying to keep up with my pace.

"Only thing required is your signature, ma'am."

Stephanie's hair is jet black and always pulled back so you can see the beautiful smile she has for everyone, no matter how her day is going. I quickly sign all the documents as we walk, continuing through the lobby until we reach the elevator.

We get off at the sixty-sixth floor, still humming the music playing on the elevator Michael Jackson's, "Man in the Mirror."

"Stevens & Silverman Law Firm" is displayed on a cream colored wall facing the elevators. People are always amazed when they first glimpse the antiques I have collected in my travels throughout the world. I have mixed them with the office's Early American décor. My secretary, Ellen, who has been working for the firm for twenty-five years, meets us as she takes my jacket and hands me a cup of coffee while following me to my office. I look at my digital watch and see "8:34," and decide to head to the boardroom. I am sure the firm's lawyers are gathered around the large oak conference table awaiting my arrival to discuss a huge case with a major airline.

"Sorry, Ms. Stevens," Ellen says politely. "Your father is on line three."

"Thank you, Ellen. I will take the call from the boardroom."

"Why is Dad calling me this early?" I wonder, as we make our way down the hall to the conference room.

Ellen walks ahead of me to open the door and I enter the large room, closely followed by my assistant. I stop to greet the bevy of lawyers who are all dressed in nicely tailored black and navy blue Armani suits.

"Why is it that businessmen all wear the same wired round glasses? I guess it makes them look important, or older, if they are younger," I think to myself, smiling at them. The men stand as we enter the room and I walk over to a small lounge area outfitted with sleek leather chocolate couches, chairs, and classic tables holding fresh large flower arrangements in tall vases. Stephanie is standing near a bank of phones lit up with the incoming and outgoing calls, holding a phone receiver. She hands it to me, then walks away to give me some privacy.

"Hello, Daddy?" I speak softly, trying to keep our conversation private, looking out of the large floor-to-ceiling windows at the tall skyscrapers in Lower Manhattan. I can immediately tell by his quavering voice that something is dreadfully wrong.

"Emily," he mumbles. Then, a moment of silence. "You must come home. Your mother is dying and she won't make it until the morning."

Shocked by the news, I suddenly feel a huge knot in my throat and I want to cry out. Devastated and confused, I dare not show any emotion in front of the men sitting around the table, glancing at me as they pretend to converse socially.

"I will be there as soon as possible, Daddy," I say, hesitating, as he whispers, "Okay."

I hand the phone back to Stephanie, still in a daze. I just talked to my mom last night and she was excited about being home from Washington.

"Something is terribly wrong!" I think, while walking away from the phone and heading for the door where Ellen stands, waiting for me. Stephanie grabs the phone from my hand and begins to speak with my father, getting information from him in detail. I walk carefully, trying to make my way to the washroom without making a scene, and with each step I take, I am reminded of my youthful years with mother that now seem like an eternity ago.

I open the door and what feels like an ocean of tears rolls down my cheeks as I dab at them with my Hermes scarf, careful not to get lipstick on it. Staring in the mirror, I notice my swollen, bloodshot eyes as I reach for the polished nickel faucet just below the mirror. I dampen and place a cool towel over my forehead and I am sure that this is an awful dream and I wait, hoping I'll wake up any moment in my warm bed.

Suddenly, I am distracted by two women in stalls having a conversation about a party last week involving, as they describe it, "Some niggas fighting over a lady friend." They don't notice me until they emerge simultaneously from their stalls and quickly change the subject. Two young African-American women I know well nod in my direction and quietly leave while I remain, staring in the mirror, recalling memories of a young girl whose mother and father once told her a story, not a once-upon-a-time story from a book of fairy tales, but a real-life, true story. It is the story of our family's history and my parents' love.

Chapter 1

Peg James is my name; born to Mr. and Mrs. James from Toledo, Ohio, in 1938. I was born the very same year and month that Germany signed the Munich Agreement with Italy, France, and Great Britain. I remember reading in my history book about the date, September 29, 1938. That was just six days before I was born. I liked to read about German history, because my biological mother was a beautiful German woman that my father met while he was playing jazz in clubs all over Europe. They got out just in time, but she died soon after. My father remarried and his new wife became my "Mama." When I was eight years old, they both died in an automobile accident on Highway 75 near Rossford, Ohio. I was given to my cousin, Sera James. She was living nearby in Columbus, Ohio, and she gladly took me in, raising me as her daughter.

Shortly after my parent's death, I was seen by a physician there and treated for depression. The doctor said I nearly had a nervous breakdown from the trauma I endured from the loss of my parents.

My cousin Sera was working odd jobs at the time with a local law firm. She was only ten years my senior.

When I became older, I was offered a part time job working for a wonderful man, Dr. Robert Carson, a local physician. I didn't want to set my eyes ever again on Toledo, so I took the job.

My cousin Sera took a job as a paralegal intern for an esteemed law firm and said she planned on being a judge someday. She dreamed that one day Negroes, particularly down South and in some places up North, would be able to vote without having to pay poll taxes or be impeded in other ways from exercising their constitutional rights and be able to live freely like other races in America.

Every Saturday evening, we would head down to the university nightspots and order cocktails and have intellectual conversations with students in the "Negro Only" section. We were articulate and poised. It was usually our physical attributes, however, that caught the attention of the young college students with whom we debated, as well as other men, both black and white.

People always said if you closed your eyes, you would think we were white women by the sound of our voices. But when you opened them, you would see two black women with the small waists and well-rounded derrieres that are typical of our race.

I have always been more outgoing than my cousin, so even though I was a member of many church social groups, I made sure we still had time to visit the city's nicer piano bars. Sera and I always enjoyed listening to the wonderful local talent, such as Nancy Wilson. I would order a vodka tonic and Sera liked gin and tonics with a twist. It was great just to relax to the sounds that came from Millie's Jazz Club, just a block from the university.

I began my studies, part time, at Ohio State in political science, while I worked odd hours for Dr. Carson. I had free room and board and signed up for night classes. After receiving my bachelor's degree, I continued to work for Dr. Carson, who by then had gotten married. Shortly thereafter, he and his wife had a beautiful baby boy that they named Robert Jr.

Dr. Carson is a nice, soft-spoken man and I never heard him speak ill of people because of the color of their skin. He has a wonderful smile with pearly white teeth and large dimples. He wears round glasses, which hide his blue eyes sometimes. His shirts are always crisp from the spray starch the dry cleaners use and he is always nicely attired in a tie and a sport coat.

He once told me that his family had owned a plantation in Savannah, Georgia, and showed me documentation showing that his great grandparents, Matthew and Betty Stevens, bought slaves right off the ships. Later, the family moved to Birmingham, Alabama, where his parents fell on hard times and lost everything. So, they decided to place him up for adoption with a family that could provide for him. It seems odd for such a wonderful man to have ties to a legacy which caused such destruction to a race of people. Could any good come from it?

Dr. Carson came home one night, exhausted after a long day of back-to-back surgeries. He had several huge files in one hand. He said he believed that a man named Ken Stevens Jr., who lives in Birmingham, Alabama, is his biological brother. He explained that he had already found a wonderful house next door to his long lost brother and wanted to relocate there. He talked it over with Mrs. Carson and they decided to move his practice to Birmingham, immediately.

I was very excited and overwhelmed with joy seeing the great lengths Dr. Carson went to, not only to find his brother, but to find a wonderful house right next door to him! I thought to myself, "This man must really want a relationship with his brother to move his entire life." He said he was offered a great opportunity there and would be the head vascular surgeon at the local hospital.

Mrs. Carson was in Europe doing research, so Dr. Carson asked me to be in charge of taking care of the family's most prized possessions during the move. He generously gave me two month's pay in advance for the move, since he could not make the trip until things were settled in Columbus. I gladly accepted the assignment.

"Wow, I'm moving to Birmingham, Alabama!"

Chapter 2

Who would ever think that I, Seth Stevens, would be a father? Emily Rose is my first child's name. I would never have thought that I would be the proud father of a healthy baby girl. I named her after my grandmother, Emily, and my mother, whose middle name is Rose. My parents, who have already made their introductions to her at the hospital today, say that she has big blue eyes with a small streak of curly blonde hair on the crown of her cute little head.

This day, May 2, 1963, is special and I shall cherish it for the rest of my life. I picked up a big bunch of wildflowers from Richards Market in downtown Birmingham to put in my baby's nursery at the local hospital. The boys at work say I've been smiling ever since I heard that Nora gave birth to my baby girl. My best friend Patrick and I smoked cigars to commemorate my becoming a father during lunch today, when I got word my baby girl had arrived.

I get off early to change, before heading to the hospital, and I notice a demonstration downtown at Kelly Ingram Park, which involves a number of Negroes who began a march for equality from a nearby church. After getting out of my truck, I am told by people who saw the demonstration that local authorities were called in to keep them in line.

I get back in my truck and slow it to get a better view. The police are beating Negro protesters with clubs and spraying them with high-pressure hoses. I know the Negroes are in trouble when I see dogs from the Birmingham Police Department being brought to the front line.

"Serves them right," I think, with a smile and the assurance that every white person in this community feels the same way I do. Folks in Birmingham don't take kindly to Negroes thinking they're equal, if not better, than whites.

When I arrive home, I quickly jump in the shower, and then put on my best Sunday suit. I grab my new camera, even though I'm sure my parents are already at the hospital taking pictures. Everyone talks about how

I'm always photographing every event and I must say, I do have tons of pictures, including some I know I must keep hidden away.

When I was younger, my grandfather taught me how to develop film in the basement of our home, where he made a darkroom. After his death, I discovered pictures he took and some just sent chills down deep in my soul. Through the years, I have taken pictures of weddings, picnics, and even some pictures of my closest friend, who has secrets I dare not tell anyone about.

I grab a roll of film off my dresser and dart down the stairs with my hair still dripping, because I'm dying to take pictures of my new baby girl. I make a quick call to the hospital and when the phone rings in Nora's room, my mother answers.

"Where are you, Seth? We thought you'd be here by now"?

"I'm on my way!"

"Check on Ronnie before you leave. Tell him I'll be home soon and there's a sandwich and some lemonade for him in the icebox."

I hang up and find my little brother at the kitchen table and give him the message. He's smiling and excited about being an uncle. After promising him I'll make sure I take a photo of his new niece just for him, I quickly go out the back door and get in my truck as a sweat breaks out on my face and butterflies flutter around in my stomach. Backing my Ford pickup from my parents' driveway, I check each side, making sure there are no pedestrians walking past. Then, I notice men moving in furniture next door at the old Whitfield Mansion.

"It will be great having new neighbors after it's stayed empty for so long," I think. The back window of my truck is obscured by my baby's birthday balloons, so I have to watch out again for pedestrians.

"It's a Girl" is printed on white ribbons tied to the five pink balloons floating inside my truck.

Excited as I arrive at the local hospital, I nervously head up to the nursery with my new camera strapped around my neck and approach the nurses' station after I exit the elevator. There is a lovely brunette sitting behind a long oblong counter that's covered with patients' charts. I motion to get her attention and she looks up, gazing into my green eyes, smiling.

"Which room is Nora Thomas in?" I ask. She points while coming from behind the counter, revealing a curvy shape that her white uniform hugs tightly.

"You can find her in Room 514, the last room on the right," she says softly, in a velvety voice. I smile and then have to shake my head slightly, focusing on the reason I'm here.

With each step I take down the wide hallway, my heart seems to beat just a little faster until it feels like it's going to jump out of my chest. I'm greeted with a smile and a hug from my mother, who's standing near the door, awaiting my arrival.

"She's beautiful, Seth, and she looks just like you!"

My baby girl, Emily Rose, is snuggly wrapped in a pink blanket; lying quietly in a hospital crib with a sign that reads, "6 lbs., 4 oz." I'm not surprised that no one from Nora's family is here. They were totally against Nora continuing with her pregnancy and wanted her to get rid of the baby. Nora always said if I wasn't going to marry her, then Emily Rose would take her parents' last name. Knowing marriage was out the question, I agreed, deciding to wait to deal with it at a later date. Even though she has a different last name, it doesn't matter. She's still my baby girl. I know her family was against her having this baby, but I never thought they wouldn't be here for their daughter.

My parents are standing over the crib, smiling ear to ear, admiring their first grandchild.

"I guess you're a father, Seth," my father says, while looking at his mother's namesake.

"Hello, Nora, can I get you anything?" I ask, a little too politely.

"No, Seth. I'm fine," she says.

I bend over and kiss Nora on the forehead, thinking, "This is the mother of my child and I'm not in love with her."

Chapter 3

Finally time to relax, and what a day it has been. Hiring a housekeeper and cook for this big house was a job in itself. I am pleased that the movers finally arrived yesterday with all of the Carsons' belongings. Moving to a new city is difficult enough, but being in charge of the move is worse. Sending me to accomplish this momentous task alone lets me know that the Carsons have complete confidence in me. I am earning every penny I have been paid. Unpacking rooms filled with boxes can really wear you down, especially when you are in charge and everyone is looking to you for direction and guidance.

I pray I packed the family china properly. Dr. and Mrs. Carson would be furious if one of the wedding plates was cracked, not to mention their Waterford crystal punch bowl and glasses. They will look nice on their beautiful mahogany table in the dining room, gleaming in luminescence off the crystal chandelier hanging from the ceiling. While I unpack towels in my private bath, I smile, thinking about how well the Carson family has treated me over the years. It was a delight watching Robert Jr., who calls me "Aunt Peg," grow up to be a fine young man, who is now attending Ohio State University. Sometimes, when he was a child, he acted as if I was his mother. Everyone always said, when they saw me, they knew Robert Jr. was nearby.

I reach in the medicine cabinet just above the bathroom sink in the plush bath next to my room on the second floor and grab a small bottle of Epsom salt to add to my bath water to soothe my aching body. I think I used every muscle in my body during the ordeal of moving an entire household across the country. Looking out my bathroom window next to the sink, I notice a young man working on his truck next door. He looks up at me, puzzled, and his face distorts into what appears to be shock, then disbelief, as he does a double-take and his eyes widen. I kindly smile and nod to him like a good neighbor, then close the curtains.

My tub is filled with hot water that soothes my cramping toes and a sigh of relief spreads through every muscle of my body.

"Ahhhhh. This is heaven."

With my eyes closed and my neck relaxing against the back of the cast iron tub, I refamiliarize myself with peace and quiet.

"Well, nice to see you again, peace," I say in my best Southern belle drawl. "And you, too, quiet. I have missed you both."

Earlier, I found a small radio under the kitchen cabinet that the workers must have left by accident while readying the house for the Carsons' arrival. I quickly confiscated it and brought it upstairs, hoping to find a jazz station.

"This is KLMH," the announcer says with a silky voice, as he plays smooth jazz by gone, but not forgotten jazz great, Billie Holiday. I become quiet and somber, listening to the haunting lyrics of "Strange Fruit," amazed that a song about black people being lynched could be so poignant and reflective. Yet, the pathos and inevitability of evil cannot be denied, either.

This house will take me weeks to complete, but tonight I am going to just soak. Relaxing is another story.

My nerves are startled by every single sound that creeps through this big house, mostly coming from a cool wind outside wafting through the house like a breeze rustling a petticoat.

I recline in the tub, admiring the wonderful handcrafted rails that swing around to the second floor and the large, domed artistically decorated ceiling, lit by a cascading chandelier. Normally, I would have never left my bathroom door wide open for fear that someone might come barging through the first floor main door. It still bothers me a little, but I am determined to relax. I can finally enjoy peace and quiet after this long and busy day. Let me just close my eyes for a second and let my mind forget all I have to accomplish before Mrs. Carson's arrival from Europe, soon after her husband's arrival from Ohio.

Opening my eyes, I notice the time on the clock on the bathroom wall and realize several hours have passed. I must have dozed off while basking in the warmth of the now cooling water. I had not realized how truly tired I was. The steam was long gone from my rejuvenating hot bath, so I pull the plug and sit watching the water as it creates a tiny tornado in the tub. Reluctantly, I put one leg over the side and drop my wet foot onto a shaggy rug next to the tub, and slowly emerge from my peaceful retreat.

My favorite soft towel, retrieved from one of the boxes I packed, absorbs the small water droplets on my face. I mentally run through everything at hand tomorrow, as I dry myself off completely and apply creamy lotion. Then, I head downstairs to the kitchen. I put on a kettle and grab a teacup from an unpacked box on the kitchen floor for my evening tea.

Passion Flower Tea is my favorite after a relaxing bath. I walk around making sure all the first floor windows are locked by wiggling each latch, and then head toward the front door to see if it is locked. Suddenly, the sound of the kettle whistling, as if to say "please come get me," distracts me and I change direction, anxious for a soothing cup of hot tea. I am reminded as I head to the kitchen of always wanting to stay up late when I was a child. I can hear my mother, as though it was yesterday.

"If you don't get to bed young lady, I'm going to tell your father!"

I scoop a teaspoon of sugar for my tea, fondly remembering the great parents I once had. Moments later, I climb into bed, positioning myself with my back against the headboard and take my first sip of tea, anticipating the sweet warmth that will soon wrap around me like a blanket, bringing sleep and sweet dreams.

"Ummmm, this is delicious," I think, as I take a small sip, and then set the cup down, grabbing a No. 2 pencil and a pad from the nightstand. My eyelids become heavy as I begin making a list of chores for tomorrow. I am again overcome by a peaceful repose and find myself calmly drifting off to sleep.

Chapter 4

It's May 3, 1963, and Birmingham, Alabama, is a quiet town. Well, everyone who lives here thinks so. Everyone here has their place in this community. When you walk into the Richards Market downtown, Mr. Richards calls my name out loud with a hearty, "Welcome to Richards, Seth!"

When we were children, Patrick, Mike, and I always loved going swimming next to Richards while our parents went shopping. We jumped clean off the Tucket Bridge next to Richards and I was crowned "King Jumper," since very few guys would even dare to make such a high leap. I nearly lost my life one evening when I was bold enough to jump from the top of a lamp post clear off the bridge and hit the water head first, nearly drowning. Luckily, my friend Patrick was there and quickly jumped off the bridge to save me.

When I finally came to, he was there smiling and asked me, "What the hell you do that for, Seth?"

I owe Patrick my life and nothing could ever make me forget that.

I gather my tools from the porch, where my kid brother Ronnie must have used them earlier, and head to the garage to begin work on my Ford pickup. I enjoy taking small parts off and fixing them to make my truck look better. Today is the day I have to change my oil, which is long overdue.

I can tell it's nearly nighttime by looking at the sun's rays fading in the Western sky and the sound of birds calling each other in the trees just above the garage, ready for a good night's sleep. I'm now twenty-three and still living at home! Thank God for my parents being wonderful Christians. I've come to grips with the fact that Nora and I will never get married and I will likely be the one who will raise our daughter alone, since her family cannot afford to take on such a big responsibility.

I lie flat under the truck so I can reach the oil tank under the engine and quickly change the oil. Pulling myself up from under the truck after my task is accomplished, I glance up at the old Whitfield house next door and suddenly I notice the second floor light on and wonder why. I haven't seen activity in that old Whitfield house in years.

Then I remember seeing moving trucks there yesterday as I headed to the hospital.

"It'll be great having new neighbors," I think. "Maybe they'll even have youngsters to play with Ronnie or maybe a daughter to play with my new baby girl, someday."

I grab an old towel to wipe my hands, greasy from working on my Ford, when I notice a nigger girl in the upstairs window. Standing and looking above, I dare not move as I widen my eyes to get a better look. "Did my eyes just really see what I thought I just saw?"

The girl walks past the window and then slowly pauses as she looks at me and smiles, closing the curtains.

"This can't be! Niggers moving into a predominantly white community? This can't be, and especially not in a house next to the Stevens family!"

"My dad will be furious," I think, "when I break the news to him tonight after he comes home from the courthouse!" I rush inside our back door where Ronnie is finishing off his bowl of chocolate ice cream at the kitchen table.

"Ronnie, did you know we have new neighbors?" Ronnie shakes his head, but his eyes get big with excitement as he looks at every move I make.

"I wonder. Do they have kids?" he asks, after taking another spoon of ice cream.

"I didn't see any kids, but I did see a nigger girl in the upstairs window."

Ronnie's face wrinkles in a frown as he takes another bite.

"You shouldn't talk like that," he says.

I walk over to the kitchen sink, looking out the side window, trying to spot more signs of movement throughout the house next door. I pour myself a glass of water while keeping my attention on the side of the Whitfield's house.

"Surely a nigger family can't afford the old Whitfield place? What black family would have the guts to move here in this community?" Upset, I grab my keys from the key hook next to the back door and dart out the door to the garage. I must've filled my engine with oil in record time, because the sun hasn't set yet. So, upset and disturbed about what I just witnessed, I decide to head over to Patrick's house.

Five minutes hadn't passed before I was knocking at my closest friend's door.

"Who is it? " Patrick replies, his voice muffled, coming from behind the big wooden door.

"It's me! Seth!" I shout.

Patrick quickly turns the knob and opens the door with a cheerful grin on his face.

"Didn't I just see you less than an hour ago?" The only thing between us is a screen door covered with large mosquitoes trying to get inside.

"You will never guess who just moved into Mr. Whitfield's old house!"

Patrick stands with his palm directed up just above his waist like he is in a prayer line at Sunday service.

"Who? I hope it's a beautiful blonde like you see on the billboards downtown!"

I can see Patrick's parents getting up from the dinner table in the dining room beyond the entrance hall and living room, awaiting my answer as they listen closely, curious about my new neighbors.

"It's niggers!"

Mrs. Grant begins walking toward the door, shaking her head in disbelief, as I look at her through the screen door that seems to undulate as she moves across the living room. She sits down on the couch with her hands over her mouth in shock. The screen door suddenly opens and I rush inside, slamming it shut to keep out the dreaded mosquitoes.

Patrick is a much bigger man than me. He walks up behind me after slamming the front door shut, making a sound like a gunshot, and I quickly turn around. I can tell he's upset. His face, which was just cheerfully smiling, is now grimacing with an angry frown.

"Are you sure you saw what you say you saw?" Patrick asks.

"Yes! I am damn sure of it!" I say boldly. Then I notice that Mr. Grant's face appears puzzled as his mind scrambles for the right words.

"Who would sell the best property in Birmingham to niggers?" he screams, his voice shaking with fury.

"I don't know," I say calmly, "but I do know what I saw."

I look over at Patrick who is speechless with rage. I can hear his younger brother Mike's voice coming from his bedroom down the hall. He must have heard every word I said, because he has his boots on and he's shouting.

"I have my shotgun!" he says, as he rushes into the living room, pushing shells into his gun, his shoelaces untied, nearly tripping him.

"Patrick, can you go get a few bottles of rotgut and some rags?" I ask, as I put my hand on his shoulder to steady him while Mike bends down to tie his shoes.

12

"Hold on, boys!" Mr. Grant says, walking over to the desk where he searches for numbers in the family's phone book.

"I don't think you boys will need none of those things until I get to the bottom of this. "

I am sure Mr. Grant is dialing the local authorities, but we are already heading out of the door toward my pickup and on our way to the old Whitfield house. The hate that fuels our hearts was recognized and ignited by the only thing we know having been taught for generations how to deal with uppity niggers who think they are equal to, or better than whites. We can't stop and wait for the authorities. We have a job to do.

Chapter 5

The three of us arrive several hours later at the old Whitfield house. We're drunk, loud, and I'm barely able to focus on the path ahead. When we arrive, bottles are rolling from side to side in the open truck bed, making a loud clinking sound. Seth and my brother and me have been drinking heavily from the bottles of rotgut whiskey we picked up on the way. The headlights shine on the big oak doors that grace the front of the old house. The doors give the old place character and the appearance of a warm, beautiful home belonging to a family of means. It enrages me to think that niggers now live here.

"We're here, boys, and I know she's in there!" Seth announces.

Seth slurs his words, driving slowly. We've been doing some serious drinking, and it has taken us an hour to get here. Focused, gripping the steering wheel to keep his hands steady, he must've barely noticed that the pickup stops mere inches away from the big oak tree that stands on the front lawn of the majestic house.

Seth is fueled with hate and anger as he presses his hands on the pickup's horn. I'm sure everyone in the county must've heard it, but his intent is not to alarm the neighbors, just the interloper. I guess they should take it as a warning, though, that something bad is going on in their lily-white neighborhood. Seth just wants the girl he saw in the window to know this is no place for niggers.

He turns off the pickup with the headlights still shining on the big house, and leaves the keys in the ignition. Mike yells out, loudly slapping his hand on the roof of Seth's truck, before jumping out of the back bed. Barely able to stand, I throw the passenger door open and walk a few wobbly steps to meet Mike at the bed of the truck.

"We have work to do," Seth says, as he shuts the door on the driver's side, and then wipes his mouth after swallowing a large gulp of warm homemade liquor. I know he instinctively hates whoever is inside this house. We stare at the windows, anticipating some kind of movement from within, but nothing happens.

"I know she's in there!" he shouts. He turns to look at Mike and me as we struggle to unload a large object from the pickup and place it on the lawn.

"No one is allowed to live in this wonderful house except a pure family," he says. Mike and me make it clear how we feel, as we laugh without a care in the world and start digging a hole on the lawn to plant our collective hate. Mike suddenly shouts out, as he looks up toward the dark house.

"Damn, Seth, looks like no one is even home, being so quiet and all!"

Seth grabs the rope from the back of the pickup and howls at the house.

"Little girl," Seth says. His voice suddenly becomes calm and soft. "Little girl, come out and play." He takes his time looking at each window for some sign of life, finding nothing.

"I know she's in there, boys!" Looking at Mike and me, he takes another big gulp, emptying the bottle and throwing it at the tree, breaking it. He then turns around and stares at the dark house, his eyes squinting as he tries to peer inside.

"Don't make me come in there after you, little nigger girl."

This time he speaks with an unsteady, booming voice that echoes in my eardrums. We stop digging and watch as he takes each step slowly up to the old Whitfield house, dragging a noose by his side, making a barely audible scraping sound as it grazes the concrete path. Dead flower leaves blow across the path from the manicured lawn, which leads to the large Victorian wrap-around porch. Each step he takes seems to start a bigger fire inside him, and as he comes closer to the doors, he is enraged. His breath is reeking of alcohol and his hair is dripping wet from the humidity. He has the appearance and demeanor of the poor white trash we hate only slightly less than we hate niggers and Jews. He touches the old door as if admiring the wonderful wood grain, causing us to cackle drunkenly at his cautious approach. He turns and puts his finger to his lips, shushing us. Suddenly, the sound of a key locking the door from the other side catches our ears and Seth motions to us again to be quiet. Seth reaches out to check the door handle and tries to gain entry, but the massive door refuses to budge. In frustration, he bursts out in a hate-filled scream as he slams his open palm on the door.

"I said come out, nigger girl!"

He puts his ear against the eight-inch thick door, listening for sounds of movement or voices. Drunk and exhausted, he drops to his knees and sobs: "You aren't' supposed to be here!"

Chapter 6

S ound asleep, I quickly awaken after hearing a sound so loud it seems like it is entering the bedroom on the second floor. Trembling with fright and alone in a new house, I reach for the clock on the nightstand next to my bed and see that it's two thirty in the morning.

Pulling back the thin sheet covering me on the queen-size bed, I think, "Who would be up at this hour?"

In a dark house alone, I dare not turn on the lamp on my nightstand, feeling it would only bring more attention. I sit up and hear the sounds of crickets and summer owls outside my bedroom window. Sheer curtains are engulfed in a gentle summer breeze making its way through the open window and gliding gracefully across me in a cool caress. I stand and grab my white robe and tie it gently around my waist. Putting on my slippers at the foot of the cast iron bed, I walk silently across the room and open the bedroom door slowly.

"The hinges need to be oiled," I think, hearing creaking sounds I hadn't noticed until then. "Why is it when you are trying to stay quiet you never can?"

Taking small, slow steps, I hear only the mahogany floorboards creaking as I walk across the room. I move slowly down a dark, unfamiliar second floor hall, touching the walls decorated with small pictures I had hung earlier in the day. I pause at each doorway to catch my breath, while placing my hand on my chest, only to feel the hard thump of my heartbeat. I'm afraid and alone; unable to reach the phone near the kitchen downstairs.

Finally, I stand at the top of the stairs, where I pause and tilt my head to one side.

"Hello, is anyone there?" I ask softly, praying no one answers, but still aware of the creaking of the old hardwood floors. I take each step with caution in the dark house, moving forward downstairs toward the enormous living room that showcases a massive marble fireplace with a large oil painting hanging above it. Turning my head in each direction, I try to determine where the sound I heard in my room came from, when suddenly a devastating feeling comes over me.

"Could someone be in the house?" I think, fear growing inside me at a rapid rate.

Shaken and motionless in the hallway that leads to the main entrance, I hear mumbling coming from outside the front door. I walk toward it slowly. Even though I am terrified, I manage to convince myself to look through the curtains, but notice nothing unusual.

"This can't be children playing at this hour," I think, as I reach for the front door handle and realize that the door was the only thing I forgot to check when the kettle screamed from the kitchen. I hear a faint whisper coming from the other side of the door and pause.

"Come out little, nigger girl," a man says.

Noticing the skeleton key still in the keyhole, I immediately lock it, fighting back tears and swallowing the lump in my throat. Then the words get louder and more forceful with a hard thump on the door.

"I said come out, nigger girl!" he screams with all the rage of a wild beast that can't get to its prey. "Now, I know you're in there, because I just heard you lock the door. How dare you! How dare you lock me out! I belong here! This is *my* street! *My* neighborhood! You're the one that should be locked out and hung from a tree until your pretty little neck breaks! Why? Why can't I get to you and put this rope around your neck? Why?" he cries.

A faint sound like someone sobbing catches me by surprise and I am tempted to open the door and look outside to see who's there.

"You are not supposed to be here," he says, sobbing with frustration and defeat.

Clinching my robe tightly, shaking my head "no," I erase any thoughts of opening the door from my mind, which is racing, wondering who is outside and why they are there taunting me. My knees suddenly become weak and I am barely able to stand. I lean my back against the heavy wooden door just to get some stability. Then, I try to calm myself by focusing on the domed ceiling above the stairs with its painted pastel sky, white clouds, and pink cherubs just visible in the blue moonlight shining through the windows.

After mumbling a brief prayer of thanks, I take a deep breath. But fear overtakes me, and I let out an indescribable cry of confused shock. I stumble over my scream, barely able to mouth the words as they finally escape my lips.

"But, I only work here! Leave me alone!"

Calming myself down again after my agonized outburst, I wait for a minute, and then I peek out the window, where I notice a glare from outside.

"They're setting the house on fire? My Lord!" I think, grabbing my robe close to my throat, while tears flow unchecked down my cheeks. "This can't be! Who would do this?" I quickly stumble back to my bedroom in terror, unsure of where to go, what to do. I fall on my bed and cry out in despair, not sure if I will live or die.

Chapter 7

Hung over from last night, I can only remember bits and pieces of the events. One thing I am sure of is that we have a disgusting family of Negroes living next door and I'm not happy about it. I must get up and head off to my job, because the construction company I work for put in a huge bid and it was awarded to us. Mr. Powers, the company's foreman, asked all the fellows to get at the site a little earlier than usual. So, I head down to the kitchen to grab a cup of coffee, only to see that Ronnie has beaten me to the cream and is putting the last cup in his hot oatmeal.

"Howdy, Seth," Ronnie says, watching the expression on my face change as I realize there is no cream for my coffee.

"Where you off to?" he asks.

"I have a new job over on 6th Street, downtown."

I open the refrigerator to see if there is maybe a drop of cream left, only to be distracted by the doorbell ringing.

"Now, who could that be?" I think, forgetting my quest to find cream inside the Frigidaire.

I walk from the back of the house to the front door, through a hallway full of framed pictures from our family outings. We always take pictures at the picnics after Sunday services and my parents make sure that we keep a scrapbook for the coffee table in the living room. My parents also have framed pictures on a dresser in their bedroom showcasing the best pictures that weren't put on the hallway wall. There are smiles on all of the faces in each picture that my mother carefully put in beautiful frames she bought downtown at Richards. Every local politician and even some federal personnel are pictured. I always feel really bad that Ronnie is never able to go to the Sunday picnics with us due to his allergies and sickness. My mom treats him to a big ice cream cone after he finishes his dialysis each Sunday. The poor guy had a bad hand dealt his way and Dr. Kemp told my parents he has to have a kidney transplant if we want him to see his fifteenth birthday. We're all nervous, because he is fourteen now.

I open the front door and, low and behold, Nora is standing there with my baby girl in one arm.

"Didn't the doctor tell you she should stay inside due to all the pollen?" I ask, rushing them inside. I see Emily smiling and looking at me with her big blue eyes. For some reason, I forget about everything at that moment. Nora hands me a diaper bag filled with cloth diapers and glass bottles.

"Look here, Seth," she says abruptly. "I can't do this. You and your family gonna have to take little Emily. My parents just can't help me at all. So you gonna have to raise her yourself."

"Do you know that I am on my way to a big construction job?" I ask, my heart racing. "Who am I gonna get to watch her?"

"I guess that's your problem," she says, as she hands me a bag of baby clothes. "You begged me not to have an abortion and now I am stuck with this damn baby that I never wanted. I gave you everything, Seth, even a child. But I can't do this."

Nora grabs little Emily's hand and kisses her one last time as she darts from the house and gets inside a car, parked outside with a male driver I don't recognize. As they drive away, I pray that this will be the last time my baby and I ever set our eyes on Nora Thomas.

Emily begins to cry as I stand on the porch, gently rocking her in my arms, trying to quiet her. I look up as the car that brought Nora with the best news she has given me since she told me she was having my child, heads down the street, driving off like they can't leave fast enough. Then I get a glimpse of a nigger girl on the porch next door watering flowers. Still trying to keep my baby quiet, I am shocked and disgusted as the girl looks over at us and smiles.

"Hello, there," she says, talking bold as brass, as if we were equals. Her smile slowly leaves her face, replaced by a puzzled look as she tries to understand my expression and the words spoken from my lips.

"Why in the hell are you here, nigger? You need to move over to the other side of town if you know what's good for ya!" I scream.

Turning to go inside with my baby, leaving everything on the porch until later, I make sure the door slams behind me, leaving her speechless, no doubt.

As I look down lovingly at my beautiful Emily, trying to calm her now frightened cries, after startling her with my outcry against the nigger girl next door, I wonder, "Who in the hell could ever love a nigger?"

Chapter 8

I awaken, thankful to be still alive, after the frightening night. I've never been so afraid. The house didn't catch fire, but I can still smell a slight odor of burning wood and wonder what was on the lawn afire last night. I sure hope it was not the large shade tree.

After staying up until nearly daylight, I feel exhausted, but I am glad I managed to get a few hours of sleep. I wonder who was at the door screaming and sobbing last night and decide it had to have been some adolescent prank or something. No mature adult would behave that way. Looking at the long list of chores I wrote last night on a pad on my nightstand, I let out a sigh, thinking about the busy day ahead. I quickly push all thoughts of last night aside, get dressed, and go downstairs to start my day within half an hour of waking.

"Now, what can I have for breakfast?" I think, as I look forward to my usual fare, reaching in the refrigerator to get a jar of strawberry jam to spread on my toast. Toast with strawberry jam is a must. I get done with preparing my breakfast quickly, trying to get out of the kitchen before the housekeeper and cook takes it over to start her work for the day. I hear her running the sweeper upstairs, getting Dr. and Mrs. Carson's bedroom ready for their arrival. There is a gnawing reminder of last night, as I begin to spread the jam on my toast and think about how the events last night really upset me.

I am so glad I took the time last week to hire ground help. This old house is in great need of landscape attention. Although in need of a lot of care, I know the lawn and gardens have great potential for natural beauty once pruned and landscaped. I always thought Birmingham was beautiful and a great place to live from the pictures I'd seen, but after last night, I am beginning to question my decision to move here with the Carsons.

Reading the morning paper with a cup in one hand, I head for the front porch swing to relax for a few quiet minutes before starting another busy day of unpacking. The morning paper's main headline describes Negroes protesting and the local authorities using force to get the protestors under control.

I wince as I look at the pictures of people of my race being drenched with fire hoses and attacked by dogs.

The workers I hired are cleaning the front lawn where the majestic big oak tree stands as if guarding the house. I breathe a sigh of relief, seeing that it is intact and unharmed.

"Was anyone here last night?" one of the workers yells, as I look up.

"What do you mean?" I reply.

"There's a burnt cross laying here and a few ashes," he says, shaking his head.

Before I can respond, Miss Bee comes from behind the front door to join me. Bee is the housekeeper I hired before I arrived in Birmingham, after being told by Dr. Carson's contacts here that she's the best housekeeper and cook in Birmingham. She is in her mid-fifties with salt-and-pepper hair worn pulled back in a bun. The other workers I hired said that Bee doesn't take any stuff from anyone, no matter what color. I can believe that, as I spy a small pistol sticking out on the side of her apron just below her tied belt.

The workers told me that her church pleaded with her to stop carrying her rifle after she started shouting in the spirit one Sunday and pulled the trigger, leaving a big hole in the roof. She nearly cleared out the entire church, including Pastor LeCroy, they said, when that gun went off.

She told me to call her Bee, like all her friends do. A formidable woman, she is not without a sense of humor at times. She said she used to work as a cook at the juke joint on the Negro side of town and men used to smile when they saw her coming.

"I had the best body in Birmingham when I was younger," she said when I first met her. You would never know that now, though, by looking at her big stomach resting under those huge breasts.

"Enjoying a cup of hot coffee, Miss Peg?" she asks.

"No, I prefer tea. Do you drink tea?"

"Sometimes, I guess. What are the workers looking at out there on the front lawn?"

"We had some visitors last night."

"Visitors!"

After hauling her wide girth to the edge of the cement path and taking a closer look, Bee lets out a piercing scream that startles me.

"That's a Klan cross!" she yells, grabbing her pistol instinctively. "Y'all take that down right now, you hear?"

"What is it?" I ask, as she rushes back to the porch and up the steps.

"That's one of the symbols that the Klan uses here when they feel threatened. Did you see who they were, Miss Peg?" Bee stands a few feet from me, looking down at me with an intense, serious look on her face.

"No. Actually, I heard noises last night, and people talking. But I didn't see any faces." The look on her face frightens me nearly as much as the incident last night.

The look on Bee's face changes, giving the impression that she is not convinced I did not see anyone. She puts a stern grip on her pistol then leans down at eye level with me.

"If you have any trouble with the Klan, please call me. Do I make myself clear? Do you think you will need me to stay the night tonight, Miss Peg?"

I try not to let her know that last night scared the daylights out of me, but I feel comfortable knowing that Dr. Carson is due to arrive this afternoon and I am no longer afraid.

"No, Bee that will not be necessary. Dr. Carson is arriving today."

"Well, I'll be here until he gets here." It is clear that she will not be leaving until she is sure I am not alone in this house again tonight.

Bee sits down next to me, looking out at the workers on the lawn and takes another sip from the coffee cup she set down when she left the porch, never taking her eyes off the workers.

"Bee, I appreciate your concern," I say, glad I have such a strong ally.

"Good!" she replies. "Because Bee don't take nothing from nobody. Everyone I know of is scared of my best friend, Cha-Cha."

I look up, sure she will tell me who Cha-Cha is. I wait for an explanation, but she continues to sip her coffee.

"Who is that that, Bee?" I ask. That second, and not a moment later, Bee looks directly at me with piercing eyes.

"Cha-Cha" is the sound that my shotgun makes when I load her up."

Bee gets up whistling as she makes her way back in the house to begin her duties. I am so confused about Bee and her guns. I get up and continue to watch the men remove the dark remains of the burnt cross from the front lawn.

"Place the ashes in the fire bucket in the back, please," I yell. "I can use them for a project." They look as confused as I feel after Bee's gun-toting diatribe, but they just shrug and bag up the ashes like I asked. Still confused by Bee's response, I open the door and go inside, thinking: "Was I right to hire this woman?"

Chapter 9

In the afternoon, Dr. Carson arrives earlier than I expected. I am so glad I hired the extra help I needed to get the majority of the house done by noon. I wasn't sure how soon he would arrive and I wanted the house to be ready.

I am excited about having half the day off, and decide to go into town just to have a cold Coke. I put on a nice summer dress with some comfortable sandals and a sunhat to keep the hot sun off my face.

"Maybe I will meet some nice people in town," I think, as I walk out of my room and head for the stairs. I hear Dr. Carson talking to his wife on the telephone in the kitchen, telling her how lovely the house looks and assuring her they made the right decision. Then there is a silence, and it seems that Dr. Carson is listening to his wife talk, as I reach the bottom of the stairs and stop to look at myself in an ornate mirror hanging on the wall.

"Wait a minute!" I hear him say, as I put on one of my earrings, tilting my head to one side.

"There was a demonstration in Birmingham, Alabama, that brutalized hundreds of Negro teenagers," the newscaster's voice says, coming from the small black-and-white television in the kitchen. I head for the kitchen, listening. Dr. Carson is standing motionless with a sandwich in one hand, riveted by what he's hearing and seeing.

"Dear, let me call you back. I think some children were seriously injured downtown."

I walk toward the television slowly, watching the screen, and stand by his side as we both look at the television in disbelief. We dare not move, afraid we might miss what Walter Cronkite is saying.

Suddenly, we hear a knock on the front door. With my mind still on the television, listening to the newscast, I make my way to the front door, where I glance out the small window, shivering as I remember peering out of that same window the night before. I open the door to see a tall, attractive white gentleman wearing a nice off-white summer suit and a big smile.

"Carson residence. Hello, may I help you?" I say, after I open the door to greet the stranger. The tall gentleman looks at me and the smile fades from his handsome face.

"My name is Ken Stevens. I'm the neighbor next door. My son told me we have new neighbors. Do you live in this house, girl?"

I hear Dr. Carson's footsteps heading for the entry hall. The suddenly rude "gentleman" seems to change his attitude when he sees Dr. Carson approach the door and stand beside me.

"Sorry I'm just getting over here," the neighbor says, taking off his hat. Mr. Stevens extends his hand to Dr. Carson and they politely shake hands.

"Ken Stevens is my name. I'm your new neighbor. We had a busy day yesterday with the birth of our first grandchild. Here comes my wife, Mary." A woman his age walks through the door wearing a nice summer dress.

"Hello, and welcome to the neighborhood. So nice to have someone finally move in next door. I'm Mary Stevens," she holds out her hand for Dr. Carson to shake, which he does, smiling politely. "Please forgive me," she says, "but you look familiar. Have we met?" I nearly faint as I hear her words.

"Oh, no!" I think to myself. "It can't be!"

"No, I don't think so," Dr. Carson says. "I am new to Birmingham. Please come in Mr. and Mrs. Stevens," he says, and turns toward the living room, continuing to talk as he leads the way.

"I'm Dr. Robert Carson, but you can call me Robert." Dr. Carson looks overjoyed, seeing his brother for the first time after wanting to meet him for so many years. I wonder how he can contain his excitement. I am sure he has not told anyone about his long lost brother, except for his wife and me, and I am sure he is just bursting to tell the world he has finally found his brother.

As they sit in the living room, Dr. Carson relates the news we both just heard on the television.

"Did you hear the national news about Negro children attacked here in Birmingham?" he asks his guests.

Mr. Stevens looks somewhat perturbed as the newscast continues, listening to Walter Cronkite's account of the day's events blaring from the television in the kitchen. Mrs. Stevens seems perplexed and eyes Dr. Carson suspiciously as if she is trying to remember something, but does not utter a word.

"Can I offer you both a drink?" Dr. Carson asks.

"Why, yes, that would be fine. Scotch, straight up."

"Peg, would you be so kind as to get Mr. Stevens a scotch?"

I walk over to the wet bar and notice Mr. Stevens watching my every move, pretending to admire the house's beauty. I'm sure living next door he knows how this house looks. I feel his eyes staring at me while I pour his drink.

"Looks like you found good help here in Alabama," Mr. Stevens says, his voice tinged with an undercurrent of contempt that makes me cringe. Overjoyed about finally seeing his brother, Dr. Carson seems oblivious to the sinister undertones hinted at in his only living relative's tone and manner.

"Well, Peg moved from Ohio with us. She's family, you know," Dr. Carson replies. The Stevenses laugh, seemingly relieved, as they relate stories about their own Negro help. They recall mammies, cooks, and ground workers hired by their parents and themselves over the years that they said also seemed like family.

I direct my attention back to the television after handing Mr. Stevens his scotch, enduring the pointed look he gives me as if we have a secret. Mrs. Stevens looks on apparently used to her husband's inappropriate behavior and resigned to live with it.

"I wish I could find a good Negro to work for the family, especially since we will be raising our grandchild," Mrs. Stevens says pointedly, directing her statement at me with an air of irritation that baffles me.

Dr. Carson changes the subject as I walk toward a chair near him with a smile on my face, feeling protected, knowing Dr. Carson is here. I would never have dared smile if I was alone with his brother.

"So, Ken, are you originally from Birmingham?"

"Yes, born and raised here in Birmingham; lived here my whole life. The house next door was passed down from my parents who moved from Savannah just before I was born."

"That's great, Ken," Dr. Carson says. "They left you a legacy." Dr. Carson's manner indicates his certainty that the man sitting in the living room of his new home talking to him is his biological brother. Hearing that Ken Stevens' parents are deceased is all the corroboration he needs.

"I think I made the right decision about moving my practice here," Dr. Carson says, his face gleaming with a broad smile. "I'm the new director of the vascular department at the local hospital."

"You don't say?" Mr. Stevens replies, as he takes a swallow of his drink. "I practice law here and have been practicing for thirty years now. The law keeps me busy."

Dr. Carson takes out his hanky and wipes his forehead.

"Work is always good."

Mrs. Stevens looks around as if anticipating Dr. Carson's family to come out of one of the rooms to greet her with a kindly smile, and makes a point of ignoring me.

"So, where is your family, Robert?" Mrs. Stevens asks, with her hands folded primly and properly in her lap.

"Oh, my wife is coming soon. She is working on research for her dissertation for her doctoral degree in Europe, and my son is attending Ohio State University," Dr. Carson says, beaming with pride. "How many children do you have, Mr. and Mrs. Stevens?"

"We have two sons, Seth and Ronnie, and now, a new granddaughter, Emily Rose," Mrs. Stevens says, equally proud.

"You have to see her; she is so adorable. We became grandparents!"

Robert takes his wallet out to show pictures of his family, grinning from ear to ear as he shows Dr. Carson several photos. Seeing the pictures of a young man who looks familiar, I am confused. Where have I seen him?

"We're going to have to invite you and your entire family over when they arrive and get settled. My Mary makes the best pot roast Birmingham has to offer. Better yet, the finest men in Birmingham are meeting for drinks. We would love to have you come, Robert, and join us."

"That would be wonderful. I have to go to Mobile tomorrow, but I will be back in a couple of days. Leave your information with Peg. I will call you when I get back."

"Will do!" exclaims Mr. Stevens, with a hearty laugh. "Well, we won't take too much more of your time today," he says, as he and his wife rise and head for the front door after he downs his drink, tilting his head back to get every drop.

"Thanks, Ken, I look forward to hearing from you soon," Dr. Carson says, walking ahead of the couple to show them out. I walk up and stand next to Dr. Carson at the door, as we watch his brother and sister-in-law walk down the path that leads to the sidewalk.

"Dr. Carson, I think you made the right decision moving here," I say, disingenuously, not wanting to dampen the joy of meeting his brother.

Chapter 10

I have been busy all morning making sure Dr. Carson has everything needed for his trip to Mobile, Alabama. He is attending a seminar there required for his state licensure and is soon on his way. When Bee found out Dr. Carson was leaving me alone in the house again, she went home to take care of some things there, so she could come back and spend the night. I did not argue with her, grateful that I will not be alone in this house another night.

I love peeling apples for my famous family apple pie. I am nice and comfortable sitting on the back porch, settling down after all of the hustle and bustle of the morning. Noticing a young boy playing with his trucks in his backyard next door, I wave and he smiles back, continuing to play with his toys. It looks like he is around twelve or fourteen years old. I continue peeling apples so I can start baking the second batch of my family's double spice apple pie recipe, passed down to me by my mother.

Looking on the back porch ledge, I count each one, my finger pointing as I judge each one carefully. Ten pies and I have five more to make. The neighbors will love them! This will be a great present to give our newest friends and a great way to get to know each family. Just as I am wiping my hands on my apron, I hear the front doorbell.

"Wait a minute! Wait a minute!" I shout, as I run to the entry hall. "Hello, Mr. Stevens. How are you today?" I am surprised to see him, since he knows Dr. Carson is out of town. He looks at me with his piercing sky blue eyes.

"Hello, girl. Is Dr. or Mrs. Carson in?"

"Well, no, Mr. Stevens, Dr. Carson went to Mobile this morning."

Mr. Stevens moves through the front door and pushes me aside. My temperature is rising, but I dare not say a word.

"You're not from this part of the woods are you?"

"No, I'm from Ohio."

"Well, it's custom here when you speak to white folk to address us as 'sir' or 'ma'am.'"

I close the door and walk behind him to the living room, thinking to myself this is not the same man I just met yesterday, although I remember being uncomfortable with the way he stared at me. I dare not upset this man, so I speak softly.

"Sorry, Mr. Stevens. I was unaware I offended you, sir."

Turning around with a smirk on his face to let me know he is in charge, he seems to be staking a claim on property that is not his. He smiles, his mustache so thick I can barely notice his upper lip, and looks at me, not saying a word for what seems like an eternity. Before I can react, he slaps my cheek with his large hand, just hard enough to make it sting.

"Do you have any Idea what kind of trouble you can get into here in Birmingham?" Too afraid to move, I do not make a sound.

"What kind of trouble would that be, Mr. Stevens? I don't bother anyone here, sir."

Mr. Stevens starts to admire the art in the Carson's home, acting as if he owns the place. He removes a pipe from his side pocket and slides it between his lips, clenching it with his teeth. He puts tobacco from a pouch he takes from his jacket pocket into the pipe's bowl, pushing it down with his thumb, and strikes a match to light the pipe. The pungent smell of the tobacco fills the air, along with smoke that nearly chokes me, but I am afraid to cough, thinking if I keep quiet, maybe he will forget I am here.

"Tell me more about Mr. and Mrs. Carson. What kind of people are they? Are they Christians?" he asks.

"Yes, sir, they are wonderful people," I say with a measured voice. "They were among the 'Who's Who in Ohio.'"

"Good, because we're looking for quality families here. Remember this, girl. If you address white folk the wrong way again, you might find yourself not coming back to this wonder-ful house. We have special social groups here."

He laughs, showing his full set of teeth, but I am not amused.

"Hell, even the local sheriff's department is part of our organization!" He laughs uproariously at some joke I do not get.

I put my head down, not letting Mr. Stevens notice how upset I am.

"Yes, sir," I can't believe how quickly I have submitted to this man's power over me and I refuse to believe the words I hear coming from my own mouth.

"Now that's more like it, girl. I can pretty much do anything I like here in Birmingham," he says arrogantly. "My wife may leave for New York this Monday. It would be good if someone keeps my sheets warm when my boys are asleep. Do you understand me, girl? What I want you to do tonight is meet me downtown by the Tucket Bridge at midnight.

29

Come alone and on time, if you know what's good for you. That is, if you want to see this house again. And I suggest you keep this to yourself." He pauses, as if letting what he has said sink in.

"My wife and I are looking for some niggers to take good care of our boys and the baby. Can you recommend anyone from Ohio?"

"No, sir. I come from a small family. It's just my cousin Sera and me. I do not think she would like that kind of work, sir. She is due to arrive soon. You can ask her yourself, if you like, sir."

Mr. Stevens walks over to the front door, as if he has not heard me, and then pauses.

"Well, make sure I speak to her when she arrives," he says dismissively, then says with a deliberate voice, "You know what, nigger girl? I don't like your kind. That nigger Martin Luther King is starting to ruin this wonderful country and it's making plenty of people around here damn mad. He's trying so hard to get your black asses equal rights."

Mr. Stevens takes a few steps toward me and leans down in my face, trying his best to intimidate and humiliate me even more.

"It will be a cold day in hell when that day comes. He's nearly ruined this country. You used to be a peaceful race of people with enough common sense to stay in your place."

Mr. Stevens laughs with a sinister grin that accompanies his maniacal mirth.

"The law was right, letting dogs attack your black asses and spraying water hoses on them. Were you downtown with them?"

"No, sir. I only just arrived in Birmingham that day," I reply, afraid of what he might do if he thinks I was part of the demonstration.

"Well, you can say you're lucky then. The sheriff put over five hundred teenage Negroes in jail and they're still sitting in jail now. I will try my best to keep them there or even get them transported to prisons. The only thing is the economy couldn't stand it if we did that. We need your kind to do the work too dirty and lowly for good white folks to do."

Mr. Steven opens the door and starts to finish his conversation from the porch, while I am careful not to step outside.

"We really need to get that nigger-loving President Kennedy out of the White House and get a real Southern gentleman back in there like it used to be. Did you know that President George Washington had a nigger slave working for him? Now, that was a great President! He was so great; we even put him on our currency."

Mr. Stevens makes his way down the first step from the porch, laughing loudly as he finishes his last comment and I am relieved to see Bee in a taxi that is parking in front of the house. Bee looks at Mr. Stevens as she shuts the cab door while putting one hand on her hip and gesturing slyly at Mr. Stevens. I think Mr. Stevens knows that this lady carries a pistol. It looks like someone popped the starter pistol to signal the start of a track race, as Mr. Stevens moves quickly off the pavement onto the grass just to get out of her way. I cannot help but laugh quietly; turning my head to keep anyone from noticing me, as the fear and degradation that has just consumed me subsides. Bee finally reaches the porch with a small satchel, wearing a new maid's outfit. It is the uniform I asked her to wear and I can see she is not fond of it.

The first words from her lips when reaches me are "Now, what the hell he want?" Then she walks past me, mumbling under her breath and I think, "Yep, I was right to hire this woman."

Chapter 11

I smile as Bee continues to voice her opinion of Mr. Stevens while she goes about her chores, but I am hurting inside, knowing his plans for me tonight. Everyone knows what power a white man has in this country and what he can do and has done in order to get what he wants. I try to pretend everything's fine, noticing the dress I got Bee for work looks pretty snug and I am sure I bought the wrong size. I was told from Bee's own lips that she is a size 16, but I can clearly see now that she is every bit a size 20.

"Bee, can I ask you a question?"

"Why, yes, child."

"How do the Negroes here in Birmingham put up with ignorant people like Mr. Stevens?"

"You should really attend church with me this Sunday, and then you can find out. Let me tell you something, Miss Peg."

Bee sits on the couch next to me and puts a hand on my knee.

"One day, a few years ago, I was on a bus in Montgomery, when I lived there taking care of an elderly relative. I sat in the back because I didn't want any trouble, you know. My friend Rosa, who made dresses for my aunt and me, got on the bus, so I got up and sat next to her up front. The bus had plenty of seats and I didn't feel it would be a problem if white folks were to get on. Rosa said she was tired, having worked hard sewing all day. I knew I had no business sitting in the front, next to her, but I didn't see any trouble, there being so many empty seats. The bus driver was known to give black folk problems, calling the law on them for the least reason. We laughed and talked about my crumb cake recipes—oh, you ain't had a taste of one of my crumb cakes, yet, have you? Girl, you just wait. I'm famous for my crumb cakes!" I smile, thinking about my own pies.

"Anyway," Bee says, continuing her story, "low and behold, white folks started getting on the bus and demanding that we get up out those front seats and let them have them. I said, 'Rosa, don't get up! The hell with them!' My big mouth gets me in trouble all the time, you know. Then sweet, quiet Rosa asked that white man demanding her seat, 'Don't you see all these empty seats on this bus? Why do you want the seats we are in?' Next thing I know, the bus driver stopped the bus and the police came and took poor, little Rosa off to jail. They asked if I wanted to go with her. I said, 'Go where?' The police coming talking about, 'Go to jail!' I said, 'Hell, naw! I got Bible study tonight. I promised the church ladies I would bring my famous crumb cakes tonight.' And then I took my time getting up and moving to the back of the bus. The next day I'm reading in the paper that my close friend Rosa started a movement, child!" Bee looks like she could kill a tiger as she finishes her story; one I'd heard in a different version in Ohio. She gets up and starts dusting the marble on the fireplace, moving the bric-a-brac on the mantle, humming, "We Shall Overcome."

"When was the last time you went to church, smart lady?" she asks suddenly, continuing her cleaning. "I think you will like what my pastor has to say about what's going on in Birmingham." Pausing for a moment, she turns to me. "Miss Peg, you mind if I invite some of the ladies over next week for my famous crumb cakes?" One thing I'd been told by Dr. Carson's contacts here in Birmingham when I got recommendations from more than one of them, was that Bee is a wonderful cook but she is seriously lacking when it comes to baking. According to one person I talked to that has eaten her crumb cakes, they are outright awful! How is it that a lady can cook but cannot bake? I just do not understand this to save my life. I do not think anyone here in Birmingham has the guts to tell her just how bad her crumb cakes are.

"No, I do not mind at all, Bee. We just have to make sure to ask Mrs. Carson if it is okay with her, when she arrives."

"Can't wait to meet her, Miss Peg," Bee says. "There are many Negroes missing here in Birmingham and you will hear all about it tomorrow morning at church." Suddenly, her mood changes and she instinctively reaches for her gun with one hand while holding the dust rag with the other. Her voice becomes hoarse with emotion and her bottom lip trembles with rage.

"This is nothing new to us," Bee says, and then starts humming again as she moves to another room to clean.

Chapter 12

Taken off guard by the story Bee just told me, I get up to shake off the memory of my harrowing encounter with Mr. Stevens. I walk back out on the front porch to get some fresh air and I hear a soft, gentle voice coming from outside on the porch as I open the door.

"Hello, lady," the voice says. "My name is Sammy. Do you have any odd jobs around here for me? I really need the work."

Bee stops in her tracks as she comes out of Dr. Carson's study, glancing out of the window to see who is at the front door. Sammy is a little girl around ten years old with an almond complexion. Her hair is in two pigtails. It looks like her mother took joy putting them up for her, braiding the ends and tying pretty ribbons to hold them tight against her scalp. She is wearing a floral-printed sundress with a lace collar. She wears dark brown polished shoes with a nice shine that gleam brightly against her small, lace-trimmed socks. She did not appear to need anything.

"Hello, Sammy. My name is Peg."

"How are you today, Miss Peg? Nice to meet you," Sammy replies. "I was told a Negro family lives in this big house, so I had to come and see for myself."

I walk out on the porch, and bend down just to get on an eye level with her, and then place my hands on her shoulders.

"Is that right?" I ask, laughing, hoping she will laugh with me so I can see her beautiful smile. My ruse works, as she smiles up at me. I stand up and take her hand, leading her to the door. "You just come right on in here and sit down and tell me more about yourself, Sammy." We hear the door close as we plant ourselves on the couch. Sammy looks around the room with the most darling expression of curiosity mixed with delight on her face. She jumps up to look around the Whitfield house, now the Carsons' home.

"Wow! I always wondered what it looked like inside this old house!"

Bee has finished her dusting and starts to fold clothes from the basket next to the couch. She is listening to Sammy while trying to figure who this young lady belongs to, since she knows everyone in town and everyone knows her.

"Who are your people, Sammy?" Bee says in a firm voice, as she folds a thick bath towel. Sammy walks over and looks up at her with the courage of someone much older.

"Well, my daddy works on the railroad and my mama teaches at the local grade school on the other side of town."

Sammy pulls another towel from the basket and starts to help Bee with the folding. A huge grin replaces the suspicious look that was on Bee's face a few seconds earlier.

"Oh, I know your parents," Bee says succumbing to Sammy's charm. "They're wonderful people and I do know you, young lady. I remember when you were born. I was the midwife that delivered you." Bee continues to fold the remaining laundry, as Sammy looks puzzled, as if pondering a question.

"You know what, Sammy? I'm on my way to the kitchen," Bee says, taking the basket of laundry off the sofa and carrying it to the linen closet near the kitchen with Sammy in tow. "Would you like a nice cold glass of milk with a nice piece of Miss Peg's apple pie?"

Sammy does not say a word. She just smiles. Her eyes are as big as the saucer that will soon hold her pie. As they head to the kitchen, Bee seems just as excited as her little charge. I am quite sure that she intends to cut herself a hefty slice of apple pie, also. Bee returns a short time later with Sammy, who has a small piece of pie, while it looks like Bee sliced herself half a pie. She sits down with a fork in one hand and continues a conversation she and Sammy must have started in the kitchen.

"Sammy, you were the perfect little bundle of joy when I put you in your mother's arms! Now, you better start eating that pie before your milk gets warm," Bee mumbles as she puts a fork full of pie in her mouth. Sammy starts to giggle sitting on the edge of the couch.

"Is this all mine, Miss Peg?

"It sure is, Sammy."

"Miss Bee says a midwife helps mommies have their babies. Do you have any babies, Miss Peg?"

Before I can shake my head "no," I look over and see Bee's plate is clean and she is nibbling on the crumbs as though this is the last meal she would ever eat.

"No, I don't have any children, but if I did, I would want a little girl just like you!" I say, smiling at the girl looking up at me with a mouthful of pie. "Tell me more about yourself, Sammy."

Sammy takes another bite, chews it briefly before swallowing, and then wipes her lips with the cloth napkin, fresh from Bee's laundry basket, before she speaks. She makes me smile at her deliberate and impeccable manners.

"Well, Miss Peg, I have two brothers, Mark and James. I wrestle my younger brother James all the time, and can you believe that I win? That rascal can't get out of my grip," she says with a laugh.

She brings a large glass of milk up to her face. The only things visible are her big brown eyes overlooking her glass.

"So, Miss Peg, is this big old house yours?" Sammy blurts out.

"Oh, no, young lady. I work for the Carson family."

"Well, do *they* have any kids?" Sammy takes a quick swallow and the white foam from the milk settles on her upper lip.

"Yes, they have a son, Robert Jr. He is a student at Ohio State."

"It must be nice to go to college. I want to be a biologist when I grow up."

I can see Sammy means every word by her sincerity.

"How're your grades, Sammy?" Bee asks.

"Oh, I get straight A's. "

Bee puts her hand to her face and smiles as she walks toward the stairs with another full basket of folded laundry on her hip.

"Well, young lady, you're off to a great start!" she says proudly, then heads to my room with my clean laundry.

"Daddy always says if I study hard, I will not have to answer to anyone but the good Lord."

"Your father is right."

"Miss Peg, were you here for the big march the other day? Everyone I know that lives here was there while the young people marched."

"A little while ago, I did have the great pleasure of meeting Dr. King and his wonderful wife, Mrs. King," she shares. "She said I was going to become someone special when I grow up."

I pinch Sammy's cheeks and look into her eyes.

"I do believe that, young lady. Is Sammy your real name?"

"Oh, no. My brothers and Daddy gave it to me because they say I'm a tomboy," she says, and then gets distracted as she walks past the music conservatory.

"Wow, you have a piano? I love the piano! I take piano lessons. I may be a concert pianist when I grow up. My teacher says I'm a *pro-te-ge*." The last word is pronounced carefully, as Sammy makes sure she enunciates each syllable properly.

"Oh, my, Sammy! I must say I have never met a protégé before. Well, future concert pianist, you can play this piano anytime you like."

"Thank you, Miss Peg!"

Sammy runs into the conservatory where a grand piano sits in the center of a room filled with art and musical instruments and looks around for a minute like a kid in a candy store as I watch, reveling in her delight.

After taking it all in, she comes out and heads to the front door in a better mood than when she came.

"Do you mind if I come over tomorrow?"

"Not at all, dear child, but you have to tell me your real name."

Sammy turns, just before reaching the door, and smiles.

"My real name is Condoleezza!" she says proudly, as if she has just announced that she is the Queen of England.

I have a strange feeling she will become someone special one day. Little Miss Condoleezza turns and heads out the door, skipping down the sidewalk for what I am sure will be a long journey home.

Chapter 13

I walk in the kitchen just as Bee comes in with a fresh basket of clothes pulled from the clothesline. I glance through the open doorway and see that the summer sun is starting to fade, along with the intolerable heat. Then I look back at Bee whose mouth is sprinkled with crumbs and can tell she has been nibbling on one of my pies again.

"It seems this house is the house to come to today, Bee."

"Well, let me know if you need anything. I'll be on the back porch in the cool air folding laundry, soon as I get me a cold drink of water."

I look at my watch, knowing I only have three hours until I have to meet Mr. Stevens downtown tonight. My heart wants to call the local authorities, but my mind is saying if I know what is best for me I had better go where he told me to go. I am about to walk up the stairs to start my hot bath when the doorbell once again rings.

"Who is it, now?" I think, nervously heading to the door. I look out the window and notice a Negro couple in their mid-thirties. The woman appears to be carrying a gift.

"Hello," I say, greeting them as I open the door. "May I help you?"

"Yes, my name is Thomas," the man says, "and this is my wife, Mattie."

"Well, come in, Thomas and Mattie," I say, moving aside for them to enter. "My name is Peg." Thomas removes his hat as they come into the house.

"Please, come in and have a seat."

I direct Thomas and Mattie to the living room, where we engage in polite conversation.

"So, what has you beautiful people out at this time of night?"

"We heard about your move to Birmingham," says Thomas.

"And we wanted to bring over a gift," pipes in Mattie, her soft voice barely audible. "We're the welcoming committee at our church."

"Reverend LeCroy is our pastor," adds Thomas.

"Why, thank you, Mattie," I say, taking the nicely wrapped gift.

"We had to come up here personally, Miss Peg, just to see for our-selves. The buzz around Birmingham is that a rich Negro woman now lives in the old Whitfield house," Thomas says.

I notice while we talk that they are constantly looking at the cathedral ceilings and the beautiful craftsmanship exhibited throughout the room. Mattie is a short pretty lady, but seems a little shy.

"Is this wonderful house yours?" she asks, her voice just above a whis-per.

"No, this is the Carsons' home," I reply.

"Well, every Negro family, and I'm sure the white people in Birm-ingham, believes there is a rich Negro family living in the old Whitfield house. It's shocking to know how news travels in this town. Never in his-tory has a Negro family moved to this part of town where the most pow-erful people live. We were hoping and praying it was true because we would like to get some justice around here. So, we had to come over to see for ourselves."

"I only work here for the Carsons and I must tell you something."

"What is that?" Thomas says, leaning forward.

"Last night I was visited by some people who really wanted to do some harm to me. I did not get a look at them, but they left a burning cross on the front lawn. I am still shaken and fear that they may come back tonight. Earlier today I was also visited by a man by the name of Ken Stevens. Do you both know him?"

"Why, yes, ma'am," Mattie replies, still speaking barely above a whis-per. "He is our district attorney and the most powerful man here in Birm-ingham. Some say he is even more powerful than the mayor. Why? What did he want?"

"I really would rather not say right now, but he did request me to do something for him. What is your advice? Should I do what he asks?"

"Yes, ma'am, I think you should do what he asks or he can make your life a living hell here in Birmingham," Mattie says, her voice even softer.

I find it odd that Thomas does not comment, as it seems most men would be concerned about a stranger making requests of a young woman like me.

"Enough of all that. Where are my manners?" I say with a slight grin, trying not to let my true feelings show. I am terrified of even thinking about what Mr. Stevens wants with me tonight.

"Let me get you both a piece of my famous apple pie." I see Bee has closed the back door. I hear her voice loudly singing a hymn I like, "Just a Closer Walk with Thee," as she tackles the tedious job of folding sheets. I asked her to wash all of the sheets for the beds because they smelled musty after the long trip in the moving truck. There are two sets for each of the beds in the ten-bedroom house with twice that for the queen-size bed in my bedroom and the king-size bed in the master bedroom. I hum along with her while I slice the pie and put it on the blue Delft china that Mrs. Carson brought back from Holland after one of her many trips to Europe. She was there studying the court systems and how they affect international relations, the subject of her dissertation.

"Should I have Bee come in to help me entertain my guests? I am sure she knows them," I think. Then, thinking about how much pie Bee has already eaten, I decide to let her continue folding the laundry.

I return to my guests with a tray holding three small dessert plates, each with a slice of apple pie. I am shaken by the thoughts starting to form in my mind about what I feel may be the worst night of my life. My hands tremble slightly as I serve each of my guests, causing them to look at me curiously.

"Is everything all right, Miss Peg?" Mattie asks softly, glancing in Thomas' direction with a confused look on her face.

"Yes, it has just been a long day."

We eat our pie in silence. My mind is at ease when I hear the sounds of forks scraping against the plates. Less tense, I start asking them questions about the area and the religious community, while we finish eating.

We continue talking about local society as I they admire the house and tell me about its history. I let them take me on a tour of this house where members of each of their families had worked for generations as maids, cooks, mammies, and gardeners. Some rooms are still full of unpacked boxes. During our conversation, I hear a sound outside the front door as if someone is turning the doorknob. I am so thankful that I have a man in the house now, even if only temporarily.

Then I hear a voice I recognize! The voice most familiar to me!

"Peg, are you here?" the voice asks, and suddenly I am facing the wonderful countenance of my cousin Sera, walking into the dining room from the front of the house.

"Sera! What are you doing here?" I ask as we hug each other joyfully. She is wearing a beautiful camel-colored dress with red heels and a small fitted hat, looking like a photo from Vogue Magazine. Her long hot-combed hair hangs off her shoulders and moves as she hugs me, gushing with excitement. After we embrace, she casually takes off her fitted cream gloves and tucks them inside her small, compact purse.

"It is so nice to have you here, cousin," I say, relieved to have my family with me at last.

"Oh, Peg, I am so sorry to disrupt you and your guests," she says, as I grab her hand, bringing her closer to my visitors.

"Let me introduce some wonderful people I just had the pleasure of meeting. Sera, this is Thomas and his wonderful wife, Mattie. Sera is my cousin, who I was expecting, I thought, in another week. What got you here so early? It doesn't matter," I say laughing as we continue to hug each other, barely containing our excitement. "Why don't we go back to the living room so you can get acquainted with Sera?" I say to Thomas and Mattie as I lead Sera to the living room, our arms interlocked. Two suitcases, a cosmetic case, and a hatbox are sitting beside the front door.

Thomas and Mattie follow us, a little disquieted about seeing two Negroes residing in a house this grand. I sit on the couch, where Sera joins me. Thomas and Mattie take seats on the nearby Victorian loveseat.

"So what brings you to Birmingham, Sera? Mattie asks.

"I finished my studies earlier than expected and I so desperately wanted to see my family," Sera says, taking my hand and smiling broadly.

"Thomas and Mattie, I am blessed to have my only family here. Our mothers were sisters who were born in Toledo, Ohio," I explain. "So, tell us more about your dissertation and the bar exam," I say, turning to Sera and leaning my head on her shoulder like I used to do when I was a young girl and we would share our secrets with each other.

"Well, I passed my bar," Sera said, as she smiles.

"I knew you would, cousin," I interject.

"And I completed the research for my dissertation on English Common Law and other European judicial models that affect international relations for my Juris Doctor degree. Now, all I have to do is write the dissertation."

"Who in Ohio would have ever thought that my cousin would be one of the few up and coming Negro lawyers in America?" I say proudly.

"Thank you, Peg. And now, I'm working on passing the Bar in Alabama. Do you think I can be of service here?" Sera asks, directing her question to Thomas and Mattie.

"Why, yes!" Thomas says emphatically, as he leans forward, his face sternly serious. "This community is in need of a great lawyer who will fight for every human being. My mother always told me when I was a boy she remembered her grandmother saying, 'success is for everybody, it does not have a color.' It's our obstacles that bring out the best in us and show us who we really are. My mother worked next door for many years at the Stevens residence. Years ago, I can remember as a child when Mrs. Emily Stevens was sick and on her deathbed, my mother was there for the family night and day. Ken Stevens and I even played as young boys in the back yard, even though his parents forbade us from being seen together publicly. Our family will always have a place with the Stevens family, even though we are Negroes. They still give us all the pig feet, pig ears, pig tails, snout, and chitlins when they slaughter a hog each fall."

"As I recall, the slaves were given those same scraps," Sera mumbles. I stifle a laugh, punching her in her side. "Ouch!"

"So, what you are saying Thomas, is that we must go through days which challenge us and look at it as a way to growth?" I ask, trying to keep a straight face as Sera whispers, "You did not tell me Uncle Tom's cabin was located in Birmingham."

"Absolutely!"

"Tell me more about your experiences here in Birmingham, Peg," Sera says, making a valiant effort to join the conversation, obviously confused and insulted by Thomas' statements.

"People are different here," I say cautiously. "Well, some people are."

"You don't say."

"What makes us different?" Mattie asks softly.

"Being new to Birmingham, I am running into white folk that act different than white folk in Ohio. The hatred is so obviously outspoken. They really do not like Negroes here."

Sera gently touches my knee and looks around at each of us, sitting there in the living room.

"Look, do not let that get you down. The day will come when we will be respected in America. There should be a hate crime law. I will work very hard to create one. President Kennedy is doing everything he can to change things here in the South. He is trying so hard to make sure we have equal rights. I read reports about the march here, while I was in Europe, and could not believe it. Dogs attacking children and police turning water hoses on them? Things have got to change in this country!"

"Sera, let me get you a piece of Mama's famous pie," I say, getting up, scooping up the empty dessert plates and heading to the kitchen as the conversation continues.

"I couldn't believe they let dogs attack those youngsters," I hear Mattie say. "And not only did they spray them with water hoses as they marched, those poor children endured beatings with clubs by the local police. It was awful!"

I slice a piece of pie, then put it on a dessert plate and grab a dessert fork and a clean cloth napkin so I can return quickly to my guests and my family. Instead of hearing a lively conversation, all I hear is silence. Returning to a silent room can only mean one of two things: Either everyone is enjoying the conversation, or they are at a loss for words due to some type of disagreement or discomfort about the topic at hand. The tension that fills the room is palpable, as Sera's voice cracks with emotional conviction.

"The day will come when we *also* shall make and govern the decisions that will affect America. The day will come when we will not be called niggers, or spooks, or coons, or even colored, or Negro. We will proudly call ourselves black and African."

"What's wrong with being a Negro? I'm not black and I'm not from Africa. You ladies can call yourselves whatever you want and buck up to white folks. That's a lot easier for you with all your degrees and education, Sera, than it is for us poor, pig feet and chitlin-eating, colored Negroes!" Thomas rants.

"What do you mean?" Sera asks boldly, getting her hackles up as well.

"You have the opportunity to come home to this wonderful house," Thomas says, as he continues to make his message heard, while admiring the house somewhat bitterly. "It burns me when a Negro family has money and then forgets where they come from. Especially a fair skin Negro like you, Sera. I believe you can pass as a white woman. I wouldn't think you should walk downtown with a Negro man as you may get him in a heap of trouble. This town don't take kindly to seeing a white woman in the company of a Negro man."

Now, I know this man has just made Sera quite angry, but only I would know this, because she never lets anyone see her lose her composure. I knew Thomas was getting ready to get an earful. Sera puts her elbow on her knee and looks Thomas in the eyes without hesitation.

"Trust me when I say every woman or man of any color will know that I am a proud black woman, Thomas."

Thomas' male ego swells, as his lips speak the most ignorant words heard tonight.

"I look at how you both prance around here like this place belongs to you."

I can feel my blood pressure rise to about 190/120 and my tongue refuses to hold back.

Without notice, Sera stands and start to return fire, so I have to dive right in headfirst like I am at the public swimming pool on a hot summer day.

"What the hell does that mean, Thomas? First of all, I treated you and Mrs. Mattie here with nothing but respect. Thomas, how in the hell do you think you can come up in here and eat my pie and disrespect us?"

"Hold up, Peg," Thomas sputters.

"That's Miss Peg to you, Thomas!" The sweat starts to roll off his forehead as he sits looking nervously at his wife. "Now, please leave!"

Thomas stands up, looking at us while adjusting his sports jacket, making gestures as he tries to restore his dignity. Poor Mattie continues to look as if this is just another in a lifetime of humiliating moments.

"Mattie, I knew we made a big mistake coming way over here to introduce ourselves. I don't care how big your house is or if you do live in a white neighborhood, you still will be niggers!" he says, directing his statements at his wife.

I politely walk over to the door and hold it open. "Mr. Thomas. You have got to get the hell out this house—now!"

"You lucky you're a lady, because I don't think you are big enough to do anything," he says blustering as he walks toward the door, Mattie trailing behind.

"No, I'm not, but I know someone who is!"

By now, his blood pressure is rising. I can tell by his shiny face. He looks just like a kid eating a fried pork chop.

"Bee, can you come here for a minute?" I say, bluffing, knowing our housekeeper and cook is outside on the back porch folding sheets and cannot hear the commotion going on inside the house.

"Wait one minute! Bee works here?" Thomas says, stumbling over his words as he looks toward the kitchen, expecting Bee to come out with a butcher knife in one hand and a potato in the other.

"*Joshua fit the battle of Jericho, Jericho, Jericho!*" We all freeze in our tracks hearing the loud voice singing, and then a door slams! No one moves. The singing continues and then we hear water running.

Before anyone reacts, I call out loudly, "Bee, come here, please." Thomas jumps up from the loveseat, but stands frozen in his tracks as if waiting in horror for Bee to come through the door. He does not have to wait long. Bee is still singing when she comes in and looks around the room, frowning at the expressions on our faces.

"Hello, Deacon Thomas. Mattie. I didn't know you both were here!" Bee says, coming out of the kitchen, wiping her hands on her apron.

"Bee, I see you already know Thomas and Mattie," I say, breathing a sigh of relief, noticing the perplexed look on Sera's face.

"Oh, yes, we are all members of the same church."

By this time Thomas is soaked with perspiration and he takes a handkerchief from his jacket to wipe his face. Bee looks at me and I can tell from the expression on her face that she has never seen me this upset before. I know Bee welcomes confrontation and I expect her to pull her pistol out any minute.

"Can you please help me remove this man? He has insulted my cousin Sera, who just arrived this evening and been rude to me, despite my hospitality to him and his wife."

"Deacon Thomas, I see you been running your big mouth again, feeling like you gotta tell everybody what you think. With a pea-head like yours, I be surprise you got more than two thoughts in there at the same time. Don't know how poor Mattie put up with you!" Bee tells the frightened man off with one hand on her hip and the other pointing a finger at him. "Yes, Miss Peg, I will gladly take out the garbage. Come on, ya'll got to go!" Bee strides the distance between her and Thomas in a few steps and grabs him from behind by his collar and belt.

"Mattie you can stay, but your ignorant jackass husband has to go," Bee says as she shoves Thomas toward the door. Mattie stands, then sits back down again as Thomas pulls his car keys from his pocket and tosses them to her. Bee somehow pushes him to the door on his tippy toes. It is difficult to understand how a huge man can be manhandled by a woman old enough to be his mother. But I forget. This is no ordinary woman. This is Miss Bee.

I hold the door open as Bee tosses him on the porch. No one would ever know this man attends church, hearing the words he uses. I shut the door behind him and he continues to scream obscenities at us through the door. I know Thomas is upset, but he is spouting words that only a drunken sailor would use. Bee has already made her way back to the living room and introduces herself to my cousin Sera. She is on her way back to the kitchen when the door opens slowly. My back is to the door as I walk toward the living room and I do not see Thomas enter, looking around to make sure Bee is gone.

"Mattie, bring me my keys! We're leaving!" he says breathing hard, snot coming out of his nose after his profane tirade.

Mattie gets up as ordered and Bee comes back around the corner, reaching for her pistol.

"Mattie, I think I'll just walk home! You take the car!" he sputters.

Before anyone can say a word, Thomas bolts out the door, quickly followed by Mattie, who darts her eyes at me, clearly embarrassed. I slam the door behind them, locking it, and then lean against it trying to calm myself down. Bee smiles and nods at us, and then goes back to the kitchen. Sera and I start to laugh and I tell her about Bee and the pistol she carries and how she accidentally shot up the church's roof with her shotgun. I tell her that no one in this city messes with Bee. We are laughing so hard, we can barely talk as I help Sera take her luggage upstairs and show her the master bedroom.

We sprawl on the big canopy bed like a couple of teenagers, catching up on all that has happened since we last saw each other in Ohio, when I glance at the clock and suddenly realize it is nearly eleven o'clock. Nervously, I try to find a way to leave without being asked too many questions by my cousin. I am sure she would be upset if she found out what I must do and why.

"Sera?" I say, helping her unpack her luggage in her bedroom after procrastinating for over an hour. "I have a very important engagement tonight. Would you be insulted if I excuse myself?"

"Peg, at this time of night?" Sera asks, her voice sounding concerned, although she is distracted, trying to get silk blouses and delicates organized in the multiple drawers and bins of her antique chifforobe. Taking advantage of her distraction, I breathe a sigh of relief, knowing if she was not distracted she would notice my nervousness and question me intently about my late-night assignation.

I assure her that this appointment is very important. My cousin glances over her shoulder as I slowly walk down the hall to my bedroom, knowing deep down within I am terrified. But, I also know deep down within my soul, it is important that I do this for the peace of this house tonight. I made this engagement before I knew Sera would be here tonight and I feel ashamed of lying just to keep from being asked questions by my cousin.

After changing clothes and returning to the hallway, I discretely walk past Sera's room where she is dressed for bed, picking out a book to read before going to sleep. I silently pray that no harm comes to her as I leave her alone.

I shut the front door quietly, trying not to attract the neighbors' attention, and head toward the cab parked in front of the house that I called earlier and arranged to pick me up. It is eleven forty-five, just fifteen minutes until midnight, the time I was told to be downtown. I glance at the Stevens residence next door, where I am shocked to see Thomas having a conversation with Mr. Stevens on the front porch. Neither of them notices me. I guess what he said earlier about knowing Mr. Ken Stevens is the truth. I cannot believe what I am seeing, as they laugh and engage in conversation. Just before shutting the cab door I wonder if Thomas knows what his dear friend is plotting tonight. Maybe Mr. Stevens will get distracted and forget to meet me tonight. It would be nice to get back in my own warm bed and relax after a long day working and not have to be alone with Mr. Stevens again.

"Driver, please drop me off on 6th Street, downtown."

I wonder where Thomas and Mattie's car is and realize he must have told her to go on home while he visited his friend, probably telling him about the "uppity" Negro women next door.

The young driver, a white boy who appears to be in his mid- twenties, briefly tells me about his family and how his uncle is a judge here in Birmingham.

"Are you sure that is where you want to be dropped off, ma'am?" he asks.

"Yes, sir, I am sure." Glancing at my watch that I can barely see in the dim light coming from the streetlights, I see it is two minutes before midnight, just as the driver finally pulls over.

"That will be a dollar, ma'am."

It occurs to me that this driver seems concerned about my safety. I see a look in his eyes that has my heart racing and hope it will soon return back to its normal rhythm. During the ride, I saw that his eyes were a beautiful green, as he carefully looked through his rear view mirror.

I hand him a dollar and look briefly out the window before opening the door.

"Are you sure this is where you want to be? This area is dangerous at night. During this time in the evening, a lot of Negroes come up missing," the driver says, again his voice full of concern.

"Yes, this is the place, sir."

"This is no place for a young lady to be during the night. I can drop you off in a much nicer area where there is a diner open all night if you like?"

"Thank you, sir, for being so kind, but this is the address where I have an appointment."

"Thank you, ma'am, and here is my uncle's card who is a judge here. If you ever need him, he would be fair and will listen to you. We are aware that some Negroes are treated unfair sometimes here in Birmingham."

I take the card and get out of the cab, looking around briefly, glancing back at the brake lights from the cab driving off; then watch as they disappear around a building at the corner. I am alone and afraid in a new city. I think, "I really shouldn't have gotten out that cab." I can't help but wonder how did I get myself into this dilemma? I look inside store windows as a few pedestrians walk past me, looking at me as if this is no place for my kind. I'm walking slowly, watching each car's lights that pass. Was I right coming here? Should I just go home and deal with the consequences later? Should I just go back to Ohio and live a normal life?

I think about what went through the minds of the Negro children when the local authorities began spraying them with water hoses the other day.

I can't imagine being attacked by police dogs like those teens in downtown Birmingham. Had it not been for Rev. Shuttlesworth and Dr. King getting the money from Harry Belafonte and Robert Kennedy to bail those poor children out, they would still be in jail. If it was left up to Mr. Stevens, they would be there forever. Now they're trying to get back into school. They were expelled by the Board of Education! I sure hope those children get to continue their studies. It is hard enough for our race to succeed *with* an education; there's no hope without one. Some may pursue academic pursuits and others may do as Booker T. Washington advocated and become skilled laborers. Either way, they will have a much better chance of living productive, happy lives with some kind of training.

But, what about justice? A Negro with a Ph.D. is treated no differently than a Negro that picks cotton in a white man's field. With Mr. Stevens being the district attorney here, would the Negro community in Birmingham ever get justice? No, I think not. I think Mr. Stevens picks and chooses which people he believes are not a threat and that's who he allows in his company. It seems that this man has too much power in this town, so I must continue with this tonight and deal with my feelings later. I am aware of what he wants to do to me. I do know he doesn't take kindly to Negroes, so why me? The questions he asked me earlier about the Carson family make me wonder if he is looking for answers, also. What other reason would he want with me at this time of night? Deep within my soul I already know and I am afraid.

Chapter 14

It has been an hour and no sign of Mr. Stevens. I exhale and find my nerves starting to relax, and I smile hopefully, thinking maybe he forgot about meeting me tonight. Starting to feel relieved, I realize my feet hurt, so I take my shoes off, knowing that will keep my feet from swelling. It seems like I stand there in my stocking feet for hours and, although cabs drive by, there are none that will stop to pick me up. Each driver slows until he notices I am a Negro woman and then quickly drives off. I pray that the kind driver that dropped me off comes back this way. Taking out the card, I try to read the name on it in the dim moonlight. A car passes by with its lights on bright and I see the words "Judge Rives, Circuit Court" printed on a plain business card. I know there is at least one white man interested in giving Negroes justice in this godforsaken place!

Walking at a pace that would win a gold medal, I think to myself, "If I can just get home, I will be fine."

A block from home, I am pleased to see that my cousin has left the porch light on for me. I finally feel safe. I walk past beautifully manicured lawns and from a distance I can see Mrs. Stevens is standing in her living room smoking a cigarette and looking out the side window. Our eyes meet. I turn from her gaze, distracted by headlights from a car that slows as it approaches me from behind.

"Get in, girl," the deep dark voice says. I hesitate as my heart sinks.

"I said get in, girl!" The now threatening tone in his voice frightens me.

"No, thank you. I work here." I politely reject the offer with a kind voice, hoping with everything within me that I will make it inside my house. I pick up my pace until I am inches from the first sidewalk that will lead me to my steps. I dare not look at the car again.

"If you know what's best for you and that family you work for, you better get in this car," the deep strong voice says, getting louder.

This time, I can hear a car door open. I am hoping someone from this nice community or even Mrs. Stevens will turn on their porch light and get this man scared so he will drive off, but it does not happen. Trembling, I slowly turn and walk to the car that's sitting there less than five feet away. I get inside, looking straight ahead. Deep down within, I realize I do not need to look at the man in the driver's seat. I already know this man and it is confirmed when our eyes meet in the rear view mirror. Mr. Stevens has the very same smile he had in his window hours earlier when he was talking to Thomas. The person I was hoping I would not see tonight is driving me off to some godforsaken place.

"How could this married man get out of his house?"

I am sure his wife must know he left. What married woman would not notice that her husband was missing from the bed at this time in the morning and not do or say anything about it? Mrs. Stevens has to have seen their car when she looked out of her window and saw me only a few minutes ago.

He never says a word, looking straight ahead to a destination only he knows. His hands grip the steering wheel while we ride down a dirt road with him not saying a word until we reach a cabin off of Highway 12. I can hear my own heartbeat pounding like a loud bass drum and I know he must hear it, too. Then reality hits me, but I know it is too late to turn back. Here I am out in the middle of nowhere in the early morning hours with a stranger. There is not a single person who knows where I am and what this man is getting ready to do to me. I dare not scream, knowing that he may kill me. I dare not even cry, knowing that is what he is expecting me to do. I dare not give this man one inch of satisfaction. I am sure now, as the car stops at our isolated destination miles away from home, that I am not the first, nor will I be the last frightened Negro woman he will bring here; wherever "here" is.

Mr. Stevens open the cabin door with a key dangling from a keychain that he retrieves from his glove compartment. It jangles with what sounds like at least a dozen keys. It's crazy how he knows what key to use, as he shoves it into the lock and pushes the door open.

"Walk in, girl." It is a summer cabin with little furnishings inside. A bed is a few feet away from the door, with a table holding a washbowl and pitcher.

"Take off your clothes, nigger." Doing what he says, I notice a mirror on the wall that reflects my body and the expression on my face. Who is this woman? This cannot be Peg James from Toledo, Ohio. A girl loved by her parents and constantly by her mother's side. A girl who learned how to cook favorite family dishes and listened to stories read to her by her father each night until she unwillingly fell asleep, listening to the sound of his voice. This cannot be the same girl who was taught how to love everybody no matter the color of their skin.

Yes, this is the same woman so far from home who was once told by her grandmother the stories of millions of men and women who were slaves, and even some living free in America, who were raped, beaten and even killed. Looking at my cold, naked body in the mirror, my conscious mind is quickly drawn back to this cabin when I am thrown onto a sheetless mattress. He quickly removes his clothes and sits on the edge of the bed to take off his boots. He looks at me lying there naked and nearly still. I curl up to keep warm, shivering from the coolness of the early morning air.

"I can run!" I think for a moment. "Am I strong enough to fight this man?"

Then for a few seconds it crosses my mind that other women like me have been here at the mercy of this man and I wonder how many may have been taken away from their loved ones because they may have said something to someone. I think this man who brought me here must from time to time bring other Negro women here secretly. They are alive because they never said a word, or dead because they thought their voices would be heard if they told the authorities.

There is a small oil lamp near the bed. Mr. Stevens lights it with a match before he lies next to me. He notices my small body trembling, and places his huge hand softly on my cheek.

"You are the prettiest nigger I ever set eyes on, but your kind will have to know your place in this world we live in," he says.

He holds me firmly with his strong hands as his lips touch my shoulder, then makes his way past my breast to an area I thought no man would go to with his mouth. I can feel my vagina open and a flow of fluids exits my body as I shake uncontrollably with great pleasure, reaching a climax I never knew existed. I am speechless and discovering sensations my body never knew. He takes me again, this time thrusting his penis deep inside me. I am in a place again that has never been explored before, not even by a man I once loved in Ohio. My body and mind, over which I have always had control, are confused. This man who is raping me and I am wanting dead, takes me to a place a man never has before. This cannot be—a man I hate with all my soul and every negative word I can find in the Webster's Dictionary; a man I want to die a slow, painful death   has my body feeling incredible sensations and my mind terribly confused. I can feel the confidence exuding from me as he brings me to climax, over and over, knowing he has me totally at his mercy and completely at his will.

I will only address this man as *"He."* "He" will never get the pleasure of occupying my mind again. I want him dead. I am completely lost, damaged and helpless now. I want to be in my soft bed listening to music from the small radio on my nightstand. I want to be in bed talking to my cousin Sera about our lives. I close my eyes while he continues with me and I am brought back to my childhood on my first day of school in Toledo, just across the Maumee Bridge from Rossford, Ohio. I can remember my teacher, Mrs. Peoples, standing next to me at Pickett Elementary School, teaching me how to read and understand difficult words that I had problems deciphering. Mrs. Peoples always had a ruler in one hand and stood looking over our shoulders while we read from our small desks in our classroom. Some words I did not quite yet understand as a child, so I was asked by my beloved teacher to look them up in a dictionary where the words became alive. I learned words have meaning when you place them in sentences. Some words, I learned, did not need the help of other words, since these words stood alone with clear meaning.

I am brought back to the present when I hear water splashing. "He" finishes washing himself with water from the pitcher poured in the bowl placed on the table not far from the bed. We silently get dressed. It is now early Sunday morning. My mind thinks of a word I am sure "He" knows from his job as the Birmingham District Attorney. This word will someday seek him out and exact payment for his crimes. "He" who never thinks I will get "Justice" will be shocked when it overtakes him and "He" has to answer to an authority higher than any court or rule of law.

Chapter 15

"He" drops me off just blocks away from home and tells me to walk the rest of the way.

"Hey, Peg, my wife leaves tomorrow after she finishes with my son's visit from the hospital. I want to pick up where we left off tomorrow night after she leaves. Do I make myself clear, girl?"

"Yes, sir," I reply softly.

I arrive home minutes later and while making my way to the back door, I notice Mrs. Stevens staring at me from their side kitchen window with a coffee cup in one hand. "Whore!" she says, as I pass her window heading toward the back porch of my new home. I can tell she must know exactly what her husband is doing, but she just turns her head to it all.

I open the back door with keys in one hand, holding the other hand to my mouth to keep from screaming. I sigh with relief as I turn the knob. I am devastated, leaning on the back door, lost for words, finally feeling safe inside my new home. My ears hear a familiar voice singing a sweet church hymn and I hurriedly fix my tousled hair before facing Bee. I enter the kitchen, trying not to burst into tears, as I see her fixing breakfast at the stove.

"Good morning, early bird! I came in first thing this morning before going to church to make you a nice Sunday breakfast and here you are already up and out."

To my relief, Bee does not turn around to look at me. I feel dirty and I'm disgusted about what happened to me and how I cannot do anything about it.

"Do you want to tell me anything, Miss Peg?" Bee says, flipping over the bacon in a cast iron skillet before finally turning around and looking deep into my eyes as she wipes her hands on her apron. I want to let out a cry for help, but I am too afraid of the consequences if I dare tell anyone what transpired last night.

"No. I woke up before dawn and just wanted to enjoy the early morning air before the sun came up and brought more of this Alabama heat." I avert my eyes, unable to face this formidable woman as I lie to her, knowing she sees through my façade and hoping she will just let the matter drop before I break down and start crying uncontrollably.

"Okay, but know this young lady," Bee says in her strong voice, speaking softly and kindly, making me want to just run to her and cry on her broad shoulders. "If you ever need me, I am here for you. Love you like my own daughter, Miss Peg." She pauses briefly as her words sink in and I know that if I ever need her, Bee will defend me to the death. "Now, let me get some green tomatoes from the garden in the back for breakfast," Bee says with a laugh, her booming voice nearly startling me as she returns back to her usual self. "How did you get them to grow so fast?" she asks.

"It's a family secret," I reply, relieved that Bee isn't pressing me further. She opens the back door and notices Mr. Stevens or "He," as I now call him, pulling his car into his driveway. I see him from the window and pull back quickly, fearing "He" will notice me or that I will see his smirking smile reminding me of his power over me.

"Hello, Mr. Stevens!" Bee yells loudly enough to wake up anyone still asleep in the neighborhood. "You up early on this Sunday morning!"

"He" gets out of his car and walks to the back door of his house, stomps up the steps of his back porch, and slams the screen door. Bee turns around and looks at me from the doorway where she has just faced an enemy I am unable to face. When she sees me looking at her, I quickly turn away. I hear the door slam shut as she goes outside and I breathe sigh of relief. Bee's lack of fear both amazes and frightens me. I am afraid of what she might do if she ever found out what "He" did to me.

A few minutes later, she returns to the kitchen with a few small green tomatoes resting in her apron. She cradles the freshly picked fruit until she gets to the sink where she dumps them all into the sink, seemingly agitated. She grabs a knife and starts to cut the tomatoes after rinsing off the soil.

"It's said around town that that man next door has fathered several Negro children. For some reason, people around here are scared of him, but not me. I know two girls he's said to have had babies by. One is only fifteen and the other one is twenty and missing. The churches here have all got together to help find her, but can't, and her mother is now caring for the poor child's baby," Bee says, continuing to slice the tomatoes, wielding the knife with such force that the juice from them sprays all over the kitchen sink, counter, and wall.

"I knew when I delivered them children that they weren't from no Negro men. Everybody in this city keep quiet about Negro girls and boys who been missing for years. I tell ya, something is just not right about that man."

Bee stops slicing as she pulverizes the last of the tomatoes. She seems to calm down a little as she sprinkles paprika on the sliced tomatoes and resumes singing the church hymn she was singing earlier when I came home to sanctuary.

"*Come ye disconsolate,*" I sing under my breath, in concert with Bee's surprisingly soft soprano voice that melodiously sings the soothing words of a favorite hymn. My body is hurting terribly as I leave Bee to finish breakfast. My aching body longs to go to bed, but all I want to do after last night is take a nice hot bath. Lost in my thoughts and oblivious to anything but the pain racking my sore, abused body, I am oblivious to Sera descending the stairs, wearing her Sunday best.

"Peg, I did not realize you were already dressed for church."

Bee, who is setting the table in the nearby breakfast nook, pours orange juice into glasses as she listens to our conversation.

"Well, I...I don't think I will attend church this morning Sera. I was awake most of the night." I so desperately want to tell her I never came home last night. I so desperately want to explain what "He," this evil man next door, did to me last night.

"So, take a nap after service," Sera says teasingly, oblivious to my pain and the distress I mask, fearing for her safety. Bee just listens, and now I know she knows what happened, because she does not say a word about me being out all night.

"Good morning, Miss Sera," Bee says.

"Good morning, Bee," Sera says, smiling as she walks to the breakfast nook and sits down to drink some juice. I am left feeling awkward as Bee looks at me knowingly before heading back to the kitchen to finish serving our breakfast.

"What a nice breakfast before service," Sera says, as Bee brings out a platter holding two plates piled high with eggs, bacon, homemade biscuits, and fried green tomatoes.

"Our new friend Mattie invited us to church service this morning. Would you like to go with us, Bee?"

"Well, seeing as I already attend the very same church, that's an invitation I'd be obliged to accept, Miss Sera!" Bee says as she laughs uproariously, shaking her big belly. I had no idea that I would attend Sunday service in the filthy attire I still had on from the night before. I hang my head as I eat, silently praying and asking God's forgiveness for going to His house stained with guilt and tarnished by a sin I never planned to commit.

Chapter 16

We arrive at Bee's church along with the other churchgoers. Bee waves at several members of the church she sees, chatting with a couple of them briefly while Sera and I greet them with a smile. Mattie said before her abrupt departure the night before that she and Thomas would meet us outside the church, but we are unable to find them. Bee catches me off guard and convinces me that the workers around the house are telling the truth about her handling firearms.

"Praise the Lord Saints! Miss Peg, do you mind storing my short arm in Miss Sera's rental car? I was told not to bring any of my guns in the church. It took months until some church members finally came back to church after my shotgun went off."

Bee reaches inside her purse, pulls out a small pistol, and hands it to me just outside church doors. Since we were about to walk inside, I have no choice but to place her pistol inside my purse.

I am not surprised when we finally see Mattie, but Thomas is not to be found. I am sure he is still upset about last night and since he knew we were coming, he must have decided not to attend church today. We sit next to Mattie after we locate her inside the church. I notice a worried look on her face as we nod at each other. Neither of us wants to disturb the service that is just starting. We listen to the associate pastor speak about unity and love and are informed that a peaceful march on Washington, D.C., sometime late in the summer, is being organized under the leadership of Rev. Martin Luther King Jr. from Georgia. I am pleased and smile hearing that. It will not be too long before we as a people will be treated fairly. I still sometimes read Dr. King's "Letter from a Birmingham Jail" that was published in *The Columbus Dispatch* right before I left for Alabama. It is one of the most important letters ever written, and its words both inspire and sadden me. Why must our lives be a constant struggle for the basic human and civil rights that whites take for granted?

The church choir sings as Bee's sweet soprano voice leads another favorite song, "Christ is All."

I reach for a church fan to cool myself off from the humidity as Pastor LeCroy's message about God's forgiveness sinks into my soul and I am grateful for the Lord's grace and mercy. I am so delighted to be in service with my cousin Sera, who came to Birmingham earlier than I anticipated. We have so much to be grateful for. We were a little late getting to church, because just as I was going out the door, the phone rang. It was a call from Robert Jr., who is still in Columbus, where he attends college. We spoke briefly about his studies and how excited he is about a new chapter in his life. He confided in me that he is going to surprise his parents and come to see them at their new home in Birmingham. He asked me to keep his surprise a secret. I told him his secret is safe with me.

Chapter 17

Father Michaels leads the Catholic congregation in prayer as members of the parish kneel. On this Sunday morning, holding my new baby girl Emily Rose while sitting with my entire family, I am really needing blessings from up above. I prayed this morning that my little girl would have peace and love in her life. Since I don't pray often, I asked this from the man upstairs as a favor. I will do anything for my child and to keep her thoughts pure with the Klan traditions. It's only been a few days since Nora left town. She said it was too much for her to raise a child and placed my baby girl in my arms. My mother has been so kind. She sees that my baby girl gets all the love she needs as only a mother truly understands. She always wanted a girl and I guess this is God's way of giving her one. She has insisted on taking little Emily to New York City with her when she visits family and friends there. I am relieved that she's taking Emily with her, since I don't have a babysitter and no knowledge of caring for a baby myself.

After Ronnie's birth, the doctors told my parents that they wouldn't be able to have more children and after trying unsuccessfully for many years, they gave up. My brother sits next to me while we listen to the choir lead us in a wonderful hymn, "Close To Thee." I giggle inside as I try to hit each note unsuccessfully. My mother always says that my best listening audience is in my shower at home.

Listening to the wonderful voices, I trouble the man upstairs again, asking him to find a kidney donor for my kid brother. Out of all our friends in this town, I would have thought some would have come forward to be tested to see if they're a match. Shockingly, my closest friends, Patrick and Mike, who I would lay down my life for, didn't even come to our aid to see if they're a match. We were all shocked and dismayed when the doctor told us know that none of our family, those closest to Ronnie, are willing to save his life. So my mother decided to go to New York tomorrow for a few weeks to plead with family and friends there to get tested to try to find a donor.

During service one Sunday morning, years ago, while Ronnie was lying sick in a local hospital, Father Michaels gave my parents a few minutes to address the congregation in a plea for someone to get tested to find a possible donor to save their son. I sit in church today remembering a Saturday not long ago when my mother spent the entire day baking small cupcakes, pies, and cookies to draw people for a discussion after mass. She was sure that some of her closest friends and other churchgoers would be the first ones to offer their help, but was heartbroken after service when the entire congregation avoided her that Sunday.

My dad hugged her afterward as we packed up all the wonderful delights she had worked so hard to make. We placed them in the back of the family station wagon to take out to the lake for the weekly picnic after church where some of the same people that avoided her that day so eagerly placed her delights on their plates without one word about Ronnie's illness. I watched her as she smiled and talked to people while watching the entertainment that day without one mention of poor Ronnie's need of a donor.

This Sunday is like any given Sunday in Birmingham. We will hear a sermon and after service we will pack into our vehicles, eager to attend our weekly entertainment out at the lake. Father Michaels addresses the church, saying we are all God's children and we should love one another. The entire congregation agrees and claps in concert.

After church, we head to the weekly picnic at the lake and I really can't wait, because I was told the entertainment this week would be better than normal. I can hear my stomach growl from not eating breakfast as I smell the wonderful fried chicken my mother packed. Before we head out to the lake, my father makes a quick stop at the local hospital to drop off mother and Ronnie for his dialysis. She made sure they packed a small lunch for their long appointment there. The only thing different this week is that she is taking my baby girl with them because she dared not to leave us men with the responsibility of a baby. Before shutting the car door, she pleads with my father to please be on time when we pick them up tonight. Dad waves her off, smiling at Ronnie, as we pull away, eager to get to the lake before the show starts.

We arrive at the lake where my father has to park the car on the two-lane country road. The sun is high and you can hear faint sounds of children playing while they swim down at the lake. The adults are laughing and dancing as music plays in the background. Couples pass the car, holding hands, the girls dressed in Sunday dresses with flat shoes looking over their shoulders just to say "hello." I couldn't help but notice and admire all the beautiful women that turn and smile at me as e continue to the main entrance.

"Now, Seth, that's what got you in trouble before and gave you that baby girl," Dad says, as he grabs his keys. I reach in the back seat to scoop up my camera and my mother's picnic basket full of goodies, only to be surprised by an old girlfriend. I get out and shut the door.

"How are you stranger?" Mary Joe says with a smile. "I haven't seen you in days, handsome."

"Mary Joe, how have you been? You know my little girl keeps me busy now."

Mary Joe is sweet and will always have a place in my heart. We grew up together and attended grade school and high school together, and then she continued her education at a University in Atlanta. She later became an assistant district attorney in Birmingham and works closely with my father. My parents wanted so desperately to have Mary Joe as a daughter-in-law, but her best friend Nora and I betrayed her when we secretly had a sexual relationship behind her back and now have a child together.

I am amazed and surprised that this woman I once dated never stopped caring for me and I think she will always want a future with me. Mary Joe insists that I walk her up the path. We follow my father, who is slightly ahead of us, stopping just before the path forks off to another path that leads to the main house. We are not far from the lake where the entertainment is scheduled.

"Go ahead, Dad. I will meet you at the house," I shout out to my father. People pass us, walking fast; eager to get to the main house to get a good seat for the entertainment. I am overwhelmed by the attendance, as car after car idles before a sign saying "Private Property" at the main gate entrance that keeps out strangers. Young men carrying instruments pass us, joking and smoking cigarettes. They are all excited about today's picnic and entertainment events.

"Wow, Mary Joe, it looks like a big crowd today." We notice license plates on cars from local sister counties as they line up on the side of the two-lane road.

"I hear your dad has something special for us today, Seth," Mary Joe says, grabbing my hand gently and just holding it.

"I also heard that the ladies from the church are hosting a pie-eating contest. I bet this is the only chance the men here in Birmingham whose wives can't cook get a chance to eat wonderful pie," she says laughing. I smile, happy to hear the tinkling sound of her laughter.

"Everyone from miles around will try to beat my best friend Patrick's mother's apple pie recipe. She wins first prize at the County Fair every year."

"I must agree, Seth. After trying many pies, I have to say that Mrs. Grant does make the best!"

I think of the many evenings I was invited for supper by women I've dated. They always brought out a nice slice of pie after the meal to try and win my heart. Sometimes, I had to spit out the pie and politely call it a night, because some pies are downright awful. It is amazing to me that some women, born and raised here in Birmingham with some of the best cooks in the country, can't cook worth a damn.

Mary Joe and I take leave from each other, following separate paths after a quick buss on the cheek mine not hers. My guilt prevents me from showing her affection. I ask her to take the basket full of goodies to the lake before the good picnic spots are taken. I filch a chicken leg before she goes and greedily consume my mother's delicious fried chicken as if I hadn't eaten in a week. We look at each other, laughing, and continue laughing as we walk in separate directions. We keep looking at each other, laughing and smiling until we lose sight of each other.

I continue down the path, walking at a faster pace until I catch up with my father, surprised he hasn't gotten that far. I wonder if he was watching Mary Joe and me, hoping the two of us would get back together. I smile, amused by my father's optimism and a little sad at blowing the opportunity to have the perfect wife. I am not sure why I didn't stay faithful to Mary Joe. I didn't love Nora. I wasn't even attracted to her at first, but she kept trying to seduce me. It was only after I succumbed to her seduction that I realized she only wanted me because Mary Joe loved me. What kind of person would hurt a best friend like that? I am so thankful that Patrick is my best friend. He'd never do anything to hurt me. I'd stake my life on it.

Dad and I continue walking toward the main house. We can see it from a distance, surrounded by tall pine trees and fields of wildflowers of many colors. I can see young and old ladies carrying baskets, plucking wildflowers to place on their dining room tables for the week. As they bend to pick flowers, they create a scene that reminds me of the Impressionist paintings Mary Joe has decorating her walls. She lives in the house next door to her parents, Mary and Joe, who gave her both their names.

The air is filled with the aroma of barbecue, the sounds of people laughing, music, and the clinking of mason jars full of illegal moonshine. I shake hands with my father's closest friend of many years who catches up to us. As we continue, we follow a dirt path in the forest that leads to the main house. We finally reach the area where the main house sits by the lake and come to the front porch. It has an exterior designed like a log cabin, but is the size of a plantation mansion.

"Hello, Sheriff!" My father says, as he walks up the steps to the house to shake the local county sheriff's hand.

"I see you brought your son with you to this great picnic, Mr. District Attorney. It is great to see young men spending time with their fathers," he says. The sheriff surveys the festivities below on the beautiful lake with a watchful eye, looking for possible intruders on these private grounds.

"Would you ever run for office, young man?" the sheriff asks, spitting tobacco off to the side of the porch, directing his statement toward me as he continues to survey the landscape.

"Well, Sheriff, I don't know. I really have the desire to take pictures for a living. My father and his father before him took pictures at every picnic here on the lake for two generations. My father says that before the war with the Germans, there were pictures made of our weekly picnics. Is that true, Sheriff?"

"Yes, son that is true. Before America joined forces with England to defeat Germany, Hitler was given information from us here in Birmingham and other cities across America. Germany had groups like ours supplying them with photos and all kinds of information. There where neo-Nazi organizations across America, like the German-American Bund, who gave them information about the good work we were doing here. When the world finally found out about what the Nazis was doing in camps to Jews, Hitler told the world that what they were doing with the genocide was no different than what we were doing here. Can you believe them fools up North thought we joined the war to end genocide? Hell, no! We were all for killing them damn Jews, niggers, Jehovah's Witnesses, retards, and homosexuals! You know they call it the Holocaust? We joined the war with England, because Hitler was getting too strong. Hell, we were fighting Japan in the Pacific after they bombed Pearl Harbor in Hawaii. There wasn't a country in Europe Hitler wanted and didn't get, except for England and some of her neighbors. He wanted England, but she had the big guns. I think if Hitler would have gotten her, America would be different today."

"Are we no different than them, Sheriff?"

"What do you think, son? I would love to show you some pictures and maybe that will motivate you to continue our legacy. Come by my house sometime. I would like to show you something."

"That's great!" I reply, suddenly realizing I need to relieve myself. "By the way, can anyone tell me again where I can find the washroom? I always get confused and turned around in this big house." Mr. Johnson, who is the owner of the property and my father's best friend, points to the washroom down the main entrance hall. I see the familiar hall that reminds me of the smaller version in our own house, only twice as long and several feet higher. This hallway holds dozens of pictures of previous picnics, many of them showing my father and his friends and those who lived before them, enjoying themselves.

Who would think that Mr. Johnson would have so many photos chronicling the history of the favorite pastime of the good people in our community? Walking further down the hall, I notice a picture of my mother and father in their younger years holding a baby I know is me. They're smiling with the entertainment in the background. From the looks on their faces it seems as though they were having a wonderful time. One photo I always look for shows my teenage father and my grandfather grinning ear to ear, holding fishing poles, taken at a picnic many years ago. This is a family tradition, held each week, that we have cherished for many generations. I find it strange that in the many times I have attended the picnics here, I've spent so little time in the main house. The lake house below, located down near the water, is where we youngsters usually gather each week and rarely does anyone my age get to set foot in the main house where our venerated elders gather. Only men are allowed there, so I feel honored to be in this house with my father and his friends.

Chapter 18

M y father and I make our way from the main house down to the lake. We are occasionally stopped on the way by kind "hellos" and handshakes from locals and visitors from other counties who know my father. Watching my father in action, I am assured that he is dedicated to closing the gaps within our counties. It feels good to know that this community loves my father and the title he holds here. He works hard with the justice department as the district attorney trying to get felons convicted. I've heard him say that the majority of the city crimes are committed by Negroes and that one day, with his help, all our jails will be filled with them.

He always says if we can suppress the Negro men by incarcerating them whenever possible, they will never get a hold on their dreams. If the men are all in jail then who will father Negro children?

My father's theory is that we can soon have all the prisons across America filled with Negroes. That's our dream. My father is excited today about something special and I want to see again firsthand how strong a true leader he is. Some men from the neighboring counties brought down a fellow who requested that my father give him some advice in a legal matter. My father told them to bring him to the lake to see how we do things in Birmingham!

We arrive minutes later to hear some of Alabama's finest local musicians finish a rousing number. The local sheriff's deputies are also in attendance to make sure we have no disturbances while hosting a huge and well-attended function. The good old boys, wearing their proud uniforms with shiny badges pinned just above the neatly pressed shirt pockets, smile proudly, taking a big part in today's activities.

The mayor steps up to the microphone and greets everyone with a loud "hello." Everyone is so excited; they can't wait for the festivities to begin.

One year, we received so much rain it hindered us from having entertainment. That was when we were having our functions at Willie's Farm.

Everyone had to go home because of all the muck and the disgusting smell of hogs and livestock and all the mud the women got on their nice dresses. The ladies refused to attend any further gatherings due to complaints about Willie's Farm. So, the men got together and built a new platform on Johnson's Lake just for the entertainment.

I always wondered why everyone would come to the picnic every Sunday still dressed up. My father says the reason that people come in their church clothes to the weekly picnic is because they want to feel and look good after a hard week of work. Everyone seems to be in great spirits as they take part, eating from baskets placed on top of nice blankets spread out neatly on the open field near the platform we built. This week, one family went so far as to place a red and white checkered blanket just inches from the platform with babies in tow. I turn to look at my father. He appears to be in deep meditation while Mayor Stocks is addressing the town about some small taxes the city council is trying to put on the next ballot. His shirt is drenched with sweat, but he manages to keep his face cool by occasionally fanning his face with his hat. He replaces it back on his head nicely just to keep the hot beaming sun from his face. My mind drifts until I hear the mayor say he is pleased to be the man to introduce my father this Sunday.

"Ladies and gentlemen, it gives me great pleasure to introduce a wonderful man who holds the city's greatest law position in Birmingham," the mayor says proudly, holding one hand on the microphone stand.

"This organizer of our weekly picnic has made us all proud. We are here today due to his commitment and dedication. Let us our pray that this function continues and that God Almighty grant us peace. Amen. Birmingham and sister counties, please give a great applause to Ken Stevens!" My father steps up to the microphone with the entire audience clapping and yelling his great name.

"STEVENS! STEVENS!"

My mother would have been as pleased as I am to see how this entire crowd displays their appreciation of my father. Stepping up to the platform, Dad waves to everyone like he's running for President of the United States. He wears a kind, gentle smile as he grabs the microphone. I am almost overcome by the heat of this summer day. Damn, it's hot! I repeatedly wipe my forehead to prevent the sweat from dripping in my eyes.

"I want to cherish this moment and pass this day down to my baby Emily and her children," I think, while looking out into the crowd, on their feet clapping and cheering, awaiting a word about this week's special entertainment from my father.

"This week is special, ladies and gentlemen. We are gathered here today because of the values and love that we show throughout our communities," my father states proudly into the microphone, his voice booming across the lake. "It is great to see so many wonderful people from our sister counties and all the wonderful people from Birmingham, Alabama!" A roar comes up from the crowd as people who were sitting just a moment earlier, jump to their feet again. It takes a moment for the howls of excitement to subside, as people sit again to listen to my father.

"This year, and on this special weekend, we are providing at this picnic, demonstrations that will join us together to make our chain stronger. Working as a district attorney in Birmingham I see cases where loving people are taken advantage of throughout the day. This week, I witnessed a group of individuals gathered in the city to ask for equal rights." Loud boos and shouts of disdain and disapproval ring out at these words.

"I was born and raised in Birmingham, where my parents married young, feeling at times that they could not afford a good life for their family. My oldest brother had to be given away to a family that could care for him properly," my father says, choking a little as the crowd remains respectfully silent. Most of the audience has heard this sad story quite often, but it still saddens the heart.

"They made the hard decision to give their baby, my brother, a good life. So they gave him up for adoption. They found a wonderful family up North, I was told, that gave him opportunities to succeed in life and I am sure he is out there somewhere in this beautiful country helping people like the ones I see in front of me today." Again, the crowd cheers, congratulating themselves on being recognized by a man they all esteem.

"We have today one of the demonstrators that I know well. I recognized him during his walk for equality downtown the other day. I also watched Walter Cronkite on the national news last evening as he spoke about how the Negroes here in America are reportedly mistreated." The crowd starts shouting so loudly at the mention of Cronkite and his lies about the South that my father has to wait for them to quiet down for several minutes. During that time, my closest friends, Patrick and Mike, arrive and stand next to me waiting for my father to continue speaking. Shortly after the boys show up, Mr. and Mrs. Grant approach us, holding hands and carrying a huge picnic basket I'm sure contains some of her famous apple pie. We gather on the side of the platform and watch my father speak. I am so proud of him.

"So I brought a friend today that will give his views of how he feels about history and about how the wonderful city of Birmingham has been good to him. I've known this man my entire life. Hell, I know his entire family. His mother worked for my parents for many years, caring for my mother during the illness that caused her death. This man marched proudly downtown just the other day as they demanded that we all move forward." The crowd grows deathly quiet as my father turns and nods, signaling for the entertainment to begin.

The sheriff approaches the stage escorting a man I recognize. The deputy sheriffs keep away some hecklers on the side, ensuring no one does harm to the man. The man I recognize is Thomas, my father's Negro friend that he has known for years.

"What is he doing here?" I think.

My father stands tall next to his friend Thomas. The look of confusion on Thomas face strikes me as odd, though. Last night, I went past our living room and saw my father and Thomas discussing the events that happened downtown with the Negro march. I overheard Thomas explaining that he thinks that the Negroes here were making ground on gaining equality in America. I now notice that Thomas is wearing the same clothes he had on last night and find it strange that it appears he never went home.

"Tell them how you feel, Thomas," my father says, as he stands next to his longtime friend, holding the microphone for him.

"Better yet, you don't have to say a word. I've known you all your life and without your mother, we wouldn't have had those final days with my mom."

Quickly, before anyone can react, the sheriff places his hand on Thomas' shoulder and with the other hand slips a noose around his neck. He shoves him roughly off the platform that we built for this very purpose.

"Die, nigger!" my father shouts, as his friend's feet dangle from his now lifeless body hanging from a rope attached to a gallows in front of the platform. I hear the sound of Thomas' neck snapping just before the crowd starts to roar in frenzied excitement. The expression on Thomas' face as his body hangs motionless, still shows emotion. It's as if he is pleading to live. The crowd continues to let out cries of joy and enthusiasm as they watch the hanging body. Justice is served and everyone here, including children, is so greatly pleased. What a day for a picnic or better yet, as the Klan calls it in the United States, to *"pic a nigger."* The festivities continue for hours as Thomas' body sways in the hot summer breeze, his neck stretching a foot long.

We dance and eat while I take pictures with my new camera of Thomas' lifeless body. I am not surprised to see almost every family posing for photos with this amazing entertainment in the background. I watch the friendly smiles as they pose, some getting daringly close to the star of our Sunday picnic. I watch the children, amazed at seeing this dead body without any fear, having grown used to the weekly displays of violence and sometimes death at the lake.

Later, during the picnic I walk over and touch Thomas' feet just to ensure he's really dead. No question in my mind that this man who was once full of life is now dead. His body is cold, even though the hot sun beams down on his lifeless body. This is the lesson every generation of children is taught in order to preserve our race. What a day for all children to learn as I did and my father and his father before him!

I can't help but think, though, that poor Thomas who was kind of like an uncle to me growing up will never go home to his wonderful wife Mattie, or come by our house ever again with his warm smile like he did when I was young, bringing me a piece of penny candy and later doing the same thing for Ronnie. I always assumed that he was different and almost like a very close friend of the family. I never looked at Thomas as a Negro.

Watching his lifeless body dangle in the gentle, southern breeze leaves an emptiness that invades my cold, Klansman's heart. I then realize a part of me has died along with him today. Is it right that my father just helped kill a man who would have laid down his life for my entire family? I think about Nora's betrayal of Mary Joe, who would have done anything for her. My father, who is so well respected by everyone in this county and the counties all around us, can't be as treacherous as Nora. He can't be!

My father and I head back into town to pick up my mother and younger brother from the hospital, talking about the day's events with our friends and folks from the local communities.

"Wow, what a day! You are awesome, Dad. I have never seen you head up the picnic before. Being in charge of the Klan you always have your fellow brotherhood do the honor. I found it a great honor and can't wait till the day comes when I can do the honor," I say, placing my hand on his shoulder as he drives toward town.

"Yes, son," he replies. "Your day will come soon. I don't like niggers. My family always made sure that we would have nothing to do with them."

We continue laughing and talking until we reach the hospital where my mother and younger brother are patiently waiting outside. My mother was in New York City to plead with her family for a donor for Ronnie. I am thankful for having good parents. I am also relieved that Mom took my baby girl with her.

Chapter 19

We return home from church with Bee and see Sammy on the front porch awaiting our arrival. My cousin Sera, exhausted from her travels, decides to go upstairs for a nap after meeting and being impressed by Sammy. Bee is in the kitchen cooking dinner. I explain to her that Dr. Carson is soon to arrive this evening, so I ask her to please set the table for dinner in the dining room.

I want to teach Sammy how to plant a garden. I get her working in the backyard and even though the sun is beating down on us, I insist that we plant flowers. It will really feel like home once we have some wonderful flowers in the backyard. I love beautiful flowers and if I had it my way I would fill the entire yard with them.

"Now, Sammy when you plant flowers you have to make sure they get plenty of water after you cover the roots with soil."

"Yes, Miss Peg. Like this?" Sammy says, while standing with a water hose in her hands, soaking the roots of the plantings.

"Yes, that is wonderful!" I watch her from the shade of my big summer hat. I am barely able to see Sammy's face, hiding under her own floppy sunhat. The only thing I can see are her pearly whites as both of us laugh with the excitement of giving life to the plants we put into the fertile soil. Then suddenly, a shadow passes over me, laughing with us.

"Hello, ladies," a voice says, and both of us become silent, looking around to see who's there.

"Well, hello, young man. We didn't see you here with us" I say, looking around to make sure no one sees us speaking to a white child. I know it would be hell and hot water if someone gets the wrong impression.

"Do you need any help? My name is Ronnie Stevens and I live in that house," the pale child says, pointing at the house whose owner I know all too well. "My dad is the district attorney here in Birmingham."

This is the son of the man who raped me and will continue to do so as often as he wants. Ronnie is a small-framed boy who wears glasses and has a hairstyle that reminds me of one of the children on that television show, "Little Rascals." As Ronnie speaks you can tell something is terribly wrong with his health. His breath is ragged and labored.

"Hello, Ronnie, my name is Peg and this is my new friend, Sammy." I look over at Sammy who is confused and her face shows it. "Sammy," I say softly. "Stop staring. Ladies don't stare."

Part of me wants to have nothing to do with this boy, but my heart is softened by his nice smile and his politeness and good manners.

"Miss Peg, nice to meet you," Ronnie says, extending his hand toward me. My guts become tangled as I am quickly reminded of my meeting with this young man's father. My mind slips back to last night when I felt my body betray me during an act of violence, not love. I am brought back to the present as I realize I'm being asked if I need any help with the planting.

"Miss Peg?" Ronnie says, again.

"Yes, that would be wonderful. Can you get me that bucket of ashes next to the garage, young man?"

"Sure can," Ronnie says, as he turns and grabs the bucket.

"Now, what you want to do with these ashes?" Sammy asks, as Ronnie hands me the bucketful of ashes.

"Well, you see if you put the ashes in the soil with the plantings, it will keep some insects away and this will keep them from eating your beautiful flowers when they bloom."

"Oh, I never knew that Miss Peg!" Ronnie says, putting a small shovel in the bucket. Then he starts mixing the ashes with the soil.

"Looks like you both have a green thumb," I say, my mind not understanding why Ronnie's poor body is so fragile.

"What is a green thumb?" Ronnie asks. It seems to take everything Ronnie has to muster up a few words. His smile is bigger than life, even though his body is fragile. We continue to plant flowers laughing about nothing in particular.

"So, what part of town are you ladies from?" Ronnie asks. Sammy looks at him for a brief moment and it comes to me why I think that one day this young girl will be great when she finishes school.

"Now, you know I'm not from *this* neighborhood," she says, a sweet smile following her words.

"I am from the Negro section of town. I know your folks don't allow you to go over there. You know. Across the bridge."

"Oh, I see! So you think because I am white that I haven't been there? I just want you to know that I always go with my father to see his good friends, Thomas and Mattie. I go to their house and play with kids in their neighborhood. So I guess I do know that side of town, Sammy."

"I'm sorry, Ronnie. I thought you were like some of the kids from this neighborhood."

"It's all right," he says. Ronnie seems exhausted after his long statement to Sammy. "I know about prejudiced ways of thinking."

"Prejudice?"

"Yes, prejudice. Do you know what that word means?"

Sammy laughs and tilts her head back. "Ronnie, I do know what the word prejudice means. I try not to prejudge anyone without knowing the facts. So, I am sorry for saying what I said earlier."

"Not all white people here in America want bad things to happen to Negroes. If I live to be a man, l will fight for everyone's equal rights. I believe in the peaceful demonstrations of the Rev. Martin Luther King Jr."

"That's nice to hear, Ronnie," I say.

"Sammy, do you come over here often and do you like to read books?" Ronnie asks, after giving me a big smile, finally catching his breath.

"Yes, I love books," Sammy says, with the biggest smile I have seen on her face yet.

"I have tons of them that you can have, if you like. I don't think I will need them much longer."

"Why would you say that, Ronnie?" Sammy asks.

"Because I have been ill for a long time and I overheard my parents talking about how they think I don't have much time to live. My mom went to New York City to visit her family in a plea to have someone donate a kidney. So far, no one is a match or they don't want to help."

"Ronnie, I am sure your mother will find a donor," I reply.

"I hope so soon, Miss Peg. The doctor said today he has done all he can do. I can feel my body getting weaker each day. I look from my favorite spot on the back porch and think how great it would be to run with the wind and laugh, but my body feels so bad."

Suddenly, as I listen to Ronnie's struggle to live, the pain I felt last night because of this young man's father seems like nothing. Who would ever think that I would feel for the abuser's son? But I do. Love has no boundaries. I know now that meeting Ronnie has changed my perspective on life. I know deep down within that I can't be responsible for how people treat me, but I will be judged by the way I treat them. It is easy to treat someone nice or even with gestures of kindness when they treat you with kindness, but when we walk with Christ, we will be tested.

Why is it so hard to treat someone with love when they treat you so wrong? I must do right and treat this young man with love, even though his father hates me for no reason whatsoever, except for the color of my skin.

"Miss Peg, I think we have a new friend," Sammy says, after Ronnie goes home. We laugh and I look forward to having the opportunity to get to know my new friend. I also look forward to helping Ronnie and Sammy learn to use their green thumbs.

Chapter 20

Ifinish my bath after a busy day planting flowers and head down to make a pitcher of cold lemonade. Bee has the table set and is finishing up supper in the kitchen. It is so nice to have my cousin here and I know over dinner we will talk about old times in Ohio. I am surprised to see Sera is still asleep and hasn't made her way downstairs. Bee is frying up some hot water cornbread and boasting that she makes the best in Birmingham.

"I will be the judge of that, Bee," I say, as I rinse the lemons in the sink.

"So, young lady, how you feeling this evening?" Bee asks, placing a plate of her "best hot water cornbread in Birmingham" on the table.

"I'm rested and feeling good. Sammy and I met a young man named Ronnie Stevens earlier today."

Bee turns sharply toward me with a look on her face that surprises me.

"Be careful. If that young man's family gets wind you talking to him, there will be trouble!"

"He told me he will only visit when his family is working. It is so strange to know that he does not have the same values as his family. I think he is the black sheep of his family."

"That may be true, but you can't trust a book by its cover." Bee says, mangling the metaphor. "So just be careful, that's all I'm saying."

Dr. Carson interrupts and surprises us, clearing his throat. He must have been listening to our entire conversation while standing in the entrance hall that leads into the kitchen.

"Dr. Carson, you scared us. We had no idea you made it home. This is Miss Bee, our marvelous cook."

"Nice to meet you, Miss Bee." Dr. Carson says, shaking her hand.

"Yes, sir. The pleasure is mine. I thank you for this job."

Suddenly, a voice comes from behind Dr. Carson and his eyes are covered by two small, delicate hands.

73

"You will never guess who this is!" the voice says. Bee and I watch the tiredness fade from his face as he lights up in a surprised smile.

"Could this be a movie star?" Dr. Carson teases. Laughter like tinkling glass comes from behind him, then Sera's smiling face peeks over his shoulder and she kisses his neck, standing on her toes to reach him. Turning around, he embraces her as their eyes meet. It is like watching a love story when Sera and Dr. Carson's lips finally touch. It's like a love scene from a movie, only this is real life, not a fairy tale. Bee drops her spatula in shock and confusion.

"Miss Sera!" Bee yells. "You a Negro woman! Kissing a white man? What's going on! Why you digging 'round in the woodpile?" This last statement is directed at Dr. Carson as Bee's shock turns to anger.

"I am quite aware that I am a Negro woman," Sera says sharply, then turns to Dr. Carson, her voice gentle and loving. "Baby, I have been lonely without you." Sera rests her head against his chest as he gently embraces her, kissing the top of her head.

"Miss Sera, you ain't married to this man! Is you?" Bee finds the notion of Sera and Dr. Carson as a married couple to be incredible.

"Bee, do you really think I would behave this way with anyone but my husband?"

"I'm sorry, Miss Sera," Bee says, trying to absorb the shocking revelation. "I mean, Mrs. Carson. I had no idea." The expression on Bee's face shows she is already thinking that Birmingham will not like this one bit. "Your secret is safe with me," she says.

"I was unaware it was a secret, Bee," Sera says, as she and her husband continue embracing each other. Sera is no longer just Sera. She is now "Mrs. Carson" and Bee calls her Mrs. Carson from that moment on.

Bee, still recovering from the shock of finding out my cousin is married to a white man, quickly adds another place setting to the table. When Dr. and Mrs. Carson go upstairs and stay, however, we soon realize Bee and I are having dinner alone.

"Now, I set this wonderful dining room table and there is no one to enjoy it."

After eating another one of Bee's delicious meals, Bee and I pack up the remains to put in the icebox for lunch tomorrow. We both know that those two will not be coming back downstairs tonight.

"I never seen a white man kiss a Negro woman before," Bee says, as she clears the table. "Why didn't you tell me your cousin Sera is Dr. Carson's wife?"

"I didn't think it mattered," I reply.

"Well, here in Birmingham, folks, black and white, don't take kindly to Negroes having relationships with whites. Even the governor is for segregation, you know. He is trying his hardest to keep the schools separated."

"When you love someone it does not matter. Dr. Carson is a wonderful man and he loves my cousin."

"I do believe that by the way he held her. I just don't think this city will embrace how they feel about each other." I am speechless and after a few tense minutes, Bee continues her lecture on Southern "hospitality."

"You see, Miss Peg, it's hard when you see how we been mistreated and denied the freedom we been taught to believe in. It's hard to know we can't do anything about it only because of the color of our skin. Not being able to drink out of water fountains or even shop in the very same places that white people use."

"Let me tell you this, Bee. Dr. Carson is not an average man. He is kind and he does not judge you by the color of your skin. He is the one who will listen without judgment and he is the one who is putting food on your table every night."

"And I am thankful that he is a kind and gentle man, Miss Peg, but you'll find out if you haven't already that some men here will abuse you." This last pointed remark silences me as Bee continues telling me about Southern ways.

"They'll take your soul if they can. Don't take it to heart when you find that the Negro community will not take kindly to this. Young men are coming up missing and young Negro girls being raped and often killed. Me being a midwife, I know a Negro child when I see one and I do know a biracial child. Men here in high places and one family in particular will say one thing but do another."

I know now that Bee knows. She may not know the details, but she knows "He" is a rapist. But does she know he raped me?

Chapter 21

Bee finishes cleaning the kitchen and heads home shortly after our conversation. She seems to feel bad about telling me the cold, hard facts about life in the South. Since it was getting late and her commute is on the other side of town, I decided to call her a cab. I knew it would be easy since the cab company had no idea I was a Negro calling for one from this neighborhood.

About an hour after her departure, I notice Bee has forgotten to take the trash out after the big shock. I do not want it to sit inside the house all night, so I take it out and deposit it behind the garage where I am startled by the sound of a match being struck and the familiar smell of pipe smoke.

"Sir, you scared me," I say. Of course, that did not matter to him. "He" grabs my arm tightly and pulls me closer to him.

"We have some unfinished business to take care of, girl," he says, ignoring my remark. I feel my heart sink into my stomach like I am going down a steep roller coaster at Cedar Point in Sandusky, Ohio. Before I can get another word out, my throat is clinched with one hand and he clamps his other hand over my lips. I am reminded of the talk with Bee and I am suddenly horrified, thinking I will become one of the missing women she spoke of earlier. I am shocked as he removes his hand from my mouth and kisses me, bruising my broad lips with force as he seems to swallow my tongue. I feel the breath leave me, nearly fainting in his arms as "He" pulls me violently closer to him, gripping me so hard that I cannot move my arms or legs. "He" grinds his erect organ against me as if trying to push it through my thin dress.

"You are mine," my tormentor whispers softly. The sounds in my ear flow over me like a rushing wind, overcoming my will to stand and I bend to his will. "And don't you forget it."

I remember from the conversation I had earlier with Ronnie, that Mr. Stevens' wife is far away from Birmingham. But this man does not give a damn about his wife or his family's feelings. I cannot believe this man would take the time away from his dying son and think only about his selfish needs. Just when I think he might stop and let me go, "He" continues his mission while I remain helpless and silent. "He" removes my bra and panties, then turns me around, keeping me tight in his grip as he bends me over and enters me from behind. He moves inside me with a hard thrust that vibrates my whole being, almost making me scream in ecstasy and anguish. My mind wants this moment to be done, but once again I find my body confused by the sexual pleasure that I only wanted to experience with the husband I've dreamed of having some day.

"He" finishes with me and pulls his pants up, leaving me alone in the dark. The moon is full and clouds seem to dance in the sky. They drift swiftly across the heavens in a jagged cosmic rhythm, seemingly in concert with the voices of crickets, owls, and other creatures that pierce the silence of the night.

My face is drenched with tears and I beseech the God I serve, asking "Why *me*? Why do I have to endure this and why am I not able to tell anyone? Why is this man, who I do not know, having his way with me?" My silent inquisition of the God I know loves me ends with me sobbing silently, wanting to scream hysterically, and stifling my protests in shame, remembering the pleasure I felt while being raped again and again. Adjusting my clothes, I wonder how long these attacks will continue.

I feel so alone and completely helpless. Then I feel a stirring in my spirit and an internal voice speaks to me. *God* answers me: "You did tell someone. You told Me and I am always here. Vengeance is Mine."

I make my way back to the porch, crawling past my garden, bruised and in tears. My first step is painful, because my body is not used to what it is being put through. I stop and hug the pillar that supports the porch and I somehow feel that its purpose there is to keep me from falling.

"What's wrong, Peg?" The voice coming from inside the house sounds concerned. I quickly wipe away the remaining tears from my eyes, but it is too late. Sera knows I've been crying.

"I'm just missing Ohio and Robert Jr.," I say, opening the screen door and quickly passing her.

"Let me make you some Passion Tea," Sera says, grabbing the kettle and putting water in it while she lights the stove in quick succession. She doesn't notice as I continue my way up the stairs.

"No thank you, Cousin. I'll see you in the morning. Good night," I say, my voice shaky and hoarse from crying as I continue up the stairs, headed for a hot bath and bed.

Chapter 22

Mondays are always hard at the construction site. It's so darn difficult to set your pace when supervisors are crunched to stay on schedule. I decided not to take a lunch today so I can spend time with my kid brother Ronnie, who is home alone. I'm so grateful that my baby girl is with our mother in New York City. I decided to park on the street this time since I know I will only be a brief second cleaning up. I want to take Ronnie to the park and then get a chocolate ice cream cone at Rose's summer ice cream stand downtown. I park and head to the house. I cannot find Ronnie. I want to surprise him this time, but instead I find myself calling his name throughout the house.

"Ronnie! Ronnie! Little rascal, where are you?"

I make my way through our hallway full of family photos and l hear the sounds of birds chirping outside on this nice summer day from the open back door.

"Hey Ronnie, where are you?" I yell, like I always do when we are getting ready to head to the park to throw some baseballs. I'm hoping to get a response back from him, but there is still no answer. I know he is here after finding some of his prized toys scattered on the kitchen table. He'd never leave without his GI Joe collection. After still not getting a response, I figure maybe he is in his favorite spot on the back porch. I glance outside and see his empty wheelchair, but still no sign of Ronnie.

My mind begins to race and I start to think something is terribly wrong. The screen door shuts behind me and I suddenly hear the sound of Ronnie's laughter. I turn around wondering where he could possibly be. I rarely hear my kid brother laugh, because he is always in pain. I crack the screen door open just enough to look through, being careful that the squeaking rusty door hinges don't make a sound. With one eye peeking out the screen door, I see him next door with two nigger girls.

"What is this nigger saying to have Ronnie nearly crying from laughing?" I think.

They are all eating pie and drinking milk from tall glasses while listening to the radio and moving to the music. I watch closely, unable to keep my eyes off this nigger woman. I can't help but notice her pearly white teeth as they all laugh in her backyard. Then I remember seeing that face before. This must be the girl that smiled at me from the window next door, and again from the front porch when Nora brought Emily Rose to live with me.

A little nigger girl is also there and the three of them seem to be involved in some kind of masquerade, pretending to be characters in a fairy tale or a movie. Even though I am focusing on my kid brother, I can't help but notice how beautiful the older girl appears. As she smiles, my eyes are drawn to her smooth, pretty face and her small-framed body.

"How could this nigger be so beautiful?" I think, wondering why I hadn't noticed her beauty before, or had I? How can I be attracted to this woman who I was taught to hate and never have anything to do with?

Maybe that was why I wanted to hurt her when I first saw her, because her beauty doesn't fit with what I've been taught. Maybe I can't face the fact that I found beauty in someone I'm supposed to despise and even kill.

Seth attracted to a nigger? What would my family and friends think of me? I dismiss the notion and try hard to remember what I have been taught since I was a child.

Despite my efforts to concentrate on those teachings and trying to keep them foremost in my mind, I feel a sudden, overwhelming attraction to this woman's smile and curvy body. I am attracted to her beautiful brown skin and deep brown eyes. "How can this be?" Troubled and confused, I quietly leave and return to work.

I start secretly coming home early each day at lunch just to get a glance at her. I think about gently caressing her and softly kissing those full lips while she reads Charles Dickens and Lord Byron to the children. These are my two favorite authors. I chose to work instead of attending college, since I hate classrooms and sitting still, but I am an avid reader of classic literature and poetry. I used to recite Byron and Shelly to Mary Joe, but she preferred Frost and Thoreau to the Romantic poets. Now, I suspect that the lady I once wanted dead the very first day she moved into the old Whitfield house is probably kinder and more cultivated than anyone I have ever known.

This woman who I once called a "nigger" has a name. Is it that niggers aren't really niggers after all? Is it that some of them are wonderful, caring people, just like some white people, and that all they want is to be given the chance at equal opportunities like everyone else here in America? Is that what all this protesting is about   people just wanting better lives for their families? Who are we to feel like we are better than others? Am I better because I can come home to a big house every night and eat a wonderful meal? Am I better because society looks at the color of my skin and quickly gives me opportunities? Am I wrong after all these years? Can I possibly be attracted to this lady I now know is named Peg? Can I love a lady who is black? A nigger? No, a Negro. My dad will have nothing to do with me if I do. He will kill me dead first!

Chapter 23

It is so strange to find we have to fend for ourselves while our mother is out of town. I am not a cook by any means, but I find it easy to make grill cheese sandwiches served with potato chips. Ronnie is pleased to see we don't have vegetables with dinner and he gladly asks for seconds. My father, the famous district attorney, arrives just as we sit down at the kitchen table for what Ronnie calls "dinner."

"Hey, Buddies!" he says, as he opens the icebox to get a cold beer.

"How was your day?" Ronnie asks, while biting down on his sandwich.

"It was good. We put some 'innocent' niggers in jail where they will spend the rest of their lives busting rocks on a chain gang. Whoever said that our justice system is fair really *is* blind."

I can't help but ask, "What did they do that got them sent to jail?"

"Does it matter?" he responds.

I think of all the wrongfully accused black men sitting in jail, thinking differently than I did before. Our father told us just a week ago during dinner that it was his idea to use dogs and water hoses on the blacks that peacefully demonstrated for equal rights downtown last week. Then, I thought he was right, but now I remain silent as he boasts about his efforts to imprison every black male he can incarcerate on trumped-up charges. I am starting to feel differently about Negroes.

"So, Dad, how do you like the grill cheese?" I say, when he changes the subject to our weekly "picnic." I think if he continues to talk about "killing niggers," I might just vomit grill cheese and potato chips all over the kitchen counter. Thinking back on all the poor, innocent black men I've seen the Klan kill for sport, I start to wonder how many more were killed that I don't know about. I am thankfully successful in getting our father to change subjects. He pontificates on the fine art of making the perfect grill cheese sandwich with bread buttered just so and cheese melted to the right consistency on bread toasted black around the edges, "like a nigger at midnight." I pray that Ronnie won't mention anything about his visits next door with Peg. At the table, we talk about the New York Yankees and how we think this baseball season will play out and, of course, my father remarks baseball hasn't been the same since they let "that coon, Jackie Robinson, cross the color line." He goes on, saying they should have kept the niggers in their own league, because no nigger could ever hit as many home runs as Babe Ruth. If I've heard him say it once, I've heard him say it a million times: "The day a nigger hits more home runs than Babe Ruth, I'm leaving your mama for Aunt Jemima!"

"I spoke with your mother today and she told me she's having trouble finding a donor for you, Ronnie," Dad blurts out with a mouthful of chips, ending our jovial dinner conversation.

In the silence that ensues after his thoughtless statement, all I can hear is my father crunching chips in his mouth as if he'd just commented on the weather. As usual, he has no regard for how his words or deeds affect other people. I think about what will happen to my baby brother if he doesn't find a donor soon. The consequences are too dire for me even to consider. What are we going to do if no one steps up to donate a kidney for Ronnie?

I know it's irrational, but I feel guilty that I'm not a match for my brother. The feeling of helplessness starts to flood over me, when Ronnie suddenly breaks the deafening silence and starts to dance in his chair, moving his arms and shoulders doing a seated version of the "Twist." This strange behavior only occurs when Ronnie is happy. Today, I'm sure it's because he had a wonderful visit next door. Dad and I both laugh at my goofy brother who makes faces at us, sticking out his tongue, then stops his crazy dance to catch his breath.

"Hey, Dad, what would you think if I started to take pictures with my new Canon at our picnic next week?" I ask, careful to keep my tone light and casual.

"I don't know, son. I think the other Klan members might not like that," he replies.

"What would you take pictures of?" Ronnie asks.

"Nothing, son!" Dad says quickly. "We can talk about it later tonight, Seth. Let's see some more of that dancing, Ronnie!" Dad starts moving around in his chair like a caged monkey and Ronnie and I laugh so hard, Ronnie's eyes water and my sides hurt.

Ronnie is fast asleep when my father wakes me from a sound sleep around two in the morning.

"Seth, grab your camera! We have a special night tonight!" my father says softly, his voice excited but low, trying to keep as quiet as possible to keep from waking Ronnie who is sleeping soundly in the next room. I'm told to get my truck and I hesitate briefly, concerned that Ronnie might get sick and no one will be home.

Chapter 24

We drive to Mike and Patrick's house where Mr. Grant is awaiting our arrival.

"Hello, boys," Mr. Grant says in a whisper.

"What you got your rope for? You won't need it tonight," my father says.

Minutes later, we arrive at the main lake house where we have the Sunday picnics, but this time just the men are there. They are all men from Birmingham the mayor, the baker, teachers, principals, bankers, and the sheriff, of course. I happily take photos of everyone there, glad my father changed his mind about me photographing the Klan. I now have a great photo of each member of the local KKK; every one of whom would publicly deny they were ever part of the organization. My father calls the meeting to order. He discusses the urgency for the Klan to be stronger than ever. He says he has received a message from Washington stating that the federal government will crack down on all organizations that are committing crimes.

"This memo came directly from President Kennedy. So, boys, we have to crack down on the niggers in this city. We have to keep them in their places. We cannot have again what we experienced during their so-called peaceful march downtown. We can NEVER let niggers have equal rights here in America. If they want equal rights, they can go back to Africa and be with their own kind!"

While speaking, my dad raises his hand, forming a fist that he slams down on the coffee table, nearly breaking it. "This week at the picnic, I will call on my son Seth to conduct the entertainment. This will be Seth's introduction as an official member of the Ku Klux Klan."

The men all stand and clap, smiling at me and lifting glasses of whiskey in salute. My father has the biggest, proudest grin I've seen on his face since the day he first saw his granddaughter, my little Emily Rose. If only he and the rest of the Klan members knew how I feel about this organization now and what they stand for.

My father and I arrive home around four in the morning after a quiet ride home, both of us too tired to talk.

I immediately go to the basement to develop the film and make two prints of the photos and let them hang out to dry until morning. I'll hide the second set of prints for safety. They may come in handy someday.

I am awakened again at seven, this time by a knock at the front door.

"Seth, I am sorry to wake you up so early. I saw your father at the courthouse and I asked him if he'd mind if I came by this morning."

"Sheriff, what can I do for you?"

"I'll be needing those negatives from the photos you took a few hours ago. Your father said you also developed them, so I will need the prints, as well. Those pictures can't get out. Do you have them?"

"Yes, Sheriff, come on in and have a seat. Let me get them for you."

Walking to the door off the hall just before the kitchen, I make my way to the stairs leading to the basement, glad I had already developed *two* sets of photos. I grab one set of pictures and quickly shove them underneath an old trunk in the corner where a tattered rug hides a crack in the floor. Just as I get back to gather up the other photos and negatives, I hear steps behind me.

"Here you go, Sheriff," I say, turning and seeing him standing there with a suspicious look on his face.

"Thanks, Seth," he says, as he holds the negatives up and counts each frame, then looks through the photos, counting to make sure he has all the prints made from the negatives. He then looks up at me with a smile, before turning to go back up the stairs.

"See you, Sunday, Seth. Can't wait to see the entertainment you have planned for us this week!"

Chapter 25

This morning, I am glad I did not hear from the man next door. "He" told me to be on my porch around midnight, but was I relieved when my oppressor never showed up. Bee is already in the kitchen cooking breakfast while I sit in my robe at the kitchen table.

"Are you alright, Miss Peg?" Bee asks.

"Oh yes, I just do not feel good today. Matter of fact, I do not think I will be having breakfast this morning. Bee, would you be so kind as to make sure everyone completes their duties around the house. I will be in my room if you need me."

"Why sure, Miss Peg."

I start my morning bath water and open the curtains just to feel the warmth of the sun. I pour in bath salts with a wonderful scent I recently bought at Richards Market downtown; "Peach & Plum" it says on the bottle. I pour the colored crystals into the water and it quickly fills with bubbles from my creamy vanilla-scented soap. While placing the bottle back in the cabinet next to the window, I catch a glimpse of a smile, followed by a shy little wave. It's not Ronnie, but his brother who greets me. I realize I don't even know his name. I smile tentatively and nod, then close my curtain. Is this the same man who tried to attack me and burned a cross on the lawn that awful morning; the day after I saw the mother of his child dropping their daughter off? Is this a trick by his father to use his son to hurt me?

"I want no part of this!" I think, as I lie in my bath, tears rolling down my face onto my chin, dropping silently into the water.

"Hello, Peg," a voice says outside the bathroom door.

"Do you mind if I come in?"

"Please do, Sera," I reply, as I try wiping my tears away with hands covered in soap bubbles and succeed only in getting soap in my eyes.

"Bee told me you were not feeling well this morning," Sera says, walking in dressed in a pretty summer frock. "Can I get you anything from the store this morning?"

She immediately knows something is wrong by the look on my face and grabs a sea sponge next to the tub and then gently wipes my face.

"What's wrong, Peg?"

"Silly me. I tried to scratch my eyelid and got soap in my eyes!"

I want so desperately to tell her the truth, but dare not. If I did, she would storm out and take justice into her own two hands. Why must I keep quiet about being raped by our neighbor, her husband's brother? Maybe if I tell Sera, she will tell Dr. Carson and he will confront his brother about his crimes. Then reality sets in and I know I dare not say a word about any of this. What could she possibly do if I decided to tell her? What could Dr. Carson do with his brother having so much power? Absolutely nothing.

Chapter 26

What a beautiful woman! How could I have ever hated her? How could I have let that kind of hate fester within my heart for so many years? I am sure it's in my heart because of my upbringing. How could my parents instill in me such a world of confusion? I'm sure almost every white young adult here in Birmingham has been subjected to the hateful teachings of their parents and friends. I'm sure our parents were taught to hate Negroes by their parents. I'm sure some feel the very same way I do now, but can't voice their thoughts because of the fear of how their family and friends would react.

I watched the world news just last night and wondered, "How could the governor of Alabama have such hate within his heart for other human beings?"

I'm sure he has read the Constitution that guarantees equal rights for all citizens. This man has the audacity to not allow Negro students to attend public schools because of the color of their skin. The governor announced that segregation is here in the United States of America to stay. Can I break the hate that the Stevens family has held on to for many generations? I don't want Emily Rose growing up with this hate ingrained in her! I have to stop the cycle of hate! But how?

Before rushing off to work, I notice the open window that started the fire in me. I remember thinking that no black woman should be in my neighborhood and feeling the blind fury that drove me to my friend's house that very same evening, because I wanted this Negro woman hung on her own front lawn so the world could see that if you dared to step foot in this community unwelcomed you would pay the consequences. What was it that changed my mind and my thoughts toward the Negro race? Now, I see how the Kennedy family and other white people understand that we all are equal, regardless of skin color, but I haven't seen any white man or woman here in Birmingham able to demonstrate the zeal to be bold and stand tall openly for *all* people.

I have found not one person, including myself, who is willing to stand up and say, "This is wrong! What we're doing is wrong!"

No, we all smile and laugh and then eat and dance in the very same hour that a Negro man, woman, or child is hung from a tree for entertainment. Can I change this community to my new way of thinking, persuading them that this is the right way? My dad vowed that the Negro race must always be held inferior to the white race. He will never have anything to do with a Negro man or woman. The only Negro man he was ever close to was Thomas and now he is dead at the hands of the man he thought was his friend. The trust between Thomas and my father throughout their lives was the closest I have seen between him and any Negro. To see how my father betrayed him shocked me more than anything he's ever done in my entire life.

The evening before the picnic, Thomas had come by to discuss doing some odd jobs around the house. Thomas sat in our living room, talking about how he appreciated my father giving him work just to help feed his family. He mentioned that he and his wife Mattie had visited the new family next door and said the young Negro woman's cousin was living there, too. So my father called some of his brotherhood from the organization to take Thomas, his lifelong friend, home that evening.

"Uppity Negroes act like they white. Talking like white folks and putting on airs. No respect, Mister Ken. Make me think if Negroes up North act like white folks because they go to school with white folks, maybe there's something to all that marching for equal rights. I don't want to be white, don't get me wrong. But these young folk deserve a chance to better their lives. And if that mean learning what the white children learn, maybe that Martin Luther King Jr. right. What you think about it, Mister Ken?"

"I think Negroes have a place and they ought to stay in it," my father said, his face red with rage as he tried to keep his voice calm, talking to his old friend. "You never had any problem taking care of your family have you, Thomas?" Thomas shook his head, realizing he had stepped over his bounds and a look of fear crossed his face. "That's because you stay in your place. These young Negroes like that gal next door itching for a lynching rope you ask me. What do you think, Thomas?"

"Sure you right, Mister Ken," Thomas said, standing up. "I best be getting on home now. I told Mattie to drive on home 'cause I had some business with you. Got a long walk 'head of me." Thomas looked like a cornered rabbit, literally shaking in his shoes.

My father told Thomas it was too late for him to walk home and that's when he called some members of the Klan, telling Thomas some of his friends would take him home. The look of resignation that came over Thomas' face still haunts me. He bowed his head as if praying and just stood there in our kitchen awaiting his fate. Thomas couldn't move when the two sheriff's deputies showed up to take him away.

"Time to go home, Thomas," my father said. But Thomas still didn't move. It was as if his feet were cemented in our kitchen floor. He just stood there with his head down, holding his hat in his hands in front of him as if guarding his groin. It made me think of all the Negro men that had been castrated by the Klan and I realized why Thomas had taken that stance.

"Come on, Thomas. Time to go!" said one of the deputies as each one grabbed him under one of his arms and literally dragged him away. He never looked up when they pulled him across the floor, but from where I sat at the kitchen table, I saw his cheeks were wet with tears. I felt a little sorry for him, knowing he was about to get a severe beating for suggesting Negro children should sit in the same classrooms with white children. Hell, he might be missing some fingers and toes after saying Martin Luther King's name in our house!

"Those deputies were going to work him over real good, then drop him off at home for his wife to tend his wounds!" I thought to myself. Thomas never made it home.

The next day, I noticed that the same men who had escorted Thomas onto the platform during our entertainment were the very same two men who picked him up that evening. I wonder if his wife suspected my father. The last time she saw her husband, he was talking to his lifelong friend. Maybe she knew if any man or woman dared testify in a court of law that my father was the cause of Thomas' death, then *their* life would be in danger.

The day after Thomas' death, poor Mattie came by the house crying, almost on the verge of having a nervous breakdown. She asked if we had seen Thomas on Saturday evening. She was sure that Thomas stopped by to visit my father, since he lived next door to the new family in town that they visited that evening. But she was confused and couldn't remember Thomas telling her from our front porch to drive on home. She said she and Thomas couldn't believe that a Negro family had moved next door and wondered how could that be possible? She talked about the marches and all the national attention from the media and went on to say that Thomas believed the Negro would finally have a voice in America.

It never occurred to Mattie that saying those words to my father ended her husband's life. When Thomas talked to him that Saturday night about Negro children going to school with white children, I saw a certain look in my father's eyes; the very same look he has had just before he's ordered the lynching of hundreds of Negroes at the picnics. Thomas was unaware, even though he knew my father his whole life, that his trusted white friend was responsible for the deaths of so many Negro men across this state. If he had known, he wouldn't have said a word about segregation. He wouldn't have said a word about the changes coming to America because of men like Martin Luther King Jr. He wouldn't even have mentioned the name of the most hated Negro in America, had he known the danger he was in. The words Thomas spoke that evening were like nothing I've ever heard from him. It seems that seeing Negroes that had the benefit of being educated like white people and living like white people, free and equal, emboldened him. His words were the words of a man that was free from oppression. The words he spoke pierced my father's heart. The words Thomas spoke caused my father to start worrying that if the day came that Negroes in Alabama had equality, this very same man that he had known for years, and who he had told what to do, would be equal to him in society. He must have seen that Thomas' grandchildren might one day be great and powerful in our world. My father and his friends had kept Negroes in their place for generations by giving them piecemeal jobs and just enough money to subsist. Did my father feel within his heart that one day the "We" they shouted about in marches would someday include Thomas? Would Thomas someday march in Birmingham, singing in a chorus with his Negro brethren, "We shall overcome?"

Thomas would be alive today if only he hadn't said a word that night. So how can I stay silent knowing that Thomas dreamed of great things for every man, woman, and child of his race? I can't keep silent any longer. I have work to do and the world will see how events in this town will change the world as this chapter in my life unfolds. I remember years ago, a Negro woman named Mrs. Parks was bold and stood tall as she refused to give up her seat on a bus in Montgomery, right here in the state of Alabama. I think how I had the very same feelings of hate that my friends and family still hold within their hearts; hatred that had me on the same path of trying to kill off the Negro race the way Hitler tried to kill off all the Jews. I look at life now, thinking, "Why?" Why was it that I and other whites felt so superior to people just because of the color of our skin? God created us all in His image, so who are we to hate another human being? We all bleed the same color. We all walk upright like men. We all breathe the same air. We all love our family and friends.

What was it that changed my thinking and how can I make a change without letting the people I love so dearly know? Perhaps, what changed me was the kind and gentle way that this beautiful lady, Peg, has treated my brother. Does she know that this may be his last year of life if we do not find a donor soon? There has to be a reason why my kid brother likes spending time with this lady next door. Knowing Ronnie, I suspect he doesn't look at her color. I watch her interact with my brother and see the love she has in her eyes, both for him and the little black girl, too. I watch how Ronnie's eyes shine with happiness when he is near her, forgetting his serious illness. Then I see him later, holding his head down when he hears our father speak about hating Negroes. Am I starting to feel the love that my little brother has towards this kind and beautiful lady? Or am I falling into a different kind of love with her, deeper and quicker than I ever have before in my life?

Chapter 27

Dr. Carson arrives home from work, still a little upset about some of his more seriously ill patients. He opens the front door with his key and sets his briefcase next to the intricately carved mahogany coat hanger Sera brought back from Europe. I watch him pour himself a shot of bourbon from the bar in the parlor.

"Good evening Dr. Carson. Dinner is almost finished," I say, bringing him his slippers. Sera rushes past me, beaming as she embraces her husband and gives him a quick kiss.

"Are you okay, Peg?"

It seems both of them are concerned about me. I assure him that I am fine, but I know this is far from the truth.

"Dr. Carson, can you do me a big favor?" I ask, after Sera goes to check on dinner. "I have a dear friend that is seriously ill and I would like to ask you if you would ask his father if you can look at him for an exam. I would also like to ask you if you would examine me to find if I would be a match to give him one of my kidneys."

"Peg, are you sure you want to give this young man your kidney?" Dr. Carson asks, as he sits his empty glass down, looking serious and concerned. "What do you know about this young man you say is your friend?"

"Dr. Carson, do you really think in order to save a person's life you have to know them?" I reply.

"Okay, if you feel like that I guess you should come by the office tomorrow and let me run some tests on you."

"Wait one minute," Sera says, as she walks in from the kitchen, having overheard part of our conversation. She comes over to the large fireplace where we are standing and faces us. I can tell by her voice she is seriously concerned.

"Do you think this is a safe operation?" she asks her husband.

"This procedure is common and successful," Dr. Carson assures his wife, telling her that everything will be fine as she rests her head on his shoulder.

"Can you both do me one more favor?" I ask them. "I do not want anyone to know about this, please. The person I am wanting to help is Ronnie."

"Who is Ronnie?" Dr. Carson asks.

"Ronnie is our next door neighbor. Your brother's son. Can you both promise me that this will be our secret?" Both of them nod in agreement.

"We can do that, Peg," Sera says, then walks over and closes the door that leads to the kitchen. She wants to make sure Bee cannot hear what she wants to talk to us about.

"So what can you both tell me about the family next door?" she asks, while taking a seat in a wing-backed chair near the fireplace. "I know you know that Mr. Stevens next door is my husband's biological brother. What do you think of him?"

I want to scream and tell them that we should move far from this place, but I know Dr. Carson wants so much to know his brother. I know it would hurt them both if they ever found out that this man they both know as family is repeatedly raping me. I decide to tell a lie.

"Well, I think he is a wonderful man. I don't know much about him, but from what I can tell it seems like everyone respects him in this city," I reply with a straight face.

"Robert, how are things going with getting to know him?"

"We went out for a drink with some of his friends and they all seemed like decent human beings. I really want to take this slow, not letting anyone know that he is my brother. I will tell him in due time."

After our conversation, we decide to watch the local news before dinner. The weatherman says it is going to be nice all week. Bee walks in the room dressed in her maid uniform that I know she hates, but pretends to like.

"Bee, who made you wear that dreadful uniform?" Sera asks with a laugh.

"Mrs. Carson, I was directed to wear this uniform ma'am, but if you would like for me to wear something else tomorrow, I will surely do so."

"Yes, please do so," my cousin says, while we all laugh on our way to the dining room, ready to enjoy a wonderful dinner. After the meal, I dare not walk outside to take out the garbage. It's like music to my ears when Bee offers to take the trash out. I am sure if "He" is outside by the garage he will get a rude awakening when he reaches out and finds Bee! I am hoping he will, knowing that if "He" does, "He" may not live to tell the tale or at least get shot where it counts. I imagine him grabbing Bee and the pistol in her apron going off as she whacks him upside the head, hitting his "weapon" of choice that he uses in his repeated rapes of me. It almost makes me giggle out loud as I serve myself a second helping of Bee's pot roast and potatoes.

Chapter 28

After I see Bee off and ensure all the windows and doors are locked, I head upstairs to take my hot bath and sip my Passion Tea in my room while reading a new magazine. Before I know it, I am fast asleep in my warm bed.

"Wake up! Wake up!" a raspy voice whispers in my ear. I am awake, but think am I dreaming.

"Wake up!" the voice insists. "I said wake up! I let you have the night off last night, but not tonight, Peg!"

This man is in my room standing over me. All I can make out is a silhouette against my window, a dark figure that looms over me, barely visible in the moonlight. My body trembles as my mind realizes who the intruder is. "He" climbs in my bed. Confident I will not make a sound, he does not even cover my mouth.

"Peg, you are so beautiful. Did you miss me? I want you every night and I will never take no for an answer. Do you hear me, girl?"

"I hear you loud and clear."

My voice is but a whisper as I pray silently, asking God to please send Dr. Carson into this room.

"God, can anyone hear what this man is about to do to me?" I am sure my prayers will be heard. I am sure Sera will come through my bedroom door any moment. I watch the door handle with hope in my heart, while my mind retreats into the past, back to a time when I was a child, dreaming that when I became an adult I would fall in love with a man who would be loving and caring.

"Don't do this, sir," I whisper, barely able to let the words escape from my quivering mouth.

"I do what I want here. I own this city and I own you." Again, "He" takes me to that forbidden place within minutes as his tongue darts in and out of me, bringing wave after wave of pleasure that both shames and excites. I find myself unable to resist, willingly yielding to him, overcome by the sensations he arouses in me. He causes my entire body to writhe uncontrollably in spasm after spasm until my bed is soaked with my own juices.

I look into his face, now hovering within inches of mine, smiling in satisfaction, and I know I do hate this man for this. I hate him for not allowing me to experience these feelings with a man with whom I am truly and deeply in love.

"Peg, I think I love you," "He" says moments later, as he exits my window.

Love.

"Love is patient, love is kind."

This man rapes me night after night.

"It does not envy, it does not boast, it is not easily angered, it keeps no records."

He wields his power like a sword, subduing any and all around him.

"Love does not delight in evil, but rejoices with the truth."

His entire life is a lie. "He" pretends to be a family man, a leader of his community, but "He" is the epitome of evil.

"It always protects, always trusts, always hopes, always perseveres."

The only thing "He" protects is himself. Where is his love for his wife? For his dying child?

"Love never fails." (1 Corinthians 13:14)

"He" dares speak of love to me? After he repeatedly takes me against my will and forces my own body to betray me? How can "He" speak of love when all "He" knows is hate! But I refuse to feel hate for this despicable man. I refuse to harbor hate in my heart, because I know the true meaning of love. Love, true love, is my salvation and my peace.

Chapter 29

My appointment with Dr. Carson is at noon, today. I wake up early, feeling awful after what "He" did to me last night. The last words I heard him say, "I think I love you," filled me with just anger. How can a person say he loves you when all he does is hurt you? Love does not inflict pain. How can this man who calls people with dark skin of many shades "niggers," and has nothing but contempt for other human beings, speak with the same mouth and say the word "love?" What "He" loves is being in control of my body. But the one thing that he cannot control is my will.

I step out on the back porch hoping to see Ronnie and Sammy, but I'm surprised to see neither child waiting for me. I told Bee to take the day off due to all of the hard work she has done this week making sure my cousin is comfortable in her new home. Standing outside in the cool early morning air, already starting to warm up under the hot Alabama sun, I notice that the flowers the children and I planted last Sunday evening are starting to bud. I grab the water hose and water them just before the sun turns the morning breeze into a scorching wind. Otherwise, I will have to wait until the sun goes down to water them, because the water would be too hot and it might scald the delicate buds.

"Hello, Peg! How are you this morning?"

"I'm fine, thank you," I reply, turning around, not expecting to see the man standing there smiling at me.

"Hello. My name is Seth Stevens. I live next door."

I drop the hose and the water creates a puddle on the walkway. I am surely ready to move back to Ohio if this young man plans to harass me like his father. I recognize him from our previous encounters. I look at my back door and wonder how I can get to the house without causing a scene.

"Hello, Mr. Stevens. How can I help you, sir?"

"Please call me Seth."

"Okay, Seth."

I watch warily as he extends his hand for me to shake. He looks directly into my eyes. We shake hands and I feel myself blush as he caresses mine gently.

"Let me turn off your water, Peg."

"Sure," I reply, somewhat confused by his kind demeanor. "How can I help you, Seth?" I ask.

"I know that you been here for weeks now," he begins, his face flushed as he tries to find the right words, "and I would like to tell you that I am sorry for how I treated you when you first arrived."

His words stumble forth as he looks back at his house. I am sure he is making certain that his father is not home while we are having our first real conversation. This is my first opportunity to really look at his face and I notice his pleasant smile, which fades away as he becomes more serious.

"The evening that you moved here, I was furious and I hate to admit it, but I wanted to do harm to you. I wondered why a Negro woman would move into this community, where we never in history had a family of your kind. I got scared when I saw you standing in the window that evening. I did what I've been taught and that was to create havoc to try to scare you away. I wanted to prove to this city, or even maybe the world, that I wanted you gone. But when I looked at you the other day with Ronnie and I saw compassion and love, I saw something that I never saw before or was just too blind to see. The truth. For the first time, I realized that the people who say they love my brother, but will not even take the time to visit him, don't really love him. I saw his happiness and joy when he was with you and how much you cared about him and that little girl he plays with. I am deeply sorry for my actions, Peg. I just hope someday you'll find it in your heart to forgive me."

I move closer to Seth as a tear rolls down his cheek and I gently wipe it away, looking into his eyes and seeing the sincerity there. Seth turns quickly and starts heading for his back porch, as if running from the embarrassment of shedding a tear in front of me. But he turns back and smiles, his face telling me how he really feels and why he has to leave in a hurry.

"Peg, would you be so kind as to accompany me on a picnic tomorrow at noon?" I hear these words and am reminded of the genteel Southern gentlemen I have read about in books, surprised to finally meet one in Birmingham.

"I…I don't know if I can," I sputter. My heart races, wanting me to speak the words I truly feel. Finally, I manage to say, "I would like that, Seth."

I watch Seth return home, humming a tune with an upbeat rhythm. This man, who I was not at all fond of when I moved here, is somehow a changed man. I have to wonder why.

Chapter 30

I have completed all of my tests with Dr. Carson and sit in his office awaiting the results when he comes out and advises me that I am a suitable candidate to donate a kidney to Ronnie. I am excited and filled with joy!

"Now this young boy will have a chance at life," I think to myself. "Now this boy will become a man and have children of his own one day!" I think about him finishing junior high and starting high school in the fall, where he will meet some wonderful girl and perhaps have his first kiss. I imagine all of this just moments after I realize Ronnie no longer has a death sentence, but a whole life ahead of him.

"When would it be good to do the operation?"

"I spoke with Mr. Stevens' family physician and advised him that I had found a donor for his patient. I was honest with him about the race of the donor and we agreed to form a team in Ohio that will come here to perform the surgery. This is the only way we can keep this quiet in Birmingham. With local physicians, we run the risk of his family learning that the donor is not white and rejecting the kidney. I hate to think of my own brother doing such a thing, but this is the South. It's the only way we can do it, Peg."

"I understand completely," I say, tempted to tell him the truth about his brother, but not wanting to spoil this joyful moment.

I am thinking about my conversation with Seth just hours ago. I am excited about our picnic tomorrow and decide to wear my cream dress with the matching sandals. Dr. Carson sits behind the large oak desk in his office looking at my chart. I know there are a few more tests that have to be done, but Dr. Carson seems hesitant and a bit uneasy. My joy starts to evaporate as I fear bad news may follow the good.

"Peg?"

"Dr. Carson, what's wrong?" I ask, standing. He looks at me, with a puzzled look on his face.

"Peg, you're pregnant."

Shocked and confused, I grab the arm of the chair to keep from falling. My mind races, searching for an answer. I sit back down and try to make some kind of sense of this.

"Are you sure I am pregnant?"

"Yes, I am one hundred percent sure. May I ask you a question, Peg? I think it's still very early. How is that possible? You've been here in Birmingham for just over a month. How could this be, Peg?"

"Dr. Carson, it is complicated. Do you mind if I excuse myself?"

"No, not at all."

I slowly walk through the lobby of his office, dazed and numb. What did I do to deserve this? I realize "He" is the father of my unborn child.

Can I have this child?

What would "He" do if he ever found out?

Chapter 31

I wake up worrying about this child I am carring inside me. I am thankful that I did not have to deal with anyone last night after getting the news yesterday. I head down the stairs deep in thought and remember that this is the day I am meeting Seth for lunch. I am sure this operation is still a secret in the Stevens family and I make a mental note not to mention it to Ronnie.

I am in the kitchen making a cup of tea when I suddenly hear chatter in the living room. By the spirited, down-home nature of the conversation sprinkled frequently with "Thank you, Jesus!" and "Praise the Lord!" I realize Bee has arrived with her friends from the church. She asked me before if she could have her mission circle over for their monthly meeting and her famous crumb cakes.

"Miss Peg, please come in and meet the ladies," Bee says, when she hears the teakettle full of boiling water whistle, letting her know I am going through my morning ritual. I really just want to stay in the kitchen and enjoy my tea quietly before getting ready for my "date." Date? I'm going on a date with a man that not too long ago was calling me "nigger" and resented me for living in this house. But you never know what God has in store for you. I hear a chorus of "Hallelujahs!" coming from the living room and I am reminded that I am on my way to meet the mission sisters.

Bee stands in front of the group of ladies, hands on hips, as they place small cakes on their plates, but with odd little frowns on their faces.

"Ladies, this is Miss Peg," Bee says. "Now, she's from up North, so let's show her some real Southern hospitality. She ain't had much of that since she moved to Birmingham. She just needs to be around some good Christian folks. Amen?"

"Amen!" the ladies respond in unison and rush over to shake my hand and give me friendly hugs, happily leaving their plates of some sad-looking crumb cake behind. I am overwhelmed by their kindness and acceptance, having already experienced the same hearty welcome at the end of the church service that Dr. Carson, Sera, and I attended with Bee. I recognize several of the ladies I met at the church who seem genuinely glad to see me. As they finish greeting me, each of the ladies gingerly tries to slip back to their seats, but Bee keeps saying, "Don't forget your crumb cake!" She forces them to reluctantly return to the table to retrieve the pitiful pastry perched pathetically on small dessert plates. Each of the ladies pretends to be pleased with Bee's confection as she watches carefully to make sure each of them has a plate.

"What time is it, Bee," I ask, distracting her.

"It's around ten-thirty, I think, Miss Peg. Let me check the clock in the kitchen," Bee says as she ambles away. Several of the ladies take advantage of the opportunity to put their pieces of what is supposed to be crumb cake back in the pan, and leave their empty dessert plates on the table as if they have finished eating.

Bee returns with another pan of that awful crumb cake, nearly catching a couple of the ladies in the act of putting their cake back. They pretend they are getting more cake when they see her.

"Don't worry, ladies," Bee says with a satisfied smile. "I got plenty more crumb cake." She looks around at the mission sisters and zeroes in on the one lady in the group she is sure is ready to eat by now.

"Sister Goings, I see you don't have a plate," Bee says to one of the ladies whose rotund body is even larger than hers. "I know how much you like sweets. Go ahead, have a piece. It's not like it's gonna make you fat!" Bee laughs as some of the other ladies giggle. "All them pig feet, fried chicken, beans and cornbread you cook so well already done that! Not that I can talk, mind you. I put on a lot of weight eating these crumb cakes, let me tell you! Here, I'll get you a nice big piece."

"Just because you cook and clean for these uppity Negroes, it don't mean nothing, Bee," Sister Goings says. "You still ain't nothing but the help, even if you do have a key to their house. They ain't no different than the white folks in Birmingham, hiring black folks to clean up after them like they better than us!"

Bee stops in her tracks and her nostrils flare as she turns toward the woman who is nearly twice as wide as she is, as the other ladies quickly move aside. Beads of sweat form on Bee's forehead and start dripping down her face.

"Now, you know what Pastor LeCroy said that the Bible say? To mind your own business and leave Sister Bee business alone! Right, sisters?" One of the ladies tries to get the others to stay calm and motions to Sister Goings to sit down.

"I ain't scared of Bee just because she carry that gun around with her! It's probably empty anyway!" Before she can finish the sentence, Bee pulls her pistol from her apron and starts shooting it above her head as Sister Goings runs screaming out of the front door, her backside bouncing like a ball. She is quickly followed by the other ladies reacting to the loud bang when the chandelier comes crashing down on the table on top of Bee's crumb cake. I stand with my mouth wide open, not believing what is going on and realizing the same mayhem must have occurred when Bee's shotgun "accidentally" shot the roof off the church! What is it with this woman and firearms aimed at ceilings?

"My crumb cakes!" Bee moans, putting her pistol away and surveying the pile of glass from the chandelier and crystal punch bowl. The gummy-looking pieces of what was supposed to be crumb cake cover the beautiful tapestry rug, underneath what used to be a fine mahogany table. The mess spills over to the hardwood floor in places.

"I made these wonderful crumb cakes just for the ladies. Sorry, Miss Peg. You didn't even have a chance to try my delicious crumb cakes."

Seemingly in shock, Bee starts to clean up the mess mechanically, humming a familiar song, stopping occasionally to bemoan the loss of her crumb cakes and to assure me she would pay for the damages. I think to myself, Bee will have to work for Dr. Carson and Sera for the next twenty years without pay to pay for the destruction she's caused.

Feeling sorry for Bee, I take a deep breath, turn toward the kitchen and come back with two pieces of Bee's "famous" crumb cake on dessert plates and two cups of tea on a tray with cream and sugar.

"Bee, it's going to take a while to clean up that mess. Why don't you sit down and eat a piece of your cake with me. There was another pan in the kitchen."

"That's right," Bee says, smiling. "I made that pan for Dr. and Mrs. Carson. Don't guess they mind if we have some."

Bee and I sit down and I muster up the courage to put a fork full of the gummy mess covered with brown sugar crumbs in my mouth. Surprised at the taste, I spit Bee's crumb cake out, right in her face.

"What is wrong, Miss Peg?" Bee says, wiping her face with her apron." She seems more concerned about me than the mess I just spit all over her.

"Bee, did you cook your crumb cakes here?" I ask, already knowing the answer. Bee nods, confused since Sera gave her permission to use the kitchen and anything in it to bake for her mission circle. I never had a chance to warn Sera about Bee's baking. Poor Sera assumed that since Bee is such a good cook, she had to be a good baker, too, being the logical thinker she is.

"I realized when I went to sweeten my tea this morning that I put the salt in the sugar jar and the sugar in the salt jar when I filled them both yesterday." A long silence that seems to last an eternity follows.

"Can you imagine the look on that greedy Gladys Goings' face if she had put a whole one of them cakes in her big mouth?" Bee says, laughing so hard, tears well up in her eyes.

"There'd be bits of salty crumb cake all over the walls." Bee's mouth drops as she realizes the full impact of my having confused the two canisters.

"She probably would've picked up the punch bowl after tasting that salty cake and tried to drink the whole thing full of salty cherry punch!" A fresh round of laughter starts with both of us holding our sides. "This whole room would've ended up cherry red! Lord, have mercy! That would have been harder to clean off the walls than the rug! Looks like either way, I was 'bout to wind up cleaning a mess."

Bee wipes tears from her eyes and looks at the plate in her hand and takes a bite, trying not to frown as the salty taste overwhelms her taste buds.

"A little salty," she says, as I start giggling uncontrollably at the contortions her face makes as she chews and forces herself to swallow. The cake tastes like cornmeal used to coat fish dipped in egg. Each grimace she makes sends me into peals of laughter and pretty soon she's again laughing with me. Had anyone come into the house at that moment and seen the two of us sitting in a room that looks like a tornado hit one side of it, laughing like a couple of drunk hyenas, they would have thought we were both insane and in need of serious psychiatric treatment. And that includes Dr. Carson and Sera.

"I still make the best crumb cakes in Birmingham!" Bee exclaims, as she finally gets control of herself, her uproarious laughter subsiding to a chuckle as she gets up and goes back to her cleaning. I start upstairs to get ready for my "date." This time, instead of humming, Bee sings as she tackles the mess she's made. I'm sure wondering how Dr. Carson and Sera will react when they find out that the elegant chandelier, solid wood table, and expensive Waterford Crystal punch bowl have all been destroyed.

"Walk with me, Lord. Walk with me. Walk with me, Lord. Walk with me. While I'm on this pilgrim journey, I need Jesus to walk with me." As I go upstairs, I say a silent prayer using those same words.

Chapter 32

"Hello, Miss. Peg. How are you today?" Seth says with a warm smile when I answer a knock at the back door and find him standing there.

"I'm fine, thank you. How are you, Seth?"

"Wonderful, now that I am here." I grab my shades and a pretty sun hat to guard the sun from my face.

"I have never been in a truck before, Seth," I say, as we walk toward his driveway where his pickup is parked.

"I hope you will like the drive," he says as he opens the passenger door for me. "I visit this spot often and I know that there won't be any interruptions while we get the chance to know each other."

A momentary feeling of uneasiness overtakes me as I think about his father taking me away to an isolated place. I quickly shake off such thoughts, confident that Seth is nothing like his father. Not anymore.

"So, what did you pack for our picnic today?"

"I packed a wonderful chilled salmon with crackers and cheese and a bottle of Chardonnay."

"I am impressed, Seth. That sounds so gourmet. I love salmon, and Chardonnay is my favorite wine."

"Thank you, Miss Peg. My father gets it from California. I'm glad to hear you like it."

"Please call me Peg," I say, pushing back thoughts of the way my body reacted when his father raped me and the pleasure I felt.

"I will, Peg. I called you 'Miss' to make sure you're not a Mrs.," Seth says jokingly. We arrive at the place that Seth planned for our picnic after about fifteen minutes that seem to pass quickly.

"Let me get the door for you, Peg," Seth says, relishing saying my name as much as I relish hearing the sound of it coming from his mouth.

"Why, thank you," I say, stepping out of the truck onto a dusty dirt road marked with the tracks of the tires on Seth's truck. I realize as we approach a cabin that this is the same place his father took me the first night that "He" raped me. Suddenly dizzy, my head spinning as memories of that night flood my mind, I swoon, fainting, as Seth grabs me and lifts me from the ground. Just before I pass out, I realize he's carrying me to that house and try to let out a scream, but cannot utter a word as I sink into darkness.

Chapter 33

I wake up in the cabin and stifle a scream, as I realize I am lying on the same bed where I lost my virginity, only now it is covered with a chenille bedspread that hides the bloodstains on the mattress from my first rape.

Seth sees the horror on my face and a look of deep concern creases his brow as he leans forward. I nearly recoil seeing for the first time a resemblance between him and his father and for a split second I think "He" is there.

"It's okay, Peg. You just had a little heat stroke," Seth says, puzzled by my reaction.

"I do not faint like that," I say. "I am no shrinking violet. In Ohio, I used to go hiking and I love fishing and boating and working outside in the yard. I am an outdoor person. The sun does not bother me."

"The sun's different down South, young lady," Seth says, mocking my indignant Yankee spirit.

"Well, are we having a picnic, or not?" I ask rhetorically, as I attempt to stand, only to fall back. Seth catches me and holds me in his arms looking directly into my eyes. I feel arousal and desire like I have never felt for any man before, and pray that Seth does not try to make love to me in this cursed bed, knowing I will not be able to refuse him.

"I know of a beautiful spot near here on this dirt path that leads to a quarry," he says softly, his voice sending chills down my spine. I think I may faint again. He gently pulls me up and I am still in his arms when we stand. Looking up at him, I see a vision in his eyes, a vision of a future forbidden in states with laws against miscegenation.

We silently walk out of the cabin, arm in arm, and Seth leads me down a path toward a grove of trees.

"So, what brings you to Birmingham, Peg?"

"I wanted to be near family while I finish my education," I say. "At first I wanted to go into business and management, but now I am leaning towards law."

"That would be great," he says. Seth's words are supportive, but he seems less than enthused about my choice of profession; probably the result of having a father in the same field. However, I know I will never misuse the legal system the way his father does. Seth seems deep in thought as we continue walking.

"I must tell you that white folk here won't think too kindly on a wonderful lady like yourself pursuing an education in law. My father is the district attorney and I know for a fact that they will kill any Negro that tries to become part of the legal community here. He knows judges and others who will stop you here in your tracks."

"That may be, but I am optimistic," I say flippantly, making a feeble attempt to allay his fears, realizing now why he was troubled when I mentioned going into law. We continue to walk in silence, thinking about the possible consequences of my decision to follow in Sera's footsteps. I have been thinking about the law for some time, but it was not until I arrived in Birmingham and saw all of the corruption and the disregard that the city's district attorney has for the very law he is sworn to uphold that I knew I would have to spend my life fighting for justice for my people and all Americans. We come to a curve about a hundred yards from the cabin and I do not notice the quick turn.

I nearly fall off the path, but fortunately Seth is there and grabs my waist, this time keeping me from a deadly plunge. I look below and see a hundred-foot-long drop. Right on the edge of the precipice stands a relic pine tree I am sure is over one hundred years old.

"Peg, you have to be careful around here," Seth warns. "There are plenty of life-threatening drops here. I should know. I played here when I was a child and know them all. Do you see that oak tree on the path just before the drop?" We turn around as he points at an old oak tree. I nod, amazed at the tree's beauty.

"You have only five good steps before this deathly drop occurs."

"Oh, I see," I say, mentally taking note of the short distance from the tree we just passed to the drop. I was so lost in thought a few moments ago, I did not notice it. "Thank you for telling me that, Seth. This seems like a dangerous place for children to play."

"We Southerners are a fearless lot!" he says, laughing. "Or just too stupid to take precautions. We were pretty reckless when we were children, but our parents always taught us when and where to take risks and we knew this was not the time or the place. If any of us had fallen here, we would not be alive to tell about it."

"This is a peaceful place," I think, concentrating on its beauty rather than on the ever-present dangers here, none of which rivals the hell on earth I experienced the last time I was here. I cannot help but compare the beauty of this natural setting to the ugliness of the last man that brought me here. My thoughts about a place I prayed I would never see again have taken a 360 degree turn, not only because I am here with Seth, who is nothing like his father in thought, deed, or gesture, but also because of the wonderful wildlife that I see during our hike.

"Okay, we are here," he says, setting the picnic basket down for the second time during our walk. He set it down before on the edge of the precipice when I nearly fell, nearly sending our picnic fare over the ledge.

"This is my favorite place to get away from everyone," Seth says, as he spreads a blanket on a shady spot of grass. He empties the basket, taking out our meal and all of the accoutrements. The food smells delicious and the crystal glasses, china plates, silverware, and cloth napkins make me think about Bee and the mess she is tackling this afternoon. He hands me a wine glass, then picks up the bottle of Chardonnay, popping the cork and pouring me a glass of chilled wine in one smooth motion.

"You have to taste this cheese, Peg, " he says, after pouring himself a glass of wine and picking up a round of cheese, which I hope is sharp cheddar, my favorite. "Close your eyes and open your mouth."

I laugh and open my mouth with closed eyes to welcome the flavors, which are new to my taste buds.

"That is wonderful, Seth." Before I can ask him what kind of cheese this is, I open my eyes and stare into his face, only inches away. The tenderness I see in his eyes overwhelms me as he moves toward me while holding my gaze. He gently kisses my lips, pressing his mouth gently against mine, wrapping me in the moist wetness of his open mouth. My lips eagerly part to let his probing, tensile tongue enter in search of my mine. Our tongues wrap around each other, writhing in a rhythmic dance, exploring and caressing each other for what seems like an eternity, but is only an instant.

"I'm sorry. I just had to kiss you," Seth says, as he pulls away to look at me and tell me with that look how he feels.

"Can I be honest with you, Peg? I never in a million years would have thought that I would ever have feelings for a Negro woman. Then, I met you. A woman who is beautiful, kind, and smart. A woman. Not just a Negro woman. The woman I realize I've been looking for all my life. When I'm near you, my heart races. I never loved a woman before. I never felt the way I feel when I'm with you, Peg. So, I am following my heart. I know now, that you are different from the rest of the ladies here in Birmingham, black or white. I've been watching you interact with Ronnie every day, treating him with so much kindness and love, like no other lady I've ever known. Do you know that I come home every day just to watch you? But, Peg, I can never let anyone know how I really feel about you, because they will hurt you if they find out."

Seth's words tumble out of his mouth in a rush, falling all over each other in a heap of emotions and thoughts that confuse and amaze me with their sincerity and honesty.

Wrapped in the security of our own private little world, we eat and drink between kisses and caresses, then sit for what seems like hours, holding each other, looking at the beautiful quarry below.

We pack up and head back to Seth's truck, surprised that it's not later. The sun is far from setting when we end our *tête-à-tête*. He is the perfect gentleman, the first man who ever opened and closed my car door. He laughs about some memory of his brother, placing the picnic basket in the bed of the truck, just in the nick of time as one of his friends, who he says is named Patrick, drives up behind us. I watch through the rearview mirror while Seth walks back to his friend's vehicle. I'm sure he is trying to keep his friend from seeing that a Negro woman is sitting in his passenger seat.

His friend says, "You sly devil! I see you stay busy these days. I haven't seen you since the last picnic." Patrick tries looking through the back truck window, trying so hard to find out who the woman in Seth's truck is without being too obvious.

"Who do you have there? Is that Mary Joe?"

"Yeah, it is," Seth lies.

"Hello, Mary Joe," Patrick shouts loudly, with a wave.

Seth tries to distract Patrick by sitting on the hood of his friend's car, redirecting his attention back toward the country road he drove in on, but Patrick starts walking toward the truck. I hear Seth say, "Mary Joe got heat stroke and started throwing up. It's all over my truck seat, her dress, everything."

I am relieved when Patrick makes a face, gagging slightly, then turns and walks back toward Seth who is now standing by his car. They chat for a while out of my earshot, but as they part, I hear Seth yell to Patrick that he and "Mary Joe" are going out for lunch tomorrow when she's feeling better.

A little unnerved by the close call with his friend, Seth and I say very little on the way back to my house, but he holds my hand with one hand while he drives with the other. We communicate wordlessly, expressing our feelings for each other with gestures and looks, saying more without words than most people say with volumes.

I arrive home to find Sera and Doctor Carson having coffee and pie at the kitchen table. I do not see or hear Bee and wonder how the cleanup operation went and what the owners of this stately home had to say about the destruction of some of their most precious and valuable belongings.

"Hello, young lady. Where you been all day?" Sera asks.

"I had an engagement today and now I am exhausted."

"Please sit with us, Peg."

I am sure that Dr. Carson has told my cousin I am pregnant, but I had hoped that he would not divulge my personal information. Dr. Carson glances at me and remains quiet as his wife begins small talk at the table.

"So, how did your tests go?"

I must have a blank look on my face, because she repeats her question.

"Your test for the kidney transplant?"

"Oh, my test went great. Did you not tell Sera about how the test went, Dr. Carson?"

"No, I wanted *you* to tell her about your tests," Dr. Carson says pointedly. "I did call Dr. Mason, who is the Stevens boy's physician, and I also told his father we found a donor. I informed him that we are scheduled for surgery tomorrow afternoon, due to the urgency of the boy's condition." He sounds ecstatic about the good news, as I am sure the Stevens family is, too.

"So, young lady, you are scheduled for surgery tomorrow, early in the evening. This is the best time to do this, because there will be fewer hospital staff there at that time of day. We don't want anyone from the hospital knowing who gave this young man a kidney. You will need all the rest you can get tonight, Peg. Tomorrow is going to be a long and difficult day."

"Dr. Carson, will the results of my other test affect the surgery?"

"No, not at all. Just get some rest tonight, Peg."

There's a puzzled look on Sera's face as she sips some coffee, then puts her cup down on the saucer and looks at me intently.

"All right, Bee told me her version of what happened to our chandelier, crystal punch bowl, mahogany table, and Oriental tapestry rug," she says with a look so intense it is almost comical. "Now I want to hear your version." Despite her indignant tone, I know she's not really as angry as she's letting on. Everything in the house is insured and can be replaced, but I didn't tell Bee that, because I didn't want her to think she can just shoot up the place whenever she feels like it. I smile, remembering the sight of Sister Goings running outside, and I tell the tale.

I start by telling them about my mix-up with the sugar and salt canisters. By the time I get to the part about me spitting Bee's nasty crumb cake right in her face, they are both laughing so hard, I'm sure the neighbors can hear them and think someone is either in great peril or losing their ever-loving mind! I am relieved that Sera does not know about my pregnancy. But she will soon. I will not be able to hide it much longer.

Chapter 34

After Sera and her loving husband disappear upstairs for some time alone before dinner, Bee comes into the kitchen looking tired and drained. Her dress is soaked with perspiration and her apron has cherry stains on it.

"Do you mind going with me over to Mattie's house, Miss Peg? " Bee asks, a worried look on her tired face.

"The ladies from the church mentioned that they haven't seen her lately."

"Sure, I would love to go."

Bee goes to change into some clean clothes in the downstairs bath while I go upstairs to change my grass-stained dress. I hear Sera and Dr. Carson talking quietly in their room as I pass by, then silence as I head downstairs after putting on a white linen skirt and sleeveless blouse. It is getting late, but the sun is still hot.

I call for a cab, which arrives within a few minutes, right after I write a note telling Sera where we are and that Bee will finish dinner when we return. The aroma of a baked chicken sitting in the oven fills the air with the promise of another great meal as we leave for Mattie's. When we arrive at Mattie and Thomas' home on the south side of Birmingham a few minutes later, I ask the driver to keep the meter running while we go check on our friend.

Bee is eager to find out what is going on and is already walking up to the house. She has only heard rumors from the ladies at church. I clearly was left in the dark, as I have no idea what is going on with Mattie or Thomas. I wasn't shocked when we went to church and there was no sign of him. I'm sure he is still upset with me after I kicked him out of the house for making those foolish and ignorant comments. I was not surprised that he didn't show up at church. I figure Mattie told him we were coming and he just wanted nothing to do with me. He didn't look too upset, though, when I saw him next door in the Stevenses' window that very same evening.

I step on the front porch just as Bee knocks on the door, rattling it with her large, pounding fist.

"Now, what's taking her so long to come to the door?" she says, turning around to look at me, fuming.

Mattie comes to the door after Bee peeks through the front window and yells out her name. She looks as if she does not want company, but comes to the door anyway, because she knows Bee is not leaving until she finds out if Mattie is all right. I notice that Bee's attitude changes quickly once the door opens and Mattie is standing there in front of us.

"Hello, Sweetie, we came over today because we heard that you weren't feeling well," Bee chimes in an uncharacteristically sweet voice.

The "we" she mentions is really "her," since I have no idea what is going on. Mattie is dressed in her robe and her hair is all over her head as if she has not combed it since we saw her at church on Sunday. Her face is expressionless and her eyes are glazed over like she has not slept in days. She is looking past Bee off into the distance. Mattie's appearance and demeanor are such a shock! I am speechless and just smile at her, wondering what's wrong.

"What the hell you two want?" she suddenly spits at us, her face reddening with anger.

"Excuse me, Sister?" Bee says, unfazed by Mattie's hostility. Mattie does not waver and moves closer to Bee, whose girth blocks her from my view. But I can hear her loud and clear.

"I said what the hell you two want?"

"The only reason I'm not beating you down right now is because I heard from the ladies at church that something is terribly wrong!"

Mattie apparently backs up, because Bee starts walking through the door like a bull charging through the streets of Pamplona, Spain.

I turn around and wave to the cab driver, hoping he will not leave us, as I walk behind Bee through Mattie's front door.

"You have a party in here, Mattie?" Bee asks, as we both look around at the disarray.

"I believe my Thomas is dead," Mattie blurts out as she sits down on a couch covered with clothes. "He would never leave for this long and not call me." Her voice is resigned.

"So you're trying to say that Thomas is missing?" Bee says, plopping down on a pile of clothes next to Mattie, putting her arms around her friend as Mattie starts to weep.

"Yes! I know deep down in my heart that something is terribly wrong. The last time I saw my Thomas was the night we came over to the old Whitfield house that Saturday night. He never came home. I just thought he might have stopped by his friend house next door to the Whit-field place, but when I called, Mr. Stevens said he haven't seen nor heard from Thomas. The following morning I went out looking for him right before church, but he was nowhere to be found. I couldn't help but feel that something was wrong as the days passed with no sign of Thomas. I went downtown to file a missing person report with the local police. They just laughed and said,

"Maybe Thomas left here and joined that Rev. Martin Luther King Jr., marching for your rights!" I knew then, at that moment, my Thomas was dead."

Bee and I listen while Mattie talks through her tears; her emotional state indicating she may be on the verge of a nervous breakdown.

I walk over to Mattie and sit on the other side of her on the couch, squashing some clothes piled there.

"You say the last time you saw Thomas was the Saturday night when you both came by my house?"

"Thomas never came home, Mattie?"

"No."

She wipes the tears from her face with a tissue from her robe and looks at me for a sign of hope.

"Have you seen Thomas, Miss Peg?"

"No, I haven't seen Thomas since that night." That was almost the truth. I did see Thomas conversing with Mr. Stevens that same night. Is it possible that "He" had something to do with his disappearance? Listening to poor Mattie, I am sure that "He" is somehow to blame for whatever has happened to Thomas. I go to the kitchen to start a pot of tea for Mattie and I hear her doorbell ring. I feel obligated to answer the door while Bee comforts her on the couch. When I open the door, I am surprised to see Mr. Stevens standing there with the sheriff.

"Girl, what are you doing here?" "He" says, walking through the door.

"We came over today, Mr. Stevens, because we heard that Mattie wasn't feeling well."

"How are you, Mattie?"

"She's fine," Bee says.

Mr. Stevens and the sheriff walk over to Mattie, looking official.

"Hello, Mattie," the sheriff says.

"We came over today because, well, we have some bad news," Mr. Stevens says as he sits next to Mattie where I was just sitting. Bee has not taken her eyes off Mr. Stevens. I think she already knows he is the one responsible for Thomas' disappearance.

"Mattie, we found Thomas."

"Where is he?"

"Mattie, Thomas will not be coming home."

Before Mr. Stevens can get the rest of his story out, she lets out a cry so full of pain and anger, he jumps up from the couch as if he's been struck a blow. All the while, he has been pretending to comfort Mattie with his condescending voice and his faked concern. Now we know for sure; Thomas will never come home. And the very same man that brought his wife the news is the one that has made her a widow. I'm sure of it.

After the bearers of bad news depart, I pay the cab driver and send him on his way. I then call Dr. Carson so he can come over to see to Mattie and give her something that will let her rest.

He comes over quickly and checks her pulse and blood pressure, then gives her a mild sedative to relax her. We wait while Bee puts Mattie to bed and I take her that cup of tea I was making her before the sheriff and district attorney came with the bad news. Dr. Carson gives Bee and me a ride, dropping us off downtown to get a cup of coffee, telling us to take a few moments to calm down from the whole ordeal before worrying about dinner.

Getting out of his car, I wave him off and make my way toward a busy restaurant in downtown Birmingham. I open the door and start in. I hesitate when the entire restaurant gets quiet and everyone stops eating to stare at me.

"Table for two, please," I say to a nearby waiter, wondering why the other diners and the staff are all staring at me. Do I have a stain on my blouse? Is my skirt ripped?

"Excuse me?" the waiter says, his face turning red.

"A table for two, please."

"Girl, we don't serve niggers up front here." Now *my* face is turning red.

Before I can answer, Bee rushes inside and quickly grabs my arm, smiling at the rude waiter.

"Sorry, she is new to Birmingham," she says, pulling my arm and dragging me out through the door.

"Did you hear what he said? What he called me?" I say out of the waiter's earshot, but loud enough for the customers near the door to hear.

"Listen, Miss Peg, Birmingham is a different world than what you are accustomed to."

We walk around the building to the alley and enter the restaurant from the back where there is a small room with tables and chairs without any décor of any kind. I look at the cooks while they take orders just feet away from where we sit.

"What would you like to order?" Bee says, and I mumble my reply.

It is apparent there aren't any waiters taking orders. I watch Bee walk up to an order window and place our orders with the Negro cooks. I couldn't help but think of all the pain I witnessed when Mattie got the news about Thomas just minutes before. Deep within my soul I know the real reason why Thomas didn't make it home. I noticed him that evening, the night of his disappearance. Mr. Stevens is the one who knows what really happened to Thomas.

Bee returns with two sandwiches and beverages on a tray, puts it on the table, and then sits down next to me.

"Let me tell you something and I don't mean to be rude at all," Bee says with a stern look on her face. "You are never to enter a place of business in this town through the front door. These white folks will kill you dead if they feel you think you're equal to them. I know one thing, also, Miss. Peg."

"What is that?"

Bee looks around making sure that no one can hear what she is getting ready to say.

"I know that Thomas was over to the Stevens house the night he disappeared. I believe that he is the reason for his disappearance and I know you also know that he was last to see him."

"What are you talking about, Bee?"

"Listen, young lady, I saw you when I went to the kitchen to get us tea that evening when Mattie was at the house. I witnessed you seeing Thomas at the Stevens house like I did when you left. I also know you didn't get a room that evening to relax. One thing I don't like, Miss Peg, is a liar and if you continue lying to me, well, I guess this is my last day working with you and the Carson Family."

I put down my sandwich and look around the restaurant, imagining everyone in that room knows where I was that evening.

"Bee, I really cannot get into it right now with you. If I were to say anything, I might not be able to come home, either. Do you understand?"

"I understand, Miss Peg," Bee says, as she grabs my hand to comfort me.

Chapter 35

"Hello, Mr. Richards."

"Well, hello there, Patrick, how are you? Can I get you anything today?"

"No, sir. I just came in today to pick up some sugar for my mama's famous pies for the picnic this coming weekend. Are you coming?"

Looking over his reading glasses, Mr. Richards smiles wryly, relaxing with one arm on a shelf.

"Now, you know I never miss any picnic here in Birmingham," he says. Leaning forward, the proprietor of the best store in Birmingham continues speaking softly, so no one else could hear.

"We have some of the best entertainment in the South. My brother in Kentucky always claimed theirs was better than any other state. So, I visited him last year and they had a very entertaining picnic. They had themselves a young nigger gal about 'round twenty. She had mouthed off to a fine, Christian white lady she worked for, because she didn't wanna scrub those white folks' bathroom floor with a toothbrush."

"She was drilled in every hole God gave her, including her ears and eyes, by fifty to sixty men right in front of all the white boys they could round up, so them young 'uns could learn how they supposed to keep women in line, no matter what they color. Then they tied a rope to each of her feet, hitched up each rope to the bridles of the fastest two horses they could find, and whipped them horses so they ran hard and fast. They popped that gal like a watermelon! Quite entertaining!" Mr. Richards lets out a low, gurgling laugh, relishing the memory.

"I was close enough to get one of her nipples before them rednecks picked over what was left of her, taking souvenirs. After, we took photos to make postcards to send up North, of course. My cousin in Philadelphia told my brother to save the next uppity black bitch for him, so he could pull her apart with his bare hands when he comes to visit. They can't do nothing to black folk up there but avoid them," he says.

"But good as that picnic was, it wasn't nothing like the one I saw in Tennessee. You see, in Tennessee they lynched an entire family, even the children. Hung 'em all from a bridge, after castrating the men and the boys and, of course, raping the women and the girls." Mr. Richards leans forward, beckoning me to come closer, then whispers in my ear.

"With a bull! Tore them two little black girls in two. They were dead before they could lynch 'em. Nearly killed they mama, too. When that bull rammed her, blood spurted out her mouth like water from them fire hoses they spray on them marching niggers. Boy, I wish you could've seen it, Patrick." I am thinking the same thing, hoping Mr. Richards will give more details about the castrations and the bloodletting that day.

"But that ain't all," he says, moving over to the counter to watch some niggers lingering too long around a counter, trying to catch them stealing so he can call the sheriff. The sheriff would love to throw some more niggers in jail so Mr. Stevens can prosecute them and send them to prison for a long time. I admire that man. He's put more niggers in jail than any prosecutor in the history of this county; probably any county in Alabama!

The niggers get some cheap junk Mr. Richards keeps in his store just for them that probably falls apart as soon as they get it home. They walk over to a clerk to pay what little money they have for some shoelaces and socks. Mr. Richards makes sure they give the clerk their hard-earned money, then goes back to his story.

"They weren't done yet. They saved the best for last. A pregnant nigger had the nerve to file a complaint about her husband being lynched. The nigger wouldn't sell his couple of acres to a white man that wanted it, so of course being a proud Southerner, he had the Klan hang him. His wife must not have heard the story of another nigger bitch demanding justice for her lynched husband back in Georgia. My grandpa told me all about it. A lot of other families must have passed down that story because they did the same thing to this nigger bitch in Tennessee that they done to that one in Georgia. Niggers should know better than to talk about lynching, but that picaninny come talking 'bout she want justice just the same like the one in Georgia! Niggers better learn the history of how they been treated in this country before they come talking 'bout justice." We both laugh at that.

"Like niggers gonna get any justice in the South. They oughta still be slaves, picking our cotton and cleaning our houses for nothing. Now, white folks gotta pay niggers to work for us? But that's all right. You see that flag up there?" he shouts. Mr. Richards' voice has gotten louder and he's nearly yelling when he points to the Confederate flag hanging from the ceiling in his store. "The South *will* rise again!"

His loud proclamation gets applause and whistles from the white patrons in the store, while a few niggers that are just coming in from the back to give Mr. Richards their weekly paycheck look nervously at each other and hurriedly leave without buying anything. The whites laugh and Mr. Richards gets angry.

"What ya'll laughing at! I just run out my best customers. Them niggers can't keep a dollar in their pockets if you sewed it with needle and thread! They spend ever cent they get and they was about to give me most of the money those white folks pay them to clean they houses and they yards, cook they meals, and nurse they babies until I ran my damn mouth!"

The white customers continue shopping, amused at Mr. Richards' rare loss of self-control. Visibly calming himself, Mr. Richards turns back to me.

"Sorry, 'bout that Patrick. I'm a son of the South. The only thing gets me worked up is thinking about us losing the Civil War and having to pay these damn niggers money to work for us now. Is there anything else I can do for you today?"

"Yeah," I say. "Tell me what them good old boys in Tennessee did to that nigger wanting 'justice' for her husband!"

"That's right!" Mr. Richards says, realizing he hasn't finished his story. He leans over, lowering his voice so only I can hear him.

"Hung her from a tree by her feet and set fire to her; burned her to a crisp! She was already black, but that black turned burnt black. Her howling and screaming was so loud even the birds and the crickets got quiet. Never have I seen such pain and agony and never was it so well-deserved and so enjoyed." We both laugh, thinking about how much we love to hear the screams of the niggers we beat and often kill. Chuckling, Mr. Richards continues the story.

"My cousin, who invited me there to see how they keep their niggers in line, said his little grandson still has nightmares about that nigger screaming. Wakes up yelling, 'Tell her to shut up!' Little sissy! Hope my cousin takes him out to the woodshed and makes a man of him before it's too late!" Mr. Richards' pointed remark reminds me of being taken to the woodshed when I cried because some big boys beat me up. My father made me strip and bend over and when he was finished with me, not letting up until I stopped crying and begging him to stop hurting me, I never cried again. Never! Now, I'm the one that makes others cry!

"Then, when her screaming finally stopped, we saw something moving inside her and one of the men cut her belly open. A black baby fell on the ground and started screaming! My cousin smashed that little nigger's head with his brogans until it stopped crying. It was just like what my grandpappy told me they did to that nigger's baby in Georgia when it moved and got cut out of its mama and started crying like a bitch. Got rid of two nigger families in one day!" Mr. Richards smiles, remembering the sight of that burnt body, the dead baby on the ground, and the smell of burnt flesh.

"Best picnic entertainment I ever saw! The people there say this is what they've always done, still do, and will continue to do to keep their niggers in line, even though the rest of the world thinks lynchings have stopped. Do you know they say J. Edgar Hoover wants to send the FBI to break up the KKK? Ain't gonna happen!" Mr. Richards raises his voice again, but quickly quiets back down, seeing more niggers coming from the back of the store where their entrance is located, with money in their pockets, ready to give it to him for some cheap merchandise.

"Yes, son," he continues quietly, "a hundred years from now when we travel to Mars, they will still be lynching niggers in the wonderful Smokies. Let me tell you something, Patrick, and you listen well. I watched the march the niggers had here in Birmingham and I know we have to get this community under our grip. If not, we will have Jews, Mexicans, homosexuals, commies, and God knows what all trying to have the good life we have here in America." He shakes his head in disbelief that anyone would dare encroach on our Southern traditions.

"Now, the Negroes are wanting to vote without paying a poll tax and we all know around here that day is never coming. It's gonna always be too high for them to pay, and ever year they add the poll tax from the years before, so they can't never get enough money to vote–ever! Old nigger come in here wanting me to count a bag full of pennies to see if he had enough money to pay the poll tax so he could vote for that Papist, John Kennedy. I asked him how old he was. He said he was seventy-eight years old. I said, 'Nigger, you gotta pay poll tax for every year since you turn twenty-one. That's sixty-seven times what you got in that bag!' That nigger took that bag and walked out of here, hanging his head like a dog that just got his balls kicked by a mule!" Mr. Richards laughs so hard his belly shakes.

"He had a heart attack a couple days later and his people told me he died the night of the election. Said he held out until he heard Kennedy won. Some president. Supporting niggers! I'd like to take that Mick to Tennessee! That's what I'd like to do. They know what to do with nigger lovers down there. They lynch 'em, that's what! They treat them just like they treat the niggers they love so much!"

"You said the sugar is in aisle seven, right, Mr. Richards?" I ask, not wanting Mr. Richards to go into another tirade.

"Yes, son," Mr. Richards says, answering with his usual smile.

"Nice talking to you. Let me know next time you go to Tennessee!" I start walking away, hoping to avoid another long story. Mr. Richards is known for the good quality merchandise he carries for the whites in the community and his gregariousness. He loves to talk and will always take time to talk to his favorite customers, usually other Klan members and their families. Anyone in a hurry when they come into his store usually steers clear of him, trying to get in and out as quickly as possible.

"Patrick, check out my new shipment," he yells to me, as I disappear down aisle seven. "I got new boots for hunting that just arrived this morning."

As much as he likes to talk, Mr. Richards will make sure you are out of here as soon as possible once you have your merchandise. I'm glad about that, because I wouldn't want one of the fellows coming in here and seeing me doing a woman's work. Women have their place here in America. They must be put in their place in every white family. My grandfather told me once that the only purpose for a woman is to bear children, cook, and clean. All the men in my family and most of the other men I know think the same way. The perfect example of a good Southern belle is in my own household. My mother never questions anything my father says. Even when he is wrong, she agrees, because she knows her place.

I make my way over to find the sugar and spices as directed by my mom and I am surprised to see Mary Joe standing there with a cart.

"Mary Joe, how are you?"

"Hello, Patrick. How are you and your family? It was great seeing your mom Sunday at the picnic. Out of all the great bakers here in Birmingham, I must say your mom is the best."

Holding the sack of sugar I just retrieved from the shelf, I know damn well that it will take more than one bag for my mother to make her pies for this Sunday.

"If I didn't know better, Mary Joe, I would guess you're thinking about entering this week's bake off." She laughs, looking at ingredients on the side of a cake box sitting on a shelf near the sugar, then searching for the things she needs on the shelves.

"I wouldn't dare enter an event that would compete with your mama's cooking, Patrick."

"You may not be the greatest cook, but you must be the fastest woman alive, beating me downtown. How on earth did you make it here from the quarry before me?"

"What do you mean, Patrick?"

"Didn't I just see you out at the quarry with Seth? I didn't come any nearer because he said you weren't feeling well."

"Oh, is that right?" Mary Joe replies, looking confused and angry.

"It's not surprising how quickly you recovered on such a beautiful day as today," I tell her, as I continue putting more sugar and other items my mother has on her list in the cart. I leave Mary Joe in the spice row, realizing something is amiss.

What could Seth be doing out at the quarry and with whom? Why does Seth feel like he has to lie to me about his new girlfriend? I don't know the answer, but I am damn sure going to find out tomorrow! I'll carefully hide my car just before he and his new friend arrive. Knowing him like I do, I know exactly which spot he will take her to tomorrow.

But right now, I am excited about seeing these new boots Mr. Richards said just came in. Not only are whites gathered in the new shoe section, but so are niggers holding their children while they try on the cheap shoes Mr. Richards keeps on one shelf just for them. Seeing those niggers reminds me that I need to continue collecting shoes for the Christmas shoe drive. Helping poor white children keep their feet warm is my own personal charity. I am blessed to help so many children. I have at least two dozen boy's shoes to distribute this year. Would be nice if they were made out of good leather, instead of the cheap stuff Mr. Richards keeps in stock for the niggers, but I take what I can get, whatever I have to do to get it.

"My best year collecting shoes so far!" I think, as I examine a pair of fine, leather cowboy boots that will be real nice to wear at the next hoedown at the local Elks Club.

Chapter 36

What a beautiful Saturday morning. The sun is shining and our street is full of children laughing, riding their bikes and skateboards. After taking my shower, I head down the steps for a quick breakfast with my father and brother. I start thinking that I only have an hour before meeting Peg for an early lunch at our special spot. If anyone ever finds out, it will be hell to pay for not only me, but Peg, as well. I know from watching firsthand what this town would do if people find out that a white man is fond of a woman like Peg.

I am surprised to see my father is already downstairs having breakfast with Ronnie at the kitchen table.

"Oatmeal, son?"

"No, thank you," I say, sitting down at the table.

"Then let me make you some eggs," my dad says.

"I think I'll pass on the eggs, Dad, but I will have a cup of coffee."

I get up from the table, looking at the house next door, trying to see any sign of Peg.

"Seth! Seth!" my father says repeatedly, trying to get my attention.

"Oh, Dad, I'm sorry. My mind is elsewhere."

"I understand, son. My mind was like that when I met your mother. Who is she?"

"Who is who?" I try to relax as my palms get sweaty.

"Who is the lady I know you're seeing, young man? Remember, I once was your age."

He laughs and Ronnie joins in as if he has a clue what our father is talking about.

"Oh, Dad, she's just a girl I met here in Birmingham."

"Okay, young man. Just remember, you have a new baby."

"That reminds me, Dad. I received a letter from Nora and she has now decided she wants some kind of relationship with our baby. What should I do?"

"Don't you worry about Nora? Let me handle it, Seth."

Hearing my father's words, I know that I don't have to worry about this issue ever again.

"Okay, young men," my father says, as we all sit at the table. "I do have some good news! I received a call yesterday from Doctor Mason and he informed me that they found a donor for you, Ronnie. The doctor said it is important that we move on this immediately, so your operation is scheduled for tonight."

Speechless with shock, I look at both of them, especially at Ronnie as he looks at us both with a concerned expression on his face.

"What the matter, son?" my dad asks.

"What does that mean? Does it mean I won't die now?" Ronnie asks.

"Yes, son! That means that we must be thankful for whoever this good Christian person is for giving you a second chance at life."

I hug Ronnie and we both cry with happiness as Dad gets our mother on the phone.

Chapter 37

I'm patiently waiting to see this mysterious woman my friend is seeing. I'll bet he's secretly seeing one of the nice blondes from the picnic last Sunday.

"Where you off to, son?" my father asked me, right before I jumped into my car, in a hurry to get here before Seth and his mystery woman arrive.

"I have to check on Seth."

"Okay. Tell him I said, hello."

"Will do, Dad!"

During the entire ride, I wonder why there is such secrecy about Seth's new girl. I guess we all have secrets and there are some things we don't want people to know about; no matter how close you are to them. I remember when Mike, Seth, Connor, and I went out to this wonderful new club that opened just after we finished high school. We told some girls we would meet them there and we couldn't wait to get going. Seth had just bought a new camera and he never left home without it. He once told me he wanted to be a reporter and that a picture could tell a story all by itself. We all laughed and had shots of whiskey, chasing them with cold beers the entire evening. Later, after we were all drunk, the girls we were supposed to meet finally showed up.

The girl that had her eye on me was the prettiest and I knew I would score big that evening. Since this was our first night out as men, we were trying to act worldly, knowing we'd be going to college soon. I asked the pretty blonde, who didn't seem to mind that I was drunk, if she wanted to go for a walk and when she nodded, headed with her to a remote area where I clumsily had sex for the very first time. Obviously more experienced, she took control of the situation, unzipping my pants and climbing on top of me. I enjoyed every minute of it.

Arriving near the quarry, I am relieved when I don't see Seth's truck. I carefully hide my car just beyond the tall pine trees at the Stevenses' summer cabin, anxious to get a glance at this mystery woman my friend Seth is scheduled to meet today. I take a big gulp of a cold beer I brought along for the ride. In all of the years that I've known him, I've never known Seth to be so secretive. It's a hot summer day and there is not a cloud in the sky. I drive along the path in the opposite direction that Seth should be taking. I get out my car and wonder who could be better than Mary Joe? I know one thing it can't be Nora, that's for sure. I spoke with her the morning she left Birmingham and was glad to hear the whore was leaving Seth and their baby alone, forever.

After walking about a quarter of a mile, I sit where I can see the spot where I believe the two young love birds will sit and talk. Maybe it's a New York model from one of those books that I see my mother read all the time? Whoever she is, I am damn sure he wants this quiet. What other reason would he bring her to this isolated area?

By the time my closest friend arrives with his secret woman, I've downed a six pack. They walk along the dirt path, laughing and holding hands. I am not surprised to see that this lady is wearing a big sun hat that covers her face and shades covering her eyes. She is petite, wearing pants with sandals, and carrying a big straw bag decorated with colorful flowers. One thing is for sure, she is not Mary Joe! Her body is amazing and I watch her walk, eyeing each curve as my eyes move down her body and up again, stopping at her small waist. My friend holds her as they stand, look-ing down into the quarry. She laughs. Seth pulls her closer and kisses her deeply. But who is she? I am sure I have never seen this woman before.

I lower myself on my belly like a Marine, and decide to get a better view of the otherwise occupied lovers. I must be insane to pry into my friend's life like this, but I wonder why he's kept her a secret if she's as beau-tiful as she appears to be. As I get closer, I hear some small talk about Seth's brother, Ronnie. Seth tells his secret lover that Ronnie's doctor has found a donor and they will perform his surgery this evening at the local hospital. I smile, knowing how long his family has been waiting for such good news. I know this made Seth happy, knowing that his brother will have a second chance at life. I can't imagine having to deal with the kind of dread that his family has had to endure during Ronnie's sickness.

Chapter 38

Seth and I go to our favorite spot, just in front of the drop into the quarry. It is only a few yards beyond the cabin his dad took me to the first night he raped me. My feelings are mixed. I wonder why being in this same place now puts a smile on my face? I am ecstatic about being here with Seth, and I am also excited about tonight, knowing Ronnie is going to live a full life now.

I packed some cold cuts and apple pie for us to share. I was also sure to wear my big dark shades since the sun is bright. I put on a thin sweater to keep warm in the cool breeze here. And what woman would ever leave her home without a big hat to hide her face from the sun during the summer? Not I!

Seth and I hold hands while walking towards the edge of the quarry. He tells me how excited he was about finally finding a donor willing to give his brother a kidney and save his life.

Even though I am getting so close to Seth, I dare not let him know that I am the donor. I decide to tell him I am leaving today to visit my family up North, since I know I will be in the hospital for a few days. We sit down and make ourselves comfortable while watching a hawk climb high in the sky. We watch as the hawk dives below to feed on some poor rabbit that never makes it to its den.

"Seth, I am leaving tonight for a short visit up North."

"When will I see you again?" he asks. "I'd love to see you as soon as you get back, if that's okay?"

"I should be back by Monday night."

"Then, let's meet here Tuesday. Is that all right, Peg?"

"That would be fine." I start taking cold turkey sandwiches out of my summer bag when Seth suddenly jumps up, startling me.

"Damn! I forgot the wine! Let me run back to the truck. Wait right here, Peg. I will be right back!" He kisses me on my lips and darts back up the wooded path towards his truck, which is parked about a quarter of a mile away. This is really the first time I have been able to relax and reflect about tonight's surgery. But my reverie is quickly interrupted by the sounds of footsteps coming from behind me.

"That was fast, Seth," I say, as I turn around to find it is not Seth, but a young man around his age.

"You frightened me," I cry out, rising to my feet quickly with my hands against my chest, trying to stop my heart from pumping so furiously.

"Who the hell are you? I said who the hell are you, nigger!"

I recognize this man now, standing just about ten yards away from me, from the close call yesterday. I turn around and see that I am only feet away from edge of the quarry with nowhere to run.

Where is Seth?

"I've been watching you with my friend and I must say you're good looking for a nigger. What the hell are you doing with Seth?"

Each time he speaks, he draws closer, and I notice the small pieces of gravel slipping over the edge. I am afraid I am now just inches away from falling to my death. Nervously, I watch as his large hand slowly clinches into a fist and I am trapped with no place to retreat. Before I can get one word out, his big, strong hands grab my neck and I fall to my knees. He looks down on me with an anger I do not understand. I watch his eyes as he starts to speak, spewing words filled with hate, showering me with his hot, sticky saliva.

"You piece of nigger trash! I'm going to kill you!" he screams.

His eyes bulge and his hair drapes over his snarling face and just as I slowly start to lose consciousness, I hear Seth's voice calling out to save me.

"What the hell are you doing, Patrick? Take your damn hands off her!" Seth takes Patrick by his shoulders, pulling his friend away with such force he has no choice but to release me. Then he turns him around and punches him in the face, knocking him to the ground as I still struggle to catch my breath.

"Peg, you okay?" Seth asks, helping me to my feet.

"Her name is Peg?" Patrick snarls, as his mouth fills with blood that drips from his busted lip.

"So, Seth, you're a nigger lover! I know she's beautiful, man, but how in the hell could you kiss a filthy nigger like that?" Seth helps me up carefully as I slowly catch my breath. I am sure I would be dead now had Seth not come back when he did.

"How long you been a nigger lover, Seth?"

"Patrick, you owe Peg an apology," Seth says, pulling me close, protecting me.

"I don't owe this nigger shit! This city don't take too kindly to nigger lovers, Seth. You been my friend ever since we were brought into this world. Your parents are like my very own. How could you feel this way about a nigger, knowing all we've been taught?"

"Patrick, what we have been taught is wrong," Seth says, as I lean my back against a tree, still recovering from the attack. I notice a rope dangling just above my head and just inches away from the ledge.

Patrick turns to me and with the most evil look upon his face starts shouting questions.

"Who are you and where did you come from nigger?"

"I said to address her as Peg," Seth shouts back, his arm still around my waist.

"I am Peg and I work for Dr. Carson," I say, trying to calm everyone down.

"Dr. Carson? Who the hell is Dr. Carson?"

"He's a new doctor in town and he and his family are the ones that moved next door to the Stevens."

"Wait, let me get this straight," Patrick says, trying to stand on his feet, warily watching us. "You're the nigger that Seth saw in the old Whitfield house next door. That was the evening you moved to Birmingham?"

"What is he talking about, Seth?' Patrick starts to laugh as he finishes his story.

"You see, Peg, your new friend Seth this guy here he was the very same guy that came and got my brother and me the night you moved into the old Whitfield house. We came that night to hang you in that tree, right in your own front yard."

"Is that true, Seth?"

He sighs, not looking at me, but down at the ground.

"Peg, I told you I was confused that evening," he says.

"See, nigger, your boyfriend wanted you dead the very same night he knew you moved into the house next to him," Patrick says.

I quickly grab my belongings, feeling betrayed.

"Please take me home!" I cry.

"Yeah, take your nigger girlfriend home. Wait until I tell everyone about this. I am sure your family will love the news I have for them and the whole city of Birmingham."

"Let me tell you one thing," Seth says, as he steps closer to his friend. "I think you better hold off on telling everyone anything about today. I don't want anything to happen to Peg. Do you understand?"

"And if I don't?" Patrick counters with a smirk.

"Well, let's just say that it wouldn't be the best choice you ever made."

"You and your new nigger girlfriend get the hell out of here! You're nothing but a white trash nigger lover, Seth!"

129

"Let's just forget we were ever friends!"

"Don't come by my house, Seth! You'll be lucky not to find your entire family missing!"

"You come near my family and I'll kill you dead!" Seth struggles to calm himself. "Let me tell you one thing, Patrick, if you know what's good for you. Knowing what I know, you better not say a word to anyone about this."

I watch as Patrick's smirk dissolves and his face turns ashen white. He watches in silence as Seth and I walk to the truck. When we leave, he is still standing there looking as if he's not only lost his best friend, but his sense of security. I am silent the entire trip home. Seth assures me that Patrick will not say a word about what happened.

"Seth, I would like it if you would not come by, or ask me out again."

Chapter 39

It has been about two weeks since the students marched through downtown Birmingham. That was the day when I first arrived here.

I look back at my life in Ohio and wonder why I ever agreed to come to this place. Here I am getting ready to give one of my vital organs to the son of a man who repeatedly rapes me and there is not a damn thing I can do about it.

Just when I think things might get better, I find out that Ronnie's brother is the very same man who taunted me and actually wanted me dead my first night here in Birmingham. Should I be risking my health, trying to save someone who is part of a family so full of hate?

I am scheduled to go under the knife tonight, but I am wondering if I should stop this. I could refuse the operation and allow this family to suffer. Let them deal with pain and the death of a family member. Should I make them feel the hurt that they have imposed on me? The emptiness I am feeling and the sadness that is breaking my heart makes me feel as if I am on the verge of a nervous breakdown. Now, I am as cold-hearted as they are. I have been forced to feel as hateful as the men who live next door to me. How I wish I had died the very same day my parents died in that awful car accident in Ohio. Then I wouldn't be feeling all the heartache these men have put me through. I am in deep thought, contemplating my own death, when suddenly the phone rings.

"Hello, Aunt Peg?"

"Yes, Baby, how are you? It is so good to hear your voice. How's Ohio?"

"Everything here at the University is wonderful. I hope you didn't tell my parents I'm coming."

"No, I wouldn't do that, Robert Jr. Tell me, how are your studies?"

"I am doing well. I decided to attend summer school. I was coming home this weekend, but I am afraid I will have to come next week. I will get a cab at the airport so I can come to the house and surprise my parents.

I think that is the only way I can keep them in the dark about me coming home."

"Yes, Robert," I say, giggling with Robert Jr. as we hatch our plot. I am enjoying being a co-conspirator with my nephew and I temporarily forget my own dilemma. "I think this may be the only way to keep my nosy cousin from finding out what we're up to."

"Aunt Peg," Robert Jr. says, with a serious tone to his voice. "How do you think my mother will fare making a career in Birmingham? She always wanted to work with the Justice Department. I look at the world news and see how much hate people have for us there. I just hope she can make a difference someday."

"I am sure she will get that chance, Robert" I say, sensing concern about his parents' well-being in his voice, though he'd never admit it.

"Now, promise me again you will not tell them I am coming home soon," he says in a scolding tone, back to his usual carefree, lighthearted self.

"I promise I will not tell them, Robert," I say. "Scout's honor!"

"Cross your heart and hope to die?" he counters and we both start giggling like a couple of kids. "No, I crossed my fingers and my toes! I'm not going to tell! Now, go study!"

Robert responds, "Great! I don't believe you, but I have to trust that you wouldn't double cross your favorite nephew!"

We both say our well-rehearsed chant in unison: *"One and only* nephew!"

"Love you, too, and I will see you soon, Aunt Peg."

"Love you and stay safe." I feel much better now after talking to Robert Jr. That boy has always had a way of making me smile. What if he needed a kidney? Wouldn't I want someone to be kind enough to save my nephew from certain death? I know now what I have to do.

Chapter 40

Bee accompanies me to the hospital, along with my cousin Sera, only a few hours after my lunch with Seth. Dr. Carson and his staff meet us in my room. They were all brought in from Ohio in order to keep this issue a secret. Dr. Carson doesn't trust the hospital staff; sure that they would tell the local community and then the Stevens family would be sure to find out Ronnie's new kidney came from a Negro. Dr. Carson informs me that Dr. Mason will perform the surgery on Ronnie, while he will perform the surgery on me. I feel relieved, knowing Dr. Carson will be my surgeon.

"Baby, you gonna be alright," Bee says, while helping me change into my hospital gown and get into bed. A few minutes later, a nurse comes in to give me an IV.

"Now, you're going feel a slight poke, Peg," the nurse says, as she searches for a vein. "See, that didn't hurt, did it?" I did not feel a thing.

"Peg, you know you really don't have to do this," Sera says.

I can tell she is as nervous as I am. Sera always twists her finger when she is nervous.

"Sera, think of all the good that will come out of this," I say, feeling tired suddenly. It has been a long day.

"You're right, Peg."

My cousin and Bee stay with me until it is time to go up for surgery. Before we leave for the operating room, a nurse comes in and says that the next-of-kin paperwork is required.

"Peg, I know you're probably feeling a little groggy now, but I need you to sit up and fill out these forms," the nurse says.

"I would do it, but I feel light-headed. Have my cousin fill it out, please. Sera, can you fill out the form for me." Sera nods, and I watch with bleary eyes as the nurse hands Sera a clipboard.

Thank God that Sera and Bee are here, because I don't think I can do this alone. I know deep within my heart that this is the right thing to do, no matter what Ronnie's family has done. I really don't think Ronnie could ever be as heartless as his father and brother. I must do what is right. I must do what I was taught by my parents to do. I must do the right thing by helping this young man. That's what love is all about.

Before long the doctors come in and ensure us that the surgery will go smoothly and as planned. The nurse comes back in and reminds Sera not to forget the next-of-kin document. It is still on the clipboard, laying on the foot of my bed where Sera placed it when she got up to give me some water. The attendants put me on the gurney that will transport me to the operating room.

"Sera, are you okay?" I ask. "You look a little dazed."

"Oh, I'm fine, Peg. I just think this Southern air has gotten the best of me today. I will be here when you come out of surgery."

"Are you sure you okay?" Bee asks Sera. She takes a small white handkerchief from her purse and dabs it on Sera's temple. Her forehead is covered with beads of perspiration.

"I am fine, Bee," Sera says, pushing Bee's hand aside as she looks straight ahead, as if she is seeing a ghost.

Chapter 41

I know I have to get Peg's trust back. I also know I have a visit to make to my "dear friend," Patrick. But before I do, I must go inside my home to get the evidence that I secretly stowed in the basement. I know what I have in my possession is the only thing that will keep Patrick's big mouth shut.

Patrick is sure to tell others if I don't get to him first. I drive for hours around town until I finally notice his truck parked outside the local bar just on the edge of town. It's a place where we sometimes hang out when we need to blow off some steam. I quickly park my truck and gather the photographs that I'm sure are the only thing that will keep him quiet. I've been keeping the negatives along with others in a secret location in the basement at home. Looking through the bar's large glass windows, our eyes meet briefly before I turn and proceed inside.

"Well, look who the hell just walked in and graced us with his presence!" Patrick says, as he swallows a large gulp of beer. He spreads his arms wide, as if to welcome me, while some guys playing pool nearby remain completely uninterested.

"Everyone look! Mr. Seth Stevens has arrived!"

I can tell he has finished several beers and I am sure more than a few shots of whiskey.

"How you doing, boy?" Patrick says, looking at me with the very same demeanor that he had toward Peg as he held her throat tightly, almost ending her life.

"Everyone, I have good news! Your attention, please! Everyone, I think you will enjoy what I am getting ready to say."

Suddenly, the entire bar quiets down and everyone is paying close attention to Patrick, who is obviously drunk, waving his arms in the air. "Everyone, listen!" he shouts again, and people look at each other, shrugging their shoulders trying to figure out what's going on.

"You know, boys, this is a town where we don't like it when niggers think that they are equal to us. Why, just weeks ago we all watched as the niggers had the gall to march downtown for equal rights. It's amazing to know America is changing from Washington, D.C., all the way to the Mason-Dixon Line, but here in Birmingham, we have segregation, today and forever. Even though President Lincoln demanded that every nigger be free, they still are beneath us white folks. Does anyone here think your babies could ever be sitting next to a nigger in *our* schools? The very same words that the teachers teach our children will be the very same words that the niggers will use against us for equality." A few people nod their heads while everyone waits for the big news.

I look at Patrick as he walks around the bar with a bottle of beer in his hand, wearing his cut jeans and boots and a dingy T-shirt.

"Do you want that, Seth?" he says, as he approaches me. He stands just inches away from my face and his voice lowers to a whisper for only me to hear.

"Do you want your precious, little Emily Rose learning the same as a nigger? Oh, I forgot, your children will be niggers, too." He makes sure his words are only heard by me.

"Hello, Mary Joe," he says, his voice once again loud and boisterous. "Glad you made it tonight. Seth has some exciting news for us all."

"Stop it, Patrick," Mary Joe replies, knowing that Patrick has been drinking and he sometimes gets louder when he drinks.

"Mary Joe, Seth has some news for us all." Patrick nearly stumbles and falls and finally realizing he's drunk, the other patrons return to their pool games and beer

I offer to buy Mary Joe a drink and she accepts, taking my money and walking to the bar to order it.

"Patrick," I say quietly. "I think you should take a look at what I brought with me." He looks down and notices the yellow package I hold in my hand. I extend it toward him and he takes it from me. He slowly opens the envelope and looks closely at the pictures inside. Suddenly, all the liquor he's consumed today loses its potency and he looks as sober as the proverbial judge.

"You see, Patrick, all the years I've known you I never judged you, because you've always been like my brother. I truly love you like my brother and I never thought it would come to this. But you give me no other choice."

"Where in the hell did you get this from, Seth?" Patrick's rage is palpable as he speaks to me through clenched teeth, just above a whisper.

"We were out drinking and I had my new camera around my neck. Connor went to take a leak, and then you went. You two were taking so long, I went to see if you'd both passed out in there." I pause, watching his rage subside, leaving him drained of emotion. "I never in a million years would have thought that you and Connor were lovers. You guys never even knew I took pictures in the heat of it all. No one in this town would ever believe that you are gay after all the gays you've jumped with your Klan buddies!"

Patrick looks around nervously, as if he's afraid the other men in the bar can see the photos through the envelope that he still clutches under his arm.

"You see, Patrick," I say, directly confronting him now. "Personally, I don't give a damn what you do or *who* you do it with, but you gave me no other choice. You are a hypocrite and if you say one damn word about today or if I see one Klan truck even break down on my block, this entire city, including your family, will see with their own eyes who you truly are."

Quickly recovering, Patrick puts the envelope inside his jacket and claps on a smile as he looks over at Mary Joe watching us from the bar.

"Outstanding, Seth!" Patrick says loudly, but not as loud or as boisterous as before.

"You boys finally make up?" Mary Joe says jokingly, as she strolls toward us holding a beer in one hand.

"Everyone, I want you to meet my good friend, Seth!" Patrick exclaims. "Best friend in the world!" A few people look around, shake their heads and return to their pool tables, conversations, and whatnot.

"Mary Joe, I'll have to take a rain check on that drink with you," I say to my always understanding ex-girlfriend. "I'll see you, later. "Sure, Seth," Mary Joe replies, with maybe just a touch of sadness in her voice.

As I walk away and close the bar door behind me, I feel like I did the right thing. I know Patrick will look at the photos again more closely when he is alone, and when he sees how graphic they are, he will definitely not say a word about Peg and me for the rest of his life.

"The only thing left for me to do now is try to see Peg off before she goes out of town for a few days," I think, as I get in my truck, determined to make things right with her.

Chapter 42

I open my eyes and the very first people I see are Sera and Bee with big smiles on their faces.

"The medication has not worn off yet, so your speech maybe hard for us to understand, Peg," my cousin says, grabbing my hand. "How are you feeling, Peg?" Sera asks, as Bee wipes my forehead with a damp cloth.

"She will be just fine, Missus Sera."

"Your surgery was a success and we were told that Ronnie is doing fine, also," Sera says. The nurses brought in from Ohio wheel me back to my room, where I first notice the pain in my side from the surgery as they transfer me to my bed.

It is not long before Dr. Carson, along with the other surgeons, are around my bed explaining that I must not exert myself for a few days.

"Now, Peg," Doctor Carson says, standing next to Sera. "You must take it easy and we will see to it that you are transferred home during the evening so no one will get suspicious. I have a nurse that will see to you this evening at home," he explains. Dr. Carson leaves my side and writes on my chart. It is a shame that some people in this town could make such a big fuss over me giving my kidney to Ronnie. I think I would be as good as dead if this news were to leak out. I feel at ease knowing that Bee, Sera, and Dr. Carson will keep this with them for the rest of their lives. Oh, and now I know Bee is putting everything together. I am sure her mind is running a million miles a minute as she listens and pieces it all together. I am sure the Stevens family is happy that Ronnie has a new kidney, but I am equally sure they would not be happy knowing that the donor is the very same person their son Seth wanted dead when I first arrived in Birmingham, and that his father has been repeatedly raping me and I am carrying his child. The sad thing is that I am not sure I even want to have this child. I am so confused. I must tell someone, but who can I trust?

Chapter 43

It's been a few days since my surgery and I am finally making my way downstairs to sit on my back porch. Sammy is there and she greets me with a warm smile and a kindly hello.

"How are you doing, Miss Peg?" she says, as she walks slowly up the steps. "I know you told me last week you would be out of town for a few days, but I was figuring you should be home by now."

"Thank you for coming by, Sammy. It is good to see you are up early this morning."

"Do you have any work for me to do today?"

"Yes, I do. But first, you must have a cup of tea with me."

Sammy's skin is so smooth and you can tell her mama takes her time plaiting the two thick braids in her hair. She is also wearing a nice outfit that makes her look like a picture in a department store catalog.

"Sammy, when we finish our tea would you help me with some of my gardening? It seems like the bugs are eating my flowers."

"How are you supposed to keep the bugs from eating them?" Sammy asks, as she carefully sips her hot tea.

"Well," I say, "I keep this bucket of ashes and when you mix the soil with the ashes it somehow keeps all kinds of insects from eating the flowers. And the next thing you know, you're looking at beautiful flowers growing big and strong. I think we will have the best garden in Birmingham, yet!"

I am sure to walk slow as we make our way from the back porch to the area that divides the Carson property from the Stevens. It isn't long before Sammy notices Ronnie sitting on his back porch. He is there with a nurse to assist him and I see his mother looking out the screen door.

"Hello, Ronnie," Sammy says, smiling with the warm sun beaming on us as we till the soil.

I watch not saying a word as the nurse stands up with the most unpleasant look on her face. She makes her way closer to us until stopping just before crossing the property line.

"How dare you niggers speak as if you're equal to us? Nigger woman, you should teach your child how to address white folk!"

"Ma'am, she did not know any better," I say, averting my eyes from the angry woman's face. "I am sorry if she offended you."

"Seeing as how she is still young, you may want to teach her early," says the nurse, looking at me accusingly.

"Where do you niggers live, anyway?"

I am sure this woman is cleverly trying to gain information and I have no doubt she will tell some of her friends and give them our whereabouts.

"Ma'am, I work for the Carson family."

"Well, next time, only address white folks in the right manner, not as if you're equal to us. Do I make myself clear?"

"Yes, ma'am."

I slowly grab Sammy's hand and we go back to our planting. The look on Sammy's face says it all, and I am sure I am bound to hear about it any moment.

"Why do white people hate us so much, Miss Peg?"

I slowly bend down to look Sammy closely in her eyes while holding my side.

"I don't know, child, but I know there are some good people out there. If you look at history, lots of white people during the Civil War fought for us to be free. There are just bad people everywhere and they come in every color and size. There are white people today that are fighting along with Negroes for equal rights. That is what you must keep fighting for when I am long gone. Promise me that, Sammy. The day will come, maybe not in my lifetime, but you shall be able to speak to whoever you desire, no matter if they do not like you because of the color of their skin. Promise me Sammy, to get your education, because no one can take that away from you. You can be whatever you want to be in life. Never give up on your dreams, even if someone tries to discourage you, no matter who they may be."

I notice another shadow come over us as I stand. This time, it is Mrs. Stevens, walking toward us with a coffee cup in one hand.

"Hello, Mrs. Stevens. We didn't see you, ma'am."

"You keep that nigger girl away from my boy! You hear me, girl? My boy just had surgery and I don't want any nigger germs or a spot of your blood on him! Do I make myself clear?" she says, inhaling smoke from the cigarette in her other hand.

"The last thing I need is your kind hovering over my son and tainting his blood with yours. If I had anything to do with it, I'd make sure all your black asses wouldn't step two feet on this side of town, but I know your asses are too damn poor to live without the decent jobs that we give ya. Don't make me repeat this again, girl. Stay away from my son. And that goes for you, too, little nigger!"

"And one more thing," she says. "Don't let me see any of your damn flowers growing over in my yard. Do I make myself clear, girl?"

I watch as Mrs. Stevens walks back to her porch and speaks with the home nurse. I can tell that Ronnie is still receiving medication, because he is sleeping in his chair on the back porch, enjoying the sun. Ronnie doesn't budge an inch, except to lift up two fingers to say hello.

Sammy and I smile back at him, careful to do so only when his mother and the nurse are not watching. They turn and look our way while they hold a conversation I am sure is just more hateful words about us. The sad thing is that a Negro was the only person in Birmingham willing to give up a vital organ to save her dying son. I want so much to tell her my blood is running through that boy's veins right now, giving him life! Then I sigh, resigned that this is one secret that can never be revealed.

"Come on, Sammy. Let's go have a piece of my pie."

Chapter 44

Bee is already in the kitchen fixing lunch.

"Hello, Bee, how are you today?"

"I'm fine and how are you feeling? Can I get you something cold to drink?"

"Yes, a cold glass of water would be great."

"Hello, Miss Bee," Sammy says.

"Hello, child. I wanted to cook something special for lunch today, so today we are having chicken soup. Mrs. Carson told me that Dr. Carson is coming home for lunch."

"Sammy, would you go and let me hear you play a song on the piano while I speak with Miss Bee?"

"Yes, ma'am!" Sammy's excitement about getting to play the baby grand piano has her skipping out of the room, humming a melody I often hear her playing on the piano.

"What's wrong, child? Aren't you feeling better from your surgery?"

"Yes, Bee, I am. But I am in need of your help."

Bee opens the cabinet, takes out two cups and pours hot water from the kettle that's sitting on the stove half full of hot water.

"What is it, child?" she asks, sitting at the table with me, putting tea bags in the cups to let them steep while we talk.

"Bee, I need you to listen to what I am getting ready to tell you. The only thing I ask is that you don't ask me any questions or judge me, please."

"Miss Peg, you know I love you like my own child. What is it?" Bee asks, as she leans closer toward me.

"I need you to help me find a doctor."

"A doctor? Why don't you let me call Dr. Carson?"

"Because I am in need of another kind of doctor. You see, I am in trouble and I don't think I can go through with the outcome after what happened."

"Miss Peg, I'm not following you at all. Speak plain to me."

"You see, Bee, I am in need of a doctor who can terminate a pregnancy."

Bee sits back and looks at me without saying another word and I want to crawl in a deep, dark hole and never come out. The kitchen is completely silent and sweat rolls off my face. Bee looks at me without a word.

At that instant, we are joined by Sera. She has been helpful ever since I came home from the hospital, but a little distant when she is with me.

"Hello, ladies, how is your morning? Looks like we are going to have a lovely day," Sera says, as she pours herself a cup of coffee.

"Your garden is growing wonderfully, Peg," she says, as she walks over to the back door and looks through the screen door. "Is that the piano I hear?"

"Yes, Sammy came over and wanted to spend some time with me since she has not been over in a few days."

Sera walks over to the other side of the room to listen and admire Sammy's talent while sipping her coffee.

"I didn't realize that young lady had such a talent."

"Would you like some breakfast, ma'am?" Bee asks, sipping her tea and avoiding looking at me.

"No thank you, Bee, but can I have a moment with Peg?"

"Yes, ma'am." The look on Bee's face tells me she would like to continue cooking at the stove, pretending not to listen. But she complies with Sera's wishes and goes to do some dusting.

Suddenly, the kitchen goes deathly still. The only sound comes from Sammy's deft fingers gliding up and down the keyboard in the next room. Although Sera plays very little, and not nearly as well as Sammy, the perfectly tuned baby grand piano is my cousin's pride and joy. I am wondering what Sera wants with me. She pours herself another cup of coffee and sits across from me with her elbows resting on the table. She raises the cup to her mouth and sips her coffee. She is too quiet, which makes me uneasy.

"Peg, you know we have been close our entire lives. We are practically sisters. When we were young we used to tell each other our deepest secrets. These past few days, I know you have been recovering from your surgery which, by the way, I am still not understanding. Why would you go through with such a dangerous operation when it is apparent that this family next door does not give a damn about you, whatsoever?"

"Sera, I..."

"No, Peg. Just listen to me, please!"

Now I know without a doubt that something is terribly wrong and I am sure I am getting ready to know what it is. Sera gets up from the table, looking regal in a grey dress with a skinny belt around her waist. She takes a big breath with her back towards me as she stands at the kitchen stove.

"How long you been pregnant, Peg?"

My eyes look across the room at her while I try to search for words to explain everything that I have had to endure. If I tell her the truth she will not understand.

Before I come out of the fog I am in and realize she is standing next to me, she slams her coffee cup on the table and pieces of china shatter everywhere. Suddenly, the music stops.

"Is everything okay?" Sammy asks, after a few tense minutes.

"Hello, Sammy. Would you mind visiting Peg tomorrow?"

"Yes, ma'am. I will see you tomorrow, Miss Peg."

"Okay, child," I say softly.

Sera watches until Sammy reaches the street and then continues her questions.

"How could you do something so stupid and get yourself in this situation when you're not even married, Peg?"

"Sera, it is quite complicated."

"Complicated?" Sera says, as she leans over, her face stopping just inches away from my face. "The only word you can come up with is *complicated*?" This time her volume is just above a whisper to keep Bee and the rest of the workers outside from hearing our conversation.

"Peg, this is careless and in a million years I would never have thought you, out of all people, would get yourself into something so irresponsible!"

She looks in the other room, making sure Bee cannot hear anything. I am sure if the housekeeper and cook found out, Sera would feel embarrassed. She would be even more embarrassed to know that Bee *already* knows. I find it hard to believe someone I have known my entire life would not come to me in a more compassionate way and ask me what she can do to help. If Sera knew the real reason I'm in this predicament, she would be the first to confront 'He" and everyone in this house would be dead by morning. "He" would kill us all if he thought anyone might find out that the Negro woman he has been raping is pregnant with his child.

"Do you have anything to say for yourself, Peg? I am so ashamed of you," Sera says, walking out of the room terribly upset, but still unaware of the facts. Now I am truly feeling alone with this big old world on my shoulders. Looking out the screen on the back door, I stop to admire the wonderful flowers that have brought forth new buds and begun to blossom. The ashes are doing their job, I think, keeping away the insects that would have normally devoured them.

Chapter 45

Days have come and gone and still no sign of Peg next door. I guess she stayed a few days up North, needing a short vacation. It doesn't take long for me to get home from a new construction job. I decided to take an early lunch and make it home within minutes. I park my truck on the street since I only have an hour for lunch. I also want to see if Peg made it back from Ohio. I walk through the front door heading to the kitchen for a bite to eat and a cold cola only to hear my mother and the home nurse outraged about a situation involving someone the nurse refers to as "a nigger next door."

"Where is Ronnie?" I ask, as they continue with a conversation that I want no part of.

"We should hang her," the nurse says, while placing sterile pads on a tray, preparing Ronnie's bandages to cover his surgery scars.

I ponder their words as I get a sandwich. Was I really like that, and how could I have been so blind? What I am feeling now is gratitude to the Big Man upstairs for giving my young brother a chance to have a life. I would have thought when my mother came home she would only be thinking of Ronnie, but she has quickly gone back to her hateful ways and forgotten the hopelessness we all felt before Ronnie's surgery.

I honestly think if she could get away from her hateful friends and people from this community she would be a wonderful person who would see people for who they really are. It would be wrong for me to think that every white person feels the same way about the Klan and what it stands for.

Before I walk out of the back door, I open the screen slowly, just enough to look outside. I can't help but notice the beautiful lady next door who I once began to like so very dearly. This wonderful lady named Peg is in the company of a small child and they are laughing and smiling, admiring a variety of colorful wildflowers in her garden. In all the years I have lived in Birmingham, I have never seen flowers so vibrant and healthy. I can see her demeanor is calm and relaxed as she waters her garden. I believe God knew this day, at this precise moment, that her face would be graced with a smile and it would bloom like a beautiful flower for whoever was lucky enough to gaze upon its beauty.

I am so pleased to know she made it back home and I want to take her once again to that secret place where we first kissed. I wipe the tear that falls from my cheek without my mom and nurse noticing and realize I am falling in love with Peg.

Chapter 46

I t is late and Bee assured me earlier that she would get her son to pick me up at midnight. Heading down to wait for Bee, I am stopped at the bottom of the stairs by Sera who looks at me with the most unpleasant glare.

"So where are you off to, Peg? I am sure to a place no respectable woman would go at this time of night."

"Bee and I are going to a place tonight that troubled women go to when they feel like relieving stress," I tell her.

"Oh, I see. You're going to church?" she replies. Sera's voice drips with sarcasm and contempt.

"No, Sera, we are not going to church." I am relieved when I finally hear Bee and her son pull up in the driveway.

"I will see you at breakfast, Sera. Please don't wait up for me." I dare not look around, for I know if I do I am bound to be bombarded with more questions from my cousin. So I continue out the front door, closing it behind me. When I get in the old, beat-up car that looks like it is on its last leg, I look back at the house and see Sera glaring out of the window as we pull off. I also notice Mr. Stevens looking out of his window next door and Mrs. Stevens joining him, peering out to see what or who has caught his attention.

"Miss Peg, this is my son, June Bug," Bee says from the front passenger seat.

"Howdy, Miss Peg. Mama talk about you and the Doctor and Missus all the time. Feel I already know you," June Bug says, smiling at me in the rear view mirror. I manage half a smile and a soft, "Hello."

I wonder if Bee's son knows where he is taking us and why. He and Bee talk about people and events going on in the community and I utter not one word as I sit in the back seat. I silently watch the beautiful Victorian, Tudor, and Colonial homes passing by my window and admire the dramatic entryways and sculpted lawns, softly lit by porch lights. I hope one day when I finish my studies to own a beautiful home with a wonderful and loving husband, but I know it will not be on this street. How can I ever tell my husband about this thing I am about to do? How can I make him understand that I could not bear my rapist's child?

Soon, we are in an area of Birmingham I dare not visit alone, night or day.

"This where you delivering the baby, Mama?" June Bug asks.

"Sure is. Miss Peg volunteer to help me since your Aunt Sue be busy taking care of her own new grandbaby tonight."

"Miss Peg, Mama delivered all my children. I got five girls and five boys, two sets of twins and a set of triplets! Runs in our family! Wait 'til you meet Mama's twin sister, Honey! She and Mama not identical. Mama go to church and live right. Aunt Honey do just the opposite. Men round here call her Sweet Honey. She ain't raised none of my cousins. My Mama and her other sisters and brothers raise all sixteen of her children."

"June Bug, hush, now! That baby be two years old by the time we get in there if you keep talking. Come on, Miss Peg," Bee says, getting out of the car." And you be back here in two hours. Don't you go home and go to sleep, now! I'll give you some gas money when you get back."

"I will pay him, Bee," I say, starting to open my purse as I open the door. Bee looks at me and shakes her head, so I close my purse and get out, closing the car door as June Bug smiles and waves, then drives off leaving us alone on the dark street.

"My son a good man. Good to his wife and his kids. He work hard and he drink hard. If you had give him gas money, he go straight to a juke joint and start drinking hooch and forget all about picking us up in two hours. This ain't the place we going. I just told June Bug that, so he won't suspect nothing," Bee says and starts walking away. I watch her, but I cannot move. Bee realizes I am not moving and looks around.

"Are you sure this is the right place, Bee?"

"Yes, child! Now, keep quiet and follow me."

We make our way down a dark alley where we occasionally bump into drug dealers and men sleeping next to garbage cans.

"This cannot be the right address, Bee."

"Will you please keep your mouth shut, Miss Peg? This is the only place that will help a lady like you. Matter of fact, this is the only place that will help any woman no matter what color you are. This is a place where the color of your skin don't matter as long as you have cash. You did bring the cash I told you to bring, Miss Peg?"

"Yes, I brought the cash, Bee."

"What is this place, Bee?" I ask, walking quickly to keep up with her as we soon reach our destination.

"You ask for help getting rid of that baby you carrying, Miss Peg, and this is the only place I know where you can get that done. Now, come on," she says, walking up the steps of a dilapidated structure. Bee is standing by a door with peeling paint and steps aside when I walk on the porch, nodding her head for me to go on in. I grab the doorknob and Bee touches my shoulder gently and I feel her strength pouring out to hold me up as I cross that threshold, pause, and walk in looking straight ahead.

***

Bee was giving me a piece of her mind just a few hours ago. She was sitting on the front porch snapping beans for dinner and she told me: "Miss Peg, I'm a woman who has seen a lot here in Birmingham and I have witnessed so many things firsthand that generations who are coming behind us will never comprehend them even if they read about them in history books. And they never will 'cause the only thing the history say 'bout us is we was brought here from Africa to be slaves."

"What you ask me to do for you today is illegal and I dare not be a part of it. I reckon if you do anything in life you should own up to it and live life the best you can. I sho believe a woman should have the right to choose what to do with her body, no matter what I think personally. So if you feel that this is what you wants, I won't judge you. You must do what Peg want so when your journey is close to its end you can face God for yourself and answer only to Him. My mother once told me before she left this world that the good Lord has in His word that we will reap what we sow here on earth. Because if you go to heaven and you do wrong here on earth you can't reap it there." I listened in silence to Bee's sermonizing, knowing her words were true and that enduring their sting was only the beginning of what I will reap for my sins.

"My grandmother had one sister who died young. She told me once that she gave birth to fifteen children at a very young age and when her husband and she jumped the broom the minister said not until death do them part, but until distance do them part. Slaves got married that way 'cause they couldn't marry legally, not knowing if one or the other would be sold. Some of her children, she knew, were not her husband's. They were the master's who lived in the big house. Her children were immediately sold after birth and because she didn't know which child was her husband's and which ones were the master's, they both cried and pleaded with the master not to take their children. It was apparent that some of the children were fathered by a white man and the master was afraid that word would get out that he had done it."

"One evening when he was away, his house caught on fire and all his family died. He was left without any family and found his self all alone. He then realized that he had sold all his living children into slavery. He tried to locate them, but never found a single one, and so he shared the grief of all the slaves whose kin he had sold away. He didn't give his mixed children a chance to know him and possibly do good in the world. So here am I, a black woman who treat everyone like I want to be treated. So here am I, a black woman who has been spit upon and slapped by white folks for no reason except that I'm a Negro. I'm a woman who has love in her heart that knows no matter what happen I will not be judged on how others treat me, but how I treat them. My faith is really tested when people treat me bad, but I prove my faith by how I treat them back, Miss Peg. That is why I say and I believe in my heart that all the wrong blacks do to whites or whites do to blacks we all have to reap it, if it is not right in His eyes," Bee said, looking upward, then back at me.

"Miss Peg, I dare not look at you any different, knowing I'm not perfect."

Tears made their way down her cheeks and she quickly wiped her face, changing her mood in an instant to the jovial, no nonsense Bee that I only knew until today.

Chapter 47

I finally get to have a day off tomorrow, so I decide to watch late movies with my family tonight. I'm delighted to be holding my little girl again, feeding her a late bottle. Our family is finally together, celebrating with Ronnie who is now back home with his new kidney. Having Mom back from New York is great, because Dad and I can't really take care of Ronnie properly. I still think it was odd that the doctors were able to find a donor at the last minute when we knew for a fact that Ronnie was so far down on the list for a donor. But we weren't going to look this gift horse in the mouth. My mother rejoiced when we told her Ronnie had a donor. She was pretty sad when not one member of her family in New York City was willing to risk the surgery to save her child's life. It seems like everything is working out well for our family. I pray that someday my parents will also have a change of heart about their association with the Klan. I dare not tell them how I really feel, knowing that this would be the death of me. I now have my own child to think about.

We are playing Monopoly together on the living room floor, listening to Chubby Checker singing on the radio. I pretend to dance with Emily Rose and it makes her smile. Ronnie suddenly yells, pointing at all the property he's acquired during the game and starts singing "Twist and Shout," as he collects rent from all of us. I must say, I think he will be the best real estate developer in U.S. history if he keeps this up. My mom holds out her arms for Emily Rose as she finishes her bottle. She wants to burp her little angel "properly," exchanging a look with the nurse who's joined us as Ronnie continues singing along with the radio. When the song ends, my mother changes to a station that plays all Western music since she and my father have a strong dislike of "race music," which has become increasingly popular with whites and is played on almost every station.

The Stevens family is truly blessed, and we have vowed to buy gifts this Christmas for poor white children who wouldn't otherwise have a good holiday. Although Patrick and I are no longer friends, he's always doing good works each Christmas, helping the poor by donating dozens of shoes—to white children only. Many years ago, he gave shoes to a family, but afterward he found out that they were Jews. The child had the shoes on and was walking away from the community center when Patrick found the family and took the shoes back. I couldn't believe he did it. That poor child had been smiling and his parents were so grateful. Patrick wiped the smile off that boy's face and had him and his parents in tears. If he really knew the meaning of Christmas, he would know it doesn't matter what color the child is. I don't think the Man Upstairs designed the birth of His Son for us to pick and choose who we share His love with, based on the color of their skin. Somehow, I will get my family to realize this without causing a big commotion about it.

"Okay, Ronnie, it's one in the morning and we have to get you off to bed," the nurse says, checking his temperature. Ronnie makes a face as he bites down on the thermometer in his mouth.

"We want to make sure you don't catch any fever due to the niggers coming so close to you this morning." My dad comes through the entry and hears her statement.

"What is she talking about, Hun?" Dad asks, setting his briefcase next to his favorite chair.

"Nothing to alarm yourself with, Ken," my mother says, getting up and giving him a quick kiss before heading to the kitchen to get his supper. "We just had an incident with the new neighbor's maid next door. I told her never to come close to Ronnie ever again, even though she said she only wanted to say hello to him. I give thanks to Ronnie's nurse for noticing her sneaking around, probably trying to steal something. Those people are natural born thieves. I see her watching our house trying to see if we're home. I wouldn't put it past that picaninny to sneak over here while we're at church to steal our silver!"

My father looks down at Ronnie and for a brief moment he is silent. This never happens when it comes to berating Negroes.

"I don't know why this city ever let niggers move into this community. Mr. and Mrs. Stevens, we have to do everything in our power to never have our kind mix with them. We have to keep our race pure. If not, we'll all be walking around here acting like monkeys and looking like baboons."

There is an unusual stillness in the entire house as we silently look at the nurse. "Could my parents be thinking for once this is wrong?" I think, hoping against hope. Only time will tell. The nurse departs as soon as she completes Ronnie's checkup, probably feeling uncomfortable when she didn't get the response she expected with her racial slur. I'm so glad she's gone! We continue to laugh and enjoy ourselves the rest of the evening.

Emily Rose is wide awake, refusing to go to sleep as she looks from one person to another, watching our every move. I start singing a lullaby to her and she watches everyone making faces and covering their ears in reaction to my off-key melody. A big smile spreads across her face, and then she waves her hands in glee and starts laughing when Ronnie sticks out his tongue and crosses his eyes. My baby girl is such a beautiful, innocent child and she could care less what color her neighbors are.

Chapter 48

We walk through the door into a smoke-filled room. There is a lady standing there with a cigarette hanging from her lip. We wait while she quickly counts the cash like a bank teller and asks us to follow her to a room I have dreaded seeing since I made the decision to do this.

"Take off your clothes and put this robe on," the woman with the cigarette says. Bee and I walk in and she leaves, closing the door behind us. Terrified and trembling so much I can barely stand on my own two feet, I sit down in a small wooden chair. It looks just like the chair in the cabin where "He," who is responsible for me being here in this horrid place, raped me the first time.

Why did I come to this god-forsaken place called Birmingham? Why did I agree to go out and meet this man? Why is it that the law doesn't protect Negroes the same way it protects whites? Weren't the laws designed to keep *all* Americans safe? If Negroes break the law, we should be judged accordingly. But if we need the law to gain justice it seems like the scale weighs less on our side. How can I expect to get any justice in this city when the man who is raping me is also the district attorney?

A nurse in a dingy uniform stained and splattered with blood comes in and helps me up on the table, instructing me to place my legs in the stainless steel stirrups as she straps them in place.

"Is this your first time, girl?

I nod slowly and dare not let a sound escape my mouth. I keep my lips tightly closed. In rooms adjacent to mine, I can hear women screaming words straight from hell and I am afraid the same screams will soon be coming from me. Terror rises in my throat as I anticipate what is about to happen and the pain that will accompany this act that I know must be done. I cannot give birth to the baby of a rapist! Yet, I find myself praying Bee will take me by the hand and say, "Child, we must leave this place!" But she remains quiet. Can I do this? The fear turns to dread that turns to terror, suddenly turning my stomach, making it churn and bubble. I feel a cool draft fill the air as a tall man dressed in a white lab coat splattered with blood opens the door and walks tiredly into the room.

"How are you tonight, girl?" he says, his Southern drawl as thick as syrup. "Are you sure this is what you want?"

"I am fine, thank you," I say, as I manage to form the words to respond to him, "and yes, I am sure this is what I want. "

He asks me several questions: about my last period, if I have had morning sickness, if I have been pregnant previously, and so on, while he snaps on gloves and puts a dirty mask over his face that looks anything but sterile. I am sure he works either at the local hospital or some nearby city medical facility. I have heard of doctors working on the side performing this procedure, making money illegally. I never thought I would be the one sitting in a place like this. He touches me in my private area and immediately I feel the way I did when "He" violated me the first time and every time after. His hands are cold and rough as he examines my vagina with probing fingers.

"Girl, you're going to have to relax while I exam you," he says sternly.

"Yes, sir," I say quietly. He positions the clamp and slowly twists a knob attached to it that opens me up. Even though I know this is for the best, I am nervous and confused. My mind runs a million miles away to a place my father once took me when I was a child and he told me a story.

"There was this woman who heard God's voice in her spirit tell her that she would be a playwright," Daddy said, while holding me on one knee with his hand around my waist to prevent me from falling. "She was told that the journey would be hard, but not to give up. She began with unknown actors, paying them all she could; sometimes not paying them when she did not have any money. But she continued to explain if they would only hold on, they would get a great reward. It seemed as though everyone wanted to be in her company's productions. They told her they would stick by her side and follow her dream to the end."

"She was told by others that she was foolish and that this venture was doomed to fail, because there was not a market for stage plays at that time, but she continued with her dream. Trying over and over, it seemed she couldn't get the results she dreamed of. She always thought that the next performance would be the big break she had been looking for, but she was devastated when once again things didn't go as she had anticipated. She began working odd jobs to pay everyone she owed, always smiling, even though inside she was crushed with disappointment, but still holding on to what she was told by God."

"Then one day when she was all alone and feeling like she didn't have a friend in the world, the voice again said, 'Never give up.' That became the name of a play she started writing that day. Sometime later, while riding a plane back to New York after a short trip back home, she was reading the play she'd conceived the day she had heard God's voice. She was thinking about how to stage a production of it with no money and wondering, 'Did I hear your voice right, Lord?' But there was no answer."

She then started a conversation with a woman who was sitting next to her in first class, where she was sitting thanks to one of her actor friends who worked as a flight attendant. She was a well-dressed woman, wearing expensive jewelry and a mink coat, but she was utterly distraught and in tears. She'd been told by her doctor that she only had a week to live due to rapidly metastasizing breast cancer.

She said, 'If I only had a year, I would give to the poor and help others, but I only have a week to spend with my family.' She then said she was on her way back from a hospital that offered her no hope. She was on her way home for one last try with a new radical treatment developed by a physician in New York. After hearing that story, the playwright took the lady's hand and prayed with her, despite the woman's insistence that she couldn't believe in a god that would take her away from her family. After her brief encounter with someone whose life was ending, she realized that as long as she was alive there was hope. Back in her New York apartment, unaware that she'd left the only copy of her script on the plane, she cried all night as she thought of the beautiful lady with only a week to live, asking God for His mercy and grace.

The following year she got a call from the lady on the plane. The lady explained that she found the playwright's script, "Never Give Up," on the plane. She took it to her home in the Hamptons and read it, missing her appointment with the doctor she was supposed to see because she was so engrossed in the play. She explained how it inspired her to live and not die and declare to the works of the Lord, accepting Jesus Christ as her Savior. The playwright was thrilled to hear that this woman she'd prayed for was alive and that she'd found Christ.

However, she was totally unprepared for what she was told next. It turns out the woman she'd met on the plane, that was given less than a week to live a year earlier, was the biggest Broadway producer in New York. She not only got her play produced on Broadway, but the playwright who never gave up went on to write more hit plays than anyone in Broadway history. So what I am telling you Peg is that life is full of things we can't control. Sometimes, you want to lie down and give up. Sometimes, the results are not what you want them to be. But if you hold on and don't question God, He will stay faithful to what He said. Never give up on God, because He never gives up on you.

At that moment, I find myself back on the table, spread-eagle, being poked and prodded with cold, rough hands in this dark place. I look up at Bee's face, full of tender concern as she holds my hand. The doctor announces that the baby I am carrying was conceived less than a month ago. I watch Bee's face as she realizes that I must have gotten pregnant after my arrival in Birmingham. That is one thing I did not want her to know. I am sure once we are back home, she will ask me about the father of my unborn child, knowing she has not seen me in the company of any man here in Birmingham.

"Now, this is going to hurt, girl, so I want you to bear down and grab the poles on either side of the bed. You ready, nigger?"

"Yes, I'm ready, sir."

A short while later, Bee and I sit quietly in June Bug's car, heading home while he talks about the goings on in the neighborhood and the gossip over at the pool hall. When we arrive at the Whitfield house, now the Carson house, Bee starts getting out of the car, insisting that she stay the night.

"I don't think that is necessary, Bee."

"I insist, child," she says, closing the back door of the car.

"I will be fine, Bee. But thank you. Good night."

I am relieved that all the house lights are off and that my cousin and her husband have already retired for the night. I watch Bee and June Bug drive away and I wave to her until I see the car turn the corner. I am sure Sera is still upset with me, but if she only knew what I have been going through she would still think of me as the woman she's always known. Suddenly, my thoughts are disturbed by a voice whispering nearby.

"Peg, I know you're upset with me, but please give me a chance to explain myself tomorrow. Please meet me downtown by the movie theatre in the morning at nine. Okay?"

"Okay, I will Seth," I say, too drained to argue and too tired to care.

I watch as Seth darts across his lawn and slips through his front door. Am I in my right mind to meet this man tomorrow, now that I know he was the one who came to this house my very first night here in Birmingham?

"But now, I do not think he is that same man," I say to myself as I go into the kitchen and grab the trash to take outside. When I get to the last step on the back porch, I am quickly grabbed by the man I have been trying to avoid for days.

"Where have you been hiding, Peg?" "He" says, just above a faint whisper in my ear. I try to turn and walk back up the steps to the back door, but he refuses to let me go. I sigh and resign myself to what is about to happen as "He" walks me towards the back of the house. It is where the servants once stayed, but has since been converted to a garage that's rarely used except to store trash. This time "He" does not have to ask me to take off my clothes. I know the routine so very well and know that the less I resist, the gentler "He" will be. I do not say a word and all "He" does to me is just a blur. The pain from his intrusion inside me just adds to the humiliation I suffered earlier at the hands of an abortion doctor. I can't believe I've just been to a man who illegally performs abortions in a back alley in unsterile conditions and now I must suffer the indignity of rape. I really expect to get some horrible infection that will either make me infertile or kill me, if God is merciful. Now, if I can only forget about this evening and get some sleep, that would be wonderful.

Chapter 49

It's Sunday morning and I refuse to go church this week knowing what will follow at the picnic. I can only imagine which poor Negro man, woman, or child the Klan has picked up this week. I'm sure they will be lynched at the event; an act I now recognize as outright murder. My mother knocks at my bedroom door, asking softly what I would like for breakfast, while I hold my daughter in one arm with a bottle in her mouth.

"Nothing, Mama," I reply, prompting her to open the door and ask if I am feeling well this morning while touching my forehead for signs of a fever.

"I'm not feeling well this morning, so I think I'll stay home this Sunday."

"Okay. Ronnie is in his bed and the nurse is already here. Let me get Emily Rose ready for church and I will check on you after we come home from the picnic. Make sure Ronnie eats all of his lunch. I left it in the icebox. He has been running a small fever so see that the nurse takes his temperature each hour."

My mother takes Emily Rose and the clothes I laid out for her to wear today and leaves my room to get them both dressed. I think about my young baby being at the picnic, but I know she is too young to really understand what is going on and I am thankful for that. I really didn't listen to my mother's instructions regarding Ronnie, knowing that the nurse is still here to take care of him. The only thing on my mind is wanting to see Peg. I can't wait to see her this morning and make this a day she will never forget. I plan to take her on a date that will make her trust me even more and remove all doubt about what she has been feeling since she moved to Birmingham. I am planning a drive to a town nearby for a quiet, intimate lunch in a small café where we can relax, clear away from Birmingham.

A short time later, I look out my bedroom window and see my father slowly back out of our driveway and head to the cathedral. It seems every white person on this street attends that church, despite the fact that most people in the South are Protestant and don't trust Catholics, especially the one in the White House. My own father calls him a "papist," a religious slur against Catholics. He says the president is the wrong kind of Catholic, nothing like the good Catholic people in Birmingham. Were he from the South and intent on legislating segregation at a national level, my father would gladly embrace him as a fellow Catholic. It's not long before I head down the stairs, only to bump into that vile, hateful home-visit nurse.

"Oh, I'm sorry I startled you," I say to the nurse, who jumps when I walk into the hallway where she is standing, closing the door to Ronnie's room. "How is my brother doing today?" I ask.

"He's been running a fever so I am keeping my eyes on him."

"We're grateful he has such a good nurse," I say, lying through my teeth as I smile at her. "Look, I need to get some work done today. I need to look over some construction plans. "Do you think you will need me to help you with anything before I leave?"

"No, young man," she says. "I will be just fine with him. But your mother says you're not feeling well yourself. Don't you want me to take your temperature?"

"Can you keep a secret?" I say, smiling broadly at the woman who probably hasn't had any male older than Ronnie smile at her in a long time. "I'm fine, but my parents don't believe in working on the Sabbath, so I told a little white lie."

"Better than a black one!" she says, laughing like a hyena at her intentional racial barb.

I continue down the stairs and head to the kitchen, where I glance out of the window and notice my family is not the only family headed to church. I'm shocked to see a beautiful older Negro woman accompanied by Dr. Carson next door. He opens the car door for her and they drive off. I am hoping to get a glance at Peg, but she is nowhere in sight. I'm hoping she'll show up at the spot I asked her to meet me at today for our day out.

"What are you looking at, young man?" the nurse asks as she takes the orange juice bottle from the ice box.

"Oh, nothing," I reply. "I'm just admiring the beautiful flowers in the garden next door. I think that garden is the best in Birmingham." I can hear our hardwood floor creak as she walks closer to me and looks over my shoulder.

"Yes, I agree. I don't know what that nigger is doing over there to get those flowers to grow so fast. Maybe I need to get her to come work my garden." My skin crawled when she said the "n" word.

"That nigger is up to no good, I tell ya! She walks around her yard like she's better than us whites. I am thinking my husband the sheriff will have to take her for a ride. I am making my recommendation that she be our next entertainment at the picnic next Sunday. What do you think about that young man?"

"Ma'am, I'm sure you have a long list of Negroes you want dead and I'm sure she's not at the top of the list."

"You know you're right! Kill 'em all, I say!" She lets out another huge laugh. "Now, let me take your brother his juice."

Chapter 50

I have been sitting in my truck for what seems like over an hour, listening to some of my favorite tunes on my broken down radio and am just about to give up on Peg, who was supposed to be here already, when I'm pleasantly surprised to hear a familiar voice.

"Hello, Seth. How are you today?"

Looking at her beautiful skin and luscious lips, she seems especially lovely on this nice, sunny, and warm day. It's a beautiful Sunday without a cloud in the sky and it seems that the sun is shining brighter, now that Peg is here. "I'm wonderful now that you are here Peg. Let me get the door for you," I say with the biggest smile on my face, while my mind is searching for the next words to say, trying not to let her know that I'm nervous. I notice her lovely sundress that moves in the slight breeze, swirling around her amazing body, the matching sunhat, and a pair of white gloves that she holds in one hand, along with a small purse.

"What perfume is that you're wearing?"

"Oh, I forgot. I bought it at Richards Market in downtown Birmingham. Do you like it?"

"Yes, I do."

"Thank you," she says, while looking into my eyes as I shut the door. While returning to the driver's seat, I look around to make sure that we are not noticed by anyone and see Negroes looking at me and then Peg with curious looks on their faces, then continuing with what they're doing without saying a single word.

"So, where are you taking me, Seth?" Peg asks with a seemingly distant attitude.

"I want to take you to a place today that will make you forget about Birmingham. Is that alright?"

"Sure," she says, still not her usual warm self.

We drive for forty minutes taking back roads, so I am sure we will not have any problems with the locals from Birmingham. We stop at a gas station where Peg wanted to use the wash room before reaching my surprise location. I think it might be a good idea to get some gas and so I stop my truck on a dirt road just before reaching the gas pump. Everyone near the station notices the cloud of dirt that makes its way past the truck from the tires making an abrupt stop. I put my truck in neutral and turn off the engine.

"Can I tell you something, Seth?" Peg says, looking out the window. We are surrounded by tall, majestic trees and open cotton fields that look like something you would see on a canvas at the local art museum in Birmingham.

"I want to thank you for not looking at me the same way you looked at me the day our eyes first met when I moved to Birmingham."

"Peg..." I start to speak, not sure what to say.

"Hold on, Seth. I know now you came to the house that night with your friends to harm me."

I watch her eyes fill with tears of hurt and resist the urge to wipe away one that falls on her cheek.

"All I want to say is that I know you must care for me now, because no white man would ever treat me the way you have, now that you have finally gotten to know me. Sometimes in life we look at what a person has or how a person looks, but when we finally know someone for who they are, we find out what is important. The heart of a person tells the story of how a person really is, no matter what color they are. I appreciate you for getting to know me," she says, gently touching my cheek.

"Can I get you some gas, son?" the attendant asks, bending down to look through the open window.

"Yes, sir. I will have three dollars of regular, please."

"Sure, son."

Oddly, he doesn't say a word about a Negro woman leaving the passenger seat of my truck. Peg slowly disappears around the building where I'm sure there is an outhouse for Negroes only.

"Where you headed?" the elderly man asks. He is dressed in dirty, oily overalls and a baseball cap. I can tell that he never washes them. I bet it's taken him years to accumulate this much filth on his clothes.

"Oh, we're headed just up the road. I'm taking her to her family," I reply.

"It's not often round here you see a nigger sitting so cozy next to a white man 'less he dating her."

I can tell this man is trying his best to figure out what is going on here. I don't think he believes me as he look more closely into my truck for any signs we might be lovers.

"You find what you looking for, sir?" I ask pointedly.

"Not yet, but when I do I sure will let you know. I see your plates say you're from the Birmingham area. Are you a nigger lover, son? I see the way you look at that nigger. That's the way I been looking at my wife for forty-five years. That's love in your eyes, son, and the only thing about yours is that the Klan here will kill you dead if they find out. Now, personally, I don't give a damn who you love. Just don't flaunt it in my face." Before I can get a word out we are joined by Peg, smiling from ear to ear, happy to be out of the sun and back in the truck.

"Here, let me get your money, sir," I say as I reach in my back jeans pocket and pull out my wallet. I grab three crisp one dollar bills and hand them over to the old man, who has taken out a bandana and is loudly blowing his nose. I slide him an extra dollar just to keep him from calling around town and starting trouble.

"Thank you, son. That's mighty white of you," he says with a knowing grin on his face.

I start the engine and quickly drive away, looking through my rear view mirror as my truck leaves a cloud of dust. I take one last look at the elderly man who stands there watching us until we are out of sight.

Chapter 51

I am glad that Seth took time out of his busy schedule to spend the day with me. I think I have now resolved the disappointment and anger I felt towards him regarding his previous feelings about me and all Negroes. He is a product of his environment and his heritage, but now, God only knows how, he has finally seen and accepted the truth and is no longer filled with the hate that made him want to harm that which he has been taught from birth to hate. I wonder how many Negroes he has seen beaten and killed and if he has been a part of such vile actions. But I cannot dwell on those thoughts now.

"He who is without sin, cast the first stone," Jesus once told those that judged another. I cannot stand on my high horse. Sure, I saved Ronnie's life, but when it came to my own child, my first thought was that I could not let it live because of how it was conceived. I am in no position to judge anyone, least of all this man who has shown me nothing but kindness and love now that he gotten to know me. Thankful that he is with me today, I pray that I can find it in my heart to forgive myself as I have forgiven him.

He will never know how much it means to me that he is with me today, especially after last night. I know his family always goes to church on Sundays and Ronnie is still convalescing from his surgery. So it must have been difficult for him to get away, knowing that the family must remain available and vigilant in case there are any complications. If Seth only knew what I went through last night in that dark alley. I can only imagine the hundreds of women, if not thousands, who have walked down that cold, dark alley and had to endure the same degradation and humiliation I went through last night. I am sure they had the same mixed feelings I had and I can only wonder what each woman's thoughts were as they climbed on that stainless steel table.

Bee told me on the way home that a young white woman died from an illegal abortion last week. Bee also mentioned that another lady in a nearby county died from an infection. She was too afraid to tell her parents she had an abortion. I imagine all the women who were rejected by the men who fathered their children, men who thought that it was alright to act out the sexual fantasies from the darkest parts of their minds and then abandon the friend or lady who is left with the consequences of their pleasure. I only hope someday that things will change in our society that will prevent women from walking down a dark alley in the middle of the night and keep them from having to give up a child that should never have been conceived in the first place. I hope communities and churches will someday acknowledge that we all make mistakes during our journey and that we can live with our choices, but they must be *our* choices, not choices made for us by society, the church, or the government.

Sitting beside Seth, as he drives us away from the gas station, I know that soon he will have to face the choice he made to spend this day out in the open with a Negro woman. Why should society make it so difficult for a person to cross the color line? God has no color line or, he would not have made us so different from each other. Why *did* He make us different colors? Is it so that we should love each other as God loves us? I think that is the easy part, but the difficult part is how you think or feel no matter what others around you may say. The people close to you are the people that hurt you most when you find out they treat you differently, not knowing the truth.

I am feeling the summer breeze fall across my face from the open truck window. Looking at the beautiful landscape, though, I despair. Instead of rejoicing this Sunday, believing that God gave us such beauty in nature, I am saddened, knowing what my dear cousin Sera must think of me. A loose woman I will never be, but that is what she is thinking when she looks at me. Am I wrong for not telling her, or is she wrong for not accepting me for who I am, instead of what she thinks I am? Pushing these thoughts away, I decide to enjoy this glorious Sunday with Seth. I am excited, but cautious; unsure of his true feelings for me and wondering if he will deny me when we both have to face the truth. My mama always said a man who will not defend his woman is not a man worth having.

Chapter 52

We arrive at a jazz club that's serving brunch in a small town just two hours outside of Birmingham. It takes me a while to find a parking spot for my truck among the multitude of vehicles parked outside the popular spot. I am hoping we won't run into anyone from home. I heard that Negroes and whites are allowed to dine at the same tables here. I'm hoping that's true, but I am still a little wary.

We are greeted by a beautiful Negro hostess with a warm smile, nicely dressed in an elegant cream dress and black high heels.

"Would you like a table for two?" she asks.

"Yes, please," I say with a smile so broad I feel stupid and awkward. I'm almost giddy about the prospect of being able to sit with Peg in a public place.

We walk through the restaurant and I can't help but notice the stunning décor. The chairs are upholstered in red velvet and there are white linen table cloths and napkins on every table. I am amazed to see so many white and Negro couples talking together and enjoying the cuisine. Some of the couples are white, some black, but mostly mixed. A waiter pulls out a chair for Peg as the hostess shows us to a table.

"Will this table do for you?" she asks, waiting for us to be seated before giving us menus.

"Yes, this is wonderful!" I say, sounding like a yokel.

"Thank you," Peg replies tastefully, as always, gracious and the epitome of class.

We have a great table up front, not far from the stage where a piano sits along with other instruments. I can't wait to hear the live music. "Wow! There is a great crowd out this Sunday," I tell Peg. "I was told a jazz artist from your home state is performing here today. Nancy Wilson. Do you know her?" She laughs and shows all her straight, white teeth as she tilts her head backwards.

"Yes, I do! I used to go to a jazz club in Columbus to hear her sing sometimes. It was always packed when she was in town! How did you find out about this place, Seth?"

"Well, it wasn't easy. Let's just leave it at that," I say, recalling the strings I had to pull just to find out where this place is located. White people who come here would never admit it to another person and Negroes definitely don't want to tell a white person about it. I ended up having to pay a Negro jazz musician from Birmingham a lot of money to give me the location of the only place I could take Peg without risking both our lives. Her broad, satisfied smile is worth every penny I had to pay to get us here. I'm looking deep into her eyes, drowning in their beauty and totally unable to speak or move. I'm so lost in them. She looks back at me with such love I just want to take her in my arms and hold her forever.

"Thanks for bringing me here, Seth," she says, putting her small hand over mine.

"I'm glad you are here with me, Peg," I reply, finally able to speak, just as the waiter returns to take our order. We order the house special, Sunday brunch: fried potatoes and ham, homemade biscuits with churned butter and molasses, scrambled eggs, grits, Southern fried chicken, sweet potatoes, collard greens, sweet cornbread, and peach cobbler, with sparkling wine and buttermilk. We dine on the delicious food, licking our lips and our fingers, while listening to local jazz artists. "How is your meal, Peg?"

"Everything is wonderful. So much food! You could feed half of Columbus with this much food! Does everyone cook like this in the South or only a chosen few?"

"I must say that my mama can cook everything on this menu. She learned from her mammy, Mabel. Mama claims Mabel could out cook everybody in the South. Restaurants used to ask for her recipes. Mama swears the Colonel got those eleven spices from Mabel," I say laughing, recalling my mother's stories about the Negro woman that raised her while her parents traveled to Africa, trying to save "savages" from their sinful ways. "The lady I marry will have to know how to cook."

My pointed remark makes Peg blush and almost choke on the wine she is sipping.

"Having children is important, too," I continue, making Peg's previously red face turn almost white.

"Seth, what is your baby's name?" Peg asks, looking down.

"Her name is Emily Rose."

***

I can tell he loves her by the way he smiles when he mentions her name. Just as I was thinking I needed to get Bee to teach me some of the tricks to Southern cooking, (although she is not very forthcoming with recipes for anything but that god-awful crumb cake), Seth has to bring up having children, a very touchy subject with me right now.

***

"That was my grandmother's name on my father's side. She was a wonderful lady who helped women here in Birmingham. She worked hard when she was alive to ensure that all women were treated equal, no matter the color of their skin, their class, or their education level. I truly miss her and what she stood for. I never knew the true meaning of her causes and purpose until I really got the chance to know you. You two would have hit it off really well."

"She sounds like a wonderful woman and it sounds like you inherited many of her qualities. I really respect the way you take care of you daughter. I remember the morning I saw you on the porch, when I watched the mother of your child drop your baby off in your arms."

"Peg, I'm so ashamed for the way I treated you that morning. I was terribly wrong for speaking to you the way I did. Can you ever forgive me for all the wrong I did to you and all the Negroes in Birmingham? I'm a changed man, Peg."

"I know that now, Seth. I am also sorry for thinking all white people here are hateful. I honestly thought all the white people in this city were evil, except Dr. Carson, of course."

"Please don't condemn others in Birmingham for how they think about Negroes," Seth interjects. "Despite having a grandmother that loved all people, I once felt the same way they do until I met you."

"I just wonder, Seth. How can people treat people wrong just because of the color of their skin?"

"I was taught by my father, and he was taught by his, to despise other races. When I was a child, we all played at a park in Birmingham, and we used to watch the Negro children playing nearby. They would look at us, but would never play with us. We believed that they thought they were too good to play with us. But it was our parents who thought *we* were too good to play with them. It wasn't until I became a teenager that my friends and I came to understand that our parents had been teaching us what they had been taught."

"You see, Peg, when I was young I had no knowledge of how my community and other cities across America were treating Negroes. I was just an innocent child without a prejudiced bone in my body. It's when I became older and no longer wet behind my ears that I realized the place Negroes had in our society, and that's when I began to embrace the ways of my parents and their parents before them. I saw how my paternal grandmother was rejected by white society and became an embarrassment to my father and his father, and I didn't want that to happen to me. It was the way of the land, and everyone in the South came to believe that treating Negroes like inferiors was what was expected, even when slavery was over."

"Seth, let me tell you something about the Negroes you see every day here in Birmingham. There are families whose grandparents were separated from one another and sold because they were considered property. The largest commodity in the United States before the Civil War was slaves. The only thing that was valued higher in America was the land itself. The Negroes you see every day are the descendants of slaves that sweat, bled, and died. They were beaten, raped, and killed building this county.

My grandmother told me the story of her grandfather who was a slave in Mississippi; about how his hands would bleed every night from picking cotton all day in the hot summer sun, only to come back to a master who made him do things he would never even dream of doing. Her grandfather was raped by his master and there was not a thing he could do about it. He had to get up each day for his entire life and look at this man who did the unthinkable."

Did you know there were places where slave owners could go to sexually abuse slaves? They called them 'sex houses.' Any depraved thing a white man wanted to do, he could do. Some of the houses had women, some had girls, and some had boys. The same thing happened on the slave ships. Men, women, boys, and girls were sexually abused. Many couldn't take the abuse and being crammed together, lying in urine and excrement. They either died of diseases or jumped overboard when they were taken on deck for 'exercise' to make sure they did not lose the use of their limbs during the long journey. Those that survived were the strongest and the healthiest.

My grandparents believed that one day, here in this great land that we live in, they would get justice, even if they did not live to see it. Here we are today, two people who care about each other, but have to hide just to eat at the same table. Here we are in a country that has fought a war across the ocean because of how Hitler wanted to rule the world. He invaded all those countries in Europe, believing his race was superior to all others. Here in America, people of my race are still being murdered, raped, and treated like they are not equal to other human beings. Would it have been better if we had never been brought here from Africa? I say, no. We were brought here for some unknown reason and I believe that out of all this mess, we will get justice and a change will come, just as Dr. King has stated.

Now we will not stand for injustice, no matter the cost. We will die for what we believe. We will get justice, even if we do not live to see to it. The civil rights march here in Birmingham last May will change how people view Negroes, forevermore. The ignorant ways of the men and women who treat people badly just because of the color of their skin or religious beliefs is wrong, Seth. I think everyone deserves a chance in life. I also believe that we can all change for the better."

"You're right, Peg. I see clearly now the reasons why my grandmother risked being ostracized from Birmingham society to stand up for this cause. You know what I think, young lady? You should be a lawyer like my grandmother!"

"How about a judge, Seth?"

"Yes, I was gonna say, after you become a lawyer, you should become a judge," he says, laughing.

***

We continue enjoying the Southern cuisine and listening to Nancy Wilson. She recognizes me from the club in Columbus and introduces her "hometown girl" to the audience. She touches our hearts immensely with her wonderful performance, singing romantic songs in her lilting voice as couples sit embracing each other, including us. Seth gets emotional as Nancy sings Billie Holiday's song, "Strange Fruit." I wonder why this song touches his heart so deeply. Suddenly, I am stunned as Seth kisses me passionately. At that moment, I know I am to marry this man who I realize I am hopelessly in love with and one day I will have his children. Am I wrong for loving a white man?

Chapter 53

It's not long before we have to leave, and when we arrive back in Birmingham, I ask Seth to drop me off not far from the house. I tell him how I really enjoyed my Sunday date and how great it feels being with him. I never in a million years would have thought I would fall in love with a white man. The local Negro community would be outraged to know about us, given our history of abuse by white men. I think that is why Dr. Carson and Sera are right to withhold this information. I always knew the love my cousin Sera and Dr. Carson have is special, but I never had an attraction to a white man myself, until I got to know Seth.

Walking home, I see all the little white children playing outside. I am sure their parents are enjoying a quiet Sunday evening with a few precious moments alone. The young boys are gathered in the street playing stickball, while the little girls play hopscotch on the sidewalks. The picture would be perfect if children of other races and nationalities were also allowed to play with them, but I know that vision cannot exist in Birmingham, Alabama, in 1963. How great it would be to see polite, smiling white faces with hands waving, warmly welcoming anyone who walks down this street regardless of their skin color! I may not live to see it, but hopefully a change will come someday. I finally reach the porch and begin to proceed up the steps, where I am approached by Sera, coming from the backyard with a bunch of freshly picked flowers in her hand.

"Hello, stranger," she says. "I am shocked to see you in so early. I thought a lady of your stature would be out all night," she says in a tone I find offensive and demeaning.

"What is that supposed to mean, Sera?" I ask, bristling in anger.

"I just thought you would be out all night entertaining the man who got you pregnant. Or is it that you don't know who he is," she mumbles as she walks up the steps.

"You know, Sera, you of all people know who I am. Well, I thought you did," I say, thinking if my dear cousin only knew of all the pain I have been through since I moved here she would have a different attitude. "I thought family was supposed to be there for you and not judge you, no matter what you go through."

"Do you think maybe you should move back to Ohio? I know you love it there and since we have not met this man who got you pregnant, I am assuming he has no idea he is the father," Sera says dismissively. She makes her way across the porch, passing by me as if I am not even here. She is only inches away from the door when I push past her, knocking the flowers from her hand as she gasps in surprise, and run through the house to get to my garden.

I did think it might be better to move back home momentarily, and then I thought about Seth and how meeting him has changed my life. I couldn't do this to him. I sit on the back porch steps and gaze at the amazing array of flowers covering the entire back yard and growing up on the fence. I can see that some of the petals are starting to close in the night air. I am amazed how big and bright they have become. The ashes did their job and I make a note to use them each year. I am so glad I did not throw the bucket away. Now it will stay full of ashes just for one purpose to maintain this beautiful flower garden. The day has been dry and hot, so I think this is a better time than any to water them.

Watering the flowers relieves my stress. I am relaxed as each leaf welcomes a drop of life-giving water. Suddenly, I am reminded of my nephew, Robert Jr., and his quickly approaching arrival. I will make sure to call him tomorrow to get an update on his arrival time this coming weekend. I am so glad he did not arrive as originally planned several weeks ago, due to the ordeal I have had to go through. What a bright and intelligent man he has grown up to be. I can only imagine all the hate he must have to endure on a daily basis, just because he is the biracial child of a Negro woman and a white man. I am sure he would be the first to tell anyone concerned that what people say about him does not define him. What a smart young man he is! I am so thankful to have him as my nephew. I am thinking differently, however, about his mother, who has shocked me with her unforgiving insults. But life goes on.

"Well, young lady, where you been?" Bee asks, closing the back door with her apron in one hand and an oversized bag loaded with trash in the other. "I haven't seen you all day and don't tell me you came to church today because I looked all over for you. You nearly knocked Mrs. Carson down coming through the door, running through the house like a heathen." There is a glimmer of amusement in Bee's eyes as she says the last. "I was coming down the stairs with the laundry I'm gonna do tomorrow and thought there was a tornado coming through here."

"Believe it or not, Bee, I had a wonderful day, despite what I went through last night."

"That's wonderful, Miss Peg. I'm sure you made the right decision. Well, let me put the trash out and get home. I have a few of the ladies coming over for my famous pie for our next meeting. I can't wait!"

"Bee, are you sure they are coming?" This time, I am the one with the mischievous grin.

"Yes, they will," she says, feigning indignation, "because I'm the president of the after church sweet pie committee." I do not think Bee's pies will go over with the church ladies any better than the crumb cakes. "How about you show me how to cook Southern food and I will give you the recipe to my mother's famous apple pie?" I offer. "But it'll have to be Friday, because I have a lot of gardening to do this week to start getting ready for fall." I can tell Bee is pleased, as she hugs me tight and dances out to deposit the trash. I notice she is still wearing her snug, and apparently too tight, maid outfit, despite Sera asking her not to. The thought of Bee defying my high and mighty cousin lifts my spirits and I continue watering the plants, smiling.

"You got a deal, Miss Peg!" Bee says, walking away from the garage. "We'll start out with something easy, like fried okra! See ya in the morning, child!" she says excitedly, as she walks toward the side of the house that leads to the sidewalk for her journey home. I chuckle, knowing Bee will not be bothered by anyone, as I am sure she has her pistol somewhere near her.

Chapter 54

Monday mornings are always hard for me, but today I really dread going to work. I was able to dodge all the bullets of questions my parents had for me when I returned home last evening. I did have a wonderful time with Peg and I'm sure she enjoyed herself, as well. I keep thinking of her wonderful smile and how we understand each other and are learning what our perspectives on life here in America and the world are. My baby girl is getting a tad bit bigger as her appetite has grown from drinking a few ounces of milk at a time up to an entire bottle. She will make her daddy proud one day! I look at this innocent child and I know I can never fill her mind with what I was taught. I have to find a place for us to live soon, for this is the only way I can be sure my parents' beliefs will not be fostered in my impressionable young daughter.

It's almost lunch time now, and I'm getting worried. Normally, Patrick sits next to me while we eat and we talk about old times growing up in Birmingham. I'm sure the packet of photos I gave him has him feeling betrayed by his once close friend. I know that this will keep him quiet for only so long. What I have that he doesn't know about yet, will keep him quiet until he is old and gray and by that time, hopefully, the world will have changed. But what I have I don't think he'll live to see, if I decide to show it.

Before long, Patrick enters the trailer where we usually have lunch, dressed in his dirty jeans. He's wearing a hard hat and holding a coffee cup in one hand.

"Hello, Patrick!" I say in a friendly voice. For a moment he tries not to notice I'm here.

"Oh, if it isn't the nigger lover," he whispers, as he walks over close to where I'm sitting.

"You know, Patrick, I really don't want to get into this with you today."

"All I have to say to you, Seth, is one day Birmingham will know what kind of nigger lover you truly are. I'll find some way to make sure you and your bastard child are hated by every decent human being in Birming-ham!"

"Have a great day, Patrick!" I shout at him. I see the shock on his face when I get up and walk toward the door. I was hoping he would have thought of all the love we have had for each other and all the history we have as play brothers. I had hoped he might say those few simple words that every human being needs to hear when they have been done wrong: "I'm sorry." I was like him not long ago, and I will not give up on my friend, but I will not stoop down to his level, either. I'm a new man who has been changed by love for the better. But I sure wanted the old Seth to come out for five minutes, just so I could kick his ass! I think all Christian people think that way about some of the people they meet sometimes. Hellions! That's what they are called, and rightly so. That kind of hate can come from nowhere but the pit of hell.

Chapter 55

It is Friday, and I am still experiencing some slight bleeding from my recent doctor's visit. Thank God, Bee was kind enough to take me there last week. I am sure I could not have done it without her. I am sure I made the right decision, knowing I am the one who will have to live with that choice my entire life. The days seem shorter and some days the temperature gets a little chilly at night, but my flowers are still surviving. Picking up the phone on the kitchen wall after checking to make sure I am alone, I call my nephew. I am excited about seeing him this Saturday.

"Hello?"

"Hello, Robert Jr. How are you?"

"Aunt Peg! How are you? I'm doing okay. It's been hard this year. I'm glad my studies are coming to a close next year."

"Believe me, I know what you're going through. So when exactly are you arriving this weekend?"

"I'll be arriving some time tomorrow evening or Sunday morning, depending on which flight I take. How are my parents? You know this is so hard not telling them I'm coming to see them and the new house!

I miss Dad drilling me about my studies and Mom always asking who I'm seeing these days." He laughs, as though I don't already know he is a ladies' man.

"I am just calling to tell you to have a safe trip and I will wait for a call upon your arrival so I can pick you up, okay?"

"Yes, Aunt Peg. Love you and I can't wait to see all of you."

"Okay, Robert Jr. Love you, too." I hang up the phone and turn around and there is Bee smiling from ear to ear, because today is Friday and she is excited about getting her hands on my mother's famous apple pie recipe. I am sure of it!

"Hello, Miss Peg, how are you feeling today?"

"I'm fine, thank you." I see that Bee has her pencil and a notebook in tow so she won't miss out on any step. We sit at the kitchen table and peel apples. Then we start to slow cook them on the stove.

"Miss Peg, can I ask you something?"

"Sure, Bee. What is it?"

"Well, you see, Pastor LeCroy was speaking this past Sunday about how in the past several young girls and boys have been coming up missing here in Birmingham. The entire community has been talking all about it and I just want you to be safe as you venture out at night. The latest news is that some young boys have been disappearing lately. The families think maybe they're just simply running away for a better life away from Birmingham. Something deep in me is a saying that it is more to it than that. You know? So just be extra careful if you go out at night, okay?"

"I will, Bee. Thank you for showing you care," I say, knowing Bee has some thoughts about how I got pregnant, but she does not judge me. "Sometimes I think you care more about me than Mrs. Carson does."

"Oh, child, your cousin cares for you deeply. She's just finding it hard to show it, that's all. Well, look who's at the back door! Hello, Sammy!"

I turn and see Sammy looking through the back door. She looks like she's sobbing crocodile tears. "Come on in, Sammy!" I say, getting up and going to the door to let her in. "Now, what has you crying and all upset?" I help her sit at the kitchen table and I dry her tears with some tissues Bee hands me, realizing she is crying real tears, not crocodile tears!

"You have to…to help my…my aunt and…and her family find…find my cous…cousin, Bobby!" Sammy is crying uncontrollably and can barely get her words out through her blubbering.

"What do you mean, child? There's another child missing?" Bee asks in alarm.

"My cousin Bobby didn't come home last night," Sammy says, calming down a little as she blows her nose. "I came over to tell you ladies that my cousin is missing and ask if you will help me find him."

"Yes, child!" Bee says before I can speak. "Let me turn off the stove and we will help you find him!"

"Thank you," Sammy says as she continues to sob, wiping her tears with her open palm. It is disconcerting not seeing a smile on Sammy's face. "Bee, please call your son to see if he can give us a ride. I am sure we will need to cover the entire city to find her cousin."

"He's at work right now, Miss Peg, but he'll be off in a couple of hours," Bee says. I am frightened by the worried look on her face. "Child, go to the wash room and freshen up your face. Miss Peg, can I speak with you please?"

"Yes, Bee," I say, watching Sammy go to the bathroom, her body shaking with sobs as she cries quietly. I have never seen Bee like this before. I can tell something is terribly wrong.

"Miss Peg, like I told you, there's been several children missing for years and I am sure Sammy's poor cousin is missing because someone is taking these babies! God only knows why and what for. We have to find this poor kid soon, or we may not find him at all," Bee says, her eyes filling with tears.

"Who do you think is the person that is taking these children?" I ask.

"I think it's the white man that's been fathering them. Raping young black women who can't afford the doctor you visited the other night. This man don't want his deep, dark secret to get out. How I know this? It's because every child missing is mixed, Miss Peg, and so is the child Sammy is speaking of. I know 'cause I delivered Bobby."

My stomach tightens in knots. Could the man that Bee is speaking of be the same man who has been raping me for weeks? I know I am not the only woman he has been raping. But how can I tell Bee and how can we get Sammy's cousin Bobby back?

Chapter 56

We head out the back door with Sammy, holding each of her hands in one of ours as we make our way from the back to catch a cab. The sun is setting and I know we do not have much daylight left. Bee is very upset, because she was unable to get in touch with her twin sister to see if she could drive us. Bee's son, June Bug, did say that Honey is wild. I think maybe Bee is starting to judge her sister the way Sera has been judging me.

"Sammy, tell me the last time you seen your cousin."

"It was yesterday. We just finished playing and…"

I do not hear the rest of what she is saying, because I notice Seth's truck pulling into his driveway.

"Wait one minute, Bee! Mr. Seth!" I am yelling from the top of my lungs, making sure he can hear me before heading into his house for supper. "This poor child has a serious problem. Can you help us?" I have no idea how he will respond. Bee stands beside me with Sammy still crying and people looking from their yards or out of their windows to see what is going on.

"Miss Peg, what's wrong?" he says, walking across to our yard with a concerned look on his face.

"This poor child has lost her cousin."

"How old is your cousin, child?" Seth says, kneeling beside Sammy as he grabs her shoulders and looks her in the eye.

"Twelve."

"Don't cry, child, we will find her. When did you last see your cousin?" he asks, taking Sammy by the hand and leading her to his truck. Bee and I follow them and the four of us are heading for Seth's truck when Sammy says something that stops Seth in his tracks.

"We finished playing stickball and my cousin Bobby changed his gym shoes and put his new brown dress shoes on because we were going to a church social."

"Wait! Your cousin is not a girl?"

180

"No, sir. My cousin is a boy. Bobby was born here and then they moved to New Orleans. Yesterday was his first day back in Birmingham."

"Describe your cousin again to me, please."

"Bobby is a twelve-year-old, light-skinned boy with freckles. He decided to change his shoes, and then had to use the outhouse near the park. I came back to look for him, but he was nowhere to be found. He left his gym shoes, ball, and stick. I thought maybe he went home without me."

"No, I don't mean that. Tell me about his shoes."

"His shoes?" Bee says, puzzled. "What do his shoes have to do with this, Mr. Seth?"

"Tell me about your cousin's shoes." Seth has a look in his eyes like I have never seen before. He speaks to Sammy patiently, but with a sense of urgency.

"His mama just bought him some brown shoes with black soles at the Richards store downtown when they got here yesterday, because the ones he wore here were all scuffed up."

"Take this girl back to the house and then call her parents and her cousin's mother and have them join you in two hours here at your house, Miss Peg!" Seth barks his orders as he walks quickly toward his truck.

"Do you know where this child is?"

"Please, Miss Peg," he says, turning to me as he opens the truck's door. His eyes are cold and he seems to be shaking with rage. "Go back and call her parents and have them come here like I said."

As Seth was speaking with Sammy, a cold chill came over me. Did Seth suspect that his father could be the cause of all this? I am sure now that he knows where Bobby is and who has him. Seth suddenly runs inside his house, leaving the truck door open and the three of us standing there looking confused for a few short minutes. He slams the screen door on the back porch of his parents' house and runs back to his truck with a few things clutched in his hand. He gets in the truck and immediately takes off without a word. Does he know that his father is the cause of all this trouble the Negroes in this city have had to endure all these years? Bee, Sammy, and I watch as his truck speeds away into the darkness, leaving us all confused and afraid.

Chapter 57

Iknow my father is at the Grants' house tonight. I overheard him talking to my mom this morning just before breakfast about an important meeting tonight with Mr. Grant. Damn it, how could I be so blind? Is the Klan kidnapping children? It can't be that my former best friend has been kidnapping children right here in Birmingham. But it all makes sense now. It explains why he always has brown children's shoes to donate to charity. And it shows how he's hiding the evidence of his crimes. I hate to think what he's been doing to these poor boys. I've known his dark secret about having relationships with men, but I would never have thought that he has been kidnapping children. Why are they all biracial? Why brown shoes? What's happened to the children that have disappeared? I cannot believe that I have been such a fool.

I park my vehicle a couple of blocks from the Grant's. The sun has set and I know any moment that the neighborhood porch lights will soon brighten each house, so I decide to enter the Grant's property from a wooded area in the back. Being very careful to watch each step, I make my way through the bushes. I flinch every time I step on a small twig, thinking it must sound like a crackling fire. I have to be wrong about this. I just have to. But deep down in my soul, I know it's true.

I finally make my way to a manicured lawn overlooking the Grant house from the back. I get a glimpse of Mrs. Grant's pies for this Sunday's picnic cooling off in the window, and suddenly realize how she gets so many pies baked. She must start making pies as soon as one picnic ends, getting ready for the next one. I pause to survey the property, trying to locate Patrick. I can hear Mrs. Grant humming, "Yankee Doodle," but I see no sign of Patrick. I know he's near, because the car he loves so much is parked near the driveway, just beside the house. He would not dare leave it parked there overnight. But where could he be? Walking closer to the house, I notice a small shed with an industrial light hanging outside, just above the double wooden doors. It's attached to a barn like you see in old western movies. This has to be the place where he is taking the young Negro boys. I am sure of it.

Looking very closely through the crack that divides the doors, I try for a better look. I decide to take my chances and enter the shed, making sure I don't slam the door behind me and attract attention.

Bent over, keeping low, I notice dozens of little boys' shoes placed neatly on hand-made shelves along a wall. I now realize that I have been face-to-face with a kidnapper, and very likely, a killer for years and I didn't even know it. Here I am thinking I know his darkest secret, and the truth is that his sexuality is not the only skeleton he has. But why? Homosexuals are not child molesters. All the ones I know of that have been discovered are married men with wives and sometimes mistresses. I never heard of a homosexual that rapes children.

If they did, as much as the Klan hates them, I know I'd have heard about it! Somehow though, they have always seemed more tolerant of those who've been caught red-handed raping a child. Unless it was a boy. But even those men weren't called homosexuals. The Klan said they weren't. They said they *knew* these men and they said they weren't homosexuals. It was just a way of tagging someone with a label that justified beating and sometimes killing them.

I grab a small pipe wrench near a tool area and proceed even further into the shed, taking notice where I place each foot on the dirt floor. Where could Patrick be holding Sammy's cousin? I am sure he hasn't harmed the child, yet. He has been working overtime at the construction site and he wouldn't have had enough opportunity to get rid of the bodies, *if* he's killing the children when he's done with them. The thought causes me to retch a little, but I fight back the desire to vomit and try to focus on finding the boy I know is here somewhere. There is a faint whistle coming from the house. I can barely hear it at first, and then it starts getting louder as each second passes.

Where can I hide? I find a tarp that they've used to cover the wood they collected for the winter months and decide to hide underneath, leaving a small crack to see whoever approaches. Just as I get settled, the door swings open and Patrick emerges from the dark shadow of the night with a coffee cup in one hand. Still whistling, he carefully closes the door behind him. He stops a few feet away from me and stands in front of a set of finely sanded and painted shelves. He is admiring the shoes he has cleaned and shined and stacked neatly on the shelves. Waiting to see what he'll do next, I suddenly hear Mrs. Grant yell from the same window I'd seen pies sitting in just a few minutes earlier.

"I hear it's going to get cold tonight, Patrick! Grab a few logs and bring them inside, please." I hear Patrick's mother shut the window and go back to working on her pies.

"Yes, ma'am!" he shouts back at the closed window, never taking his eyes from the shoes he's collected throughout the years for his own self-gratification. I can't bear to imagine the details of his crimes. I think he honestly believes that by giving numerous shoes away each Christmas to underprivileged white children, he is somehow absolved from any guilt for his perverted and, most likely, murderous acts.

Patrick grabs a few small logs just feet away from where I'm hiding, and then we both are distracted by a sound coming from behind a wall covered by a Confederate flag. Then I hear the thumping noise again, followed by a bump and a muffled cry coming from somewhere within this shed. But where? I watch as Patrick steps closer to the tarp, just inches away from me, to grab a few more logs, then abruptly drops them and walks to the huge Confederate flag draped along the wall. He pulls the flag away and I see that behind it is an adjacent stair which leads to a lower level of the shed that I never knew existed. Looking around, he pulls a long string which turns on a small light hanging just above his head and carefully proceeds down the wooden steps.

He emerges a few minutes later with a flashlight and lays it on the work bench. Then he rearranges the flag so nobody will notice his secret place. "This is not the same man I have grown to love as my play brother," I think to myself, as he continues to the house with a few logs underneath one arm.

So, this is his deepest secret. I am just hoping that he didn't harm Sammy's poor cousin. Waiting a few minutes before I uncover myself from the plastic tarp, in case he returns for something, I grab the flashlight that he left on the bench and make my way down the secret stairway which looks like the home of the devil himself. An uneasy feeling comes over me as each step I take brings me deeper within the abyss, and for a moment I'm sure I am walking into the pit of hell.

Then there's the thump I heard earlier, but this time it's much louder. I walk slowly down the stairs, being extra careful. I can only imagine what this man would do to me to keep his secret and what he has also done to so many missing Negro children. After a few moments that seem to last forever, I notice a nice-sized trunk that you might find at the foot of a beautiful bed in a master bedroom. It has leather straps that were once used during travel to keep the lid from detaching. But why have a chest down here? It appears to be quite old, and the antique trunk certainly looks out of place in this dingy, dark hole of a dungeon.

The thumping noise begins to get louder and I finally realize the trunk is its source. Examining the travel chest more closely, using the flashlight to illuminate it, I notice that this monster has a padlock on it to prevent anyone from opening it. I reach for my pipe wrench and notice a small pistol in one of my pockets. Someone must have placed it there without my knowing about it. I grab the pipe wrench from the back pocket of my overalls and slam it aggressively onto the lock and break the padlock into two parts. Nervous and shaken, not daring to imagine what I might find, I slowly lift the lid.

"My God from Heaven! This can't be!" I whisper.

A light-skinned Negro child is lying in the trunk, bloody, wet, shaken, and confused, and in tears as he looks at me, blinded by the flashlight.

"Please don't hurt me again, sir," the boy pleads, while lying in a fetal position. His hands are tied and I can tell at one time or another he was gagged, because a sodden handkerchief hangs around his neck.

"Don't worry, son. I won't harm you. Are you Bobby?"

"Yes, sir."

"Bobby, let's go home."

After I loosen Bobby's hands, he hugs me tightly. I imagine it's the same way children embraced their fathers when they came home from the war; like I was a loved one they thought they might never see again.

"Now, Bobby, you have to be very quiet."

"Yes, sir."

"Grab my hand and watch where you step, okay?"

"Yes, sir," Bobby says, still shaking from all the trauma. We both stop suddenly, dead in our tracks, as a voice comes out of nowhere.

"Well, look a here! If it ain't the white nigger lover!" Patrick says, as he walks from the dark shadows of the stairs, dressed in denim overalls without a shirt. His hair is oily and dirty from his nine-to-five job.

"Patrick, you really need professional help. I can see to it that you get help."

"You know it's too late for all that, Seth. Leave the boy and go home," Patrick says, while standing between us and the stairs.

"The only way I am leaving is with this child, so please get out of our way."

"Well, nigger lover, you picked the wrong nigger to save tonight. So turn him loose and I will let you go," Patrick says, holding up a butcher knife that he is clutching in his right hand.

I remember how caring Patrick once was. I remember the kindness he showed to children who played stickball on the streets of Birmingham. I never would have suspected that he would turn out to be a killer of so many innocents. Looking at him now, I do my best to change the subject, to get this poor child away from the demonic acts he's planning in his psychotic mind.

"Patrick, remember when we were younger and we went swimming downtown off the bridge? The day I thought I was a man and decided to jump from the light pole that stood over the bridge? I wanted to do something no soul here in Birmingham had ever thought of doing. But it all went terribly wrong, and I remember gasping for my last breath and deciding to give up on life. At the very end, I reached up and there was your hand there to save me. That day you saved my life, and I am here today because of your love and courage. You still have that love within your heart, but this time let me help *you*, Patrick. Let me hold out my hand to you like you once held out your hand to me.

I love you, Patrick, and I know you can change if you want to. Look at me! I changed. The man I once was, I am no longer. I have learned to love and not to judge people just because they are different from us. I learned Patrick that it's okay to be wrong sometimes. Everyone dead or alive has been wrong at some time in their lives. No matter how big or how small the case may be. So, this time let me help you. Can you do that?" There is a moment of silence when I think we are all going to walk outside this shed of dark secrets. Finally, my mind starts to feel at ease and then all hell breaks loose.

With tears in his eyes, Patrick speaks words that could only come from the mouth of a real Klansman.

"Sorry, Seth, but you're gonna have to die here tonight, just like the boy."

Reaching for the pipe wrench in one of my overall's pockets for some sort of protection for us, I stumble on that handgun someone put in my side pocket. "Bee must have put it there," I think, aware of her reputation for being a gun-toting woman, despite the efforts of the Klan and the local authorities, which are one and the same, to pass gun control laws to keep Negroes unarmed.

I never thought I would have to turn a gun on my best friend to defend my life and the life of an innocent child. I point the barrel at Patrick and pray that it's loaded. He stops in his tracks, looking confused. He can't seem to fathom that I'm poised to kill him, although a moment ago he was ready to plunge a knife in my chest.

"Now, move to the side, Patrick; I don't really want to harm you." Patrick's eyes become more sinister as he slowly moves away from the stairs. "Stay back, Patrick! You're gonna have to pay for all the trouble you caused those poor families, but I promise I will be there for you while you go off to jail. Okay?" Patrick keeps his eyes on Bobby, as if pleading with him to understand.

"Get out of our way, Patrick!" I watch as Patrick moves farther away from the steps, his eyes never leaving Bobby. Then he stops and falls to his knees, holding his head as if trying not to remember.

"He looked like you," he says in a child's voice. "I had just gotten some new brown shoes from Richards. Real leather shoes. Not the cheap plastic ones he sells to… He was parked outside in an old Buick and said my father told him to take me on home, because he had to go back to his office. Mr. Richards said my dad had gone down the street to use the pay phone. But I recognized the driver. He had done some work for my dad. So I got in the car. He didn't take me home. He took me to the woods and he kept me there for hours. He took off all my clothes. Everything but my shoes. He made me bend over and hold onto a tree while he…" Patrick starts sobbing and falls to his knees.

"All I could see was my new brown shoes. I passed out and when I woke up, he was shaking me. He told me to get out of the car, because I was home. He told me if I told anybody they would know what I was. That I liked boys. He said he knew I liked boys. That's why he knew I would like what he did to me. He said when he was my age a white man showed him that he liked boys. The same white man that got his mama pregnant. His own father! Then he smiled and drove away. I never saw him again. I think he left town, afraid I'd talk and the Klan would come looking for him. But I never told anybody, because he was right. I do like boys. I try not to. That's right, I have sex with men. I even buy them brown shoes to wear while we but it's not the same. It's just not the same." His sobs echo down there in the pit and my skin crawls as if his slimy, greasy fingers are touching *me*!

Crawling up the stairs from that dark place, holding on to Bobby, we make it out of the shed. Knowing Patrick as I do, I am sure he has a pistol in there somewhere. I walk as fast as I can, carrying this poor child who is too traumatized and weak to walk. I've got to get him to my truck and back to his own family, who I hope is waiting patiently with Peg for his safe return. I am sure this man I once would have given my life for will emerge from the shed with a shotgun or some other firearm and end any hope of this child and myself from seeing the light of day. Seconds later, as we make it outside, we pass the window where Mrs. Grant is setting her pies and she notices us leaving.

"Seth, what are you doing here?" she yells, as she opens the window behind us. We ignore her and continue running toward my truck. "Whose child is that? Did you see Patrick out back?"

Mrs. Grant's last question is interrupted by a single gunshot that comes from the shed.

"Patrick! Oh, my Lord!" Mrs. Grant shouts, as she rushes from the house to the shed in horror. "What did you do, Seth?" She screams as she opens the shed door and apparently sees Patrick lying on the dirt floor. I refuse to turn around, directing Bobby to keep his eyes forward toward the road that leads to safety and the rest of his life.

Chapter 58

Sammy's family sits in the front room, tense but patient. The small platter of cookies on the coffee table remains untouched. Bee and I wait with them at the Carson residence and for the last two hours I have nervously tried to make small talk about church, my flower garden, and Sammy's promise as a budding musician to no avail. When Sammy's entire family arrived earlier with a host of aunts, uncles, and cousins, we knew the stately, formal living room would not hold them all. Neither would the homier, more comfortable kitchen. So we moved the entire lot of relatives, including sixth and seventh cousins, into the largest area downstairs, a seldom used and sparsely furnished family room, which Dr. Carson has threatened to turn into a library. Sera, however, refuses to entertain the notion of the family room being anything else but just that, the family room, anticipating eventually having several grandchildren running around the house every summer.

Bee is keeping busy serving cool drinks and asking and answering questions. The family has been searching for Bobby for over twenty-four hours. A deeply religious family, they also say they've been fasting and praying, and trusting in God for a miracle. Occasionally, someone throws up a hand and shouts and they all respond with shouts of their own, or start rocking back and forth, praying or speaking in tongues.

"The Lord will bring our son back to us, Miss Peg," Bobby's father says with total assurance. "I believe with every ounce of faith that He will return him to us safely."

"Yes, sir," I reply. "My prayers are with you and your family for his safe return." Deep down, I am hoping that Bobby will come storming through the door, but he has been gone for a day now and I can only imagine the unthinkable. I am afraid that this young boy will be added to the list of children missing here in Birmingham. Who would ever want to touch someone's child? "Only a sick person in need of prayer," I think, just as one of Sammy's distant cousins raises her hand and shouts "Hallelujah!" followed by a chorus of shouts, prayers, and praying in tongues.

Sitting in a chair near the window, a petite white lady with red hair, who seems out of place in this family, has been sitting alone unnoticed the entire time, nervously twisting a handkerchief in her hands. I quietly walk over and sit next to her.

"Excuse me, ma'am, can I get you something to drink?" I ask her.

"No, thank you," she says, turning and giving me a tentative, shy smile. She turns back to look out the front window, her eyes full of both hope and despair.

"Are you family, ma'am?" I ask, wondering what brings her to this crisis.

"I am Bobby's mother," she says quietly, while continuing to look out of the window as her eyes fill with tears. Her mouth quivers slightly as if she is about to speak, but she is only able to let out a heavy sigh. Then she turns to me, mustering up the courage and the strength to speak.

"Excuse me, but what's your name?"

"My name is Peg James," I say, extending my hand.

"Nice to make your acquaintance." She shakes my hand and a big smile spreads across her face.

"Thank you for your hospitality to my husband's family and me," she says.

I remember what Bee said about a man having biracial children by black women who may be trying to get rid of them to keep his secret, and I immediately know who has to be at the bottom of this woman's missing child. "He" took that child! I am sure of it. But if the abductor is only taking children he's sired, he would not take Bobby, would he? Sitting there with Bobby's mother to give her some small measure of comfort, I keep thinking how "He" is not human and does not give a damn about others outside his race. It has to be who I have been thinking it was all the time. It has to be. No one else is as evil as "He" is. I refuse to believe it.

"Why were we told to come here, Bee?" I hear a family member ask. The family has had many questions we were unable to answer, but this one we could.

"The next door neighbors' son, Mr. Seth, asked us to call you all and have you wait here until he comes back," Bee says with her usual abrupt manner, only this time there is a touch of tenderness in her tone and manner, indicating her concern and empathy for this family.

"Wait one minute! You mean to tell me that the racist family's son next door asked you to call us about Bobby's disappearance?" one uncle asks, quieting the room. "He may be the reason little Bobby is gone!" Other members of the family nod or speak in agreement.

"That's what I said, ain't it?" Bee says, without any hint of tenderness.

"I can't believe you of all people, Bee, would have us waste our time coming clear across Birmingham on the say-so of some racists' son when we should be out looking for Bobby! I hate the white people in this town!" The family starts talking loudly, gesturing toward Bee.

"I am sure Mr. Seth will find Bobby!" I say, after getting everyone's attention by striking a glass with a spoon. "I am sure of it," I add, jumping in to back up Bee.

"Miss Peg is right. Just because his parents are racist does not mean that this young man is not sincere in his efforts to find Bobby," says a soft voice nearby. Had a pin fallen just then, we all would have heard it. Everyone turns to look at Bobby's mother, who has mustered up strength to add to her hope. "You all know how my parents felt about me marrying Bobby's father. They were just like the other people here in Birmingham. That's why we went away. But when they came to visit and saw Bobby, their hearts just melted. They love Bobby so much. I haven't had the heart to tell them he's missing. I was waiting hoping I wouldn't have to."

After a tense moment, one of Bobby's aunts goes over and hugs her sister-in-law, followed by another family member, and another, until they are all around her comforting her and telling her that Bobby will be found. Then her husband moves toward them and everyone moves aside as he walks to his wife, takes her in his arms and they both start crying cleansing tears as the family gathers around them crying and praying, and being a family.

"Excuse me, Miss Peg," Bee says softly. "Can I see you for a minute, please?"

I reluctantly walk away from the touching scene to see what is bothering Bee. She has a troubled look on her face. I did not hear the phone ring or see anyone come in, so I am hoping it is not bad news about Bobby. Bee looks more nervous than ever as I follow her to the kitchen. "What is it, Bee?" I say curtly, wanting to return to our guests.

"What should I say to Dr. and Mrs. Carson who just pulled up and are now coming around to the back door? You know they saw all those cars on the street and are wondering what's going on here."

She is right. What am I going to tell them? They had to have seen all the cars parked outside and wondered what is going on in their home. The phone rings and I am so on edge I answer it after one ring.

"Hello?"

"Aunt Peg?"

"Yes, how are you Robert Jr.?"

"I'm fine, thank you. Just making sure you can pick me up tomorrow. I have decided to catch a flight when I get through with this project that I need to finish by tomorrow morning. I will keep you posted."

"Okay, nice talking to you," I say, making sure Sera and Dr. Carson, who have just come in, do not suspect I am talking to their son. "I will talk to you soon. Good-bye." I hang up the phone quickly, not giving my "nephew" a chance to respond.

"Peg, is everything alright?" Dr. Carson asks. He and Sera have confused and anxious looks on their faces as they both turn to Bee and me, looking for some clue about what is going on.

"No, everything is not okay. Do you remember Sammy?" I reply tiredly.

"Yes! Do not tell us she is missing!" Sera says, her eyes widening in horror.

"No, she is safe, but her cousin Bobby, who she was with yesterday, is missing and I was asked by the neighbor, Seth, next door   you know Mr. and Mrs. Stevens' oldest son   to call the family and have them come over."

"Peg, why would he do that?" Dr. Carson asks. He is about to say something else, but he is interrupted by a scream from the living room.

We all rush to see what is going on. The front door is open and everyone is standing on the porch or the lawn. We can clearly see a truck parked in the driveway next door and someone getting out of it. It is Seth. He walks from the driver's side around to the passenger's side and opens the door. Suddenly, a young boy runs around the truck and moves as fast as he can to get to the front yard where he rushes into the arms of his parents. Everyone is laughing and thanking God, rejoicing about the return of this child! Bee and I hug each other and Dr. Carson holds Sera in his arms and I see a tear roll down her cheek as she watches Bobby's parents, crying and kissing and hugging their son. I feel tears welling up in my eyes, too.

I watch Seth, tired and dirty, but so full of joy that he has brought this child back to his family. Then his smile turns into a frown. Something must have happened. But before I can get to him to ask what's troubling him, he is surrounded by a host of Bobby's uncles, aunts, and cousins, who I know love him and seem to have momentarily forgotten he is a white man, as the men take turns shaking his hand and patting him on the back and the women give him big hugs. Next door, Mrs. Stevens hears all the commotion and comes outside on her porch to see what is going on.

So many people surround Seth, thanking and blessing him, she never even notices it is her son who is directly the center of attraction. I think if she saw that Seth is the person everyone is fussing over, being glad-handed and hugged by Negroes, there would be hell to pay tonight. Seeing all of those black faces is more than enough for Mrs. Stevens. She quickly turns around with a look of total disgust on her face and goes back into her house, not even noticing Seth's truck parked in the driveway.

The crowd disperses when, once again, Bobby's father walks into its midst. The tall, muscular man with the demeanor of a great African king walks up to Seth and grabs him, hugging him, as tears roll down his face. He finally lets go, and Bobby's mother is there to give him another tearful hug. When she releases him, Bobby looks at Seth and says with conviction: "Until today, Joe Louis was my hero, because he was the greatest fighter that ever lived. But you're my hero, now."

Seth picks Bobby up and hugs him tightly with tears rolling down his cheeks just as his mother looks out of the window, screams, and slams it down hard, breaking some of the glass. Everyone looks around startled, and then Bobby laughs. His laughter is pure, joyful, and contagious. Soon everyone is laughing as they head for their cars, waving good-bye to us and Bobby and his parents, several stopping to make sure everything is okay before leaving.

Seth carries Bobby to his parents' car and puts him in the backseat, while Bobby's father holds the front passenger door open for his mother. The two men stand talking intensely for a few minutes, looking very serious and concerned. After a few minutes, they shake hands and Bobby's father gets in his car and drives off to take his family home. Seth waves good-bye to Bobby and then walks toward his truck, waving good night to us. He closes the truck's doors, and tiredly walks up the steps to his porch where he sits down in the cool night air for a moment. I resist the urge to go comfort him, instead turning to go inside, following Bee, who is unusually quiet after the events of this evening.

Dr. Carson looks at his nephew proudly and I hear him say as I walk up the steps, "See, Sera, we were supposed to be here in Birmingham. I am beginning to love this Stevens family next door."

"Yes, I believe you are right," Sera replies.

I know tomorrow will put a smile on their faces when they see their son. Tomorrow, I can finally share the secret I have been keeping for weeks!

"Miss Peg, you mind if I take the day off tomorrow?" Bee asks with a weary voice.

"Sure, Bee," I say. "It's been a long day for all of us."

"I'll be here as usual," she says, grabbing her purse and walking toward the back door.

Chapter 59

It is Saturday morning and what a beautiful day it is! I am surprised to see Bee up so early, knowing that she was up late last night seeing Sammy's family off after the ordeal.

"What time did you arrive this morning, Bee?"

"Miss Peg, when I was leaving, your cousin and that wonderful husband of hers told me to just stay here last night after such a long and stressful day," she says. I wonder for a moment where she slept, then remember I did see a door to one of the guest rooms upstairs slightly ajar when I got up this morning.

"I am so grateful that young man, Mr. Seth, came through for the family last night," she says, as we both avoid discussing where and with whom Seth found Bobby. "Do you think all his family has changed like him? What am I saying! After the way his mother slammed down that window when she saw Negroes hugging her son, I already know the answer. That peckerwood just as racist as she always been!"

"Bee!"

"Sorry, Miss Peg," she says, although I can see she is not sorry at all. She knows I hate language like that, no matter who is the topic of discussion.

Relieved that I do not have to answer her question, I walk quietly out on the back porch. The sun shines directly over the Stevens house and seems to be making its way to our back porch. Bee must have awakened early, because she left us a basket full of freshly picked vegetables on the porch. I am so pleased that I added a few rows of vegetables to the garden.

"Miss Peg, your garden is wonderful! Look how big the onions are." Bee points to the green stalks coming out of the soil as she joins me on the porch, reaching down to pick up the basket.

"Hello, ladies!"

I cannot believe my eyes. It is Ronnie sitting in his favorite spot on his back porch, writing in what looks like his journal.

"Hello, Ronnie," we reply, as we wave cautiously, keeping our eyes open for any sign of Mrs. Stevens or the nurse from hell. Our instincts prove to be right. The wicked nurse from the west walks out the back door just as our hands drop after we wave at Ronnie.

"Ronnie, I hope you're not speaking to those niggers," the nurse says.

Poor Ronnie does not say a word, but you can tell he is not happy about her comments by his facial expressions. We return our attention back to Bee's basket filled with vegetables she picked earlier this morning. The colorful array of bell peppers, onions, and carrots is so appetizing.

"My garden in Ohio never produced vegetables as perfect as these, Bee."

"Let me wash them, Miss Peg, and get them ready for Sunday supper tomorrow. I plan to make a wonderful beef stew with hot water corn bread," Bee says, returning to the kitchen with a broad smile. I hear her washing the vegetables in the sink, running water from the faucet over them as she hums happily with no signs of tiredness from the day before. I return to the kitchen minutes later to find Sera at the table enjoying a cup of coffee and an English muffin. I can tell she is still pretty upset with me.

"Good morning, Peg," Sera says, busily spreading cream cheese on one side of the English muffin as Bee turns up her nose at what she calls "high class food from up North."

"Hello, Sera. How are you this morning?"

"I am fine, thank you," she says formally, as if talking to a stranger. "Peg, did you make a decision about moving back to Ohio?"

"Can I please talk with you about that at another time, Sera?" I don't want to discuss my personal business with Bee at the kitchen sink. Not that I have too many secrets from Bee anymore, but discussions between family members as serious as this one should be done privately.

"That would be fine. Maybe after church tomorrow."

"Ladies, while I have you both here, I want to ask you if you would like to attend service with me tomorrow," Bee says, as she finishes the vegetables, laying them on a towel to dry. "We have a special program and the pastor wants to get the community together to discuss the disappearances of Negro children. I think we could use some suggestions from you ladies on how we might deal with this matter."

"Yes, I would love to attend," Sera says, stopping a moment to chew the food in her mouth. "I also want to speak to the church about running for district attorney in the next election if the civil rights legislation is passed in Washington by then. Do you think you can get me on the platform to speak to the church?"

Just then, Dr. Carson takes us by surprise when he walks in and requests a cup of coffee before heading to the hospital for his morning rounds.

"Hello, dear, would you like to attend Bee's church followed by a community meeting with us tomorrow?" Sera asks.

"Sera, I promised Ken Stevens next door that I would speak at his picnic function tomorrow after church. Is there any way you ladies can meet me out at Johnson's Lake tomorrow around two o'clock and hear me speak?"

"We would love to come, Dr. Carson!" Bee gushes before either Sera or I can speak. "Should I pack a basket full of sandwiches? I really had planned to cook beef stew tomorrow, but I can wait until the following Sunday if that's okay, Mrs. Carson!"

"Yes, Bee, that would be fine," Sera says, sipping her coffee.

Dr. Carson kisses his wife on her forehead before heading out the door with his medical bag in his hand.

"It'll be great going to a picnic tomorrow," Bee says.

"According to the weatherman, tomorrow will be a wonderful day without a cloud in the sky," Sera says, seemingly as pleased about the picnic as Bee.

"Who wouldn't want go to a picnic on such a beautiful day?" Bee asks rhetorically.

Chapter 60

When I go out to sit on the back porch awaiting Robert Jr.'s call, it seems to only take moments for the sun that is so high in the sky to start heading towards the west and make its way just beyond the mountains for sunset. By then, we are all sitting on the porch talking about how Seth found Bobby last night. Had the man I now know I love not come to the rescue, we would be reading about Bobby, just another missing black child, in the Negro newspaper.

"Who would have every wanted to hurt any child?" Sera asks, while relaxing on the back porch with her feet up on the patio table. We all grow silent, trying not to contemplate the question hanging in the stillness of the night air, hoping to catch a cool breeze and wondering where Bobby had been, who had him, and how Seth found him.

"Ladies, I have to go now," Bee says, breaking the silence as she stands up and heads inside still talking. "I made the sandwiches and they are in the icebox with the other picnic items for tomorrow. Now, I'm going to get my beauty sleep."

She moves around the kitchen, gathering her things, mumbling under her breath about what she will do if she ever finds who "the low-down, dirty skunk" is that kidnapped Bobby.

"Thank you, Bee, for your hard work," I say as she comes back outside. "We will work on a new recipe on Monday evening. I want to show you how to make a moist red velvet cake."

"I would love that, Miss Peg," Bee says, while taking off her apron and placing a small hat on top of her head.

"Bee, are you sure you would not like for us to drop you off at home?"

"No, child, I need the exercise," she says chuckling. "I will be just fine. I will see you ladies at church tomorrow. Miss Peg, do you mind bringing the basket of goodies I packed for tomorrow's picnic? Just bring it to church with you, please."

"Will do, Bee."

Having given us our marching orders, Bee walks down the steps, waving good-night, as she walks down the side of the house humming. The porch is silent for a few tense minutes until, thank God, Dr. Carson pulls up in his sedan. I do not understand how Sera and I, who were once so close and used to speak to each other about everything, can now barely speak to each other civilly. It is ironic that the people close to you are the ones that hurt you the most.

Dr. Carson gets out of his car looking exhausted. I can tell by the expression on his face that he feels the tension between Sera and me as he makes his way through the dense fog that has settled on the porch. The fog seems to be pressing down on all of us like a weight, growing heavier with each passing moment that Sera and I have remained quiet, pulling us down like drowning victims in the oppressive silence that has enveloped us since Bee's departure.

"Good evening to the two most beautiful ladies in the city of Birmingham make that the state of Alabama!" His voice is a little too bright and his smile much wider than usual as he tries to cut through the dense fog of our recent enmity.

"Well, one of us is a lady, I suppose," Sera says cattily. She slams the screen door as she leaves the porch, acting as if she cannot stand the sight of me for a moment longer.

"Pay her no mind, Peg. She just thinks of you as her little sister. She wanted you to get married in her wedding gown."

"I understand, honestly I do. But the way she is treating me hurts so much."

Dr. Carson heads inside, probably hoping to plead my case to his wife. I am left alone, breathing a sigh of relief as the weight of the silence between Sera and me dissipates into the night air like ashes thrown outside, only to come back down and cover everything they touch. I am afraid Sera and I have a long way to go before things will be like they were before; if they ever are again. But I will deal with that tomorrow. Just this once, I need to relax like I did nearly a week ago when Seth took me to that wonderful Sunday jazz brunch.

I look up at the sky trying to count stars and end up counting the unkind words Sera has spoken to me since discovering my pregnancy. When I was a child, my mother taught me so much. It was as if she knew we did not have long to be together. One of the things she taught me is that if you do not have something nice to say, do not speak at all. Too bad nobody taught my increasingly hateful cousin that.

Chapter 61

The next morning we arrive at the church in time to hear the choir singing praises unto God. We thought we would see Bee there, since she promised to save us a seat. The usher greets us and offers us a seat not far from the back where the ushers sit after they are finished seating the congregation,

"Peg, I thought Bee was saving us a seat."

"Yes, I thought that, also."

We look around the church, trying to get a better look at its members. I can see that the service is high with the Holy Spirit moving in God's people.

"Wait a minute! Isn't that Bee up there next to the pastor?" Sera says, putting on her glasses to get a better look.

"Yes, Sera, I think so."

The choir finishes singing and the pastor introduces Bee who looks nervous as she stands behind the podium.

"Brothers and sisters, Pastor LeCroy has allowed me to speak to you this morning. I never really spoke before hundreds of people before, so please forgive me as I may not know all the right words to say.

For years now, so many Negroes have been coming up missing. Young boys, especially. Two nights ago little Bobby, Rodney and Phyllis' son, went missing for nearly twenty-four hours, as some of you may have heard. We were all amazed how the Lord brought him back to us through the help of a young man here in Birmingham by the name of Seth Stevens. I have to say that other young boys didn't come home. Now it's at the point that adults are also missing here in Birmingham. Well, we have to stand up and join this civil rights movement that is moving across America. The children who marched from Sixteenth Baptist Church to Kelly Ingram Park were attacked by dogs and sprayed with high-powered water hoses. Over five hundred students were arrested and stayed in cramped jail cells for over five days. Hundreds were arrested! This can't ever happen again."

Sera and I hear an occasional, "Amen!" coming from the crowded church. Tears fall from the eyes of many of those sitting there and I wonder how many in the audience are missing a loved one, thinking it could be anyone there, even someone we are sitting right next to. Bee continues to speak across the pulpit. With a handkerchief in one hand, she wipes the tears that fall from her face.

"I am proud to work for such wonderful people as the Carson family. It gives me great pleasure to introduce two wonderful women who will help this community. Brothers and sisters, it is my pleasure to welcome Mrs. Sera Carson and Miss Peg James."

The entire church stands up and applauds. We shake hands with many people on our way to the pulpit. My cousin Sera takes the microphone first after greeting Pastor LeCroy and the associate pastors.

"Ladies and gentlemen, my name is Sera Carson and once civil rights legislation passes, I am running for district attorney here in Birmingham."

The entire church continues to clap wildly and I have never been so proud of her. "I must do better," I think, while she addresses the congregation. I must continue my master's program and then get my doctorate. I have to help people as my cousin has, despite the problems I have encountered here in Birmingham. This is a day I will never forget. What a wonderful Sunday!

Chapter 62

I know it will be hard for me to keep missing Sunday services, so I decide to go to church then pretend to work overtime in order to miss today's picnic. Father Michaels addresses the congregation with a warm smile, kissing the Holy Crucifix hanging from his neck.

"I am happy to announce today that God has blessed Ronnie Stevens by finding him a donor that gave him a new kidney. He is resting at home now with special nurses. It is good to know that the rest of the Stevens are here today: Mr. and Mrs. Stevens with their son, Seth, and his new baby daughter, Emily Rose."

It was nice to see the entire church of over five hundred people stand and praise God for His miracles. I am hoping somehow God will warm these same people's hearts with love and compassion for every human, no matter their color. I know as soon as we get out of church they will all head down to Johnson's Lake for the weekly picnic. Am I the only one who feels that it is wrong for Christian folk to do the opposite of what the Bible has taught us about how we should treat one another? I am sure I am not the only one who feels this way among this large congregation. I am sure some people are silent about their feelings regarding how this city has treated Negroes; afraid to tell their neighbors, friends and some coworkers how they really feel, because of what they must fear the Klan will do to them. I have pulled away from my family's hatred of Negroes and a father who is the leader of the Klan.

Knowing Father Michaels for my entire life, I can never recall him setting foot on the grounds of Johnson's Lake where we hold our picnics, let alone participate in one. I never heard him speak ill of anyone. I have always found him to be a kind and forgiving man. He leads by example for all people a true servant-leader. Following a few moments of silence, Father Michaels' words confirm in my spirit how every person should make their walk with one another.

"Every human being God has put on this earth has an obligation to be his brother's keeper," Father Michaels says, opening up his Bible for today's message. "As long as God will have me to lead this church, I will tell you what is right, no matter whether you agree with me, or not. And if you want to burn a cross on my lawn, that is quite all right by me. If Jesus could allow Himself to be nailed to one, I can put up with a little bonfire," he says, eliciting a spattering of laughter from some of the parishioners. This last statement is directed at the sheriff and my father, who sit out in the audience looking smug and content.

"We have to stop doing that which is evil and ask God to forgive us for our sins."

"The killing has to stop! How can you refuse to love someone who you see every day, someone who does you no wrong, and still say you love God whom you have never seen?"

The entire church is silent and in the silence I can hear my father sucking air through clenched teeth as he sits seething over the priest's denouncement. Father Michaels lifts his hands unto God and asks Him for grace and mercy for the people of Birmingham.

Chapter 63

Wewe arrive home shortly after listening to Father Michaels' sermon and I know I can never participate again in another picnic. The conviction I feel causes me to ask God to please forgive me for all the wrong I have done. I make a note to go to confession as soon as possible.

"Hey, son, are you gonna ride with me to the picnic?" my father asks, just before getting into his vehicle.

"Oh, Dad, I forgot to tell you that I have to work today on construction plans. Since Patrick's shooting accident, we're now short at work."

"I understand, son. I'll see you tonight when I get home."

He laughs and for some strange reason he seems excited about today's picnic more than ever.

"You're in a good mood. Is there anything you should be telling me, Dad?"

"Yes, this week I have invited Dr. Carson, our next door neighbor, to the picnic," he says with a boyish grin, as if he's trying to hold back a secret.

"I asked Dr. Carson to speak at the picnic this week. We need to recruit good law-abiding citizens into the Klan. It's good having a good neighbor who's a doctor. Who could have asked for a better neighbor? I want him to see firsthand what we do here in Birmingham. I'm sure you'll hear about this one tomorrow!" he says, while putting a picnic basket in the back seat.

My mother has decided to stay home, since my little girl lives here now. She says the picnic is no place for a baby. She mentioned one time that when she was a little girl her parents thought she was old enough to attend our kind of picnic. Boy, were they wrong! She said the Klan had found a Negro child that wandered away from her parents while she was playing at a park one Sunday and brought her to the picnic for entertainment. Seems some of the men wanted to take the toddler down to a Louisiana bayou where they hunted alligators and use her for gator bait. But the need for some hometown entertainment outranked the need for alligator meat and she became the entertainment for that week's picnic. My mom was traumatized for years after witnessing that hanging. The child's neck snapped so hard when they lynched her, it was nearly decapitated. I was relieved when she chose to not expose my daughter to such trauma.

"Seth, help your mom and check on your brother before you go to the construction site, okay, son?" my father says as he put his car in gear.

"Will do, Dad."

I watch him drive off, headed to the picnic at Johnson's Lake and think to myself that I don't want any part of it. I decide to spend just a little time with Ronnie and my baby girl before heading off to work on a Sunday. It will be good to make overtime today, because my little girl is getting bigger and we will need to get a place of our own soon.

Chapter 64

B ee, Sera, and I greet everyone after church, getting many thank-yous and pledges of support for when the time comes for Sera's campaign. We are excited about joining Dr. Carson at the lake. He had to finish a round at the hospital due to an unexpected family emergency that prevented the scheduled surgeon from coming in. His wife is having triplets! Well, they say good luck comes in threes and God has surely blessed the three of us today.

"Did you bring the basket I had in the icebox, Miss Peg?" Bee asks, smiling and speaking to some church members walking by.

"Oh, I'm sorry, Bee I totally forgot. Do you mind going by the house and picking it up for us? We will meet you out at Johnson's Lake."

"Don't mind at all, Miss Peg. Do you ladies know how to get out there?"

"Yes," Sera says, looking at the directions her husband left her.

"Okay, then. I will see you ladies out there," Bee says as she heads for a car where an older gentleman appears to be waiting for her. Taking off her hat as she opens the door and climbs into the passenger seat, Bee leans over and kisses the man on the mouth. Sera and I give each other shocked looks, then burst into giggles as Bee and her "gentleman friend" drive away. This is the first happy moment we have shared in a while and I rel-ish it.

A few minutes later, Sera and I are heading down a country road just outside Birmingham, where summer seems to stand still.

"What a beautiful place to be today," I think, as the hot wind blows across Sera's sedan creating little whirlwinds between the seats. We hum "Amazing Grace," our favorite duet in Sunday school, where we were often asked to sing when we were growing up in Ohio.

We arrive at Johnson's Lake, our excitement growing as we anticipate hearing Dr. Carson speak to what seems like a large crowd, judging by the number of cars parked on the side of the road that leads to the entrance of the property. We can hear music coming from down by the lake. Sounds like a country band.

"Peg, would you grab the blanket on the back seat, please?" Sera says, while looking in the mirror as she puts on her lipstick.

"I like that color on you, Sera."

"Thank you. This is a new color. I will make sure to order you one."

"Why thank you, Sera." Finally, she is speaking to me. But I can tell she has not come around because our conversations are very short. I was hoping Robert Jr.'s surprise visit might help, but he never called for me to meet him at the airport and I fear he was not able to come.

Children are laughing and playing games in the open fields that lay in front of a wooded area.

"I am assuming this is the way to the lake, Sera."

"I am sure it is. Let's ask these children." It seems that we are late and all of the adults have already gathered at the lake.

"Excuse me, young lady. Is this the way to Johnson's Lake?" Sera asks a towheaded little girl.

"Yes. Are you today's entertainment?"

Sera and I look at each other and start laughing. Then we politely thank the inquisitive child, and continue down the clay path.

Chapter 65

I was very proud when I watched my nephew bring a child who was missing back to his parents. That night, I was overcome with love for my family. Without Seth's help, that child would have never seen his parents again. Speaking with Sera, we both came to the conclusion that moving here to get to know my extended family next door is the best thing we could have ever done. Sera was also excited about running for public office as soon as the Civil Rights Act passes in Washington. We both think this is the best thing for her to do to fight for equal rights here in the South.

We are also both pleased with the Civil Rights Movement that Dr. King and others have created; finally allowing the people's voices to be heard. I am glad to know that so many whites have helped with the Civil Rights Movement. I am also appreciative that so many blacks and whites, now and before this generation, have fought and died for all Americans to have equal rights.

The family I never knew I had for so many years; the family I wondered what it would be like to hug and show that I love them; the family I could only imagine; the family I dreamed of telling me stories after dinner about our parents and what they were like   that family is here in Birmingham. I am really excited about telling Ken that I am the brother our parents were unable to take care of and had to give away so many years ago.

My adoptive parents kept a letter from my natural parents explaining how they so wanted to keep me, but due to being young and not being able to feed me, this was the only choice they had. I felt honored when Ken asked me to speak to some of his friends today, and by the turnout, I can tell he has plenty of them.

"Hello, Dr. Carson. It is nice to meet you. We heard so much about you from Mr. Stevens."

"Excuse me, but what is your name?"

"Please forgive us for being so rude. This is my wife, Laura Grant, and I am Thomas Grant. We live a few miles from you. We heard you moved into the best property in Birmingham."

"Oh, really?"

"Yes, the Whitfield Mansion is one of our most stately and revered residences. We're just glad to have someone of your caliber residing there with your family. Make sure you get a piece of my wife's pie. She bakes the best here in Birmingham."

"I sure will," I promise, doubting that anyone's pie is better than Peg's apple pie.

"You're going to like the entertainment today. They've got someone special from up North." I continue walking in search of my brother, wondering about this "entertainment."

A few minutes later, I am sitting with Ken, watching the crowd while they enjoy the music and wonderful food on blankets spread out on the field in front of a medium-size stage. We listen to a local band of college students playing a few well-known tunes, while a group of pretty, young girls watches them from the foot of the platform. Nearby, some boys swing from a rope hanging from a limb.

"You see that huge oak tree, Robert?"

"Yes."

"Would you believe my father planted that tree when he was a young boy? His father used to fish here when he was young. They used to come up here before they moved to Savannah, then back to Birmingham. That tree is a symbol of something strong that survives life's storms. It's still here healthy and strong. The kids love to swing from the rope and jump into the lake."

We laugh, watching some unusual jumps as several boys shout "cannonball" just before hitting the water.

"Ken, do you ever wish you had siblings, I mean, that you grew up with?" I ask, testing the waters.

"I always wished I could meet my brother. Well, hell! My mother told me one time I used to have a brother. She and Pa was young and the only choice they had was to give him up for adoption. Look, I have a picture of them in my wallet."

My heart begins to pump faster, because I have never seen my parents' faces. Ken opens his wallet and shows me a lovely couple. These are my parents! I try not to show any emotion, but I get choked up and play it off as an allergic reaction to the pollen. Then, Ken says something that totally shocks me.

"Hell, Robert, you look just like my pa!" Ken is holding the picture up to my face, then laughing.

"Ken, is there some place I can go to freshen up before speaking to your guests?"

"Sure. Just follow this path up through the wooded area and at the top of the hill you will see the Johnsons' main house."

"Thanks, I will return shortly."

"No rush. We're going to have a little entertainment before you come back down to speak. I will send the sheriff up to get you right after it's over."

"Sure. Up this path, right?"

"Yes," Ken says, still pointing and smiling.

I leave the crowd of hundreds of people below and start up the path which first passes an open field of colorful wildflowers. I hear birds calling each other and see yellow jackets flying around open flower petals. Shortly after, the path starts to incline and my knees begin to ache with each step I take. I gaze up toward tall evergreens and pine trees like you only see on Christmas cards. The idyllic landscape prevents the sun from shining on the path ahead.

I have to admit, I almost lost it when Ken showed me the picture of my parents earlier. It was a shock seeing them for the first time. I need a moment to compose myself before speaking to what looked like the entire city at the picnic, although I don't recall seeing any black people. But this is the South. I just hope Sera and Peg don't feel uncomfortable in this crowd. I reach a huge log cabin house minutes later that has a large draped porch in front. Even the squirrels are enjoying the sunny day, gathering pine cones and pine needles in preparation for the coming winter.

I can't wait to see my wife! This will be our first time out in Birmingham together. She seemed excited about coming today. Peg and Bee seemed excited, too.

"Hello, is anyone here?" I say, looking through the screen. The front door is open.

"Hello, hello?"

"I guess everyone is down below, enjoying the entertainment," I think, while opening the screen door slowly, looking for some sign of an owner. The humidity in Alabama is like walking in a sauna. "I must find a wash room!" I think, as the sweat pours in little rivulets from my face. I walk down a hall decorated with pictures hanging along its walls. The hall leads to a family room. I am about to walk past the restroom, when I notice my reflection in a mirror that hangs above the wash bowl and a small open window near the toilet. I remember my adoptive parents telling me the agency told them the day my parents gave me up that my biological mother cried until she was so sick they had to call the paramedics. Her husband had to carry her to the car.

The only request my mother had for the agency was to ensure that the family that adopted me be a home full of love and Christian beliefs. I often wondered when I became older, how can a Christian family not have love? I decided when I married Sera that she was the woman for me and the person with whom I wanted to raise a family. Even though we were only able to have one child, that boy is the love of our life. I'm so proud of him and his achievements at Ohio State. Now, knowing my brother Ken, who also has children, it will be delightful to have family gatherings where our children can discuss issues that will someday help our community and hopefully the world.

I find a cabinet near the wash bowl and grab a towel before washing up. After drying my face, I look at my reflection in the mirror. Wow, I am getting older and the small wrinkles under my eyes are showing the long days spent in the operating room. After this weekend, I think it will be nice to take Sera and Robert Jr. on a long vacation, if he can get away from school for a few days. Hopefully, after telling the Stevens family that we are kin, they may want to come with us.

I can hear the crowd below by the lake, not far away, listening to live music and cheering. This community really knows how to have a picnic. In the North, I can't recall ever having a turnout like this, except during football season in Columbus. Hopefully, when Sera comes today she can talk about her plans to run for office, once Negroes are given equal voting rights. It will be great to complete this chapter in our lives that children will someday read about in American history books.

Boy, it's hot! I can't recall a day this hot since we moved here. I think I may want to keep this towel. I will have to see that Peg gets it back to the rightful owner. I've never seen a log home so beautiful and warm, and I notice the furniture has been kept up quite nicely, too. The pine walls hold wonderful pictures of people smiling and holding hands. I am sure they must be family and friends. As I continue toward the front door, ready to begin my walk back to the lake, I notice some family photos that get my attention. There is plenty of Mr. Johnson's history here in this house. I see pictures of family hugging each other and in one picture I notice Ken as a young boy with the same man who I now know as my father, dressed in fishing attire at what appears to be Johnson's Lake. I walk farther down the hall, where I see men dressed in hunting attire with what appears to be an animal that they just shot, laying under their feet. Then another picture of what looks like other picnics, years ago. I start to walk to the door when one picture makes me stop dead in my tracks. My body becomes numb from disbelief while I put my glasses back on.

A picture of Klansmen dressed in their white hooded outfits, sitting on horses? What is this picture doing here and who are these men? As I look closer, I see that the picture of what I thought was game under the hunters' feet was not an animal, but the body of a young Negro boy who was killed for sport. Then I see another picture of a Negro woman that had been hung from a tree at one of the picnics. Looking at the men closely, I recognize some of the faces of the Klansmen.

The ring leader looks like my father and Ken is standing next to him. That picture was taken at this lake? My family is in the Klan? The family I've been wanting to know for all these years has been murdering people here at this lake? I suddenly vomit all my lunch in a nearby trash can near a desk in the hall, and then it registers that I have invited Sera, Peg, and Bee to this picnic that the Klan is hosting.

I must find them before they get here!

Chapter 66

I could have sworn I asked Miss Peg yesterday if she didn't mind bringing the picnic basket with her to church today. Now I have to go clear across town to do something that I hadn't planned on. Thank goodness, Mr. Jameson came to church to hear me speak or I wouldn't have been able to do so. He's not a church-going man, but he loves his guns.

"Mr. Jameson, turn left at that corner there."

"Bee, when you gonna start calling me Edgar?" he says, while looking briefly to his right for other oncoming cars.

"When you start going to church!" I say.

We arrive at the Carson residence and I am surprised to see Mr. Seth sitting on his front porch with his baby girl.

"Now, Mr. Jameson, keep your car running. I'm going to be in and out. Okay?"

"If you answer one question," he says. "If I start going to church, do you think maybe someday, I'll be able to call you Mrs. Jameson?"

"Nigga, please!" I close his door, shaking my head. That man ain't never married nobody. These men say anything to you to get next to you and when they get what they want they act like a bee going from flower to flower. Well, this flower's petals are closed. Ain't no bees 'llowed here!

"Hello, Mr. Seth, how are you today?"

"I'm fine, Bee. How is your afternoon? Looks like we gonna get a hot one today."

"Yes, sir. It's a great day to go on a picnic," I say to him, just before going in the house to retrieve the picnic basket. I return to find him sitting on the Carsons' front steps.

"Now, what you do with your baby, Mr. Seth?"

"I asked my mother to keep an eye on her. So you said you're going on a picnic?" he asks, standing up with his back facing the street.

"Yes, we all going to a picnic! Dr. Carson was asked to speak today," I say, as I walk down the steps right past him in a hurry to get going.

"Wait a minute, Bee. Who all was invited?"

"Mrs. Carson, Miss Peg, and me," I say, turning and looking at him. "I'm bringing my friend, Mr. Jameson, on 'count of the driving and we have to meet them. Can you believe Miss Peg forgot the basket for the picnic?"

Mr. Seth is looking down at the steps as if trying to remember something.

"Mr. Seth, are you okay?" Mr. Jameson honks his horn and I wave at him to wait.

"I didn't realize that Mrs. Carson had arrived in Birmingham."

"Son, you met Mrs. Carson. Mrs. Sera Carson!"

"Peg's cousin, Sera, is Mrs. Carson?"

"Yes. You're scaring me."

"Bee, you're telling me that Sera and Peg are headed for the lake, now?"

"Yes, Johnson's Lake, just outside Birmingham, for food, fun, and entertainment. We gonna have a good time today. There is not a cloud in the sky."

"Bee, take the basket back in the house and have your gentleman friend stay with you until I get back!"

"Say what? Not again, Mr. Seth!"

"Please, Bee, do what I asked you to do! I just hope I'm not too late!"

He runs for his truck and backs it out of the driveway with his tires screeching as I walk over to Mr. Jameson's car.

"Mr. Seth told me to stay here while he goes out to Johnson's Lake to get Miss Sera and Mrs. Carson."

"Johnson's Lake! That's where you wanted me to take you, girl? Don't you know the Klan be having a picnic out there every Sunday and they pick a nigger to string up? Woman, you trying to get us killed?"

I reach for the door of his car and start to open it, screaming. "We gotta go get Miss Sera and Mrs. Carson! How many guns you got?"

"Not enough to fight the Klan!" Jameson says, and drives off with his passenger door hanging open. I run inside with the basket to call June Bug and everybody else I can think of!

Chapter 67

My heart is beating like an African drum as I race down the path which leads to the lake below. The humidity is so high I can barely keep my eyes open as the sweat runs down my face, seemingly aiming at my eyes. How could I have a brother and a family who I've been wanting to know all these years, only to find out that they are members of the most hateful group of people in America? How could I have been so blind? If they touch one hair on Sera's head, there will be hell to pay! I have been kind to Ken and his family and to think he would hurt my wife sends chills up my spine.

I arrive minutes later, still on the path, but not far from the base of the lake. People are laughing and asking me if I saw the entertainment.

"Dr. Carson, is everything alright?" the sheriff asks, as I approach him on the path.

"Where is Ken Stevens?" I ask.

"He is on the platform getting ready to start more entertainment," says a person heading up the path behind the sheriff, drinking what looks like a beer. "It's gonna start soon when they get the opening act off the platform. You better hurry!" That last bit is yelled at me as I continue racing down the path.

"Good, they are still being entertained," I think, while I continue quickly down the path, wondering what kind of entertainment such evil people would most likely enjoy. Then a memory of a postcard one of my adoptive parents' friends had in a family album that was sent to him by a relative from down South made me cry out in anguish and fear for my precious Sera. The picture showed a black man hanging from a tree with a crowd of white faces posing by the body for the photo. We never returned to that house again. As I get closer to the lake, I can hear music playing and the laughter of hundreds of people. Judging by the sounds, I suspect that Sera and her entourage haven't arrived yet. Thank God!

I approach the lake area minutes later and find a crowd gathered around, shouting and screaming, and as I get closer I see my darkest thoughts materialized. Sera and Peg are surrounded by a large group of white people yelling at the top of their lungs. I push my way through the crowd and try to get closer to Sera and Peg.

"Leave us alone!" I hear Peg shout. "We were invited today by Dr. Carson!"

"Niggers, go home! You're not supposed to be here!" I hear someone yell. I knock a few guys to the ground in my determination to get closer.

"Take your damn hands off my wife!" I scream, as a burly man grabs Sera.

"Wife?!" I hear from a distance, as several men wrestle me to the ground. I hear Ken Stevens' voice somewhere next to where I'm pinned down. He directs the crowd to take their hands off of me and they refuse, holding me on the rough ground.

"What the hell is going on?" Ken asks. "This is a respected doctor and a new member of our community."

"This white nigger lover is married to that nigger there!" says the man holding my legs. Then he kicks me in the head, knocking my glasses clear off my face. Blood flows from my temple and the pain is almost unbearable. I suspect I have a fractured skull. Ken, who seems to be in shock, bends down and looks at me eye-to-eye and then turns and looks at Peg and Sera, clearly confused.

"What are they talking about Robert? Is Sera your wife?"

"Yes, Sera is my wife, Ken," I say through the blood pooling in my mouth.

"What?" he screams. "You mean to tell me, this nigger is your *wife?*"

I watch his pupils dilate as he moves toward me, his face distorted with hate and contempt. He spits directly in my face, temporarily blinding my right eye. A man holding a baby a few feet away suggests they take Sera and Peg to a tree. I moan and struggle to get free, but to no avail.

"The entertainment today will put this Klan on the map!" another shouts. "They thought that spraying those niggers in Kelly Ingram Park was something. Wait till Washington, D.C., sees this on the news!"

There is a brief hesitation as I see Ken look at Peg. Their eyes meet silently, communicating something I can't understand. I look through the haze of blood and saliva, trying to find my Sera's face. Looking at Sera, not knowing if we will ever see each other again, I see tears filling her eyes as Klansmen hold her back. We are not facing the platform, but these cruel men taunt my precious wife and her cousin, turning them around so they can see what's in store for them.

"You all are going to end up just like this one!" one savage beast says, as he makes her look at the body that hangs just feet away from her. I can't see the body or Sera's face, but I can see Peg's face start to tremble and shake as her eyes look at some horrific vision and sobs are wrenched from her body. Facing the platform, she lets out the most horrific scream as she looks upon the stage. The man holding her slaps her across the face, but she refuses to stop screaming.

"This is our entertainment!" Ken says. "Let the doctor and his nigger wife see what's in store for them!"

As the men pull me up, Sera is turned around so she can see the stage and starts screaming uncontrollably, her shrieks of horror joining Peg's in a macabre duet. My wife is screaming and calling my name, but I cannot understand what she is saying. But when they finally turn me around, I understand completely.

I can barely see without my glasses. Sweat, blood, and saliva also clouds my vision, but I can tell that a young, light-skinned black man that the Klan must have kidnapped has been hung from a tree. How could so many people be this cold and heartless? The poor man's family will be devastated when they learn that their son is missing.

"You're next!" someone shouts.

The men grab me tighter, while they pull me to my feet. They move me to the platform where hundreds look at me as if watching an animal about to be slaughtered. Seeing more clearly as I get closer, my attention is drawn first to this young man's feet dangling in the air as if he's floating, not hanging from this tree just above the platform that they used earlier for entertainment. Then my eyes slowly travel up the body, confused by the familiarity of his physique and clothing, finally stopping at his face, which I see clearly.

"Robert? Robert! I know this can't be Robert Jr.! He's hundreds of miles away in Ohio, so this can't be Robert!" I think, unwilling to accept the horror in front of me.

Somewhere nearby, I hear one of the men, who seems to be of some importance, talking with the sheriff who has just arrived on the scene after patrolling the path where I passed him earlier. But what he says next mortifies me.

"We picked this nigger up at the airport," the sheriff says. "He was asking for our help, saying he just flew in from Columbus and wanted to know where the Whitfield house was. I remembered Mr. Grant called me a while back saying something about some niggers moving in there, but later Mr. Stevens told me a white doctor lived there and had two high yellow nigger gals working for him. I figured this nigger was going there to see them girls. He was just standing there looking lost, waiting by the telephone booth for someone to pick him up. Said he tried to call, but nobody answered the phone. So, we offered him a ride.

We had to pick a nigger for the picnic today, and I been hearing the niggers are trying to start some trouble because a missing nigger boy was found, and now they want us to go looking for the rest of 'em. Pastor LeCroy called me this morning talking about bringing in the FBI and that King nigger to investigate what's going on in Birmingham. So I was thinking, better not to get any local entertainment this week. We grabbed him to keep things down until we get these local niggers under control. This week, we'll set fire to a couple of crosses, maybe in front of LeCroy's church, and by next Sunday, things'll be back to normal. Don't you worry, Mr. Mayor. I can't recollect ever seeing him before." The sheriff then speaks quietly to me, but I just stand there, unable to look at his face. While the sheriff has been reassuring the mayor, some of the men have been making nooses and telling folks to go get anyone who wants to see the rest of the day's entertainment to come back to the area. Several men and women hurriedly left to spread the news that three more people are about to be lynched.

"Take my son down from that tree, Ken Stevens!" I scream, deafening the crowd as people whisper in stunned silence, apparently not used to white men claiming paternity of a black child. "If you have these men let me loose, I will kill you with my very own hands. TAKE MY SON DOWN FROM THAT TREE!" Stevens looks at me stunned, and then starts laughing maniacally.

"Your son?" he says. "Folks, we got ourselves a whole family entertaining us today!" he shouts, creating a frenzy of yells and cheers from the crowd as people start pouring in from the path. Ken walks over to me to taunt me further and I stop him in his tracks by giving him news that's even more incredible than the revelation that he and his hate-filled cronies have unknowingly killed my son.

"Ken," I whisper, my voice hoarse from screaming, "the boy you just killed is your nephew and I am your older brother, the brother our parents gave up for adoption." Ken's face contorts into disbelief and horror, realizing he is about to kill his own flesh and blood. Stunned and confused, he orders the men to take their hands off us. The crowd continues to roar, oblivious to what is happening around them. Sera, Peg, and I run as one and rush up the platform to untie Robert Jr. from the tree. His lifeless body is still warm, but we all know he is dead.

"We have to get him to a hospital," Sera says, holding him in her arms with tears pouring down her face in a flood of grief. The crowd is quieter now, but starts getting restless, waiting for the grand finale of the picnic.

Shouts of "What's the hold up!" and "Lynch the niggers!" are heard in the distance.

"You see, Ken," my voice getting stronger and louder with the emotion I feel, "we moved everything we had from Ohio, just to get to know you and your family. We didn't want anything from you, except your love. Now, please, let my family pass so we can take our son and arrange for his funeral."

The recently hostile crowd becomes completely silent, either unsure or unable to continue the day's festivities. Then suddenly, several families near the front pack up their picnic baskets and start walking away. Others quickly follow them, obviously having had a change of heart. I guess some of those that are leaving have probably wanted to disentangle themselves and their children from this weekly ritual of horror for some time, but were probably too afraid to act on what they knew in their hearts all along to be wrong. Ken orders some of the men to help us carry Robert Jr. to our vehicle where we gently lay him in the back seat.

"You see this, Ken," I say, looking at him as he stands speechless, watching the diminishing crowd as family after family walks past us on their way out. "No matter how big you think this Klan is here, not every white person in Birmingham hates Negroes."

Suddenly, we hear music and see cars pulling to the side of the road as a group of Negroes and whites appear, walking down the middle of the road, led by Pastor LeCroy and a Catholic priest.

"*We shall overcome,*" they sing. Standing next to Pastor LeCroy, we see Bee, and next to her a frail woman who looks like she can barely make it, but Bee is holding her up.

"Mattie!" Peg says, tears flooding her eyes. Before anyone can speak, the sheriff and his deputies walk past us, billy clubs in hand. As soon as they see them, the marchers stop and Bee says, "Ready, set, aim!" and several dozen shotguns, rifles, and pistols are cocked and aimed at the approaching lawmen, stopping them in their tracks. I hear sirens in the distance and watch the crowd scatter as over a dozen black cars approach. Men in black suits get out and rush to take the sheriff and his deputies into custody. They seem to be talking to a young man who got out of one of the black cars and is pointing out the sheriff and his cronies. He isn't wearing a black suit and we soon recognize Ken Stevens' son, Seth. I look around and can't find Ken, the mayor, or any of the local businessmen, or other influential men who were a part of this tragedy. They have all disappeared. The FBI agents swarm all over the place.

Seth sees Bee and they walk toward us hurriedly. A man approaches me and introduces himself as an FBI agent. He sees Robert Jr.'s dead body and starts questioning me.

Chapter 68

We buried Robert Jr. a few days later in a small cemetery just outside Birmingham where Negroes are allowed to rest. I picked beautiful fresh flowers from the garden in the back yard and instructed the funeral director to place them over his casket where over one hundred flowers were laid. All of us are still in shock and can't believe what happened last Sunday. Thank God for Bee taking care of the daily chores so I do not have to think about the house.

"Can I get you something else, Miss Peg?" Bee asks, while pouring me a cup of coffee at the breakfast table in the kitchen.

"No, Bee, but thank you," I reply. I am not even interested in drinking my customary tea these days. I think how nice it would be to just lay in bed like Sera and Dr. Carson. They have not left their room for days now. I know I must attend to the daily managing of workers here, so that will not be possible. Now I know this man next door, who I have not seen since Sunday, is nothing but evil. I do not understand how he would even want to touch me, knowing that I am the center of what he hates.

I decide to help Bee with the dusting in the family room, just to keep my mind busy, when I am interrupted by Sera and Dr. Carson.

"Would you mind dusting the study?"

"No, Miss Peg, not at all."

"Hello, Sera, Dr. Carson."

"Hello, Peg," Sera says, with a tissue in one hand to dry her tears. "Dr. Carson and I have decided to leave Birmingham. We have decided you can have this house if you want it."

"Yes, Peg, if you would like to keep this house you can, or we will put it up for sale," Dr. Carson says.

"I am lost for words. I never thought about it."

"Being very honest, Peg, neither have we. But I know I can get a director position at a hospital in Ohio. They are opening up a medical college in Toledo and I am sure I can work there."

"You are going to let these cowards get away with all they have done here in Birmingham? I know they put the sheriff and his deputies in jail, but Ken Stevens and his cronies have not been charged with anything. I heard the governor pulled some strings to keep him and the mayor and those other powerful men from being prosecuted. You cannot just let them get away with murder. What about all the rest of the people they have hung each Sunday. What about them, and the ones who they will murder after Robert Jr.?"

"Have a seat, Peg," Dr. Carson says, gesturing to a chair near the big windows that overlook the street.

"Peg, Robert Jr. was our heart. You see, we never thought about a life without him. We wanted him to marry and we could have grandchildren someday, but we know that will never happen now. He's gone."

"Here is the deed to the house and the keys to the car. You can have all of it, Peg," my cousin says.

"All my life I have loved you like a sister, Sera. I remember when my parents died and you decided at a young age to take care of me even though you were a young lady yourself. I knew you could have done so much more if you had not had to take care of me. I would like to thank you for the love you have shown me. I really do appreciate you and also Dr. Carson for allowing me to continue my education, while providing me room and board and a job. I can never repay you for all you have done."

I pause, gathering my thoughts and courage to make sure they understand what I am about to say. "After I moved to Birmingham, I was repeatedly raped and was unable to tell anyone, because I feared for the safety of this family."

"Raped!" Sera and Dr. Carson exclaim in unison, jumping to their feet.

"Yes, raped. And although all my tears are dried up now, the pain is still here inside me. Dr. Carson, the man you came here to finally meet and love as your brother is the man who has been raping me. I was told not to tell anyone, or we all would die."

"Ken Stevens has been repeatedly raping you? After all you have done for his family; giving his son your kidney!"

"Yes, that is what I am saying and he is the father of my child. I believe that this child inside me deserves a chance at life, even though it was conceived with someone who is so wicked. I tried to terminate this pregnancy, but I just could not do it. My body is still not doing so well with the transplant of my kidney. So, I think I am going to take it easy and relax for a few days if that is okay. You know, since the operation, I just have not had much time to take it easy."

The conversation stops when we hear the back door slam shut loudly, and we go to investigate. Knowing that it could not have been Bee or the ground crew, because no one ever enters the house slamming the door that loud, I fear that it might have been the Klan. We look around, concluding that we didn't hear someone coming in, but someone leaving the house. I look out of the kitchen window and see Ronnie slowly walking to his house as he leaves our backyard. Could he have heard what I just told Sera and Dr. Carson? If so, the news could be devastating to him. I am sure of it.

Chapter 69

The following day, I decide to get up with the birds. Still not knowing if Ronnie heard what was said the day before, I am concerned. If he did hear my conversation with the Carsons about his father raping me, I am not sure if he would mention this to his parents or even Seth. I am waiting for Bee to arrive which is normally around eight, because I want to help prepare supper today. I know Dr. Carson will be moving Sera clear away from this place soon. Around noon, I glance over to the porch next door and see Ronnie writing in his journal. I can only imagine what he is writing and I would dare not ask him to divulge something so private. I can tell he is getting better, because I have not seen his home nurse recently. Maybe she took some time off after her husband and his deputies were arrested and charged with the murder of Robert Jr.

I hear Mrs. Stevens talking loudly, saying she is leaving with Seth's baby. "Ronnie, I put a pitcher of water next to your chair. If you need anything, call me at Dr. Mason's number next to the phone. Okay? It shouldn't take too long, since this is Emily's first baby checkup."

I make sure she is gone by waiting ten minutes before I go over to check on Ronnie.

"Bee, please keep an eye out for Mrs. Stevens and let me know if you see her coming, okay?" I say on my way out.

"Yes, Miss Peg. I sure will," she replies, as she cuts up potatoes to make a nice potato salad. I grab a pitcher of lemonade and walk slowly, trying not to spill any as I make my way across the yard to the porch where Ronnie is sitting and staring off into the distance.

"Hello, Ronnie. I brought over a cool pitcher of lemonade. Can I pour you a glass?"

"Sure, Miss Peg, that would be great," Ronnie replies, struggling with each word. He appears to be in some kind of pain.

"How have you been, Ronnie?" I ask, knowing how painful his recovery must be, since I am the one who gave him my kidney and am dealing with my own recovery. The doctors still have to wait to see if his body accepts my kidney. I pray that it does not reject it. I want so badly for Ronnie to live. He and Seth, and Seth's little daughter, are the only hope for redemption that the Stevens family has.

"I'm not feeling so good today. I think the humidity is making it hard to catch my breath," he says, pausing to breathe in a gulp of air. "Can I ask you something, Miss Peg?"

"You can ask me anything."

"Why didn't you tell me that you were the one who gave me a kidney?"

"It is much more complicated than it appears, Ronnie." Now I am sure Ronnie knows all that was said yesterday. I am sure more questions will follow.

"Can you tell me why you haven't called the police and told them my father has been raping you?" he asks, his eyes tearing up.

"Ronnie, I have been wondering the same thing. Let me try and explain, though. Here in America it is very hard for Negroes to go to the authorities for help. Sometimes the people you go to for help can be the very same ones who want to do harm to you."

"I don't understand, Miss Peg."

"Let's just say I would not be here today if I had said anything."

"Can I ask one more question?" Ronnie asks. I nod, expecting the worst.

"Are you really having my father's child?"

"Yes, son, I am."

"How could my father do this to you? I don't understand how my father can be so cold and hateful. They act like I don't know that they hate Negroes. I hear how they talk about them, like they're not human." He pauses again. "One day, I went to the basement and found a Klansman robe and several pictures that I didn't quite understand. Is my father a racist?"

"Yes, son, he is."

"What about my brother? Is he a racist, too?"

"I think he was at first, but I know he is not now. I honestly think your brother is kind and gentle." It is my turn to pause. I decide to be frank with this rapidly maturing young man. "Ronnie, I believe I love your brother."

"Boy, is it hot out here!" Ronnie's face has turned red and he picks up a glass, pours lemonade in it, and drinks the contents in one big gulp.

"Do you mind if I read this poem I wrote," he says, changing the subject.

"Yes, Ronnie, please do." I smile at him, knowingly. I watch as Ronnie grabs his journal from the table next to him. He is still having a hard time breathing.

"Okay, here goes."

What is love…?

Love is how you feel when you think of the one you love you begin to smile.

"You know, Miss Peg, like the day we met on that sunny day by your garden and we laughed all day," he says, before reading the next line of his poem.

Love is one thing everyone wants. "Even if they're full of hate. Like my father who still wants love from his family, even though the group he is in teaches the opposite."

Love is not selfish for it lasts for eternity. "Miss Peg, don't be selfish and start to feel hate for my father who has done you wrong. For your love will out shine all the hate. Take his bad and turn it to good. Love will overcome your fear." Ronnie closes his journal and seems thoughtful.

"I've grown very fond of you, Miss Peg. I didn't look at the color of your skin or what kind of family you're from. I didn't care. Then when I found out yesterday that you gave your kidney to me, I couldn't think of anything but joy. I was preparing to die, and now I'm preparing to live! I am so grateful that God brought you into my life and gave you the desire to help people you barely know.

"Not everyone would do that. Not even my own family from New York and even some so-called friends from our church. You did this, Miss Peg, in spite of what my father has been doing to you. Promise me that you will never change."

"I promise, Ronnie." I notice that his words became clearer and his breathing steadier as he read the poem and talked to me. It was as if he was healing himself with his own words. I feel honored that I was chosen to help this young man when he needed it most. Trying to change the subject, and keep from crying, I suggest that he needs some ice for his lemonade and offer to go back home to get him some.

"Sure," he says. "But you're more than welcome to get some from our icebox. We have plenty." His smile is infectious and reassuring, but his breathing has become raspy again. It's as if he had just enough breath to read his poem and talk to me about his feelings.

Having never been in the Stevens house before, I had always wondered what it was like inside. I open the screen door that leads to the kitchen and pass a small table that is in the center of the room. Family pictures are hanging in the hall where an antique writing desk sits against one wall. Then I notice the man I call "He," smiling and holding his wife's hand in a photograph. Another picture shows him being honored for his "good deeds." "District Attorney Kenneth Stevens, Man of The Year." If they only knew! The city, that is. All the pain this man has caused this city and its constituents while keeping up a façade of respectability. The FBI should lock this man in the darkest hole and throw away the key.

"Did you find the ice, Miss Peg?" Ronnie calls from the back porch.

"Yes, Ronnie, I will be there in a second," I say, turning my head toward the back of the house so he can hear me clearly. I return to the porch where Ronnie is fast asleep.

"Wow, that was fast, young man!"

When the body needs rest, it will automatically shut down. This young man has been through so much in these few months that I have known him. He is always so kind and loving whenever I am in his presence. He looks so peaceful, sleeping in his favorite chair. I hate to disturb him.

"Ronnie, I have a glass of ice cold lemonade for you. Would you like me to help you with it?" I ask, basking in the warmth and beauty of the day. "The days are so beautiful this time of year and I am sure you have been getting lots of sleep on this back porch. What time is your mother returning from the doctor with the baby?" He remains still, his eyes closed.

"Ronnie? Ronnie?"

I cannot believe he is already worn out this time of the day, although his breathing difficulties may be exhausting the poor child. I touch his arm and look for some sort of movement.

"Ronnie. Wake up, Ronnie. Wake up," I say, as my voice quivers and I wipe tears away. My heart grows very heavy as I wait for some kind of response, but I do not get any.

"You have to wake up. You just have to," I sob.

Ronnie closed his eyes, never opening them again to what we know as life. I believe he wanted to go to a place where he wouldn't feel pain, sorrow, betrayal, and the sickness that he has had for years. This time, I believe what he overheard about his father made him give up on living. It had to cause him pain, knowing that his father, the rock that should have been his family's foundation, was not stable and not capable of providing the strength for a loving home to stand without falling in times of storms. This family's house was built on a sandy beach where the sand was blown away when the storm came. How awful it must be to trust someone for your entire life and find out one day that the person you love never existed and it is all a lie.

My heart has been broken beyond repair this week with the murder of my nephew, and now the passing of a dear friend. No more suffering,

Ronnie. "I will miss you," I whisper, looking down at his young, innocent face. Everything I went through, now seems so insignificant. A dear friend is gone, and I know if his mother walks in on me next to her dead son there will be a lynching tonight. I stop at the top of my back steps and glance over to the back porch where I first saw Ronnie and wave good-bye. After I tell Bee that Ronnie is gone, we sit at the kitchen table, waiting. Waiting to know that Ronnie's body has been discovered and that he will be tended to in preparation for burial. Waiting to hear Ronnie's mother scream.

"My son! My son!" she cries, the sound of her voice piercing the quietness of the day with the agonized mourning of a mother who has lost a child.

"I will never forget you, Ronnie," I promise to the blue sky and the white clouds that bear witness to our grief.

Chapter 70

There was a cross burned on my lawn last night. And if I find out who in the hell did it, there will be hell to pay. I don't know who thinks I have turned my back on what I've known for my entire life. Whoever thinks this is mistaken. Can I be held responsible for my brother's actions, loving a nigger and having a child with her?

It's been days since Ronnie's passing and I miss him with all my heart. We all knew when we talked to Dr. Mason that once he received a kidney he was not out in the clear until his body completely accepted it. Dr. Mason's conclusion is, that given all the years he waited, his body just gave up before it could accept or reject the kidney. But one thing I am grateful for is the donor that gave us time to spend with him, even though his body was just too tired to go on living. A man here in America should never have to bury his own children. Not a white man, that is.

I planned for him to see the world and work hard on maintaining segregation here in America. I wanted him to ensure the white race would never die. Now, for the neighbors who lost their son, if they hadn't mixed the races, their son would be here today. If Robert had just been honest with me from the beginning! I can never be part of his life and honestly I don't think they want anything to do with the Stevens family, knowing it's because of me that their son is dead and the law cannot touch me. The governor and I are from the same Masonic lodge and he called in a favor from another Mason in Washington to keep the FBI from investigating any further, after their initial arrests.

Those charges may not even stand up in court, because who's going to testify against the sheriff and his deputies? I've already guaranteed they'll be released on their own recognizance. I own this city, and even the mayor has to answer to me and that's the way it shall stay. I swear the day will come when all those niggers who marched out to the lake last Sunday will get their day at a picnic, and if for some reason I overlook any of them, they will think twice about ever doing that again in Birmingham.

I feel tears welling up, sitting in Ronnie's favorite chair. He always loved sitting on this porch. We built it when he was small, so he'd have a place to watch the world go by, since he couldn't run and play like the other kids. Ronnie used to love to just sit and write about life and all the beauty in the world. He used to love to listen to the birds call each other and watch the rabbits run and hide from Mr. Hawk. That was his name for the bird that used to rob the nests of small animals. It was really funny to see how animals, usually the squirrels and little rabbits, would just come up and eat right out of Ronnie's hands, as if he knew them all by name. I don't know how he did it, but that boy made everyone and everything love him. He was our angel.

I look up at the moon and close my eyes and I can feel him near. Even though I am feeling down and tears fill my eyes, the thought of my precious son makes me smile. I will miss you, Ronnie. I loved you so. Reaching for the tissues he always had on the stool next to his favorite chair, I accidentally brush up against the journal where he kept his private thoughts. I wonder what he was thinking in the moments before he closed his eyes for the final time. Opening the journal to the last page he wrote on, what I see pierces my heart to the core and I cry into the night knowing my son is in a place I'll never see in this life, or the next.

I'm grateful for you Lord and for a wonderful family.

I'm thankful for your grace and mercy you have shown me.

I'm thankful for the donor who helped give me life. Thank you for Miss Peg who unselfishly gave her kidney which gave me additional weeks with my family. Bless her and her family.

Oh and Lord bless the Baby Emily let her grow up healthy and strong. Miss Peg is carrying my father's child please let her have a life of change. Different from the world we live in today and may my father's unborn child find peace and love for every human being, although my father didn't. I'm tired of this family mistreating people, but if you can, let one of the Stevens feel true love towards everyone.

Peg gave Ronnie her kidney? I'm grateful for her kindness, although I can never publicly state so. But carrying my child? That can never happen. I have to find a way to get rid of her and this baby, or what I publicly stand for will be ruined and so will my marriage. I have to find a way, immediately.

Chapter 71

Morning is my favorite part of the day. I am praying that Dr. Carson and Sera change their minds about moving back to Ohio. I really want them to give Birmingham a second chance, because not all white people here are racist killers. Even some ex-Klan members helped us with Robert Jr.'s body during their mass exodus from their last picnic. That innocent word, "picnic," derived from the 17th century French word *"pique,"* or its colloquial variant *"pique-nique,"* which means "each gets a bit," has been turned into something vile, twisted, perverted, and debased by the Klan. Every American should know, what was once a nice word used mainly during the summer months, will always have a different meaning to us.

Dr. King wrote, "Injustice anywhere is a threat to justice everywhere," in his "Letter from Birmingham Jail." He wrote those words in answer to the letter from the eight white clergymen from Birmingham that denounced the sit-ins and protests held in the city last spring. They said Dr. King was an "outside agitator." But, he said he was in Birmingham, because injustice is in Birmingham.

Dr. King's statements have created one of the most powerful and motivating forces behind the Civil Rights Movement. The cry for justice is coming from the watery graves of Africans fallen from slave ships; from the unmarked graves of slaves that never saw freedom; from the torn and broken bodies of the lynched blacks that never saw justice; and from the beaten and bitten bodies of those who march for it. It is too loud to ignore, too urgent to dismiss, and too strong to defeat.

How can the Carsons give up on justice? How can they leave "the most thoroughly segregated city in the United States," knowing nothing will change unless we stand with Dr. King and Rev. Shuttlesworth and demand it? Dr. King was jailed last April 12, and within a month the stores in downtown Birmingham were forced to integrate just because men stood up and said "no" to injustice. I have lived the injustices I first read about and then witnessed firsthand. My thoughts turn to acts of injustice closer to home, as I think about all of the losses in this family that Dr. Carson so longed for.

I am still disturbed by Ronnie's death, and I know how his family must feel, having lost Robert Jr., who was like a son to me. I now understand the concept of karma and how balance is maintained in the universe. The vile human being that oversaw Robert Jr.'s execution for the crime of having Negro blood has paid for his sins. Another innocent life has been taken. Only this time, it was someone he loved just as much as Robert Jr.'s parents and I loved him. Poor Ronnie. I know he and Robert Jr. are rejoicing in heaven now, but that does not make me miss them any less.

I sit outside enjoying the sun and keeping an eye on Seth's back porch for signs of him moving about inside his parents' home, where he and his mother have been sequestered for days. To my surprise, he emerges from mourning with a cup of coffee in his hand. I want so badly to tell him I am so sorry for the passing of his brother. I think he would do the same if he knew the real truth about Robert Jr.'s murder. I am sure his sick father has told him some bizarre story about what happened at the picnic.

"Hello, Seth."

"Hello, Peg, how are you today?"

"I am alright, I guess. How are you and your family? I am so sorry about Ronnie."

"I know you are. I also know how much you loved him. I used to come home early from work to watch you all laugh and play in your garden."

"We did have some wonderful times there."

"I'll miss my buddy." His voice quavers slightly and he pauses, wiping at his eyes. "I want to take you out for a nightcap after supper, if that's possible."

"Now, where would you like to take me?" I say, hoping to lift his spirits at least momentarily.

"I don't know, but I'll let you choose a place where we can talk, if you don't mind. I just need to be in your company tonight. Let's make it around eight."

"Eight it is," I reply, smiling broadly as he forces his own smile, then goes back inside.

I continue to just sit and enjoy the warmth of the sun. It has not been a good summer. Governor "Segregation Now, Segregation Tomorrow, Segregation Forever" Wallace tried to prevent black students from attending the University of Alabama, but the National Guard sent by President Kennedy made sure the black students were granted admittance. The next day, Medgar Evers was killed in Mississippi.

However, the event that has given me the most pride and joy happened just a few weeks later. A black woman named Mary Hamilton was arrested during a demonstration in nearby Gadsden, but she refused to answer questions in court unless she was addressed as "Miss." It was a victory for all the black women in the South who have been called by their first names their entire lives, even by whites young enough to be their children. That was one of the things I so appreciated about my young friend, Ronnie. I was always "Miss Peg" to him. I hear "Miss Mary" was released from jail last week, after refusing to pay a contempt of court fine. I am sure this is not the last we will hear of this!

Seth comes out on his porch and occasionally turns around to smile at me and see if I am watching him. What a handsome man! After Robert Jr. and Ronnie's deaths, I think we really need each other tonight.

Chapter 72

Summer has passed and it's now September. My family is still grieving over Ronnie's death. Mom decided to cook her famous pot roast today for the first time since Ronnie died, and Dad and I are happy to be at the table enjoying every bite. My father has no idea that it was me that called the FBI the day the Negroes marched to the lake. I still do not know how he and his cronies got away from the authorities that day. It wasn't the first time the FBI has been here investigating the Klan. They came last spring during all the demonstrations.

Peg and I secretly watched Dr. King on television last month, when he and thousands of Negroes marched on Washington, D.C. His words were so inspiring and so eloquent; it made me realize Negroes have strong spirituality and faith in God, unlike anything I've seen in the white race, except for Father Michaels. He has organized members of the congregation, even some former Klan members to support the Civil Rights Movement and they marched with Dr. King last month. He was brave to join with the Negro minister and members of his church marching to the lake that day. I was afraid there would be repercussions for him, but some of the former Klansmen that know the KKK's tactics kept watch on the church and the parsonage, making sure he was not harmed.

No one ever publicly threatened him or tried to harm him. I guess white clergymen are not on the Klan's list, even when they are labeled "nigger lovers." The other white clergy in the city seem resolute in their support of segregation, although a couple of Protestant ministers, one from an Episcopalian church and one from a Lutheran church, marched in Washington. I read somewhere that the only denomination that condemned slavery from the start was the Quakers.

I'm just glad the worst and the best summer of my life is over. I have spent as much time as I can with Peg, but our clandestine meetings frustrate me. I want to proudly walk down the street with her and take her to a fine restaurant, but I know I would only put us both in danger. So, I have to be satisfied with taking her to an isolated spot once or twice a week to talk and hold her close to me, dreaming of the day when we can be together openly.

"Son," my dad says, laying his napkin on his finished plate. He pauses and puts his hands behind his head, leaning his chair back on two legs. "I have some good news. I want you to come with me tonight as we embark on a new era in America."

"I have plans tonight, Dad," I say, looking at him with a blank expression. I wonder where he was at my age on a Saturday.

"Well, your plans are gonna have to wait tonight. The other Klansmen have been looking at me with some doubt after finding out my long-lost brother is a nigger lover and my eldest son called the FBI to raid our last picnic, but I think after this meeting tonight they will have no doubt on how I feel." I'm speechless. My father must have used his connections to find out that it was me that called the FBI. I already knew about Dr. Carson, because Peg told me that he is the brother that my father's parents gave up for adoption.

"Why would the Klan think you're not with them?" I ask, ignoring the two bombshells he just dropped on me. I'm glad my mother is in the living room watching TV.

"The past few months, the Klan has been burning crosses on our lawn and I've been removing them before you and your mama woke up. So this meeting I am calling tonight is important, and you will have to attend in order to ease their minds and show them that we are still strong in our beliefs."

"Yes, sir," I reply reluctantly. I know there is no backing out of this one. I have to get a message to Peg that I won't be able to see her tonight, after all. I am sure she will understand. I sure hope she does.

Chapter 73

L ater that evening, after listening to the radio and also making sure that Peg knows we cannot meet tonight, my father and I smoke our pipes, and then we hop in my truck and head to an undisclosed location.

"Where are we going, Dad?"

"Turn right here, son," he says, directing me down a familiar road. My headlights shine on a man I know all too well; one who has clout with the Klansmen.

"Hello, Sheriff," my father says, opening the door. I greet the sheriff with a nod, wondering if he knows I was the one that caused him to get arrested. My father had to pull a lot of strings to get the sheriff and his deputies out so quickly. I hear they have been keeping a low profile while awaiting their trial. I understand their case is going to be heard in the circuit court.

Dad's nervous, because one of the circuit court judges is committed to giving the Negroes justice, and is not going to give any leniency to those accused of murdering Robert Carson Jr. Judge Rives is the same one that got those children's expulsions overturned last spring when they were arrested after the demonstration that had the entire country and the world looking at Birmingham with revulsion. I went to school with his son, but I never knew how they felt about Negroes until recently. I think I need to look up my old classmate now that I know we have so much in common.

"Hello, Ken! I sure hope you have a good reason for dragging me away from my family at this time of night!"

"Yes, I do, Sheriff. Just wait and see!"

We pull up not far from the cabin near the quarry where we used to go camping and swimming. I know this spot now as the spot where Peg and I first kissed. I call it our secret place. My former best friend Patrick is the only one that knows about our secret place, but I don't think I'll have any problems from him. He's been out of circulation since nearly killing himself with his own shotgun. The Grants are telling the community that he accidently shot himself while cleaning his gun, but I know better. I will find a way to make him pay for all the wrong he's done. I know now why he did it, and how he himself was a victim, but that is no justification for his crimes. I cannot allow him to continue to rape and kill children.

I direct my attention to the men in the cabin as they talk about Klan issues, smiling at me and greeting me warmly, obviously unaware that I am the one who called the FBI.

"Why are they gathered here tonight? What is my father going to do?" I wonder, while ten men take their seats around a large wooden table.

"Gentleman, I want you to know what I am getting ready to say is something that will scare the niggers for life. I was asked by our national board of Klansmen to gather a team here in Birmingham. So I hand selected Klansmen who I thought could keep the upmost secrecy. There is a church here in Birmingham that the teenage niggers marched from this past spring when they were demanding equal rights. Do you men know the church I'm talking about?"

"Yes," the sheriff says. "The church on Sixteenth Street?"

The fool is answering a question with a question, as if he really didn't know what church they marched from last May.

"Good, because we plan to bomb that church right in the middle of their Sunday service!" my dad says, dropping a bombshell that has everyone at the table gasping in shock and eagerly leaning forward to hear the gory details of this proposed act of terror. "Since that Martin Luther King Jr. calls himself a preacher, let's give him hundreds of funerals to preside over!" The men cheer and laugh like they've just been informed that the South had won the Civil War, after all.

"What God do they think will deliver them from the wrath of the white race and the decent white folks in this city after they had the audacity to march against our treasured Sunday tradition, invade our university, and sit next to us at lunch counters downtown? They are lucky the Civil War ended the way it did. What makes them think if we can get rid of Lincoln, we won't get rid of their black asses?"

My stomach turns and I feel nauseated.

"Are you okay, son?" the mayor asks.

"I'm fine, just ate something that upset my stomach." The sheriff looks at me intently without blinking, as if looking for some indication that I'm lying. It sickens me to think these men would go to this length to hold a race of people down, that they would desecrate the house of God without any fear of Him. I'd think after killing his own nephew, then losing his own son, my father would have had enough. But his standing with this community of evil men is more important to him than anything, including his own soul.

"A truck will deliver the explosives tonight. They will be planted inside the church where no one will suspect them. We will keep watch, so no whites go in the area in the morning. Sheriff, you have to set out a road block a few blocks away and pretend the city is having a gas leak. Don't worry about the people in the area; just don't let anyone enter but the Negroes. I hope they have a full house!" The men laugh long and hard, slapping the table.

I look at the sheriff and he is wearing a smile from Alabama to Virginia.

"I'll take care of the roadblock on one condition. Your son Seth rides with me," the sheriff says.

"I'm sure Seth won't mind," my father says, jubilant now that he's back leading his Klan brothers. "Right, Seth?" I dare not say a word, only nodding when I need to do so.

"Sunday morning, all you men need to be in church with your wives so you can be seen. Do I make myself clear?"

"Yes, Grand Dragon!" they say in unison. Then, they stand up, shaking each other's hands and nodding in agreement.

We all walk back quietly to our vehicles. The Klansmen have lowered their level of excitement and anticipation to prevent creating any suspicion among family and others who are unaware of the terrorist plot to kill hundreds of people. If only I could get to a phone!

The sheriff jumps back in the truck with us more excited than I've ever seen him.

"Ken, we are blessed to have you still in charge of the Klan! We won't let you down!"

"Good! Make sure you have all the men in place at six a.m., sharp. Okay, Sheriff?"

"Will do, Ken!"

I know my father is not going to let me out of his sight to get to a phone, but I have to find a way to get word to this congregation without him or anyone else in the Klan knowing. I have to figure out how to keep people away from that church tomorrow!

"I can't let them murder an entire church congregation," I think, while driving us home. My father is sleeping like a baby in the middle passenger seat, at peace now that he has won back the respect of the Klan. I have to get a message to Peg tonight to get in touch with the FBI. But how?

Chapter 74

I've been up all night trying to figure out a way to warn Peg and the others about the bombing the Klan is planning for this morning at a church near downtown. If I call the FBI now, the Klan will know it was someone within the group who attended the meeting last night. I'm sure it won't take my father long to figure out it was me, as he obviously has friends in Washington that told him who called the FBI before. And I know the sheriff is suspicious, which may explain the crosses on our lawn. That was probably a warning.

My family will be dead by Monday if word gets out that I tipped off the FBI, which is why I know my father hasn't told anyone about me calling them the day his nephew was murdered. I'm going to watch the Carson residence to see if Peg or anyone else comes outside, even for just for a brief moment. But before I do, I must keep an eye on this strange car that I noticed earlier, when we arrived home from the meeting tonight, parked next door.

"Who can it be?" I think, heading downstairs to make coffee before the sheriff is scheduled to pick me up. The phone rings just as I reach the kitchen.

"Hello?"

"I'll pick you up in ten minutes," the voice says, and then I hear a dial tone. Great! I only have ten minutes to get word to Peg. But how?

There's no sign of Peg next door as the minutes fly by. Exactly ten minutes after the terse call, I hear the sheriff's car horn, indicating he's already waiting out front. I glance outside, making sure it really is the sheriff, and I notice his car is blocking the view of the mystery car from my back entrance all the way to the Carson's home. "This is it!" I think.

I turn the porch light on out front and yell through the screen door, telling the sheriff that I will be there shortly. Then on my way out to the porch, I notice through the windows that face the Carson home that Peg is making herself a cup of coffee in the kitchen. I get her attention and gesture for to her to meet me in my kitchen. She uses caution while walking through our properties and quickly makes it to my kitchen where we speak just above a whisper, knowing if we are caught I will not be able to get us out of this situation.

"Leave this house when you hear the sheriff pull off. Okay?" I say, and she nods quickly, looking anxious. "Peg don't attend church today, and call everyone you know and tell them not to go to church this morning. Something bad is going to happen today, and I repeat, do not go to church today!"

Afraid to talk to her any longer, I quickly leave her in our kitchen and suddenly run into the sheriff who is walking through the house, just feet away from the kitchen entrance.

"Who were you talking to Seth? Is your dad up already?" the sheriff asks.

"Talking to? I'm not talking to anyone, Sheriff. Just thinking out loud." I'm surprised to see him sneak a peak in the kitchen. I'm hoping Peg is well-hidden, or he will surely see her if she stayed where she was when I left her.

"Sheriff?"

"Let's go!" the sheriff says. I'm sure he didn't see anything, but he looks back at the kitchen as we leave. I'm really hoping Peg will have enough time to warn the others!

Chapter 75

Thank God, the sheriff did not think to look under the kitchen table. He was only a couple of feet away when Seth called him. I leave immediately; making sure no one sees me as I go back to my house. I hurriedly get dressed and head downstairs, just as Bee walks in from the kitchen.

"What are you doing here today? Never mind. I am glad you came!" I say, tumbling over my words in my haste to get out and spread the news Seth has given me.

"I woke up early this morning, Miss Peg, and something told me to come here this morning. I know it was the Holy Spirit. I called a friend to drive me."

We head quickly out the door and I brief Bee while we walk out to the street.

"We have to tell people not to go to church today, no matter what church it is!"

"Not go to church? Miss Peg, have you been drinking?"

"We have to get people to stay home!" I shout to get her to see I am dead serious.

"Well, we can try," she replies with a concerned look on her face. "But don't you think it would be better if we just called?"

"No, we have to tell people so they can tell others! Every black church in Birmingham is in danger!"

"What's going on?!" she asks. As we get into the car, I happen to see the man driving is the same one who drove Bee from the church the day we went to the lake. We pull abruptly away from the curb.

"All I know is we have to warn people something bad is going to happen at a black church!"

We pull up to several churches and warn the people not to go inside. Some agree, while others continue with their Sunday routine.

A pastor of a Holiness church says it best, I think: "If we are scared to go to God's house, we should be scared to march and walk in demonstrations. How can we walk by faith in one part of our lives and not the other? So many times, we have been threatened with aggression, but we continue to walk without thinking of what a group of people would do to us as a people."

He continues with his impromptu sermon: "We often face repercussions on our walk toward equal rights. We suffer the nighttime visits from racist groups that leave crosses burning in our yards; rocks thrown through our windows; and even the nights that the Klan comes and drags our loved ones off, never to see them again. Unless we have the privilege of burying them, days or even weeks later, or not at all, because their bodies are never found. Think of all the grieving mothers who have had to bury their children in America without justice. I say we are blessed to have God's grace and protection. Rev. Martin Luther King Jr. said if we are wrong, then the Constitution is wrong!" The congregation standing outside the church bursts into shouts of "Amen," as the sermon ends. I concur.

"We have one more church to get to, Miss Peg and then I believe we've hit all the churches in Birmingham," Bee says, with a calm look on her face.

"What church is that?" I say absently, thinking about the Holiness preacher's words.

"The Sixteenth Street Baptist Church near downtown," she replies.

"Okay. We need to get to the church as soon as possible," I say, focusing again on our mission.

When we get close to Sixteenth Street, we see the streets leading to the area where the church is located are blocked off and sheriff's deputies are patrolling the area. These are the same men that were jailed for Robert Jr.'s murder and they are already out on the street. I start to feel very uneasy.

"What's the problem, officer?" Bee asks, rolling down her window.

"Oh, there's just a gas line leak and we have to block off this area. It's a small leak, nothing to worry about."

I wonder why sheriff's deputies are out on a Sunday morning, blocking off streets for a gas leak. Where are the local police and where are the firemen in case of a fire? And I do not see anyone from the gas company, either.

"Something is not right, Bee. Something is not adding up." Bee's gentleman friend, Mr. Jameson, is ready to go. "Look, ladies, this ain't my thing. My name ain't Martin Luther King!" he says jokingly, but there's an anxious look on his face and he keeps looking around nervously.

240

Chapter 76

"Sheriff, we've been out all morning, driving around making sure no cars driven by white people enter this area. The coffee I drank this morning has me wanting to use the restroom. Can you pull over at a gas station so I can relieve myself?"

"No problem, Seth. I need to piss, too," the sheriff replies.

"There's a station just a block over, close by the post office."

"Great!"

There is also a pay phone inside that station. I hate to think what will happen if Peg didn't warn the church! I wasn't able to tell her which church, because I couldn't remember the name or the location. Now, I have to make a call to the church and let them know that there is a bomb hidden somewhere inside. We arrive at the gas station and the sheriff decides to get the county car filled up.

"Fill her up, Frank," he says to the attendant. "And check the oil, why don't ya."

"Will do, Sheriff," Frank says.

I rush to the back of the station where the whites only restroom is located and flush the toilet, just in case the sheriff is listening, and then walk around to the front and go inside to buy a doughnut.

"Looks like it's my turn! Now, this may take a minute," the sheriff says, laughing.

"It's all yours, Sheriff!" I say, laughing back at him, trying to mimic his jovial mood. My eyes follow him as he disappears around the corner of the building. This may be my only chance to use the phone, but then realize I don't have any coins. Frank is outside checking the oil. I go to the door and ask him for some change to use the phone.

"No problem, Seth. Just reach inside the drawer and help yourself," he replies.

"Thanks!"

Nickels in hand, I grab the Yellow Pages and look up the Sixteenth Baptist Church.

"Yes, there it is!" I say, nervously putting two nickels in the pay phone.

"Hello, Sixteenth Street Baptist Church. How may I help you?" a lady says on the other end.

"There's a bomb in the church! Please get everyone out!"

"Whoever this is, please stop playing on the phone!"

"No, you don't understand," I say, suddenly realizing they must get bomb threats frequently. I desperately try to get her to listen, whispering to make sure I'm not overheard in case a customer or the sheriff comes in. "There really is a bomb in the church; so, please, get everyone out, now!"

"Please don't play on this phone! We've had enough of these prank calls!" the lady says in a scolding tone, just before hanging up the receiver.

"Hello," the lady says, as I interrupt her.

"THERE IS A BOMB IN THE CHURCH. GET EVERYONE OUT!"

There is only a dial tone on the other end. This lady must think this is some kind of sick joke and I know she's not taking me seriously. I look over my shoulder and I get a glimpse of the sheriff walking towards his car, where Frank is cleaning off the dipstick. I hang up immediately, hoping Peg is having better luck contacting all the churches in Birmingham. I'm praying that this Sixteenth Street Church was one on her list, since I won't be able to contact the church again, and even if I could, I can't get the lady at the church to understand that this is not a crank call this time.

I will have to stay in the car with the sheriff until he gets news or we hear the sounds of destruction that are soon to come. This city will go down as the site of one of the biggest mass murders in the history of the KKK, and I can't live with that.

"So, who were you talking to on the phone, Seth?"

I'm speechless. I had not realized he'd seen me on the phone. He pulls over a block from the gas station and parks the car.

"I want to know who in the hell you called, Seth, and I want to know, now!" He pulls his gun out of its holster and points the muzzle at me, pushing it into my side so no one walking by can see. Suddenly, there is a loud noise that shakes the entire area. The sheriff's door is blown off by the blast, spilling him out on the pavement, as his gun drops on the floorboard of the car.

Chapter 77

"**B**ee, something is going on here! This just does not seem right, at all. I am worried and I fear that someone will die today, unless we do something about it."

"Miss Peg, let's just ask the officer again?"

"Okay."

Bee's friend is so nervous he has finally dropped his happy-go-lucky façade and is now deathly quiet as he looks around for danger. He is hesitant to go back to the blockade, but obliges Bee's request.

"Excuse me, sir, but I left something at the church and was wondering if we can go in and pick it up, please. It's very important, sir." Bee is very persuasive and sincere, talking to a young deputy who does not respond. There is a line of cars forming in the street behind us. Each second that goes by, I am getting even more frightened, because we cannot do anything to warn this church. I look through my side window and notice a white couple and, looking closer, I see it is a priest and a nun. They get out of their vehicle and the priest starts asking the officer questions.

"Is everything okay?" the nun asks, as she looks into our car, while the priest talks to the deputy.

"No, ma'am. Something is terribly wrong and we need to warn somebody."

"Wrong? Let me get Father Michaels." The nun quickly returns with the priest by her side.

"Young lady, my name is Father Michaels. Sister Clara informed me that you think there may be a problem."

"Hello, Father, Sister Clara. My name is Peg, and this is Bee, and Mr. Jameson."

"Just call me Edgar, Father," Mr. Jameson says, shaking hands with the priest. "You, too, ma'am," he says, nodding at Sister Clara, who nods back, smiling.

I am careful not to let the deputy hear our conversation. We get out of the car and walk a ways along a well-worn path with Father Michaels

243

until we are clear out of the deputy's listening range. I notice some other nuns in the park, having Sunday school outside with about a dozen children.

"Father, I got word that something is going to happen at a church today, and I think this is the church where it will happen. Someone's planted a bomb and I'm afraid people are going to die."

"We have to warn them, now!" Father Michaels says emphatically, quickly walking back to talk to the deputy, sweat dripping from his face as his black clerical robes absorb the heat. "Deputy, I understand that you can't allow cars in this area, but we are going to walk to that church right there," he says, pointing to a church on the corner. Sister Clara sees him talking to the deputy and walks back to join us, as the nuns and the children leave the park.

This is so strange, because Seth never said what church was being targeted, but I know this is the church. I also know that this is truly a man of God, because of his immediate acceptance of what I just told him and his quick action to do something about it. And he is not taking no for an answer from this deputy.

"You're right, Father. I guess I can let you walk, but I can't let you drive."

"Follow me, ladies. We must hurry!" The three of us rush to join Father Michaels, while Edgar Jameson sits frozen in place, looking nervous. He apologizes to Sister Clara and me for not coming along, but he is just too afraid. He is also too afraid to drive off, because Bee has threatened to shoot off a certain part of his anatomy if he leaves.

We are walking across Kelly Ingram Park, which is located only a block from the church. We quicken our pace, trying to get to the church, when suddenly there is an explosion so loud it knocks us all off our feet. Cut, bruised, and crying for each other, we all look up and there appears to be a huge hole in the side of the church. We see people exiting out the front doors, helping women and children onto the street. Within minutes, there are dozens of people gathered outside, screaming for their loved ones and friends.

"Father, we must help them!" Sister Clara screams.

"Yes, Sister, let us help God's people!" he says, getting up from the ground and helping us up, too. We are all bruised, but there is no evidence of any serious injury. Suddenly, we hear tires screeching and look up to see Edgar Jameson's car speeding away.

"That's alright!" Bee screams at the vanishing vehicle. "Cha-Cha and me will be paying you a visit real soon! Ain't nothing but a coward! All that smooth-talking and he ain't about nothing!"

As we approach the church, we see a lady running toward us, screaming incoherently. She collapses at Father Michaels' feet, unable to continue any further.

"My child! My child! I can't find my little girl. Somebody help me find my little girl! She's in Sunday school! Please help her!" she pleads.

We soon learn, as members of the congregation talk among themselves, that it is too late. Four children have been lost forever. Four little girls.

When we hear their names, Bee starts crying. She knows their families.

Addie Mae Collins, Cynthia Wesley, Carole Robertson, and Denise McNair. Their names are spoken with solemn despair. Children have been killed. Just because they were not the right color. God help us.

Father Michaels and Sister Clara are staying with the families and praying with them. I see whites come from near and far, offering their support, after hearing the news. The sheriff and Seth arrive, too. Seth stays in the car, his head is down and I can see the sadness in his slumped shoulders. I want to go over and comfort him, but dare not. I am not surprised to see the sheriff looking very nervous, asking his deputies questions as the city police and fire trucks arrive on the scene.

Judging from the expression on his face, he was not expecting anyone to survive the blast and is surprised to see so many Negroes standing outside, alive and well no, not well, as they grieve for the four little girls. They are anything but well, but like the Holiness preacher said, they will survive. That is what we do. We survive everything thrown at us and keep on keeping on, as the old folks say.

"What happened here?" the sheriff asks Father Michaels, knowing full well he is at the center of all this turmoil. There is no way that this act of aggression toward Negroes could have happened without him not knowing about it. I am shocked to see Father Michaels scold him publicly with words that a father tells his child when he knows that he has done wrong.

"This killing and these acts of aggression must stop, so help me God," Father Michaels says, his voice firm. "America is watching, along with the world. But mostly, God is watching us! And Sheriff, you and your friends are going to pay one day and that day will come, sooner rather than later. You will all have to repent and change from your wicked ways." The sheriff just walks away without a word, joining the city police who seem to be trying to find out why the street has been blocked. I think the sheriff has some explaining to do. Seth looks up and our eyes lock. There are tears in his eyes.

Chapter 78

Afew days after the bombing that rocked the world, I find myself sitting on my back porch. The days have become shorter and the nights longer. There is a slight bulge in my abdomen now, and I know it will not be easy to hide this child from Seth. It is high noon and I gave Bee and all the ground workers the day off with pay. Today, I just want to be alone without answering any questions from employees. Today, I just want to enjoy a cup of Passion Tea on my back porch, and take time to relax my mind from all it has had to endure since moving to Birmingham.

"Hello, Peg" Seth says, looking between the wood planks that hold the banister railings on the porch. "I just want you to know, I tried my hardest to stop the tragedy that happened at the church. I really did."

"I believe you, Seth. I know you're a good man and I do love you. I am so tired of people here and the prejudices they have."

"I know, Peg," he says, coming around and walking up the steps as he talks.

"I was once like them. I know it will take time, because they have been taught for so many generations to hate, that they still think they are right. I have made up my mind that I will find a way teach my children what's truly right. Do you believe me, Peg?" He sits next to me, looking into my eyes.

"Yes, I do, but I am still having a hard time believing that they killed those four little girls. Those innocent children weren't hurting anybody. They were in the church basement, attending Sunday school. These people must pay for what they did." Seth puts his arm around me and I rest my head on his chest, hoping his mother is not home. "Imagine the anguish of the poor parents who had to wake up the next morning and realize that what they thought was a nightmare, really happened. Can you imagine waking up and not having your baby, Seth? No one will ever know what it's like, except for the families who have to live with this for the rest of their lives." I am overcome with sadness and tears well up in my eyes

"This happened to some nice families who had dreams of their little girls growing up one day and having the right to vote without having to pay a poll tax and being given the rights promised to all Americans." My voice quivers and I am crying in Seth's arms, and this time, I think he does not care who might be watching.

"Thank you for seeing that love is blind, for it knows not who it picks," I whisper in his ear. "I am so glad you opened up your heart and allowed yourself to express what you really feel outwardly. I love you for this."

"I love you, too, Peg," he says, nibbling my ear with his lips, then moving his mouth across my cheek until he finds my lips and kisses them playfully. He moans, and then kisses me deeply, passionately, until he reluctantly releases me and gently strokes my face with his hand. "I have to get back to work. Will I see you tonight?"

"Yes!" I say, brushing his cheek with my lips. "Seth, that would be wonderful." Seth walks away, never taking his eyes from me. He steps off the porch and smiles with a boyish grin, before going to his truck, getting in, and driving off with a wave.

Chapter 79

This evening, my supper is sandwiches, grapes, cheese, and a chilled pitcher of lemonade. With Bee being off today, I made a tray of cold cuts, cheese, a variety of crackers, rolls, and potato salad for Sera and Dr. Carson. This will have to be the night that I come clean with Seth about his father and all the trouble he has caused me since I moved to Birmingham.

"Thanks for the sandwiches, Peg," Sera says, while I set the tray on the dresser. Dr. Carson is taking a shower. "Robert and I appreciate you bringing our food up to our room. We have to take a day to just be alone with each other once in a while since Robert Jr.'s death."

I recall them spending nearly a month in this room after their son's murder. Now they spend most weekends alone grieving, although lately they have been in their room all day just on Sundays. This week, however, since the church bombing, they have not come out at all. I think it reminded them too much of their own loss. Sara walks over to me and embraces me and we start crying together.

"I think we have decided to stay here in Birmingham. Robert has decided he will continue his practice here and even open up a new office, dedicating the building to Robert Jr." We walk to the bed, holding hands and talking about when we were much younger.

"It seems like just yesterday when you and Robert brought Junior home from the hospital. He was so long we just knew he would play basketball, but, oh, did he fool us! He decided he would be a lawyer like his mom, and I believe he would have been nominated to sit on the Supreme Court had he lived."

"Yes, he would have been a fine man who would have been wonderful for this county. But we will never know will we, Peg?" A momentary silence settles over the room. I believe we must be thinking the same thing as we both begin to laugh and then cry.

"Remember when he could not say 'Peg' and he called you Aunt Beg?" Sera says.

"I thought that boy would never learn how to make the 'p' sound. Then he discovered pizza, but his father would only give him a slice of pizza when he said the word 'pizza' correctly."

"He learned how to say 'p' real quickly then!"

"I kind of liked being Aunt Beg and I think 'bizza' was kind of cute, too."

"It sure was. My beautiful, wonderful son. We will miss him so."

"Yes, we will, Sera. Yes, we will."

Chapter 80

Sera and I sit on the front porch and watch the children play stickball. The sun is about an hour away from setting and we decide to eat some of my pie and a bowl of ice cream.

"Mmmmmmmm, this is so good, Peg! I think I am going to lick the bowl," she says, laughing so loud the children stop and wonder what she is laughing about.

"Keep playing children! I got some ice cream up my nose!" Sera says, making the children laugh. They soon return to their game and I wonder what the four little girls that died in the basement of the Sixteenth Street Baptist Church would be doing on a beautiful fall day like this, had they lived. I think about children often now, remembering Robert Jr.'s childhood fondly; wondering what kind of child Seth's daughter is going to be when she gets older.

Seeing the children playing in the street and how they reacted to Sera's little joke, I realize they have not learned to hate, yet, and I say a silent prayer that their generation never learns that one lesson.

"Well, Peg. I think I am going to take me a hot bath and call it a night."

"Okay, Sera, I am just going to enjoy the cool breeze as the sun sets before I head in the house." I have a date with Seth later this evening and I am looking forward to seeing him. I am now four months along, so this will have to be the night I tell Seth the whole story.

"Hello, Peg." My body shudders involuntarily as I hear the voice of the last person on earth that I want to see tonight.

"I said, hello, Peg. Aren't you gonna say hello to a friend who misses you dearly?"

My body is frozen and my mouth is unable to utter a word. I am hoping that Sera did not go to bed yet, and finds some reason to come back outside.

"If you're looking for your sweet precious cousin, she's upstairs with that doctor husband of hers, my brother," he says with total contempt. "I made sure she was upstairs before I walked over here. You know, Peg, I've been really kind to you and this family or yours. I could have had the Klan get rid of all of you the day of the picnic, but I didn't. It wasn't because I found out that day that Robert is my brother. It was because of you. I didn't want another white man to ever touch your skin. I wanted to kill the ones that dared to touch you that day. But know this. If you continue to avoid me, and don't come with me tonight, there will be hell in this house by morning. I promise you that." Knowing what this man is capable of, I believe him.

"Yes, sir."

"Meet me at the corner in thirty minutes."

"Yes, sir. I guess I have no choice, do I?" I am on the verge of tears, not wanting to go, but know I cannot face losing Sera and Dr. Carson. I have already lost too much.

"Peg, you never had a choice, since the day I met you and decided you belonged to me!"

Chapter 81

We've been short staffed at the construction site all week. It's been real difficult. I told my boss that we have to get more guys on the site. I told him that I know of some Negroes who would jump at the chance to work construction if he would allow them to work for a decent wage.

"Well, Seth, let me think about it," he said. "I really don't want the Klan coming to my place of business starting trouble." Then, he pondered for a second and looked at me.

"Seth, have your friends come by tomorrow and I will give them a good job if they want one," he said with a smile that told me he knew there would be trouble, but he'd handle it. Then he went back to the plans spread out on a table constructed of two sawhorses and a board at the construction site. Henry is a good guy. He wants to do right by every human being. When I was going to the picnics, I would always invite him to attend and he would always decline my offer. He mentioned that it was more important to him to spend time with his family on Sunday than to spend it with a bunch of drunks stringing up innocent people. Once, he told me that he had decided long ago, when his father made him go the weekly picnics as a child, that he would never attend them as an adult.

Now, I believe I would like to know this man outside my job. I think when I marry Peg, he or his family wouldn't mind at all. Hell, they may even come to the wedding.

"Henry, can I ask you a question?" I ask this sunny September morning, after waiting for the other guys to leave for the day. "Please, promise me you won't mention this to anyone."

"Sure, Seth."

"What do you think about people who marry outside their race?"

"Wait, Seth. I know you and your family are in the Klan. So, are you trying to get me lynched?"

"No, not at all. I'm asking because I've been seeing a really nice woman and she's not white."

"Seth, let me show you something." Henry reaches down in his jeans and pulls out his wallet. Then, he opens it to show me his wife for the first time.

"Henry, your wife is a Negro?"

"Yes, Seth, and I love her dearly. Sometimes, you have to follow your heart. If your heart says "yes," then it doesn't matter what the world thinks, as long as you are happy. If you do that, you and your family will have all you need. Teach your children that and when they are adults they will make a wonderful contribution to this world. Remember that and be blessed."

We shake hands and I'm ready to head home to meet Peg for our date. But first, I have to turn around and hug this man, wishing that moment that my father had listened when his mother tried to teach him to love all people. Then, he would have been like Henry, a man I can respect and would be proud to call my father.

Chapter 82

What choice do I have? Either lie with this man tonight, or take a chance on his friends killing my family. I have seen with my own eyes what he and others are capable of doing to people outside their race. I have witnessed this man murder my nephew, and more recently, four little girls. I know he was behind the church bombing. I just know it.

Where is the justice? Will it ever come? I often think about what we as a people have done to deserve persecution and death for so many years. We have not been aggressive in our peaceful marches. Dr. King leads us in nonviolent, peaceful resistance. We do not use violence and torture like the Klan.

Now, I find myself once again walking into the arms of this man that I call "He." How long will this continue? How long will I have to muzzle my mouth and stay silent? How much more can I take until I have had enough?

"Lord, I lift up this child inside me unto you tonight and it is my prayer that he or she will become someone who will follow you and walk according to your will. It is done!" My spontaneous prayer causes me to realize that my uneasiness about tonight is not just because I do not want this man to rape me again. I am sensing that my child and I are in real danger. God, help us!

A familiar car pulls up to the corner where "He" ordered me to meet him.

"Get in the car, Peg."

"Yes, sir."

Once I am inside, he drives away and the sense of dread I'm feeling grows stronger. "Can I ask you a question, sir?" My eyes stare straight ahead; I dare not look at him as he drives in the direction of the cabin where he took me once before and where Seth kissed me the first time. Thinking of Seth, I want to cry out and tell this man I love his son, not him.

254

"Sure, you can ask me anything when I am done with you," he says, once again flexing his muscles, so to speak, to prove his power over me. "But I'll entertain a question from you this one time. What is it?"

"Why me, sir?"

"Why you? Why not you! I told you before that I have feelings for you, Peg, and I don't want another man to touch you ever again. I don't care if he is in the Klan. No one will touch what belongs to me."

"But, sir, you are speaking to me as if I am a piece of property. Are you saying I can never marry?"

"That's exactly what I'm saying, Peg. I will kill the man who tries to take you from me."

We pull onto the two-lane road which leads to the cabin just miles away, and I cannot utter another word. I just want this night to be over with and pray that my baby and I will survive it.

Chapter 83

I arrive home from work and I want to take a quick shower. I'm anxious and hurried because of my date with Peg. Looking out my bedroom window, I don't see a sign of Peg in her window upstairs. We have a ritual when I come home. We each go to our rooms and look out so we can see each other. Sometimes, we just smile. Other times, we make faces or throw each other kisses.

She must be downstairs waiting on me. I'll be bold tonight and ask her to take my hand, right on her front porch. This time, I really don't care what the neighbors or my parents think if they see us together. This night will start something new for the city of Birmingham.

A white man taking a Negro woman out together in public will stir up some feelings among people here, but someone has to make a stand in order to change these old, worn-out traditions dating back to slavery. If the church bombing taught us anything, it taught us things have got to change in Birmingham.

When I reach the Carsons' front door, I pause for a moment, remembering the first night I saw Peg in her window and felt such hate for her; wanting her to cease to exist because of the confused feelings the sight of this beautiful, but forbidden woman, stirred inside me. Now, here I am, knocking on her front door with nothing but love for her. I wait a few minutes, but no one answers the door.

"She has to be here!" I think, as I knock again. But there is still no answer and I start feeling fear and foreboding taking over me. I know she wouldn't have left without a word or a note of some kind. I try to shake off the feeling of doom. I convince myself she must have had an emergency and didn't have time to leave me word.

Walking back home with my head hung low, I can't imagine her just leaving. I walk onto our property and pass the side of the front porch, when I hear ice cubes tinkling in a glass.

"He took your friend to the cabin we go to every summer."

"Mom, what are you doing out here?" She takes a sip of what looks like scotch and slowly inhales her menthol cigarette.

"I said your father took your friend Peg to the cabin that we vacation at every year. Does he really think I'm stupid?"

Numb and confused, I walk up the steps, wondering what she's talking about and why she thinks that my father, of all people, is with Peg.

"I've been devoted to your father my entire adult life and I just don't understand why you and your father think I don't know what's going on around here. Seth, I gave birth to you and there isn't a mother on earth who doesn't know her own child. Seth, I've known for some time now that you care for that woman next door. I see how you look at her and how she looks at you. I know the reason that you haven't shared your feelings for her with me.

"This Klan that we live and breathe has filled our hearts from generation to generation with hate. I realized that when Ronnie died," she says, her voice cracking a little. "That boy had nothing but love for everyone. The things he wrote in his journal…" She suddenly becomes angry. "The Klan has taken true love from this family. Ronnie was my angel," she says, her voice quaking again, as tears roll down her cheeks, "and that lady that you love next door was the one that gave me more time with my Ronnie."

"Peg gave her kidney to someone she loved almost as much as I did, and I treated her so badly and I shouldn't have. I was wrong for what I did to her and the Carson family. We took a child away from them and a child was taken away from us. The Klan killed Peg's nephew and your cousin on your father's orders. I knew Dr. Carson was your father's brother the very first day I met him. He looked and sounded so much like your grandfather, I nearly fainted. I knew that they had a child who they had to give up for adoption and I put it all together. The same way I put together what's been going on with your father and Peg."

"What?!" I am dreading my mother's next words, shaking my head in disbelief.

"Peg wanted Ronnie to become a man and spread his love to the world. I see that now. We have to change as a family and it must begin tonight." She gets up from her chair on the porch and opens the door, standing with her back facing me and pauses before going inside.

"Your father has been repeatedly raping Peg for months now and I did nothing to help her. He forced her tonight to go to the cabin we vacation in every summer near the quarry. If you leave now, you can stop him and keep him from killing her and his unborn child she is carrying. My child is gone and I can't imagine her losing hers."

The door shuts as my mouth opens, and I let out a scream so loud it shakes the windows and brings people out of their houses.

Chapter 84

"Take your clothes off, Peg, and lie on the bed," I hear him say, as I stand looking at my reflection in the mirror.

"I said, take your damn clothes off, Peg."

Is this the same man who told me he loved me? Is this the same man who killed my nephew? The same man who call all Negroes, "niggers?" I was taught by educated parents that I am *somebody*. That the color of my skin does not matter and that I can be whatever I want to be.

"Sir, I am not taking off my clothes, because I am not going to be your sex slave anymore," I say with all the strength and courage I can muster. I watch as "He" comes closer and the sound of his boots gets louder. The wood boards on the floor creak under his weight.

"Once we get pass all aggression that has been directed against Negroes; once we have been given equal rights and walk in front doors, drink in the same fountains, and even hold jobs such as yours, you will be obsolete, a dinosaur from the past. But I will be a judge one day and you, and all of your friends who have been doing people wrong, will have to pay." Enraged at my insolence, "He" slaps me across my face and I fall on the floor.

"Do you think I am dumb, girl?" "He" yells, knowing that no one can hear him. "You've been alive thus far because of me!" He pounds his chest like an ape flaunting his power. "I kept you alive, not your so-called friends. The Klan wanted you dead a long time ago, but it's been me who's kept the sheriff and the full weight of the Ku Klux Klan away from your door steps each night!"

This time his fist is just inches from my face and "He" is angrier than I have ever seen him. I wipe my bruised lip and look deep into his eyes and think, "This man is going to kill me."

"Look, girl, I've gotten rid of many Negro girls who thought they could call the law on me. I made them disappear. You hear me? What makes you think I won't get rid of you and that bastard child you're carrying?" He looks down at my stomach and ponders for a second.

"Sorry, Peg, but tonight you won't be going home. You, or your bastard of a baby!"

"He" knows? How can I protect my baby? That is all on my mind. How will I get out of here alive? Without hesitation, "He" lunges at me, grabbing me by the throat and choking me with his large hands. I try to talk, to plead with him for the life of my child and myself, but he continues squeezing my neck until my vision becomes cloudy and I see a bright light as I try to fight him off, gasping for air. Where is the light coming from? Does "He" not see it?

"Stop! Please, stop!" I manage to whisper, trying to find anything I can reach that will help me. I thrash around wildly, trying to find something to fight him with, but there is nothing. I know I am dying.

"Take your damn hands off of her, Dad!" I hear a familiar voice yell. "He" looks up, but refuses to turn around. He knows that his darkest secret has just been uncovered. With his hand still around my neck, he loosens the pressure, relaxing his hands as he speaks.

"Son, what are you doing here?"

"Mom told me you were here," Seth says. I can hear him breathing hard.

"She did?"

"Yes, she told me everything."

"Everything?" I watch him rise to his feet, trying desperately to work his way out of this ditch that he has been digging himself into for months now.

"I can explain, son. The Klan wants Peg here dead. Can you help me, son?"

Seth's shirt is drenched from sweat and he is enraged as he shouts back at his father.

"Liar!" Seth lunges toward his father and they start punching each other until "He" knocks Seth out cold.

"Okay, little lady, it looks like your white knight won't be coming to your rescue, so let's continue where we left off!" "He" comes at me, laughing maniacally, ready to resume strangling me, but this time I have a surprise for him and kick him right in his groin. "He" screams, falling to the floor in pain, and I back up, looking over at Seth who is lying unconscious on the floor. Then, I run out of the cabin, hoping I can get away before "He" can get up and come after me.

Outside, the headlights from Seth's truck shine on the cabin and on the path that Seth and I always took during our private moments. I decide to run and hide among the trees until daylight. "He" has recovered from my blow and is now chasing me up the path through the trees where only the full moon is showing his dark shadow. I can hear him yelling obscenities, which means "He" is beyond rage and wants me dead.

Tired, I kneel behind some bushes along the trail where I can see his hulking body as it emerges from the hill below. He tries to make use of the light coming from the moon, shining so brightly in the night sky. He shakes and rustles the bushes, trying to find me.

"Damn you, girl! I know you're here!"

Before he discovers me just a few feet away, I decide to dash up the path that leads to the quarry.

"There you are!" I hear him say, so close it seems his voice is whispering in my ear. "He" must be less than ten feet behind me. I remember walking this section of the path before. Seth said that there should be a rope hanging just five steps away from a drop ahead. I decide to run faster, hoping "He" will continue without looking at his surroundings. "It's working," I think, as he lunges out and touches my shoulder. I know I have one chance. I have to grab the rope, or we will both be falling down a steep cliff, where we are sure to die together.

"I said this is…!" "He" yells.

I leap forward and see the rope that Seth told me about. Now, if I can only leap high enough, I know that this rope will be my life saver. If not, my baby and I will plunge to the bottom of the quarry, along with "He." This is it! After I focus my eyes on the rope, I leap up and grab it tightly with both hands.

Suddenly, there is the tug of a heavy weight holding my legs. I know it is "He," holding on to me for dear life, and I know I will not be able to hang on to the rope much longer.

"Let me go! Please, let me go!" I cry out, while trying to shake him off me. "Please! Let me go."

"Hold on, Peg!" I hear Seth say. He is at the edge, trying to reach past his father and grab me, but he can't do it. Seth starts trying to pull his father off of me, and I can feel his hands sliding down my legs as "He" tries to hold on, his body swinging over the quarry.

"Dad, grab my hand!" Seth shouts, realizing his father is about to fall into the quarry, taking me and my baby with him. He says it again, screaming as loud as he can.

My life flashes before my eyes and I know I cannot hold on much longer. I think about my parents, cousin Sera, Dr. Carson, and Robert Jr. My family seems to be there with me. Then, I remember the poem Ronnie read to me about love and I can hear his raspy voice, struggling for air, giving me hope. I thank God for all of them and think of my baby, remembering the prayer I prayed when I lifted my child to Him for His will.

I look down at the sharp rock edges, hundreds of feet below in the quarry. Then I see that "He" is looking up at me with his piercing, cold eyes that seem to say, "If I go, so will you." "He" suddenly smiles, and using every ounce of strength "He" has after hanging on to my legs so long, "He" reaches up with one hand and gently touches the small bulge of his child growing inside my belly. Then, he quickly lets go without a sound as "He" falls to the rocks below.

"Dad!" Seth cries out, watching his father's fall to certain death. In tears, he reaches out for me and pulls me to him.

"My dad! My dad!" he screams. Seth cries uncontrollably, while holding me in his arms. I comfort him with a smile on my face, knowing for the first time since I moved to Birmingham, I am free.

Chapter 85

Losing two family members this year has been hard. My father lies in a flower draped casket just a few feet from us, as we sit where we normally sit for worship each Sunday. It all feels so unreal. Even though I now know about all the wrong he has done to my mom, Peg, and others, I still grieve for him. As I look upon the lifeless body of Ken Stevens, I know his soul is no longer here with us. All we have left are the results of the hurt he brought into people's lives. Father Michaels, along with other members of the clergy, has words with my mom and me just before entering the pulpit to begin the service.

"We are gathered here today to celebrate the life and the contributions Ken Stevens has made to the city of Birmingham. We are blessed to have shared the warm heart and laughter of such a man."

My mother cries, knowing that the man she loved for years is now gone. I know it's hard for her, knowing what she shared with me the night of his death. I touch her hand to let her know that I'm here for her and that I love her. Holding Emily Rose and looking at her little smile, I vow that she will know her family history when she becomes older.

Father Michaels returns to the podium after a short selection from the choir and asks people to come forward and express their feelings and thoughts at this time. Close friends from throughout my father's years as a district attorney and others he grew up with, speak kindly of my father. Father Michaels asks if there is anyone who didn't get the opportunity to speak. The entire church remains silent and so he gets ready to say the closing prayer. The sanctuary doors suddenly fly open and a rushing wind fills the room, making everyone turn around to see what's happening.

A small woman, dressed in a black dress, black gloves, and a veil covering her face gracefully walks down the aisle to the altar. She gets to the podium and asks to say a few words. Father Michaels kindly moves aside to allow this lady to speak, as my father's friends and family look on in silence.

She removes her veil and I am surprised to see Peg, as a gasp of shock ripples through the church. She takes a deep breath and looks directly at the Klansmen and others whose words of hate are sitting on their tongues, ready to spit their venom at her.

"Ladies and gentlemen, this is God's House and everyone is allowed to be here," Father Michaels says, as he stands next to Peg.

"Thank you, Father. My condolences to the Stevens family. I would first like to say, I know many of you hate me, just because of the color of my skin. Many of you are wondering what a Negro woman is doing here today. I am here, because first I want every human being to have life abundantly. I am here today, because of all the wrong that has been done to me since I moved here. Although for his family's sake, I am sorry for the loss of this man's life. When I came here, many wanted me dead and gone, but I persevered and believed that God has a bigger plan and that plan is clear to me now. I was sent here, not only to help the Carson family, but to help you all of you to get past all the abuse and killings that have happened here.

The sheriff stands and shouts, "No one wants your kind here! Isn't that right, everyone?"

"I want her here, because I love her and there is nothing you can do about it!" I yell back at him.

I stand up, ready to fight, as several women swoon. "This is my father's funeral and we want her here, don't we Mom?"

"Yes, we do! So let her speak, as you had the opportunity to earlier," my mother says to the sheriff and others, who are looking at us with disgust.

"I am here, because I am part of this family. The father of my child is…"

"Me! Seth Stevens. I love this woman and I want to marry her and raise our child together. My father is gone and so is the stranglehold he had on this community. All of you who helped him destroy lives are put on notice today. There are federal agents parked outside of my house and Dr. Carson's house, too. If anyone tries to harm any of us, or any other Negroes, or the whites that befriend them, you will go to federal prison. My father isn't around now to keep you out of jail, Sheriff. And you and your deputies are going to pay for killing my cousin! Father Michaels, this funeral is over. Let's go, Mom and Peg!"

The church is completely quiet, as I help my mother stand and we walk past my father's casket for the last time. Then, we go to the podium and I offer my hand to Peg and help her down. Father Michaels whispers,

"I am available to officiate at your wedding."

My mother extends her hand to Peg, and with me on one side and her future daughter-in-law on the other, we walk down the aisle, oblivious to the whispers, indignant looks, and outrage of the people occupying the pews. We exit the church and head for home, leaving my father to be cremated.

A few weeks later, there was a full-fledged FBI sweep of Birmingham. The Feds hauled away the sheriff, his deputies, and many others who were involved in the murders of so many people. I am a witness in many of the cases and will be testifying against members of the Klan in a court of law, as well as providing photographs of Klan activity as evidence. Those involved in the actual killings will spend the rest of their lives behind bars in a federal prison.

I visited Patrick at his house one day after the FBI sweep, hoping to find out what he did with the bodies of the children he murdered. But as he sat there coloring and playing with some blocks like a three-year-old, I realized he had no memory of his past life. The self-inflicted shot to his head has left him with severe brain damage and loss of memory that the doctors believe will be permanent.

It is November 1963. Thanksgiving is next week. President Kennedy was shot in Dallas, yesterday, and we learned this morning that he later died. Vice President Johnson will be sworn in as the next president, and he is already promising to continue Kennedy's Civil Rights legislation. My mother, Emily Rose, and I are having Thanksgiving with the Carsons, who have offered to foot the bill for our wedding. Dr. Carson is giving Peg away and Sera is going to be her maid of honor.

Henry has agreed to be my best man and our wedding soloist is Miss Bee, who is now Mrs. Jameson. It seems she fell in love with him when she nursed him back to health after accidentally shooting him in the leg. Little Sammy, Ronnie's playmate, is learning how to play the bridal march for our Valentine's Day wedding, which may be delayed if Peg hasn't had the baby by then.

It'll be a small affair, held in the music conservatory of the Whitfield with both Father Michaels and Pastor LeCroy co-officiating. Although we have agreed that our children will be brought up Catholic, Peg wants them to also attend services at black churches. Peg and I have our entire lives ahead of us, and we plan on watching throughout the years as Dr. King's dream is realized and our children grow up to reach heights we could never imagine. We plan to spend the rest of our lives watching history unfold, as we grow older together. She is my queen.

Chapter 86

PRESENT DAY 2017

The years went by and Seth and I married and reared a family in the very same house where he grew up. We watched our waistlines get bigger as we became older. Although his mother moved to New York to be with her siblings, she stayed in contact with all of her grandchildren, until she died a few years later, having never recovered from Ronnie's death. My cousin Sera finished her dissertation and is now "Dr. Carson." Her husband, the original Dr. Carson, continued working with the local hospital and became a world-renowned surgeon and professor at the University of Alabama.

We watched the years go by. We saw the passage of the 1965 Voting Rights Act and the aftermath of the Civil Rights Movement. We were devastated when Dr. Martin Luther King Jr. was assassinated, and I decided to work even harder in law after he was laid to rest. We, as a people, have to honor his dream and it is our obligation to do everything within our means to see that there is equality for all human beings.

I ran for office as a circuit judge, replacing Judge Rives, where I stayed on the bench for several decades, before being appointed to the Supreme Court in Washington, after being nominated by President Barack Obama in 2014. I am still serving under the current administration of President Harris.

I believe I had a good life and achieved many goals in my years on the bench. I am truly grateful. I decided when I became ill with cancer, and the doctors said there was nothing more they could do for me, that I would not tell anyone until I absolutely had to. I wanted to finish my last days peacefully with my family in Birmingham, the city where I found love, after so much pain. So, I want to die here in this house, where my wonderful husband Seth and I were blessed to bring up our five wonderful children.

"Can I get you anything, Justice Stevens?" the nurse says, standing beside my bed, checking my IV, as several visitors have gathered in my room, watching with concern.

"No, child. Thank you, though." My time is almost up here. I have done all I can do during this journey.

Chapter 87

I arrive in Birmingham from New York City and the only thing I can think of is my parents. I am grateful for my assistant, Stephanie, who made sure a driver was waiting for me at Birmingham Airport.

"Ms. Stevens?" the driver inquires, as I exit the airport.

"Yes."

"I have your car waiting. My name is Curtis. He opens the limo door and I put my briefcase on the seat, tired from the flight and the recent news about my mother.

"Thank you, Curtis."

"Excuse me, ma'am?" I turn around, just as I am about to get into the limo, and see a tall man with dark glasses standing there.

"Yes?"

"Ms. Stevens, the president has requested that we pick you up from the airport and take you home."

"Of course," I say, thanking the Secret Service agent, as I grab my briefcase and wave good-bye to Curtis.

I am immediately led to a black SUV, which pulls away from the airport, escorted by the Birmingham Police Department. On the way to the house where I grew up, I think of the gratitude I feel toward the woman who is the only mother I have ever known. My heart is saddened, knowing that if my father called me and all my brothers and sisters to Birmingham, then our mother's condition must be serious. What could have my mother falling ill so suddenly? I kind of suspected something was wrong when she took a leave from the Supreme Court just weeks ago. If I could be half the lawyer she is, moving all the way up to the highest judicial office, I would consider myself blessed. In my spirit, I knew something was wrong and when my father called me earlier today at work, his command to come home confirmed what I was feeling.

We ride past Kelly Ingram Park, where our mom took us to play as children. She shared with us her memories of when she moved to Birmingham and witnessed the terrifying events of May 2, 1963. Since she was new to Birmingham, and at the time she did not have any friends, she had no way of knowing what was really going on in the city. She always explained that she didn't understand all the details of what was happening on that day, until she saw it on the news.

She talked about her life here and did not withhold any details about my father's family or her own. "Peg" is what my father called her; kissing her lips each night after coming home from the construction site. He told her that he loved her and our house was never going to be the way his house had been. He always said that he was a new man because of our mother.

Do people really know what African-Americans had to go through in order to get where they are today? Through the tinted windows, I observe some young adults with their pants hanging off their rear ends, exposing their underwear.

Wow, have times changed.

We arrive at my parents' home about fifteen minutes later and all the memories come flooding back: me as a young girl with long pony tails skipping down the sidewalk and playing hopscotch. I smile as I see children of all colors laughing and playing together. Another Secret Service agent opens the door and advises me that the president is already inside with Justice Stevens.

"Thank you."

Along several blocks, local and national news media are camped out trying to get the latest news about my mother's condition.

"Ms. Stevens! Ms. Stevens! Can you give us any information about your mother, Justice Stevens?"

I dare not say a word, because if I do, I am sure to be stopped and asked several more questions before I can enter the house. I have never been surrounded by so many reporters shouting out questions and snapping what seems like hundreds of photos every second.

"No comment!" I say, politely, but firmly.

The only thing on my mind right now is my mother and wanting to see her immediately. I am greeted inside with a warm hug from my youngest brother's son, Anthony, who is in tears.

"I am so happy we found you Anthony. The years you were missing scared us."

"Hello, Aunt Emily. Everyone is upstairs and Grandma is asking for you."

"Okay," I say, quietly.

"I get to the upstairs hallway, feeling emotionally exhausted. There are Secret Service agents standing outside my parents' door. I open the door and my father and siblings meet me, sobbing quietly.

"She wanted to come home," my father says, while embracing me.

"She just wanted to come back home," he repeats.

I hear a heart machine, loudly recording her heartbeat each second. There's an IV attached to her right arm.

"Hello, Mama. It's me, Emily Rose."

"Child, I know who you are. I am not gone, yet," she says with a smile for all of us gathered around her bed.

"I have been waiting on you, and your brothers, and sister, and their families to get here, and finally you are all here with me. I just wanted to say I love you all and I wish I could be here with you a little while longer, but my health will not allow me to do so." We are interrupted for a brief moment by the Secret Service agent standing by the door.

"Excuse me, President Harris, we have a call from you from the secretary of defense," she says, and then closes the door. My brother-in-law motions with his hand for everyone to wait for one moment.

"I always wanted the best for you children, even when your father was ridiculed after we first married. I just want you children to always believe in yourself and never take on someone else's negatives. You have made a difference in this world. I know what I taught you all and you know what your dad and I had to endure to get here."

I can tell our mother is in pain, as she stops and takes a few deep breaths, and pauses afterward.

"Promise me that you all will fight for people who are less fortunate than you," our mother says softly.

We all nod, shedding tears and hoping somehow that this is all a bad dream.

"We will, Mama," I whisper. She closes her eyes and she is gone. Our mother is gone.

"President Harris, I am sorry to disturb you again, but we have a crisis in the Middle East."

We all turn around toward the gentleman in the black suit, who never leaves the president's side.

"President Harris! President Harris, are you okay?" he asks, with obvious concern in his voice.

"No, I am not. My mother just passed away," the president says quietly. "Please get the vice president on the phone."

"I am so sorry for your loss, Justice Harris. I mean, Madame President," he says, quickly correcting himself.

"Thank you," my sister says, as she embraces her top advisor, who also happens to be her husband.

You see, my mother decided to keep her baby, even though her child was the product of rape. Even in the toughest of times, she always thought of ways that each person could change for the better. Even when my grandfather wanted to do her harm, she was able to create joy and love out of his hate. Hate is a strong word, but I know love is stronger. Who would ever have thought that the child my mother decided to have during the most trying times of her life would become the president of the United States of America? Yes! She named her baby, Justice. President Justice Harris.

My mom never let hate get the best of her. She was a wonderful woman and she always said that she, and all of us, would have Justice some day! Thank God.

Chapter 88

Being the president of the United States requires great strength of character and moral fortitude. It has been difficult to concentrate on affairs of state, since my mother is now gone, after fighting her courageous battle with breast cancer. She stood for equality for so many years on the Supreme Court. She always said that if you work hard at what you do, you will eventually achieve your goals. Her last wish was that we lay her ashes on a wonderful bed of beautiful flowers after her memorial service.

Some of the children, the neighbors, and members of our congregation have been kind enough to offer to serve us lunch at our parents' house. My father rides with me in the motorcade.

"Justice, I never rode in a presidential limousine," my father says.

"I know, Dad, and hopefully, we will get you moved into the White House with us, soon."

"Well, Madame President, I don't think D.C. is the place for me. But I will come visit my grandchildren from time to time. Your mother always wanted the children to know our families' history. Seeing you here today, I believe I can say we must have set a pretty good example for all you children."

Now that my mother has passed, I am hoping my father can experience a sense of peace. Her wish was for all of us to be together one last time. We are a family and it did not matter to him or my mother what color skin each of us had. We were taught to be compassionate and to respect others. We were shown how to never take for granted the things we have today, because we may not have them tomorrow.

I was told that my grandfather was my real father, but this wonderful man, named Seth Stevens, will always be my dad. Seth Stevens, who was once a Klansmen and fell in love with beautiful black woman, named Peg. Can hate conquer love? No, not at all. Hate can invade the darkest pit, but love can penetrate any cold heart. While waving and passing people in this long motorcade, I am at peace, too, knowing my mother made a difference in the world and taught her children to do the same.

Whites, Blacks, Jews, Hispanics, Asians, Indians, Africans, Polynesians, Europeans, and Native Americans have poured into Birmingham's most revered street to cheer America's first black female president. My mother told me once, that the only blacks that used to be allowed on this street were here to cook, clean, and garden. Equality for these "Negroes" must have seemed so far out of reach. Imagine the prestige of living on this street; this holy grail of white supremacy. Now, blacks and whites reside in these stately mansions as neighbors.

"Driver, stop the limo. I want to get out and walk the rest of the way to the house."

"Madame President, I don't think it's safe for you to be out amongst this crowd."

"Driver, we are walking the rest of the way to our home."

"Yes, ma'am. Madame President."

My father has never looked so proud, as all his children exit the limos and reach out to thousands of people with love. These people loved my mother, and they love this family. My brothers stand next to our father, while Emily and I walk along the sidewalk, thanking everyone.

"Look, Justice!" Emily says excitedly, pointing out her Israeli fiancé, Afra, who is standing in the crowd. I make a note to go watch him sing at the Met, when he opens the new opera season.

Our eyes are filled with tears, as the crowd slowly parts along the sidewalk for us to make our way toward our house. There, I see a bouquet of colors spread across not just our lawn, but across *both* our lawns. The colors range from red and yellow, to olive and ivory, to tawny brown, ebony, blue, and purple black. They reflect the dozens of colors in my mother's flower garden, fertilized by the ashes of the past and now joining two homes and two families on this hallowed street, where hate once divided and where love finally brought us together as one family.

Spreading our mother's ashes over the flowers in her world famous garden, we laugh and invite children from the neighborhood to come to the garden and talk. I'm sure the press has had a field day, taking photos of what was once the most segregated city in America as it welcomes the nation's first African-American *female* president. I do my best to ignore the cameras, as I talk to the children about Dr. King's dream and ask them to tell me about theirs.

"I want to go to Washington with you to help you run the country!" says a five-year-old Asian girl, who sits patiently on my lap.

"Do you know who helps me run the country?" I ask. "The Congress. They come from all fifty states to help me."

"Then, that's what I want to be," she says. "The condress."

"Well, I think you will make a fine congresswoman, some day," I say, knowing that this video clip will be replayed repeatedly on the evening news and most definitely will find permanent residence on YouTube. Nothing says American melting pot more than an Asian-American child sitting on the lap of the first African-American female president!

Sitting on the porch of my childhood home, I am so thankful to be alive, to have had parents that taught me to love and serve others, and to be truly American with all of the complexity, diversity, adversity, and sincerity that we as a nation possess. Only in America could a child with no royal lineage, conceived as an act of violence, descended from a heritage of hate, but nourished in an atmosphere of love and acceptance become the president of these United States. I will return to Washington tomorrow to tackle the world's problems, which are now being addressed by the vice president, who just happens to be a proud Native American. He grew up on a reservation and married a lovely Hispanic woman, whose parents worked as migrant workers. But not today. My husband and I are having dinner at a local restaurant owned by some of his relatives from India. We'll be going there, after we attend prayers in a Buddhist temple. We alternate between my Baptist church and his temple.

Knowing how faithful Mama was to her church, I was not looking forward to telling her about our efforts to respect each other's spirituality. But I need not have worried. When I told her that I go to a Buddhist temple every other week, she took my hand and looked at me with that smile of hers. It was the smile that made my father weak in the knees and had us children totally devoted to her throughout our childhood and adult lives.

"Do you know why I named you Justice? Because next to freedom, love, and joy, justice is the one thing that people yearn for most. It is hard to remain free in an unjust world. Without justice, people are not able to love who they want to. And how can a person feel joy when they are treated unjustly? Every one of us must look within ourselves to find our connection to a higher power and there are those that never do. To deny anyone that right would be unjust."

"Whatever one feels in the heart that brings peace is religion. It is not a place or doctrine. It is a connection to something higher, whether spiritual or intellectual. The vilest most despicable person on the planet who finds this out will transform in an instant, if only for an instant, and in that instant they will embrace goodness, changing the fate of everyone concerned. I have seen that happen."

"I saw a man that wanted us both dead let go of the hate that would have killed us all had he held on. Instead, he used the last of his energy to touch you, doing the one thing most difficult for him to do, claim you as his own. Then he smiled, and that smile showed a man redeemed, a man that in the few seconds he had left, after taking so many lives for so long, gave us life. Do you understand how powerful that is? If someone that did the things he did, that raped and murdered at will, found in his heart a power that caused him to give his life to save your life and mine, how can we not believe that this power is the driving force behind all spirituality and belief?"

"Just look inside you to find it. And when you do, remember a person's beliefs are determined by what is in the heart. None of us has the right to encroach on another's beliefs. At the heart of all of our religions and belief systems is humanity's desire to find that cosmic force that we can connect with and that we look to for guidance and peace. At the heart of it all is a search for peace. Once we learn to respect that, we will stop having wars to destroy each other's beliefs and learn to live in a world that is big enough for all of us to live together in peace."

She always did know how to bring beauty out of ashes.

ACKNOWLEDGMENTS

Putting words on paper was never something I looked forward to in school. Today I find it easy to express my feelings about so many wonderful people who have given me words of encouragement. Life sometimes throws you a curve ball and you end up striking it with "chapters" that move you around the bases toward home. I have always looked at life like a new inning in a baseball game, sometimes striking out, sometimes hitting a home run.

I must first thank God for his love and wonderful ways of teaching me not to take for granted the people or things I have because I may not have them tomorrow. I thank wonderful people like yourself who have taking the time to read this book. Who would ever believe that a poor child growing up in the inner city would be blessed to be a writer?

I next must thank my sister, Alisha Harris and husband Byron Harris and family. Thank you for traveling along the highways when times were difficult and I could always count on your support.

Thanks to all the wonderful people I can always go to for advice: Bishop and Mrs. Rudolph Pringle, Dr. Timothy Pringle MD, Elder Jesse Hicks, Geneva Chapman, Betty Langfitt, Jordi Bostock, Darlean Burnett, Dorthea Burnett, Charisse Palmer, Todd Reasonover, Terry & Carolyn Remburt, Mary Jones, Adam James, Clifton Oliver, Victor Clark, JR & Brittnay Baker and Lea Sullins. Thank you all for your advice when times were hard. I always know I will hear the truth from you, no matter what. Special thanks to Samantha Pringle and Scott Shah, may you rest in heaven.

Thanks to two special women Sylvia Caldwell and Vera Williams: you are incredible and I can never repay you for all you have done for me. Thank you.

There are several additional people who also contributed, but asked that their names not be used. Each of you know how much I appreciate what you have done for me.

A novel's success is directly proportional to the quality of many wonderful people on the team. And I am blessed enough to be working with some of the best, Jeanette Clint and Marketing P.R. Director, Joseph Solomon thank you for believing in me, I thank you.

To my exceptional editors, Geneva J. Chapman and Dan C. Sullins, I thank you from the bottom of my heart.

A special thanks to Tony Brothers, Founder of Still Hope Foundation: thank you for believing in me. I am forever grateful! And finally, to all the wonderful people at American Airlines Inc. (AA), I thank you.

It is 1963, in Birmingham, Alabama.

During this racially charged period in "the most segregated city in the United States," Peg James, a beautiful, educated young black woman from Ohio, relocates to Birmingham to supervise the household and ground staffs of her employers, Dr and Mrs. Carson.

Peg and the Carson family move into a stately home in an elite neighborhood, next door to a man Robert Carson believes is his biological brother, Ken Stevens. Having been adopted and sent North by parents who were unable to fully support their family during the Great Depression, Dr. Carson unwittingly returns to a South divided by race and a brother deeply involved in the politics of hate.

Ken Stevens, a Birmingham district attorney and Imperial Wizard of the Ku Klux Klan, wages a war of terror against blacks in Birmingham and quickly singles out Peg as his personal target for rape and humiliation.

Tending to a garden where she uses ashes to grow an array of beautiful flowers, Peg enlists the help of a precocious young black girl and the ailing son of her tormentor. Peg's emotional battle to survive is like her beautiful garden only showing the beauty on the surface, but not the ashes underneath.

In spite of her fear, Peg finds herself becoming entangled with a man she is forbidden to love. Her secrets can never be revealed because she must protect the lives of the people she holds dear, including the young Klan member who risks everything to fall in love with her.

CPSIA information can be obtained
at www.ICGtesting.com
Printed in the USA
FFOW01n1419041214
9231FF